Francis B Nyamnjoh
Stories from Abakwa
Mind Searching
The Disillusioned African
The Convert
Souls Forgotten

Francis B Nyamnjoh & Richard Fonteh Akum
The Cameroon GCE Crisis: A Test of Anglophone Solidarity

Dibussi Tande
No Turning Back. Poems of Freedom 1990-1993

Kangsen Feka Wakai
Fragmented Melodies

Ntemfac Ofege
Namondo. Child of the Water Spirits

Emmanuel Fru Doh
Not Yet Damascus
The Fire Within

Thomas Jing
Tale of an African Woman

Peter Wuteh Vakunta
Grassfields Stories from Cameroon

Ba'bila Mutia
Coils of Mortal Flesh

Kehbuma Langmia
Titabet and The Takumbeng

Ngessimo Mathe Mutaka
Building Capacity: Using TEFL and African languages as development-oriented literacy tools

Milton Krieger
Cameroon's Social Democratic Front: Its History and Prospects as an Opposition Political party, 1990-2011

Sammy Oke Akombi
The Raped Amulet
The Woman Who Ate Python

Susan Nkwentie Nde
Precipice

The House of Falling Women

Rosemary Ekosso

Langaa Research & Publishing CIG
Mankon, Bamenda

Publisher:
Langaa RPCIG
(*Langaa* Research & Publishing Common Initiative Group)
P.O. Box 902 Mankon
Bamenda
North West Province
Cameroon
Langaagrp@gmail.com
http://www.africanbookscollective.com/publishers/langaa-rpcig

ISBN:9956-558-25-7

Rosemary Ekosso 2008
First Published 2008

DISCLAIMER
*All views expressed in this publication are those of the author
and do not necessarily reflect the views of Langaa RPCIG.*

Dedication

To my father, Lucas K. Ekosso,
who did not reap where he sowed

Acknowledgement

I have two people to thank (or to blame) for this work. The first person is S. Dibussi Tande, who, since the early 1990s, has always encouraged me to write and has always been instrumental in finding outlets for my work.

The other person is my husband, David A. Woodward, whose moral and other support, in this and other aspects of my life, I now find indispensable.

Author's Note

I have taken some liberties in writing this book. To my knowledge, there is no Centre for Soil Sciences in The Hague. The nearest location where soil science is studied is Wageningen University.

Legal practitioners in Cameroon will probably cringe when they see what I have done with the rules of procedure in the Cameroon legal system, at least in the English speaking part of the country.

Prologue

The Weekly Correspondent 16 May 2007 Women's House in Trouble – Again

The impressive green and gold wrought- iron gates of the Women's House (WH) were sealed at 11 o'clock yesterday morning in the latest episode of the drawn-out drama that has pitted that establishment against the Douala city council authorities, our Littoral correspondent reported.

Created in 1998 by the self-styled philanthropist, Martha Elive, ostensibly to improve the lot of those she called "poor, downtrodden women", the WI rapidly became a haven for runaway wives and lazy, headstrong girls determined to get on in the world with minimum effort on their part and maximum cost on others'. Pseudo-intellectuals and women of easy virtue regularly swarmed around its founder to indulge in futile discussions about the need for societal change.

The promised "empowerment centre", as some of the Centre's unsurprisingly female minders glibly describe it, has become a badly-run seventies-style commune full of foul-mouthed, sluttish women, biting and kicking and scratching, each scrabbling for a foothold on the slope of a society they are paradoxically doing their feminine and inadequate best to destroy. The schools and workshop which were to produce the firm-minded, focused craftswomen and hardworking professionals have instead spawned half-baked, inefficient trainees with vague but nonetheless violent ideas about attaining what they consider to be their rightful station in life, unemployed and unemployable, not to say totally unmarriageable.

The boastful, smug and self-congratulatory attitude of these former inmates of the WI has spawned domestic upheaval on a scale never before experienced in our society.

Lest this be construed as an attack bordering on misogyny, we hasten to assure our readers that this publication has nothing against decent, God-fearing women who recognize their proper role in the scheme of things. However, when a group of frustrated man-haters decide to go against the grain, nay, rip apart the carefully woven fabric of a society which, though not perfect, certainly has its organized merits, then responsible citizens must be alarmed.

It would be disastrous for our society were we to allow the iconoclastic Centre to open its doors again. Destructive, self-serving initiatives, which seek to unravel a status quo developed and painstakingly established over centuries, should be squashed without compromise. It is not by accident that women have always played a subordinate role in this world. If God had wanted woman to fulfil a different role, she would have been created before man. Initiatives such as these should be nipped in the bud. This newspaper holds the opinion that the mere (though thorny) sapling the WH has become is not yet too sturdy for the righteous axe of concerned, right-thinking citizenry.

Part One

1

The phone rang.

Martha unplugged it again with a sigh and went out to her bedroom balcony, gazing out at her lawn of expensive narrow-blade grass, nurtured and primped with surly and inefficient dedication by her ground staff of one underachieving male. The pale gold sunlight and the dry, tight feeling in her mouth reminded her again that it was seven in the morning, and mornings were a time for putting on masks and going out to face the world. The world did not approve of clay-footed crusaders skulking in their well-appointed bedrooms. If she did not go out and face them, then they would come and get her.

But she could not talk to anyone just yet.

She needed a little more time. She needed to find out where Ophelia had disappeared to, and get her support. Where was the girl with her jokes and her sharp mind when she needed her most? And there were still a few pieces lacking for the puzzle of her strategy to be complete. The mosaic of her reaction to this newest and biggest threat ever was still headless; the body was good, but its legs were a bit unsteady; she needed more time to make the final adjustments. Another hour and I'll knock it into kilter; find the spittle to swallow down the fear, she thought, observing the yardman scratching his crotch. Filthy bugger. To think that a creature like him would actually believe that he was born superior to her in all things.

She remembered an old folk tale about the animal-head that borrowed body parts from its friends and went wooing in a village where it was unknown. As it returned home on a dark night with its new bride, its friends called to it from the bushes and took back their body parts until only its head was left. The moral of the tale was that foolish, proud women who refused to marry the men they knew ought to beware of good-looking suitors from strange lands.

2

The cautionary tale had another meaning for her, though. This was the time to be the borrower of body parts. But she would not give back what she took. She needed it to buttress her own strength. Never considerable to begin with, it had failed her at this crucial moment. Now was the time to build up a body of public reaction, to show resolve. This was the time to be resourceful or else let all fall into ruin. However devastating this was, she had to dress her wounds so that they did not bleed in public.

She wished Ophelia had not chosen this time to go away. She would have had some great ideas, or at least brought the crisis to a level where it could be laughed at.

She did not know for how long she stood looking without seeing at her expensive greenery and her yardman's exploration of his person, but when she turned around to go back into the bedroom, she was at last aware of her body. During the four days in which she had unplugged the phone and burrowed into this room, she had let despair and her body odour grow like mushrooms on a dead thing. Her eyes were dry and hot, the legacy of overwork shedding tears. Once she started crying about one thing, she tended to line up a string of tribulations and cry over them in great detail until she could cry no more. Her mouth felt dry, her tongue raw at the edges where she had clenched her teeth against it. It was now coated with the thick, evil-tasting residue of disuse; despair had silted up in her mouth, grainy, insidious, like fine beach sand on a swimsuit gusset, clogging her taste buds. She could smell herself. Rancid, dry sweat and soured juices. Unwashed. Unclean.

Her brain had boiled and cooled, congealed into a gluey, days-old pap of stale, unworkable ideas. She had oozed semisolid runnels of distilled fear.

She had done her penance.

It was time to be Martha again. Martha the good and brave. Martha the intrepid, the tall and fearless, taking on the world. Forget the dry gnawing in her middle. Ignore the limbs trembling with hunger. Swallow down the quaking monster that threatened to surge up from her innards. Take a shower. Be the borrower of courage. But first take Hortense's call and get the machine running again.

3

She walked across the room and plugged in the phone. After a few moments, it purred throatily from its grey marble nest.

The Martha routine was back on track. The third way, not Blair's but hers, the straight and narrow between plump housewife in voluminous boubou and anorexic call-girl in figure-hugging trousers. The price for self-respect.

"Yes, Hortense."

"*Marthe! Ça va, dis-donc? Je te dis que les journaux...*"

"...Are in their element. In high dudgeon. Outraged. In a righteous tizzy. *Je sais tout ça.* I read it all, Hortense *ma chère.*"

"So what do you think we should do? *Je t'assure que* I paid all those council taxes. They were properly declared. *Il n'est pas question pour moi...*"

"*Absolument.* I know you did. *Je sais, Hortense, t'en fais pas.* It will all blow over within a month. Trust me. The papers are in their element now, but it will pass. I know the Establishment must have rubbed its hands raw in satisfaction by now. But they are only rats in a maze, Hortense. We shall overcome yet." She paused to draw breath and iron out the thin edge of trembling that was about to creep into her voice. "I saw them. I saw them all, but I needed to draw up battle plans, and now I have. So let's move on.

"So what else did the bastards take? Give me the facts." Good. Struck the right note there. Put fire into the troops. But trailblazers, said an Owen Meany voice in her head - one of the many which fought daily to fuel her fear - trailblazers do not hibernate in their bedrooms, cowering under the counterpane, soused to the gills, waiting for divine intervention. Lord take this cup away from me, the Son of God (and of Man, by his own admission) had begged. But *His* father was God, after all, said another voice. He had a direct line to the ultimate crisis centre. I have nothing but myself, and I am afraid, and even more afraid to show it.

"I cannot really say for now," Hortense was saying. "The premises were sealed immediately after the raid, as you no doubt know. My office, I mean. I went in there for the first time today. There was so much disorder, papers on the floor, files scattered everywhere, and everything so disorganized *que je ne*

4

sais même pas quoi d'autre ils ont pris. But I know the tax records are gone. This will ruin our reputation forever. All those papers. I cannot believe the things they are saying. *Je te dis que* enh –" Hortense sighed. Martha could imagine her reaching for a tissue. A faint sniffle came down the line.

"Hortense, you forget something. We were fallen women from the day we started this thing, remember? We have no reputation to speak of, much less uphold. We are morally bankrupt. A woman's wealth is her reputation, never mind that landlords do not normally accept that as payment for rent. So, do not worry about the opinion of people who are determined to believe the worst about you, whatever you do. No worry, no worry. I am coming down there. We will talk in a few hours. I know how to handle this. We'll talk. Just wait. Sooner or later, some minor functionary will find the records in a back drawer. They are hoping that in the meantime, frail, dithering women such as us will just fall apart. Which is why we will not, okay?"

"Okay, *je t'attends.* It is just that I've been trying to call you for ages."

And I was cowering in my bedroom like a frightened rodent, and smelling twice as bad, Martha thought.

"I am coming. I'll call you when I arrive. Be strong. You are strong, you know it. Just think positive. Calm down."

Click. Now we are resorting to the American psychobabble we normally abhor, are we? How the mighty have fallen! said a snide little voice, the least likeable and most persistent of them, somewhere behind her headache. This one, she was sure, was the voice of a girl she had hated in high school.

Now you made your bed, Martha dear, added the voice she considered closest to her real self, the pep-talk voice with literary pretensions. Go and lie on it. And keep those little worms of doubt tightly shut up in your jam jar of a mind eh? A mind full of worms, full of doubts, full of fear, squirming and swarming and slithering, feeding on itself, threatening to break free and poison the world you built forever. Your *fine* mind, which displays a strange resistance to the fingers of logic trying to pry it open.

5

Well, we do not make ourselves, said her logical voice with the slight edge. God made us, male and female he made us, then either he or someone else added a crippling dose of self-doubt to the primordial soup I was fished out of, and that is why I, who have found crutches for so many, am now nothing but a jellyfish. But I must not falter. Even if my knees are jelly and my ego mush, I must be seen to be strong and there's an end to all discussion.

Riding on the temporary strength of this last thought, she bustled into the shower stall and turned the water on full blast, icy cold. Cold water gives you a nice rigid backbone to face things with.

2

Martha careered wildly down the driveway in her Mercedes. In her haste, she almost missed the wide curve, and bumped onto the red brick kerb. A couple of fuchsia-coloured dahlias with yellow hearts went rather suddenly to flower heaven. She succeeded in getting the car back onto the driveway, and reduced speed. She could just imagine the headlines. Beleaguered head of WH takes own life – severs the heads of two dahlias in the process. The yardman, who also did duty as gateman, pulled open the heavy iron gates, head bowed. Martha wondered what he thought of all the furore about her in the press. Probably couldn't read. But that would not stop him from gloating over her misfortunes, she knew. His type probably thought that a single woman in her thirties with no children was an aberration, a thing against nature. But he was careful never to reveal his true feelings to her. She buttered his bread, after all.

That was the thing with male help; as long as you paid them, they would despise you and cheat you when they could, but they would take the money and be polite in your presence at least. He probably thought that she was a woman kept in some style by some shadowy rich idiot. It would not matter that he had never seen the keeper. Women of her type were *kept*.

Mindful of this underground contempt, the policy she had adopted with her male staff was one of cool politeness and no intimacy at all. Some of them had been known to make passes at their female employers on the assumption that no woman, however exalted, could be beyond the reach of any man, however lowly. She made them understand without words that they were asexual in her view, that they were hired hands. In any case, it was no use trying to be nice to them; they would only feel more contempt for her.

In keeping with her mood and these dark thoughts, she did not wave to him as he held the gate open. She did not tell

7

him where she was going or how long she would be away. He was her servant. He would wait.

It was the same with the garage that she used when she was in the capital. She knew that they were deferential because they saw that she was a woman of means, but they overcharged her outrageously, secure in the knowledge that women knew nothing about cars and that her money came from a man and there was therefore nothing bad about returning it to the brotherhood of men. Dust to dust. One day, she had overhead a mechanic telling one of his colleagues: "if I can take money from a woman, I take it. After all, *she* gets it from another poor fool who thinks he is in love. It is our money in any case, so it should go back into our pockets." Later, when the car was being cleaned, the same man had come over, bowing and scraping and generally making himself agreeable, and she had derived some transient, impotent pleasure from chilling him with a glance.

The traffic on the road out of the city was hellish, drivers shooting across junctions without looking left or right, braking hard to avoid collision and lurching forward again, trading insults in the heat.

"*Face de rat*! Where did you buy your driving licence?"

"*Ta mère pond!* Did you finish school?"

It was a normal day in a cursed, driven city. The Highway Code simply did not exist for most drivers. There are two types of traffic lights in Yaounde. The advisory and the purely decorative. Right of way is treated as a concept developed by stupid, idealistic white men out of touch with the reality of men's true instincts. Forcing her way into the inside lane, Martha reflected that if one considered the car as an extension of the driver's will, it all became obvious. Naturally, the driving force was centred somewhere in the tenebrous nether regions of men's torsos, hence the blunt, invasive, thrusting snouts at crossroads. Of course. Cars as an extension of intrusive, demanding male sexuality. Hence their long, blunt bonnets. Phallic underpinnings in auto design. Good seminar that would make, when all this blew over, of course. She should get Ophie to do something in that line. It was the sort of link Ophie liked to create. Anything to do the men in.

It was just after midday on a Wednesday afternoon, and since this was a half-day for schools, the kids went home at noon. Consequently, the streets were thronged with hundreds of youngsters in uniform who shambled in and out of the way of cars with the manifest intention of evading, once and for all, the responsibilities of adulthood. The normal anarchy was worsened by the absence of traffic lights, which had broken down again, and anxious taxi drivers who had thrown caution to the winds in a bid to make up for the shortfall occasioned by rising fuel prices. At junctions, she pointed the bonnet of her Mercedes 300 at imprudent twenty-year old Toyota taxis and flashed her headlights. The taxi drivers grudgingly made way. No one wanted to tangle fenders with an expensive Mercedes like that one. Kiss of death, that.

The big, silver-grey car emerged unscathed from the fray, and Martha gave it steam, streaking past the old airport-turned air base, which, with the kind of air force the country could afford, was really just for show.

Well, she had her own problems. They did not include the air force.

Her mind returned to the Women's House like the tongue to an elusive wisp of mango fibre stuck between one's teeth. She had to sound coherent when she got to the coast, so she had better marshal the can of worms that was her brain into some kind of marching order. Mustn't disappoint the audience, me girl, won't do at all. You have to get there alive, so put a damper on all those thoughts roiling about inside your head and focus on your driving.

At the tollgate, the sour-faced woman attendant took her time, dragging heavily from car window to car window. Martha examined her in annoyed impatience. Shortish, average build, if one could judge what was under those shapeless, faded orange overalls. She had a pointed face like a porcupine's; blotchy and multihued from abrasive skin lightener. Hydroquinone casualties, Ophie called her type. Her hair was short and stringy, falling off at the temples; her perm needed touching up. The woman had the battered-wife look down pat. And hard as it was to believe, it all came out of plastic tubes. At least if your man beat you and ruined your looks, Martha thought, then you could blame him and a few people might even condescend to feel sorry for you. But what was the point in doing violence to your own person and then turning around to moan about male brutality when some Hulk Hogan tried to assist you? Sometimes it was hard to understand the hierarchy of pain that women kow-tow to.

The woman thrust a grubby ticket at her. Even her hands looked ugly. Dirt-rimmed islands of ancient nail polish stuck on a sea of henna-discoloured nails, with edges serrated by manual work and neglect. They looked fit to saw through a two-by-four. Martha took her stub, drove past the barrier and forgot about her. She had her own problems.

Like how to get your life's work back on track when reactionaries are trying to derail it. Reactionaries with culture, tradition and a sense of innate superiority behind them. She was the maverick lamb that had wandered away from the fold and fallen into a pit, breaking her leg. And now her enemies were round her, rifles cocked, ready to shoot her and eat her, stony-faced and pitiless, these male pillars of society. Sow the wind; reap the whirlwind, said a hectoring voice in her head, her own personal Book of Proverbs.

For a full three seconds, she wondered whether she was going mad. These gabbling voices chasing each other in the sinuous mazes of her overheated brain, calling out insults, berating, manipulating, offering frantic advice. It was as if her mind had been taken over by malevolent rodents.

And yet she had been, in the early part of her life, before her transfiguration, a star lamb, bleating the mantra nice girls learned practically in their mothers' wombs, toeing the line, going where the male sheepdogs wished, snuggling back, suitably chastened, against the warmth of society's approval when the dog barked in warning. It had all been so innocuous, so normal. She was born normal, whatever that was. All toes and fingers okay, to normal, if unprepossessing parents.

10

3

Her father was a nurse. A State Registered Nurse, mind you, not your lowly bedpan-wielding foot soldier. Nursing Superintendent when he retired, secretary-general of the tribal development committee, member of the Junior Service Club, a luminary of some note in his hopelessly obscured view. She got her height from him. Tall, fair-skinned, already bald in his mid-thirties, he was a nurse not out of nobility of motive, but because at the time he went to school, sons of middle-level villagers did not have many other options available.

So he went to nursing school in Nigeria after his Cambridge School Certificate, and studied in Ibadan. He was a man who scrimped and saved as a matter of habit, a weak animal feathering its nest, a plodder who never looked up, who would never see the wood for the trees in the landscape of his life. Life had not given him wide-screen vision, and he never felt the need for it. In this wilderness he rambled and meandered, he stubbed his toe on the exposed root of minor disappointments, and, muttering imprecations at the careless protuberance, would beat away the clinging twigs and low-growing branches of care, and then promptly blunder into a full-grown tree of outright, insurmountable disaster. Winded, he would nevertheless go on, forever in circles and forever unaware of his lack of true purpose. Lacking any talent for discernment, he would slowly wither and one day die of a heart attack in his own little wood, never given to selfless or noble sentiment, never coming upon a clear track to anywhere but the mundane. He was just a man, a normal man, lost in the mindless labyrinth of mere routine and the done thing. And so he plodded on to his end, not a bad man, a dutiful, even loving family head, never questioning, just content to live the life his ancestors had prepared him for, and therefore understandably upset that his daughter *would* go her own way.

11

To his eternal chagrin, this normal man would have only one child, the Lord (for he went to church; he was a decent Catholic) not having judged him fit for multiple fatherhood. Which was in some ways a good thing, for since he had only one child to mould, he did not need to make the effort to educate five or six children on a nurse's small salary, State Registered though he might be. Also, his wife could stay at home and look after the family as was her duty, not gallivant all over the place pretending to earn extra money as some guy's secretary. Everyone knew bosses often took liberties with their secretaries, married or not, and how was a man ever to tell, women being such treacherous devils?

Anyway, she came from a decent lot, his wife; her grandfather had been a quarter head, a sort of neighbourhood chief, under the British. Sixteen when he had seen her first, or at least when his uncle had sent for him and told him about her, she had aged well, and had kept his house well for him, even if she had borne him only one child, and a girl at that. He would have liked to have a son to go on and be the doctor he himself would have given his right arm to be, but the Lord giveth, and if you made too much ruckus, even the little you had might be taken away from you. And Mr. Elive never took risks, so he shut his mind to his hopes and went on with the business of being a nurse (State Registered), a minor provincial luminary and the head of his small family.

His wife, the smug, submissive and corpulent Mrs. Elive, programmed before birth never to question, accepted her fate willingly, and it could not be said to be a particularly trying one. She was married to a man who had gone to school, who was a *personality*. She enjoyed the furtive, illicit, unchristian power that came her way as the wife of a nurse (State Registered). Nurses were almost as good as doctors, her husband said. Sometimes, even better. She had one regret, however, though this was not the sort of thing you brought up in Catholic Women's Association meetings: she would have liked to be more fruitful, to have actually multiplied, rather than merely replicate herself unsatisfactorily through one skinny daughter. What other function did a woman have but to be fruitful and multiply?

Beyond these uncrystallized hopes that occasionally misted over the clear sense of having done right by her God, the society she lived in and her husband, Mrs. Elive had no loftier ambitions. She could enjoy the sneaky satisfaction of being better dressed than some of her more fecund fellow matrons, and keeping a cleaner household. She had elevated sly insinuation and a prurient interest in the mild scandals of provincial life to a fine art: Mrs. Elive was a normal woman and a good wife, for she had never even contemplated adultery, she went to church, she was not forward, and was never prey to abstractions and crazy things like ideas. She was content just to be a wife; not only faithful but perceived to be so by all, she would never disgrace anyone or be herself disgraced, that is, until her only daughter went to study abroad and the devil took up abode in her over-questing soul.

4

Twenty or so kilometres out of the city, Martha pulled up behind a foul-breathed bus at one of the innumerable improvised banana-republic roadblocks that dotted the highway like the friable droppings of some giant animal. In the opposite lane leading back to the city was a yuppie type with the regulation weekend dress of geometric-patterned African print shirt. Probably returning from a weekend in his village, she told herself. Local boy made good. The sort Ophie called the endangered species, as there were too few of them to go round all the single women. Has the mandatory slim, young, hostile mistress dressed in fashionable black (waiting for him back in his suburban villa in a monumental sulk because he has not taken her to the village to meet his people), the streamlined Japanese car, two cell phones and numerous beige suits. He glanced out of the window and saw her watching him. He had the thin, pencil-line moustache that was back in fashion these days and the blank eyes of a mythomaniac, she thought, wanting to hate him because she could not have him. Rather dishy, said her ageing-woman-of-the-world voice, but a bit young for me.

These days, she thought bleakly, now that Samuel had left her, her most likely possibilities were plump widowers with waning, inept virility, decent savings accounts and moronic teenaged children. She hated teenagers. It was a sign of the times that the rotting society produced these brainless nonentities with their strange tastes in music and their habitual cheating in public exams. The sons followed in the footsteps of their thieving, grasping fathers.

Young or not, she stared boldly at the yuppie, daring him to desire her. Just let me see that fabric-peeling, half-contemptuous, lascivious look I know so well and I will wind down my glass and hand you my card across the white line, teach you to look at solitary women, you -!

Haven't had a real man for a bit now, said her wistful voice; too busy crusading, and the men are frightened of me. They think I have teeth between my legs, you see.

And indeed, this was one of what she called her dry periods. At such times her mid-cycle intimations of wasting fertility bowled her over, coming at her as they did with a violence that left her weak and willing, her days floating by in a daze of impracticable sexual fantasies, her lower belly boiling softly in futile anticipation. At times like those, she felt more alive, colours looked brighter, smells were more distinct, the clear, mellow notes of a solo *guitare sèche* gave her goose bumps, made her scalp tingle. She rode on a high of desire. And that was as high as she ever got, these lean days.

The traffic began to move at last, the yuppie removed his gaze from her with no effort at all and sped off to his younger mistress. Bang, she thought. And surged forward, overtaking the wheezing bus on a dangerous bend.

5

There had been a time in late teen-age when she had enjoyed the new power of having them want you and fighting them off. When she came to University for the first time, virginity and morals intact, mind pulsing in a mixture of good-girl reserve and secret anticipation, everyone, or so it seemed, wanted to have a go at her.

There were those odious Francophones who either said in would-be Parisian accents unfortunately marred by strong tribal overtones: a) you speak good French for an Anglophone girl, one can hardly tell you are one, or b) recited their high school philosophy classes at her (*je pense, donc je suis*), or even c) borrowed their friends' leather jackets to come to her stuffy student room and act the moody lover at her in.

There were the Anglos who thought themselves the *viveurs*, the ultimate in urban chic, the sons of your parents' friends who waited for you to say hello first and made cutting, late-adolescent remarks about you the moment your back was far enough down the dusty street, and then sneaked back to your room to 'state their case' when they were sure none of their friends could catch them at it.

There were the decent ones who came trembling with their hearts on their sleeves and the ones who kept on at you because, with women, no really meant yes; they wanted to help you make up your mind because you were congenitally incapable of doing that for yourself.

There were young civil servants looking for educated wives of suitable youth and earning potential. There were older men on the prowl for a chance to recapture their lost youth, but in those days when student bursaries gave girls more honour and allowed them a chance to sleep with young men they actually loved, these were not as many as they might be. And besides, in addition to the limited possibility of getting a girl, if they were imprudent enough to park around the student neighbourhood, the male students let out the air in their tyres, or just punctured them outright in indignation at being challenged on their turf. It all amused Martha. It reminded her of the stories girls from mixed boarding schools told, of boys who waylaid and beat up on the football field boys from other schools who came, bearing gifts, to chat up "their" girls on visiting days.

There were all sorts. It was an unprecedented thrill to be wanted with such single-minded desperation and have the power to say no. And she fought them off in good-Christian-girl disdain, dutifully letting 'I dare not' wait upon 'I would', till she met Tom. And then the boarding-school nuns' pet devil ("if the devil should speak to you through a man who wants to possess your body, girls, all you have to do is say: 'sorry, I don't do things like that'") obligingly relieved her of any control over her libido.

So far, life had treated her well. In boarding school, she had more or less fitted in (more less than more, if the truth be told – she was too much of a loner); during vacations, she had unquestioningly followed the warp and weft of ordinary provincial existence. Unquestioning might perhaps be too strong; rather, she whiled the holidays away with dog-eared Mills and Boon, Pacesetter and Harold Robbins paperbacks, and watched and judged in silence. Keep yourself for your husband, warned her mother softly, during those painful, embarrassing mother-and-daughter talks when father was away at work. And she had. That is, until she came to the university and met Tom.

Not long after school began, she went to the university library one day to withdraw her library card. He was there for the same purpose, a tall, thin, dark boy in fairly neat clothes, fingering a pack of faded brochures thrown carelessly on a table, looking about impatiently for the attendant, who had taken one of her numerous unscheduled breaks.

From Martha's timid manner and the over-curled new perm, he could tell that she was an Anglophone, and so, to pass the time and also because she was rather pretty in an unobtrusive way, he said:

"Are you waiting for your library card too?"

"Yes." Martha was not good with first meetings, and she feared she had been too curt, but let him go to hell. She had not asked him to talk to her.

The attendant came in. She had discovered that her stingy boss had left his office door open, and had sneaked in to make all the unauthorised phone calls to the hinterland she could possibly manage before he got back. As a result, she was flustered and on the defensive when she came out.

"*Noms?*" she demanded, settling her drably clad thin frame on her chair, not even looking at them.

They gave their names and she picked their cards out of a pile held together by a plastic band and flipped them across the table.

They walked out of the library together.

"Where do you live?"

"In a *minicité*."

"Me too," he said. They discussed the various merits of living in a *minicité*, student housing provided at unjustifiable high cost by private individuals, as opposed to the "*bâtiments*", which were the original student hostels. His room was not far from hers. He pointed out his building to her and walked her to her door. It was after he left that Martha realised that, unusually, she had not felt after a while that he should go away and leave her alone. She was surprised to notice that he did not bore her like the others inevitably did after five minutes, however flattering their attention.

Two afternoons later, she was walking back to her room with a group of friends when she saw him sitting in a bar at the main junction, around which were cluttered most of the wooden and mud-brick shacks housing the photocopying, hairdressing, second-hand goods and furniture businesses. He saw her and came out into the sun. She dropped back from the group and he took her hand.

"How?"

"Fine."

He invited her to come in and have a drink with him. Martha was about to refuse because back home, girls like her did not sit in bars, but then she saw that there were many other girls there, so she gave in and took a soft drink. He was finishing a small Guinness, which he made last until she had downed her Sprite.

Then he invited her to his tiny room. It was simply furnished, but no less crowded for all that. It had a medium-sized bed covered with a single flowered cotton sheet, an indoor showering stall with a door, which probably signified that there was a toilet in there as well. He had a small bookshelf of unvarnished white wood loaded with his high school books and a few new textbooks he must have picked up from the notoriously inadequate university bookshop. Directly beneath his single window was a bare table of the same soft pale wood, just like the one she had. The general impression was one of tidiness without fuss, which was refreshingly different from the stuffy boys' rooms smelling of dirty feet that she had visited so far. On a small, lopsided bedside table was a medium-sized radio-cassette player.

Martha sat on the chair next to his reading table. He offered to get her another drink, but she refused, fearing that she might have to pee soon and not wanting to have to ask to use his bathroom. They chatted about the university and the difference between the Francophone and Anglophone ways of life. He was from a large, dusty market town further inland from her hometown.

After a while, she began to feel the need to use the bathroom, and decided to leave. He saw her to her door and hung around as if he hoped to be asked in, but she said a firm goodbye and they agreed that he would visit the next day. Too much encouragement wouldn't do, and she did not yet know where all this would lead.

The next day, he came and ate at her place and from then on, it was up, up and away - or downhill, depending on where you stand. She had a boyfriend at last.

She gave herself to him with a total lack of introspection. When, three weeks into their budding friendship, she decided that she would have him, all her good Catholic inhibitions burned away like paper lining off cigarette foil, and the fire overwhelmed her, consuming them both. She did not even wait a month after their first meeting (the rule amongst her clique was two or three months, though it was doubtful that anyone waited that long) to lie in bra and panties on Tom's narrow student bed in the half-darkness, the overhead light off, the

19

luminous wedge from the half-open bathroom door cutting a revealing swathe out of the nearer shadows, leaving the bed on the other side of the room in modest dimness.

The first night, she lay under the sheet in apprehensive expectation, Tom was a dim warm shape coming to lie beside her and materialising into soft warm flesh with muscle under it, hard and gentle, as she relinquished ownership of herself in the sweltering tropical darkness, and kept back nothing. That was normal. He was her first love and she had not yet learned caution. Later, with more experience, she would realise that he was, though gentle, rather inexperienced and more capable of deriving pleasure from their union than stimulating it. But the idea of having a boyfriend all to herself, someone to feel close to, made up for any shortcomings, which she did not notice in any case, not knowing that they were there.

And she found the do-not-let-him-take-your-clothes-off-before-two-months wisdom of her girlfriends tiresome in the extreme. If you enjoyed being with someone, why on earth would you pretend otherwise? And what did it matter when she took off her clothes if she *did* take them off in the end? And all that nonsense about not showing a man that you enjoyed doing what you did with your clothes off! What was the point of doing something so important if you did not enjoy it and let it be known?

"No, I'm telling you, it's not nice", said Nora, her provincial friend-of-sorts to whom she confided her intentions, "He will wonder where you learned to like such things."

"And where would he have learned his own *such things?*"

"Men always know these things, they do it first with loose girls who let them. But girls like us are different."

"How?"

Upbringing, said Nora. Education. Religion.

"Why did God give us such desires if we may not fulfil them? All that is nonsense. We learnt in biology class that such urges are natural. It is okay to have them. The important thing is to indulge yourself responsibly, you know, pregnancy, AIDS and all that."

20

"Martha, let me tell you something that you do not know. It is not good for a woman to show all she knows. People will think she is bad or too experienced."

"So the idea is that you can be as bad as you want, but do let anyone know, especially men?"

"Yes! Ask your mother whether this is not true."

"I do not discuss such things with my mother, and I am not going to live in hypocrisy. Sex is a natural thing that is enjoyed by both male and female. It is above all a biological function. Its social aspect is secondary."

Nora, wiser in the ways of the world, said: "Okay, go ahead and see if biology classes will get you a husband. I have a tutorial at four." And they parted in mutual disgust.

Martha, who had stopped going to church in her final year of high school anyway, because she had begun to find organised religion irrelevant and hypocritical, went on and showed Tom what she could do, and to hell with Nora! All those things the nuns said - they were in no position to make pronouncements - what did they know about such things?

At that time in her life, Martha had begun to judge the discernment of the Mother Church in sexual matters by what (as she read in a book on marriage purloined by one of the more daring girls from her father's library) one Christian saint is purported to have said about women. A woman, thundered Saint Clement of Alexandria, should expire with shame at the mere thought of being a woman. She would not listen to people who beatified men who uttered such nonsense, and certainly not people who had themselves never been in love! What had the time when you let a guy see you with your clothes off to do with real love? For it was real love she felt for her Tom. Such strength of feeling could only be love.

She had never felt such tenderness for anyone. The inherent *specialness* of his dirty socks, the firm, yet delicate curl of his upper lip, the way he waved his fingers in the air when he explained things to her with his head on her belly, the way he steepled his fingers and glanced at her distractedly when he was worried. And oh, God the way he looked at her when that mood came upon him! The way he complimented her on her cooking. Martha, who had never been much interested in anything

21

culinary, had suddenly discovered that she liked cooking for her man. She would wonder about it later. Was the urge to cook for a man one was sleeping with nature or nurture? Was it the nesting instinct or mere convention? *Was* there a nesting instinct?

For the time being, such considerations had no place in her life. The guy was special, everything about him was delightful. Even his nail clippings were special to her. How could anyone think to condemn anything so beautiful?

Things became rather achingly beautiful when Tom announced a few months later that he had to go abroad at the end of the year on a scholarship, and she realised that he had been planning all this – filling forms and sending faxes - without telling her. She who had told him everything, even about cousin Molombe, who had been ostracised by the family because he had made his sister pregnant, and they, such a Catholic family, had had to arrange a quick abortion, and it was her father who had gone to see that young, unscrupulous pup of a doctor they just sent to the General Hospital; she who had told him that she shuddered at the thought of another man pawing her after him; she who, having given all, having made him the centre of her existence, had nothing left for herself, and had to reinvent herself again, going back to peer into the forgotten corners of her psyche for alternative reasons to live.

She realised that she did not really know him, and he was leaving.

He left her before she could reach cruising speed, before she could learn to be self-possessed in love, and so a part of her - the frothy exuberant trusting love, or desire to love, of girlhood - went with him forever, because there had been no time to let the bubbles burst.

She went back and told Nora because she had to tell someone.

"Ah-ah! But did he say that it was finished between you two?"

"No, he just said that he had a scholarship and he would be going to Italy."

"But he did not say that..." Nora paused significantly. Martha shook her head.

22

"Then there is no problem. If he has not said anything, don't say anything either. He might go there and send for you. He might send you things." Nora thought some more.

Her eyes lit up and she jumped up from the edge of the bed where she had been perched, eating dates. "Look! He might even want to marry you. Don't say anything to make him think that it is over between you. That way you still have a chance. Do you know how many girls end up marrying their former boyfriends who went abroad? Many! So you can write to him, send him postcards, if someone is travelling you can send him an *Afritude* shirt, you know, that sort of thing." She bit happily into a date and sat back down, her eyes dreamily fixed on vistas of manhood trapped in holy matrimony.

"You don't understand."

"Understand what?"

"Look, my problem is not that he is leaving. I love him too much to tie him down. He needs to be free. My problem is that he did not think we were close enough for him to tell me of his plans till he was sure they would not fail. He does not trust me."

"Aaaaah Martha, you too! Enh! Men don't tell women everything. They have to be men, you know, keep something back for themselves to surprise you with. In fact, nobody tells anybody everything in this world. You should learn that fast if you do not want someone to hang your dirty linen out in the street one day.

"The important thing is to find out if he wants to settle with you. And my advice to you is that you should not say anything to frighten him off right now. Just keep calm. If you start acting jumpy-jumpy like a jigger, you could miss your chance in life just like that." She snapped her fingers.

"I don't want to be married to a man who does not trust me."

"Trust is what, when you can find a husband? You this Martha, you sabi foolish sometime them bad! Get your foot in the door and the rest will follow. Trust comes afterwards."

But Martha was not convinced.

She picked up the bits of her ego she could find, discarded here and there like her clothes on the plastic-covered floor of Tom's room, and moulded and welded, so that when she mended, her soul was seamy like an over-patched bedspread. But she lived, and resolved to be more careful. She learned that love was inextricably linked to fear, the fear of being left alone, the fear that the other person might not be as much in love as one was, fear that love does not conquer all, least of all personal ambition.

Tom left just before the end of her first year in Sociology/Anthropology. Before he left, she did not go back to see him, and he, with his eyes fixed on other sights, did not come to see her. She flung herself into schoolwork with the angry energy of one who is trying to scrabble out of a pit they dug themselves and then forgot. She asked many questions. How can a person forget herself and surrender to another human being to the extent that when he leaves her, she no longer knows who she is?

Take her mother. She lived only for her father. He defined all the policies that governed her life, he determined the frame of reference, and she submitted to him without question. Why would an apparently normal woman like her mother, in full possession of her faculties, choose to define her life goals in terms of another man's ambitions, drawing her happiness from the fountain of another's potentially transient desires? Did she never feel that she was taking a risk? She had no money or livelihood of her own. How did she manage without being in control? Did she never worry about what would happen to her if her husband died or left her?

Look at Nora, crazed with the idea that one had to get married, get a man to cover one's head, as she put it, or else life would not be worth living. For her school was just a way of increasing the possibility that you would get a husband higher up on the social ladder. Was that all there was to life?

Tom had been everything to her: friend, lover, fellow student and partner. Her mother had told her that fidelity and good conduct were a woman's capital, the ultimate bargaining chip. Freedom from blame should be the major ambition of any woman. But she had never *dreamt* of cheating on Tom. She was blameless. What had it earned her? What was the point of surrender when the winner of the booty walked away and left it lying there like a dead animal in the sun?

She sought answers in books and theories. She found none that satisfied her.

She resolved to have nothing more to do with that sort of thing till she knew some of the answers to her questions. But her instincts and her needs, laid bare as they were by her first love, gravitated inexorably towards their own fulfilment.

Throbbing nipples, as anyone knows, have been known to display a singular lack of interest in healthy scepticism.

And so, in the course of her undergraduate years, she lay down again and again in the darkness, but this time she kept some of herself back to take home after the party, in the predawn half-light, through the rabbit warren of tiny verandas and dead-end passageways smelling of untreated sewage that were the student quarter's side streets. All through these dalliances, once with a classmate with a passion for Middle-Eastern perfume and a marked reluctance to allow his body to come into contact with water (and because of that, just the once) and more regularly with a young civil servant and, after him, a doctorate student, she was smug in the knowledge that she had got the better of them. She was in control, whereas they thought she was all theirs.

By trial and error, Martha had finally learned the expediency of allowing a man to think you were in his power while you did as you pleased, within certain limits. She began to understand how her mother lived with her father. She realised that men were attracted to helplessness, and threatened by unfeminine efficiency. She found out that they liked being flattered, they liked you to ask them to explain what really caused the Gulf War: asking meant that you were a modern sort of girl who listened to the news; asking *them* meant that you knew who knew more than you did, you knew who was boss and who would mould your ideas. She became the ideal of the age: a woman who could pass exams and serve a civilised dinner, a woman who could tell you about the history of Latvia, say, but who knew who was the real boss.

She played the game well, went through the motions of thraldom men liked to see, washed their socks on Friday nights

25

and their sheets on Saturdays, accompanied them to bars and chicken parlours where they explained the workings of the world to their mates and expected her to be quiet. So she was quiet, and judged them, punching silent holes in their arguments, and feeling smug because they would never know what she was thinking.

But she did not know herself as well as she thought she did. She had not covered all the angles. When the whirlwind came and snapped the tent pegs of her new smugness, she was out in the cold again. She had sheltered herself under a flimsy lady's parasol in anticipation of a drizzle, and instead there came a storm.

In the meantime, she got her degree easily. Her parents were pleased. At twenty-two, their daughter had come a long way.

Now she could find the right husband.

Instead, she went to postgraduate school and met the King of Rats.

6

The King of Rats was one of her *maîtrise* teachers who went on to teach her class for the *doctorat*. He was short, balding and bouncy, with a hard basketball of a belly. The day he took his clothes off, she saw it was covered in a field of very kinky hair. Before she met and bedded him, Martha had thought she hated men with kinky body hair. Tom, for instance, had had none at all. Moreover, she had difficulty understanding what any woman would see in a potbellied man. What could possibly be desirable in a man who looked pregnant? Men had no excuse for protuberant middles. Women at least had the excuse of repeated childbirth. *Ergo*, a man with a paunch was sloppy and self-indulgent. And how did his body fit a woman's anyway, you know, *that* way?

But all that was before she learned the body's capacity to adapt, to betray itself into impossible postures when reason was on holiday and the juices ran the house. It was before she learned the self-serving logic of unreasoning passion.

The first time she had tutorials with him when she was doing her *maîtrise*, he was just another lecturer with atrophied research instincts and unrealistic perceptions of his own intellect. In her experience, university lecturers were creatures of twenty-year-old lesson notes, mangy dogs snapping and snarling at each other over petty faculty positions, essentially creatures of habit embittered and frustrated at the world's strangely persistent blindness to their finely-honed and potentially vice-chancellor abilities. That is what he seemed. Another idiot who thinks he is smart and hates the world for not agreeing with him.

She knew some gossip about lecturers, who was sleeping with whom, who exchanged marks for female students' sexual favours, who had once slapped the Dean, who was caught having a knee-trembler with a plump female student who had finally seen the light after failing his course three times in a row. But she had steered clear of all that. There was a class of girl in her view, dead from the neck up, who went through university basically on her back or kneeling before the spread legs of male lecturers. She, Martha, was living proof that brains counted, even in a dusty, mismanaged banana-republic university. She did not need to sully herself by sleeping with a man perhaps twice her age just to get on in the world. How utterly disgusting! At least, no one could accuse her of sleeping with anyone other than because she felt attracted to him. She would never go with a teacher for good grades or with any other man for money. In Martha's eyes, the reasons for having sex were what decided its legitimacy. There was honest sex, which she had as often as she could, and then there was sex with an agenda, which amounted to undeclared prostitution, the sort Nora advocated. Against such sordid pecuniary temptations, she was armoured. Impregnable. She did not doubt her ability to overcome all temptation if she really wished.

But she had never met the other kind of sex, perverse desire, the incubus of unbridled wanting that swept away all scruples and made you do things you disapproved of. Temptation, the insidious, soft and sibilant, unreliable need, the whiny Gollum who wears you out, she had not known that. She knew that she could face it boldly and ultimately triumph. That was what the nuns said. Pray for guidance, and the Lord will give you strength, they said, rosary rolling between thumb and forefinger. But she did not know that temptation is a coward. It sneaks and sidles, it comes at you from behind, it is ungallant. It fights dirty. And it can snap your conscience like uncooked spaghetti and flick it aside. And you would not even notice.

So, when, one drizzly afternoon in her third year of postgraduate studies, as she was walking up to the university gates in the rain, the King of Rats offered her a lift in his ancient Nissan Stanza, she was grateful and vaguely flattered that he remembered her from a class of thirty, twelve girls, eighteen boys. He dropped her off at the traffic lights. He was going right, he said, sorry I cannot drop you off further on, but I have to pick up my wife, she has gone to a meeting in the *Quartier du lac*, and they close at five, it is already four forty-five.

What do you need to fear from a man who talks about his wife so openly?

She liked his voice with its vestigial American accent. Later, much later, she would realize that in his boundless vanity, he was fighting an eternal battle with his tongue to maintain some vocal reminder of his stay in North America many years ago. That had been the sole defining moment of his life, which he sought to recapture by telling her carefully-preserved anecdotes about his stay in the white man's land, where things worked as they should and a man's real worth was recognised. He had a rudimentary North American accent not because he could not help it, but because he did his level best to keep one. In his ears it made him sound, well, imported. Erudite.

"And do you live far away?" he asked as he manoeuvred his car to a stop. Such an idle query.

No, she told him, just down the there, behind this tall building.

She went home, grateful, she thought, for having been spared the long walk home in the rain. That was all. Indeed it was.

He wove his web, the King of Rats. Little kindnesses. More lifts. A rare textbook. Subtle praise. Offhand compliments. Later, she realized that he had weighed her, told her what she wanted to hear, flattered a vanity she did not believe she possessed. She thought she was past the stage of gullible provincial seduced by some city slicker. Anyway, she *knew* this about herself: she would not be caught dead in a married man's bed.

He was rather kind, really, just like the nice big brother she had never had. It was also refreshing to talk to an older man who treated you like his intellectual equal. She did not realize when she started looking forward to chats in his office with more anticipation than was healthy in a platonic relationship. She did not even notice when she began to dress for him. Unknowingly, she went down Mrs. Sparsit's stairs until, when she reached the bottom, she did not know that she had actually taken the last three steps at a jump.

7

Then a man who claimed to have worked with Margaret Mead in his student days came to give a lecture. The Department of Sociology and Anthropology was in a tizzy. The King of Rats knew the visitor; who had taught him in university. As one of the more serious students, in her view, but more likely because everyone had by now surmised that the King of Rats was either sleeping with or about to sleep with her, Martha was invited to the small post-lecture gathering in one of the cleaner chicken parlours. The aim was to give the visitor a taste of local spice.

Sitting around low rattan tables adorned with faded plastic flowers in graceless mass-produced wooden vases, eating the roast chicken and fried ripe plantains, Martha listened to the conversation, and admired the way the King of Rats seemed to steer the conversation with effortless ease to just what the visitor was likely to be interested in. She wondered whether she would ever be that sophisticated. The air was thick with anthropological jargon, the reek of beer and cigarettes and the underlying smells of clayey dust mixed with male aftershave sprayed on too thick, too fast. Martha liked it. She liked to listen and pass judgment without being forced to participate.

When, at about ten, most of the department people rose either to go home or to repair to another bar for boozy post mortems about each other's performance in the presence of the foreign visitor, the King of Rats lingered till most of the others had gone. Sensing that he wanted her to come with him, but that he hesitated to declare his intention of leaving with a young woman at such a late hour, Martha went out onto the veranda and waited for the goodbyes to end. There was a cool breeze blowing. The chicken parlour was on a slight promontory, and in the dark, the city was almost, but not quite, beautiful.

When he finally extricated himself, the King of Rats was naturally going Martha's way, but if she didn't mind, he would stop over at his office to pick up some tapes of local music for the man who had worked with Margaret Mead. She didn't mind. A part of her mind welcomed the possibility of indulging in a little post-prandial dissection of the faculty people, and another, unacknowledged part shivered with anticipation of what late-night meetings would bring.

The campus was mostly deserted, except for the night birds heading for the amphitheatres for a night of swotting. Security fluorescents dimly lit the corridors, which were redolent of the sweat and fear of thousands of student ghosts. He let himself into his office, turning on the light, and she followed him. He rummaged in a drawer and found the tapes. Put them in a small stack on his desk. He walked towards her, and next thing she knew, he was licking her tonsils, holding her jaw open with his hand. His belly was a hard ball pressing into her midriff. She could not breathe. His tongue darting about in the back of her throat, he reached out and put out the light. His erethismic member was a large, springy knob against her upper thighs.

She shoved his face away, drew in her lips and clamped her mouth shut, breathing rapidly through her nose. Unperturbed, his tongue darted insistently at her lips. She squirmed in his grasp. He stuck his hand down her cleavage into her new nylon bra, her best. Later, it would come to her that she had worn it for him. He pulled out her right breast and bent his head to suck at her nipple. She shoved at his head with her fists.

All through this, there was a part of her, not involved in the fray, which was thinking. Congratulations, he likes you. He *wants* you. You are desirable to this man, with his power and importance; a university professor is in lust with you! That part of her, the secret little-girl tease, would have been quite content to go home and clasp the new knowledge of its power to itself, but this was not to be.

The security lighting lent a cold, bluish glow to everything.

"Stop. Please stop it, please!"

He raised his head and looked at her in the twilight. His eyes were dark and hooded, but she could feel their heat.

"You want me, don't you? Hm? You want me."

31

"Yes"

Her voice was the whisper of the dying. Her lower belly boiled softly in treacherous acceptance. He tried to kiss her again. She clamped her lips shut. This time he did not insist. He locked up and drove her home in silence. He knew when he had won.

Back in her room, she lay down or her bed, closed her eyes, and tried to think about all this. So this was what passion was. That insistent heat that made you feel scared and exhilarated all at once. All the men she had slept with, none had ever made her want to sleep with him just because he kissed her. For the first time, she understood some of the emotions described in romance novels. One *could* actually feel desire to the point where it made one dizzy.

Another thing surprised her. She had thought that there was a natural barrier against unseemly temptations that would block any waywardness in decent girls like her. There were things decent girls just did not do. You know, like go with married men. She had felt that the reluctance to do such things was hammered so far into your brain that your body would take care of itself and could not let itself be drawn into relationships your mind did not approve of. So why was she desiring a man when she knew, consciously and otherwise, that he was married?

Behind her closed eyes dark red and black shapes flowed in and out of each other, mutating. Her mind was floating on an unreal sea dotted with vague imaginings of their bodies, his and hers, twined and heaving together.

She sat up. This could not be happening to her. She could not want this man. It had to stop.

For the next week and several more after that, she avoided his eyes in class and hurried away afterwards. She would not give in to a married man. It was enough, she hoped, that she knew how much he wanted her. She held out for five whole weeks, and then, one afternoon, her body took over. Her hands went to her plastic closet, picked out her nicest skirt, long, black and flared with belt straps just above her hips, along with a colourful Mexican blouse, and her legs took her to his office.

He did not refer to the last time she had been there. His shiny black pupils reflected her Mexican blouse. She looked at him once, and looked away. They did not talk at all. Then he leaned forward and dialled a number to cancel an appointment.

"Walk up to the gates and then start walking down towards the traffic lights. I'll pick you up there."

Martha nodded. She did not ask where they were going. She went out of the office and walked up to the road.

In the car, they did not talk. He drove them to a small hotel in the hills and asked her to wait in the car. He went in. Then he came back out and asked her to go to room 217. It was up the stairs on the left.

"Close the door, but do not lock it. I shall be up in five minutes."

The receptionist was reading the paper and listening to the racing news. He did not look up as she walked to the staircase, convinced that she was on a huge stage and the whole world was looking at her. Near the staircase was a rack with condoms, toilet tissue and porn magazines on sale. The logistics of sin, she thought, and giggled nervously to herself.

Upstairs, the room smelled of the old sweat and hurried encounters of other lovers; the sheets looked used, but the bed was perfectly made, with hospital corners. There was a small TV on the scratched brown table. A thought flashed through her head that this was the appropriate beginning to a sordid extramarital affair, but she pushed it away and undressed. She used the bathroom and came back to lie on the bed in her bra and panties. There was a dry, tight feeling in her stomach, a lot of anticipation and a little fear. Her heart thudded slowly, heavily.

The door opened a crack, then wider, and he came in. He went to the window and pulled the blinds shut. Then he took off his clothes and hung them carefully on a hanger, and did the same for the clothes she had flung on the back of the chair.

Stark naked, he came to stand next to the bed. His short, thick penis bobbed impatiently, speaking its own language, dancing to its own music. Then suddenly he pulled her up and propelled her to the chair, against which he took her roughly, with no preliminaries. It was over very quickly for both of them. Then he led her back to the bed and she lay down.

He lay next to her; one arm crooked, his head borne on his hand, and looked her slowly up and down. There was no shyness in his gaze, and Martha met it with unprecedented boldness. She had never really looked directly at a naked man when she knew he was aware of her scrutiny. Usually she stole looks when a man was undressing or getting up to go to the bathroom, and kept her eyes demurely shut during sex, but this one invited her gaze, he revelled in it. He was proud of his body and he knew his power.

Kneading her breast, he said, "That one was for me. Now I am going to do it just for you. And I want you to tell me how you like what I am going to do to you." His hand slid lower, teasing. She was incredibly aroused by his shamelessness, and she felt the heat pulsing, right up to her scalp.

He mounted her and she welcomed his hard weight. His eyes gleamed at her. Then he invaded her with silky savagery, quickening the tempo till when she thought she would burst, and then stopping suddenly, only to begin again slowly, building up. She heard someone gasping and mewling in a most undignified manner, and thought it might be her. She did not care. Then he thrust at her violently and cried out his name as he stiffened and shuddered for what seemed an age, and rested his full weight on her.

He was not heavy; she welcomed the oneness, the slick sweat between their bellies, and the heat in the air.

They slept. He woke her up again, for what he called "one for the road". While she lay there exhausted, he rose and went to the bathroom, leaving the door open, and she could hear him urinating noisily into the bowl and afterwards she could see him washing his genitals in the sink. He came back into the room, briskly towelling himself about the crotch.

"Get up, lazybones. That how lazy you are? A little exercise tires you out. Wait till I decide to give you some real good treatment. You ain't seen nuthun' yet, baby. This is the beginning of your sexual education."

"You call this a little exercise?"

"You go see. Go and tidy up."

34

While she washed, he dressed, humming to himself. He sat on the edge of the bed and watched her as she dressed, and when she was finished, he pulled her to him, standing up as he did so, and stuck a hand into her bra.

"This is mine, hm? No giving it to those young puppies sniffing about you, enh?" he raised her skirt and put his hand into her panties, his fingers moving with the sure touch of a person finding his way in his own dark bedroom. Martha arched towards him and he chuckled.

"What is that? I thought you were tired." His arm around her, he looked at his watch over her shoulder. His voice changed and he said shortly: "Okay, time to hit the road." He picked up his keys and handed Martha her bag. "You wait here five minutes and come down after me." Not waiting for a reply, he eased himself out of the room. When she followed him downstairs, he was sitting in the car, the engine running. He pulled away as soon as she got in and they went down the hill. The city was spread at their feet, lights twinkling. It was a cool evening, and Martha wound down the window and let the breeze cool her face. She sighed happily.

He glanced at her. "We'll have to keep the office visits short, you understand. I'll work something out. We have to handle this thing like adults, hm?"

When they approached her building, he pulled over to the kerb and, looking straight ahead, pulled up her skirt again and scratched her pubis like a dog defining its territory.

"Take care."

And thus, she joined the club of serious, dedicated sinners. People often underestimate the wayward power of their own bodies.

In the first weeks of unfettered blithesomeness, she flitted airily through all the clichés: *nothing so right could ever be wrong*, said her father's old Cliff Richard record. We are not hurting anyone. What his wife doesn't know can't hurt her. All of those. Plus the ones about her unprecedented desirability, the feeling of triumph when one can have and hold a man belonging to someone else. And her ego stretched, took wing and soared, finally freed. Human beings are not really made to stick with one partner. Society, religion and a spurious decency can convince them to stick at it for a while, but you cannot go against your own nature. If a wife is inadequate in so many ways, then why should a man be deprived of smart, sexy solace elsewhere?

Why indeed?

Because, of course, she was smart and sexy. He made her feel so desirable, so near-perfect. On one occasion, when she was telling him about a minor disagreement with one of her girlfriends, he said: "I can't imagine anyone having a problem with you, you are so easygoing."

She glowed brighter than tungsten. When he left her room that evening, she lay in the dark and thought that she was not such a bad person after all. In fact, she was rather special. She sat up suddenly, put on the light and counted her good points on her fingers, one by one.

She was good at school

She was beautiful in a simple, natural way (he said so)

She was sexy (he said so, and in any case, it was obvious; he *always* had an erection around her)

She had wisdom beyond her years (he said, supporting his head on his crooked arm and studying her breasts). To her this was almost the best thing.

She was easygoing

In addition to her natural intelligence, she was possessed of an intellectual curiosity rare in other women. This was the best thing. She had a mind he recognised.

And so on and so forth, until she ran out of fingers and was secure in her new faith. She threw caution to the winds. Discretion she eschewed as being the product of small-minded hypocrites. She accosted him openly in the corridors. She went to his office and sat there for hours on end.

At first, she thought she recognised what was happening to her for what it was. This was animal desire in its purest form, not tainted by social considerations; that is why her physical responses were so strong. This was what the romance books called passion. Tough on morality, true, but a person was permitted to sin seriously at least once in her life. What else was forgiveness all about? But soon the search for approval from her lover added to the passion, and then came craving for affection, and then she was in love. This shocked her, but only a little, because:

Love is a pure emotion. Why stifle goodness? God is love, said the hymn,

And the one who lives in love, lives in God, and God lives in him...

There are many forms of love, all recognized by the Church – remember the Song of Songs? King Solomon had many wives. Jacob had Rachel and Leah. Look at good ole Abraham and the concubine! Muslims can have four wives if they wish.

I don't want to marry him, but by God, I will be free to love him as I please. Nobody knows but me what he is going through at home. His wife is limited to her mindless social climbing and silly women's meetings, like my mother.

Society condemns adultery, but the majority is not always right. Pious flat-earthers actually roasted Galileo's toes for God's sake, and they turned out to be wrong. And who are they to judge me anyway?

And she flew higher, this Icarus.

8

Everyone smelled the burning wax before her, of course. Another cliché. By the time she noticed that her wings had become molten, misshapen stumps, she had plummeted back to earth, badly winded by her fall, unable to catch her breath. There were no king's men to try to put her back together again. In this respect, Humpty Dumpty was luckier. The King of Rats just walked away without a backward glance, to another vulnerable, self-deluding little idiot. Unscathed, he gave his lectures and surprise tests while someone lay dazed on the ground and tried to figure out which way was up.

Moulting was due. But nothing had prepared her for this new kind of pain. Sloughing off old skin takes a while, and the new skin is tender and fragile, and easily wounded. She had thought that she knew pain when Tom, dear, dear Tommy, left. No one had told her that a bruised ego is worse than yearning for love departed, and takes infinitely longer to mend. The King of Rats just moved on to the next girl in the class, a stupid, hairy creature whose shoulders were wider than her hips, a damn improper fraction!

Dear Kingsley, (she wrote, to slip under his door)

I do not know what is happening to us. I say us because I still feel that we have something going, even if you seem not to realize this. A bond such as the one we have forged between us over the past six months cannot be severed in a few weeks. Therefore, I will fight, as we women have always done, in the face of the dilettantism of you men, to preserve this bond. Otherwise, I do not know what will become of us.

What has she that I do not have, I am tempted to ask.

Nevertheless, I shall not, for the ways of men are inscrutable to women. The ways of women are also inscrutable to women too, especially the ways of such uptight and vapid pretties as you seem to now prefer, but that is not the point at issue.

Suffice, then, to say that whatever she has, I shall have more, be it love or hate. Be well advised. I shall not give up. I think you need guidance and I believe it is my noble duty as a woman, though no less exacting for all that, to make you see the light.

I also think you should call me when I leave messages on your phone. I think it is the height of rudeness to ignore the distress call of a woman, especially one you have slept with with such passion, frequency and delectation. I shall come to your office tomorrow at noon. It is close to midnight as I finish this note. I will slip it under your door soon, and you will read it in the morning.

Please have the goodness, out of the kindness of your heart, if you have one under all that fat, to reply.

Do not do this to me, please.

M.

Mingled with the anger and pain was fear, the fear that she had always lived with, a vague, unreasoning fear that she was not good enough. The end of the affair seemed to confirm the sneaky feeling that she was not good for anything, even for keeping a potbellied middle-aged idiot who should feel lucky that she loved him. She had not been good enough for Tom, who had upped and left, and who had never written again. She was good for nothing. She was unable to have an easy relationship with her own parents. She had no close friends she could confide in. In those dark days, Martha felt that the world had rejected her because it had looked at her and found her wanting. If her love life was always going to be like this, then why take the risk?

Going to class and sitting through tutorials became an ordeal. The hairy girl and her friends sniggered and looked daggers at her; the boys examined her with sex in their eyes. She was fair pickings now the teacher had finished with her. A few tried, but she was too wrapped up in her misery even to feel insulted. Tom had left her sense of personal honour intact. The others had barely touched her. The King of Rats had wiped himself with it, flushed it down the toilet and walked away. The King of Rats dented and gouged, scraped and scratched. And walked away to other, unconquered interests.

Kingsley,

I do not know what you think you are playing at. Standing in the sun for half an hour talking to a colleague you yourself have described as a moron on several occasions when you can clearly see me waiting to waylay you by the stairs smacks of escapology of the worst type. And while we are on the issue of escapism, I think your affair with me has been a fine work of art in that regard. For you are seeking to escape from the tarnished existence you lead as an unrecognized professor in a small university that is worse than backwoods. It is not even backwoods, for backwoods as a word connotes a certain degree of fertility, however stupid. It is an intellectual desert, and you are the poisonous cactus in the distance masquerading as the suggestion of an oasis.

Enough.

I do not think you are treating me right. And I am beginning to think that you know it and don't care. Why else would you punish yourself by staying in the midday sun for half and hour and after the tutorial give me that smile as if you smelt a rotten banana skin? If you are not careful, I will be the banana skin on which your career will slip. I am not the rotten banana in the basket.

I want you. You know how it can be between us. Why dither?

Call, if you do not wish these pained attempts at levity on my part to become something else that will land on the Rector's table.

Boomerang primed and ready to fly.

M.

Martha lost weight and developed acne, which she had never had before. The hairy girl glowed and developed a waist overnight.

Kingsley,

The following are facts.

I followed you to the Rectorat today.

The Dean has just been having at me.

I conclude from the above facts that this is war. My country, not having Kitcheners, will not tell me it needs me, but I need myself, though a part of me wishes to make sure that I no longer exist.

I will resist that part of me. I wish to see you one last time, so you can tell me what I have done to deserve such pain. Have you never felt it? I think you have, for even men, who can sleep with whom they want with both fear (of commitment) and favour (of their nether erectile unmentionables) can and have felt the pain of loss and betrayal.

Reporting me to the authorities in your own probably untruthful words is not the sort of thing I recommend. You do not know what I will become in future. I am already in university in a country where sending women to school is still an aberration in some parts, where a man can still have two wives or more if he pleases, and where Fons and Lamidos marry children of thirteen. That also will change, as sure as I have come to university.

So I will not be weak forever. The time will come when men like you will pay. It is not as far off as you think. It may even take a swipe at the tail-end of your sordid little life.

Call.
M.

The inexorable finiteness, the house-of-cards-ness of desirability she now knew. You could wear the shortest skirts (she tried) expose as much cleavage as you dared, be as witty and profound as you pleased, humans are not monogamous. One tends to forget this when one is the object of someone's passing monogamous fancy, and then it is easy to feel sorry and contemptuous about poor, dim-witted, uncomprehending wifey. But usually the facts are brought home to one on a bed of choice nails, such as she now lay on.

Telling things about me to your elephant skin, hirsute (a quality you share with her: what do you guys do in bed, run combs through your joint stomach hair to create the magnetism needed to make the current flow between you turgid souls?) current whore and causing her to snigger as I wend my way through the midday crowds hardly reflects the learned associate professor that same people would like to believe they are.

Respect yourself!!!

41

She lay on her bed and analysed her feelings endlessly. Her ego was one large bruise. She indulged in self-flagellation. This was the punishment you got for thinking that you were entitled to someone else's husband just because your body said so. She was not the holy, safe-sex, tread-the-beaten-path, decent middle-class, good-at-school, intellectual-in-a facile-pop-fiction-way girl she thought she was. She was wanton, lacked self-control, had zero perspective, was stupid, suicidal, gullible, easily swayed by flattery (of the subtlest kind, true, but who needed excuses?) immoral, bestial, selfish, a downright ninny, an out-and-out weakling, a moral coward, an ostrich. Worse. An utter fool. She made futile comparisons.

What you have	What I have
Your age	My youth (absolute and relative)
Experience in these matters	My naiveté
Your maleness and its attendant imagined superiority	I am a female in a society that thinks we are only half human
Your money	None of my own, but we'll see about that later
Your secure tenure	You can fail me, but I will protest
Your cunning and cynicism	I will be wiser from this experience
Your network of male colleagues to support you	My equally powerless female friends
A hairy girlfriend	No one but you, and you don't want me
A car (ageing)	My two legs and money for taxis
A wife	Ha!
Your education (limited, in spite of your pretensions)	My education, less now, but with time I will be your equal at least
Your house with the leather chairs you boast about	My student room with its cheap furniture
Your invincibility (not real: imagined)	My vulnerability (never imagined but real enough

	now)
TOTAL: WE WILL SEE	

She did not know how to start to recover. So she went about her business, dumb with pain, crazed with the unrealistic hope of rekindled affection on his part, full of self-hate that part of her, a large part, still pined after him. If he had so much as smiled in her general direction during those first painful months, she would have gone to him. But he did not. He did not exactly cut her out; she was a member of his class and he interacted normally with her, as a student. Whenever she went to his office hoping to see him alone, the hirsute creature and her friends were all over like large rock spiders, clinging to every surface.

She began to gain a vague understanding of why people killed themselves. But there was something else about herself she did not know. She was resilient.

And so, more or less on autopilot, she obtained a good DEA (*Diplôme d`Etudes Approfondies*), went through the motions of applying for doctoral scholarships, and was dazedly surprised to get one from the Dutch development organisation.

9

While waiting for her travel arrangements to be made, she packed up and left her room. She had lived there for three years after leaving the main student residential area, and it was as comfortable as student rooms went, but memories of the King of Rats, lurking like old smells in dank corners, had poisoned the air forever. So she sold her bed and her cheap dark red carpet, and packed up the rest of her stuff, got on the inter-city coach, and went to wait for her departure in her parent's house.

Her mother, only sixteen when she had been married off to the nurse, had not yet lost her baby fat when she was introduced to the more intimate, invasive aspects of married life. She was never to lose it, for pregnancy, aided by dear Mr. Elive's insistent and ardent attentions, came soon after, followed by childbirth and nursing, and nursing mothers were supposed to be plump full breasted. So she had matured into a heavy-breasted, full-bodied matron, a sixteen-year-old semi-literate mind trapped in a fat-clogged grown woman's body. When she had married the nurse, she had just finished her first year of typing school. She left it with no regrets, for marriage conferred more status than pecking away at an antediluvian Remington that often refused to do her bidding.

Now her daughter had come to stay. It was not that Mrs. Elive did not love her, God forbid, but the girl was rather difficult and conversation with her always a chore. She would not talk about the ordinary things that girls wanted to discuss. As a teenager, she had spent most of her long vacations in a corner with a book and refused to help her in the kitchen. When she had broached the subject of taking care of one's body as puberty loomed large on the horizon, the girl had snapped at her: "I know all that. They told us in school." And gone back to her book.

There she now was, come back here glowering and snarling at everyone, and not even noticing that there was housework to be done. And the way she stayed in her room for hours, and would not even go to visit her old friend Nora, now safely ensconced in the mansion of the profligate son of the richest man in the town (after all, what he spent, his father replaced: Nora was happy with her twins, her teaching job and her young-matron social status). Really, Martha was just too difficult.

Martha ignored her mother's reproachful glances and concentrated all her efforts on just walking upright without falling flat on her face with despair. There was a permanent ache somewhere around where her stomach was supposed to be. Scientists said that in times of stress, the stomach sometimes dropped several centimetres; Martha doubted that hers was anywhere around her abdomen, she felt so empty. Her father was perplexed by her moodiness, but he left her alone. Woman's business, probably. Best leave her to sort it out by herself. The hormones made them unpredictable, volatile. Plus, he had never really talked with his daughter before. What could he possibly say to her? What did people like her talk about?

To pass the time, Martha went to visit Nora in her large new house. Nora, short and rather heavy to begin with, was now almost as wide as she was tall. Never one to spare the details, she regaled Martha with tales of her bedroom life - I rub soapsuds on my hands, then I sneak up behind him when he is shaving and I grab him, she said, and squealed. Martha wanted to ask her where a decent girl like her had learnt *such things*. She maligned her sisters-in-law (that Ma Julie likes to put her mouth everywhere) and complained about the social politics among competing young matrons. Her twins hovered around her, alternately drooling and whining. Looking at her, Martha wondered whether she would ever be able to settle for so little. It was common knowledge that Nora's husband had hands that roved in many directions, including over the maid's body, but Nora seemed oblivious to all that. She had reached the apex of her expectations in this world, and she had no complaints. The fact that her husband slept around Nora might have been ignorant of, but Martha suspected that she knew and either did not care or was not telling.

So this was the alternative to being hurt by the King of Rats. Was this the grass on the other side? Martha was not sure which was worse.

Some dark nights she woke up suddenly wondering whether her feeling of superiority to people like Nora and her mother was not just imagined. Are we defined by what we see ourselves to be or by the idea that people have of us? Were these women wrong to settle for what they could have without fuss, or should they demand more and risk losing even the little they had? Look at her; she had gone about sniffing at Nora's mercantile pragmatism and here she was groaning in pain while Nora lived surrounded by her children and a man to call hers, up to a point.

Whatever the actual facts were about his philandering and his non-existent money-making abilities, he was officially Nora's and at least no one would be shocked if she put her arm around him in public. She was settled. And Martha was not. Nora showed every sign of being happy. And Martha was withering inside with unhappiness. Nora was not alone. Martha was lonelier than she had ever been in her whole life, and there was no one to share the pain. She felt that Nora as a married woman would take a dim view of dalliance with a married man. People like her, with limited mental abilities, could have very strong convictions about their perception of right and wrong. So she did not tell her, even though Nora probed about who her new "guy" was.

"I don't have a boyfriend."

"Nonsense. I know you and your secretive cat-like ways. You probably have a fiancé snuck away somewhere. Every woman needs a man in her life; it's not all book, book, book. And you should start thinking of having children. Very soon it will be too late."

"Too late for what?" snapped Martha, cut to the quick.

"For a lot of things. Let me tell you enh, I know your ideas, I know that you think you can change the world. But you cannot oh! You cannot. So stop dreaming and come down here on earth and be like the rest of us. You take what you can get and God takes care of the rest. What else do you want? You can get married, have your children, maybe get a job at the

46

university here – you know. A teaching job is good for women with children, because the demand on their time is not so high, and they are free during the holidays. Now, all that school, school that you are going to, what are you going to do with it, enh? Book no be man pickin, my sister. Find yourself a man and settle down.

"So who is he?"

"No one. We broke up."

"Ah, that is why you are making sad-sad things. But get yourself someone else. Use your bottom power. What do you think God gave you that thing for, to have periods? Use it. Chop life, Mama! That is your capital. Find a man and screw him well-well, and you can lead him about by the nose, then you people go to court and sign."

Unable to resist, Martha asked: "So if I screw him well-well, as you say, won't he think that I am too "experienced"? Won't he wonder where I learned such things?"

"Ah, that was childhood *naïveté*. Things have changed now. You don't go into a man's bed and lie there like a log of wood. Ensnare him with your privates." She giggled. "That is why you have muscles down there. And you have to maintain your body", she said, glancing at Martha's lacklustre hair. "You get to keep skin. My husband is attracted to fat women, that is why I put on weight, but I make sure that I do my hair at least once every week and that I dress well. He has to be proud of me in public. Use something with aloe vera to remove those pimples. I'll take you to Priscilla's salon. And I think there is someone I can introduce you to, one of his friends. Yes! Let me call and invite him." She darted towards the phone.

Martha begged her to stop.

"Why? You do not have a boyfriend. I am about to get you one. Where is the problem?"

She came over and sat next to Martha on the sofa. "Martha, let me tell you something that you do not know. I know that you have a loving family and all that. But the bible says that a man shall leave his father and mother and be one with his wife. It is not for nothing. Let me tell you, don't mind what people say: fuck is thicker than blood, ya! It's thicker. Even God knows this. Don't sit there and think that the love from

47

your family is enough. And I cannot sleep with you. Your parents cannot. So find yourself someone who can, because it is not good for a woman to stay like that. You go get sick."

"I shall be going abroad soon," blurted Martha, who would have blushed if she could.

"For what, more studies?"

"Yes, I got a scholarship. I'm going to the Institute of Social Studies-the ISS-in The Hague." She told her the details.

"Hm! You no go ever stop book."

On this disapproving note, Martha escaped and went back to her room, somewhat comforted that even if she remained manless and barren, a life of such deliberate, mindless coarseness would never be for her. She wondered why she had not noticed before just how coarse Nora was.

When the final word came that she had leaving for the Netherlands, Martha was relieved to get away. She had hoped that home would bring her some solace, but there was an unbridgeable gap between her mother's world and hers. Mama could never understand what evil impulse could push a young girl with her prospects into the arms of some overweight married dwarf, risking her reputation in the process. And in any case, she had never thought of telling her mother. She would not understand. Her mother's temptations were of an entirely different kind: some church member buying her kind of wrapper just days after she bought hers, country cousins turning up in droves without warning and expecting to be fed (which kind *ba'luck* this? she would moan in the kitchen), house help talking back to her. There was no talking to her mother.

10

The scholarship allowed her to travel early, and Martha did not dither. All she had at home was her mother's shy, slug-like pride and attempts to introduce the subject of marriage "to one of our country boys", and her mother's friends looking her over like a bundle of greens in a market stall. Is she fresh enough, Felicia? I hear she took up with some boy, not of our tribe, my dear, with all these diseases…!

So Martha flew off to the Netherlands, dented rather badly but still in working order of some sort. Tougher, more suspicious, and determined not to fall in love again.

But what do we know about these things?

She arrived in The Hague, white man's metropolis, city of myriad, unconscionable freedoms in midsummer, with a couple of months to spare before school. She took up abode in the student hostel in Dorus Rijkersplein, a few minutes' walk from the ISS. The ISS was on Kortenaerkade. The "kade" suffix was, she later learned, an indication that the location was along a canal.

In the summer, the city was beautiful with its tree-lined streets and countless canals. The natives were largely friendly, if a little abrupt in their speech. Martha had never seen so many bicycles in her life. Everyone, young or old, cycled everywhere. Martha resolved to get a bike and join them. When she got lost (as she often did), people gave her directions when she asked. Within walking distance was a huge wood, the Haagse Bos, which the occupying Germans had used to launch V1 and V2 rockets during WW2. Martha spent a lot of time there, walking and learning how to cycle.

There was a lot of time for introspection, and Martha looked long and hard at herself, or so she thought. She had been surprised at what she had found herself to be. The mixed blessing of self-knowledge is not available to most of humankind, and there are some who can peer into the murky well of human desires and be shocked but strengthened by the new knowledge floating about within. Martha believed herself to be that type; she would have been shocked had she been told that she had not even taken the cover off the well-hole. One day, she would begin the real journey to the centre of herself, and the landscape would be both strange and eerily familiar. She had caught a glimpse of herself, and though she had been hurt and demeaned by what she found, it was only the beginning.

She had yet to deal with the fear.

When she got to the Netherlands, in the first strange and lonely weeks she convinced herself that she had expiated her sins. She had washed her conscience in the blood of the lamb, and felt she had become as white as snow. She had come to terms with her treacherous sexuality.

She knew sex could be a trap for the unwary, but she was yet to know just how brutal it could be. She did not know how it crusted in nooks and crannies and refused to be scrubbed off, like old soot under a saucepan handle. She did not yet know how it would wedge itself into corners and wait, and putrefy, and then one day, when it was wet enough, it would seep out and dye your life indelibly; and that if you were not careful, you would not even notice what was giving your life its new hue.

So she walked alone on the clean streets and in the beautiful Haagse Bos during the day, thinking about what direction her love life would take. Perhaps an empty, sex-only affair would be the best thing. She did not venture into the city at night; she was too timid to enjoy the nightlife alone in a strange city, thousands of miles from home and full of strange people.

School began. Three weeks after formal commencement, she met a tall, thin blond Dutchman in the Haagse Bos.

They met, in fact, because he did not see her. He was walking head down. Later, she would joke that in summer it was his nape which tanned first. Cornelius de Graaf was studying something very arcane about soil, which, he claimed, is what he was always looking at.

She was walking on a footpath one day when he bumped into her. They both apologized. They both smiled, and Martha went on, forgetting the incident almost immediately. He had direct, yet preoccupied pale grey eyes. She was not interested in beginning a new relationship so soon after the King of Rats, and yet white men as a group intrigued her. White people who visited African were types, either unwashed tourists in faded, sweaty clothes heading for local handicraft centres to be cheated by wily artisans, or odourless, fervid, aseptic Christian types in mission houses. Or even, more recently, rich expatriates driving around in expensive four-wheel-drives and ignoring the natives behind their air conditioning. She did not know them. The good-looking ordinary protagonist of most western fiction did not come to Africa. He was a normal man, and normal people did not leave their homes to travel thousands of miles to a continent where outdoor plumbing, or just outdoors without the plumbing, was a distinct possibility. Only people with a taste for adventure, on the run from unwelcome emotion, or lusting after the benefits of shrewd exploitation of other people's raw materials (minerals, timber or souls) bothered with Africa. The ordinary type western fiction usually described stayed at home and dealt with their own dilemmas.

On the whole, therefore, white people were an unknown quantity; not within the realm of her experience. Back home only prostitutes or daughters of rich, liberated, much-travelled people got involved with white men. There were of course, the new Internet brides, the girls who found love on the web because potential husbands were too scarce or too poor. And of course, there were the usual parish scandals about lonely, uprooted, sun-dried priests interfering with young female (or male, for that matter) parishioners, but that was infrequent and not to be counted. The general middle-class feeling back home before the economic crisis was that white men as boyfriends or husbands were unusual enough to be an aberration.

She, not knowing them well, was awkward around them. She either spoke too little or smiled too much, while in her mind she berated herself for acting like the typical grinning nigger faced with white superiors.

As it was, matters were taken out of her hands.

A couple of weeks later, Cornelius de Graaf went to the ISS to see a colleague who was a fellow there. He saw the black girl at the ISS restaurant, and recognized her immediately. He was in many ways a creature of impulse, and his current impulse was to go over and chat with the girl, so he filled his tray and walked over to where she was sitting at the end of a long table, with her back to the wall and a coffee before her. On the next table, two women were whispering earnestly to each other over an early lunch; he sidled past them and went to put his tray opposite her coffee. She looked up when his tray clattered onto the table top.

"Hello, may I sit here?"

"Of course, if you wish."

"I do wish," he smiled at her and sat down. Martha eyed him. Tall and blond, with those startlingly pale eyebrows and paler eyelashes. Funny grey eyes like a cat's.

"I recognized you from our collision the other day. May I buy you a drink to apologize for my clumsiness?"

This was really the first time a white person was talking to her about something that did not involve train schedules or classrooms or course content. She wondered what he wanted.

"Well, actually it was my fault. But if you insist, I'll have a coffee, Mr.-?"

"Oh! Sorry. Cornelius de Graaf" He smiled and stuck out his hand.

"Martha Elive." She took his hand. Long, warm and dry.

They chatted about inconsequential things. School, lodging, the city, soil. He sounded nice, and if he had sought her out to sit with her, then he was not one of those racist types. But the thing was, you could not tell whether a white man was just being polite, satisfying his curiosity about black people or coming on to you. Her supervisor, a small, greying fifty-something, was pleasant enough, and had taken her out to coffee, displayed great curiosity about her, and then invited her home for dinner with his erudite wife, herself a teacher of disabled children. The evening had been spent discussing avant-garde painting, a subject about which she knew less than nothing, and drinking something that tasted strongly of an unnameable flavour. But it was interesting for all that. Back home, your superior at the university did not take you out to coffee except as a prelude to taking out some part of his body and invading yours with it.

This Cornelius was young as well. What did he want? She was afraid of misconstruing his attention and making a fool of herself. Well, she would see. If he asked to see her again, she would agree. But she would make no forward moves, initiate nothing. Passive but willing, go along and see where it led. Because, after all, she had decided not to have any more affairs.

An hour later he glanced at his watch, exclaimed, and announced that he had to leave. These people lived by their watches, she had found.

"I must see my friend in five minutes. I did not notice the time pass. Did you?" There was a definite *look* in his eye as he asked this.

Martha just smiled. She had travelled down the road of show-me-you–are-interested-first; she knew its milestones. He stood up.

"Er, do you think we could meet again for a drink? Not here." He looked about him. "Maybe we could go to a place in town later this week. I could show you some of the city's sights."

"Well I have not really mastered my schedule –" Martha thought. Agreeing too soon might look too encouraging. So perhaps she would give him the hostel number, and if he called and did not get her, he could call again. Giving him her cell phone number would be too obviously willing. She did not know where this was going. He might be one of those polite types who kept on apologising, and all this might be a way of making up for bumping into her. He could be the front-man for a prostitution ring; that had happened to many African women who left home for Europe to find rich white husbands and ended up walking the streets for someone with their passport in someone else's hands.

"Call me in a couple of days and we will arrange something if I am free."

He took his leave and Martha studied him dispassionately. No rear end to speak of, of course. White men were not especially well endowed in that department. But his legs looked slim and strong under the faded black jeans. She could make out a hint of muscular calf. That was usually a good sign. If you could discern a man's calves through his trousers, his legs had good potential. Though sometimes you could be mistaken. Men were lucky, Martha thought, finishing her third or fourth coffee. They could hide a lot under their clothes, and before you knew it, you had fallen for some spindleshanks with shitty body hair and chest eczema.

Oh well. In any case, she was not looking for a prime specimen to father handsome children, just someone to pass the time. Indeed, it was a good sign that she was actually scheming to get this yellow-haired white man into bed. Her glands were beginning to work again. It was a good thing that memory of pain is highly evanescent, else everything would grind to a complete halt. How many women would go through childbirth again if they could remember exactly how it hurt? People would refuse to fall in love again after the first broken heart. She would wait for his call then.

She gathered her things and left.

Cornelius called the next evening at six. Martha was lying in bed pretending to read a Dutch magazine before going in to dinner downstairs. She was polite, putting just the right amount of smile into her voice, but she was sorry, there was some work she had to hand in the next morning and she hadn't even gone through half of it. She wasn't quite sure yet, but she might be in by four next afternoon, so if he called after that... He sounded crestfallen, but he would call as suggested. Bye.

Bye. If he was attracted to her, he would call again. If he was just being polite, he might feel that he had done his duty and leave it at that.

One Saturday, Martha was strolling towards the Blauwe Lotus restaurant in the small Anna Paulownaplein when she came across a white-haired woman in her seventies standing under the trees opposite the restaurant looking worriedly around her.

"Can I help you? Have you lost something?"

"I don't know. I thought I had my sunglasses with me, but I appear to have lost them or forgotten to put them in my bag. Oh well. Age catches up with all of us, doesn't it?"

She looked up at Martha. "Bertha van der Aa. Call me Big Bertha, like the gun," she said and smiled. Martha told her

54

she was going to the restaurant, and Bertha decided that it was a good time for her to have lunch too.

"And where are you from, young lady? Cameroon! Ah, I know. In West Africa. Oh, *Central* Africa. Used to be under the Germans once, was it not?" The old woman chatted amiably all through lunch, adroitly keeping the conversation from herself and focusing on Martha. Talking to white people she did not know made Martha a little nervous. She tried to keep from grinning like an idiot. By the time she finished lunch, Martha felt like a wrung dishcloth. But it had been pleasant to have someone notice her and admit it. Sometimes, these white people acted as if one were not there.

Besides, the older woman sounded intelligent. They talked about Mobutu and the rape of Zaire by the Belgians. They talked about mad cow disease, and consequent British exports of beef to Africa. The woman's clothes and accessories were discreetly expensive, and Martha wondered idly why an obviously wealthy woman of advancing age was wandering around on a Saturday afternoon looking lost. No relatives, no friends? Ah well, not her business. Bertha invited her for coffee at her home on Thursday, and Martha agreed.

Later in bed she thought about her new romantic possibility lying in bed next to her. She had no previous experience with people of his culture to draw on; it was a new chapter she was about to begin. She felt the cold of apprehension and a little anticipation inch down from her midriff to her loins. She wondered how it would be with this man. Would he smell different? Were there things she ought to know that she did not, things he would take for granted?

She stirred on the bed, snug and warm, shut in from the outside.

She fell asleep and her dreams were peopled with unfulfilled, uncompleted acts of lust in a pale grey, indistinct landscape, the fruit of her vague imaginings.

Next day, Cornelius called as she was hurrying to leave for her first tutorial. He hoped she remembered their date. He just wanted to say good morning. He would call at about four. He sounded cheery and a little hesitant, like a man who was reasonably sure of how his proposal would be taken but knew that life was full of disappointments.

A little after four, Cornelius called. He was lucky, she told him. She had just come in. They agreed to meet in the Blauwe Lotus for a drink and perhaps move to somewhere else later. On the way to the restaurant, Martha was already drawing up a seduction schedule, having completely forgotten that she could not be sure that he was not on the prowl for gullible black women to be dragged into prostitution. The thirst for affection, any kind of affection, had come to the forefront. Handholding in five days, she told herself. First kiss in seven. Bed in a fortnight, perhaps.

At that point in her life, she could still allow herself romantic anticipation. She was well short of thirty in a society where women waited to have a career first before having children. It was okay to wait awhile. Later, back home, she would remember her insouciance with a kind of wonder. In Cameroon, with emancipation, girls mostly went to school first and when they came out, they found out to their dismay that their friends who had not been to school had married all the men and available ones were a little thin on the ground. If you waited two weeks to bed a man, there was a good chance that when you were finally willing, a friend of yours with more immediate needs would have beaten you to it.

She stuck to her schedule. In a fortnight or so, she surrendered gracefully and allowed herself to be taken to his flat in Bentinckstraat. She did not hear violins or erupt in volcanic release; it was too strange sleeping with a white man for her to be totally relaxed, but there was a quiet contentment to feeling something for a man who was not the King of Rats. She had feared that Cornelius would be somewhat less well endowed than black men, but this turned out to be another myth. He was gentle and considerate, even skilled. Later in life, having had many specimens to compare, she would conclude that this business about black men being better was all nonsense.

Many black men felt that being supposedly well-endowed in that department meant that all they needed to do was mount you and pump away, and, in the abject gratitude of the chronically deprived (women waited for sex to be proffered;

so of course they did not get as much as they might like, which was just as well, for who ever heard of women *liking* sex or admitting that they did?) women would be begging to wash their socks and cook their meals to buy themselves some more bed time, so to speak.

She remembered a classmate who boasted that he could satisfy any woman better than any white man could. Martha had wanted to ask him: these men you have such scorn for are inventing machines and going to the moon; they run your life pretty much as they wish, and all you have to boast about is your sexual prowess? Have their women complained? Are they unable to have children? Have you slept with a white man yourself? Where did you get this from?

The refreshing thing about Cornelius was that he asked for nothing. He did not want to know whether he was good or not. He did not ask how it was for her. He did not ask her to go to the kitchen and get him a glass of water, or to the bathroom for a towel to wipe off his sweat, or tissue to blot his penis. He just gave generously of his deliciously firm young body.

She remembered how, when the King of Rats slipped into her cramped room of a sultry evening (he was always more concerned about being seen with her than she ever was), she had to fan him with a magazine afterwards: men do all the work, he said, you girls just lie there and enjoy.

His needs were always stronger, more urgent, so she had to comply whenever they came upon him or when his tight, important schedule of meetings with important people permitted him, however inconvenient it was for her. He was, after all, a *lecturer*. He never actually stated it, but the implication was that if she didn't give it to him, some other woman would. All the women lecturers in the faculty of arts were after him, of course, plus a frightening number of student twenty-somethings. His stories were more interesting than her girlish gossip; his accounts of faculty squabbling were infinitely more absorbing than her tawdry little litany of broken hearts and septic abortions that university girls had to suffer. His life was more interesting than hers was. He was older. And he was a *man*. He was a more important human being, someone who mattered in the scheme of things. He could redirect government

57

policy to considerable national advantage, if only those political idiots would listen to the intellectuals like him.

And as he often said, all women were the same.

"If women are all the same, why are you not in bed with your wife?"

He waved that aside. "Your body is younger."

Martha was so far gone, she did not even feel insulted. He went on with his theory.

Each man was, of course, unique. Inimitable. A man had the right to be judged on the basis of his actions, who he slept with or married had no bearing on what direction his public life would take, but a woman was only as good as her sexual activity, or the lack of it. Good women were cast from one mould. They were not sexual. They were motherly. They cooked well. They did not challenge the authority of men. When women digressed, it was their sexuality that led them astray. Whore, wanton, *cheerful giver*. A man could sleep around and still be considered a great statesman, and be respected for distinguished service to his country, he said. A man with a voracious sexual appetite was a hot *lad*. A woman with a voracious sexual appetite (he rolled the phrase around his mouth, proud of his English) is a whore. A woman who has had several lovers should do her best to conceal the fact; it was no source of pride. She was a prostitute. Period. Not a good administrator, an excellent magistrate, a good mother. Just a whore. One of his female colleagues was a whore because she had slept with another colleague while engaged in a dalliance with an older student.

Martha, who had been getting a little tired of his post-coital holding-forth, reminded him that what they were doing together right there in her room amounted to the same thing; besides, the woman was not even married. He said it was different for women. A woman who gives herself like that...no. The male colleague he could understand. But for a woman of her status to sleep with her student! "It is alright for men to sleep with younger women; society sanctions that, as the pattern of marriage shows, but a mature woman and her *student*!" And he curled his thick upper lip in righteous disgust. "A woman must respect herself."

Sometimes he sounded like her mother.

"So what am I then, I who have given myself to you, knowing full well that you are married? What do you call me? And I remind you that you are in bed with your student."

"That is different. I am a *man*. And you are my own little sweetheart." He settled his important bulk on his elbows and leered at her, panting in renewed anticipation. She attended to the pressing matter at hand, and forgot all else. But it came to her later that she had been his own, featherbrained little whore letting her lust override her misgivings.

Cornelius, thank the Lord, was quite refreshingly single. His ego did not need propping up at her expense. He betrayed no intimations of innate superiority. He had no ground rules for sexual behaviour. When she went down on him for the first time, he did not look at her with suspicion and ask, like the colourless young civil servant in her distant past: "Where did you learn to do that? Is it from those books you are always reading?" And when she expressed an opinion, he did not say she had read too much. He expected her to have opinions. He was a man who welcomed her ability to think, and not just when it came to stretching two weeks' worth of housekeeping money to cover one month.

But she did not lust after him with the all-consuming madness with which she had wanted the Rat. They shared many interests, and they were good together physically. The thing with the King of Rats had been a raging forest fire, destroying all. With Cornelius it was like a fire in a fireplace, tame, useful, and deliciously warm. There were no errant sparks. The King of Rats had burned all to the ground. Her affair with Cornelius burned with a quiet and steady flame. Martha was, if not deliriously happy, at least content. At peace.

The King of Rats did not inspire peace. He was always at war with himself, fighting to keep reality at bay in assessing himself. By no stretch of the imagination could more than a few of his traits be found attractive by anyone but himself, but he had so succeeded in viewing himself as an important part of the scheme of things that the world was forced to take him at his word. He had made himself attractive to her because he had convinced her that he was as important as he said he was. This was what women back home mostly lacked. Their view of themselves was: we are not terribly cerebral and our opinions do not really count, but we sure can cook and have babies. They did not reinvent themselves to suit their desires; they let other people force them into moulds. Men like the King of Rats broke moulds and recast them to suit their wants, and forced the world to accept them.

She told Cornelius that she had been recovering from an affair with an older man, a lecturer. He was silent while she talked, and then he said:

"You do not choose who you fall in love with, you know. Stop blaming yourself. This has happened to a lot of people. You are in no way unique. You just met your first real philanderer. He is older, he has more experience. You did not stand a chance."

"Maybe, but I had my upbringing that told me how to distinguish right from wrong in these matters. I should have listened to my conscience."

"Everyone is allowed to fail at least once. Do not be too hard on yourself. In fact, that is a kind of superiority complex you have there. It is as if you consider yourself to be so far above mere mortals that you cannot make mistakes. That is the wrong approach to these things. If you go on like that, you will become a nervous wreck in no time at all."

"I don't know…"

"I do. Forget about it. Think of it as a learning experience, and get on with life. There are worse things you will do. You are still young, and you have to learn to forgive yourself."

"You sound as if you have gone through this before."

"Not exactly, but women are supposed to have so much to apologize for, so if you go on punishing yourself for something that in my view is the responsibility of someone else, then you are just adding uselessly to the burden you carry through life as a woman, especially in a society like yours, which seems to force the role of custodians of morality on its women, but does not thank them for the task. And do not forget that this man is older than you by far. Why could he not use the wisdom of his years and leave you alone? He capitalised on your respect for him as an older, more educated person. And you did not pursue him."

"But I did. I went to his office."

Cornelius laughed. "You are very innocent. He planted his seeds well. What is that amusing expression you used the other day? That courtship is referred to as 'throwing corn' to fowl? He knew you were a hen, and he threw grain for you to peck. Hens *will* peck grain; they cannot know it is poisoned until they swallow it. Now you know. Look at the whole thing like that. And try to move on." He chucked her playfully under the chin.

"Why are we talking about another man when you are in bed with me? I am jealous!"

"No need to be. He cannot hold a candle to you."

"Flattery will get you everywhere. Come."

He pulled her closer.

11

Back in her room the next day, Martha thought about what Cornelius had said. Maybe it was time to relax about the whole affair. She had been used to feeling that it was normal for women to bear the more unpleasant consequences of any sexual encounter, licit or not. Thinking that it should not be so was new. It was a little frightening, the mental freedom that it promised. But the physical bondage remained. If you slept with a man when you were not 'safe', you got pregnant, he did not. If you were a student, you might be thrown out of school, he went on. You got morning sickness, he did not. You got complications during delivery. He did not. If you died in childbirth, he might mourn you, or in some cases, not; but he stayed alive. You got called a whore; his friends patted him on the back. You could miss out on marriage, he could marry when he wanted, or he could go on with his marriage. So why should you bear all the guilt, as well as all the risk?

She wondered why she had never thought of this before. So the key to real freedom was to keep one's body in check, wasn't it? And refusing to bear any guilt. Here she was. That bastard had hurt and humiliated her, but she could walk away from it all; there was no physical bond to link them now the affair was over. She was not pregnant, she had not caught anything unmentionable from him, because they had almost always used protection. And it was over; she was seeing someone else. So she had come out of it more or less intact. She was furthering her education, she had gained valuable experience. It was time to forget, as Cornelius said. The important thing was to keep one's mind and body intact, and pray that one did not fall in lust/love with bastards.

Martha went to visit Bertha on the Thursday as agreed, and was not surprised when the address in Wassenaar turned out to be a substantial house, with a beautiful thatched roof and a manicured garden, set well back from the road behind an elaborate wrought-iron fence painted dark green. Thatched roofs were fairly uncommon, and only old, well-preserved houses had them. It quite intimidated her, and for the first few minutes, she was tongue-tied. It was alright to talk to an old lady in the street or in a moderately-priced restaurant, but to think that this woman might be some kind of aristocrat! Martha hated herself for this feeling of inferiority that overwhelmed her when she came into contact with the high and mighty. Then it occurred to her that she had been able to relate easily to this woman when she thought she was a confused old lady, so why not continue to behave as she had before? This helped her relax somewhat, but not entirely. What did a rich old white woman want with her? Sex? Martha thought of that soft, wrinkled body and shuddered. Or maybe she was just an interesting new specimen to be studied to pass the time. Her father always maintained that white people were strange. Why leave your beautiful country thousands of miles away to come crawling about in the bush, wanting to draw plants and spy on birds, creeping through thorn groves, oblivious of pain? Why come all that way to tell people about a god they had known about before your own ancestors were born? What did this woman want?

She had told Cornelius about the meeting and subsequent invitation, but he did not think it odd. He said old people here were often lonely because they did not have the extended families the older people could count on back home. Back home, there was always some idle cousin, some kind aunt, to visit the old people. But here people were too busy. Maybe that was it. The old woman was lonely. Well, she too was lonely sometimes; she missed the noise and dust, she missed okra soup with liver, she missed the spicy food. Sometimes she even thought of Nora's pithy pseudo-wisdom with affection.

The visit, in spite of her fears, went well. Having obtained all the information Martha was willing or able to give about herself, Bertha began to talk about herself during Martha's visits to her house, about her life as the daughter of a landowner in Venlo, a small city near the German border.

She talked of growing up in the age between the wars. Her father was a big fish in a small provincial pond. As the squire's daughter, she had known a life of ease, and the respect of her father's tenants, whose sons she could not date; she *was* the daughter of a rich man. She knew, because her parents told her, that she was cut out for better stuff than the callow bumpkin sons of the local farmers; she would not fit in a homely cottage.

So when the war came and the Dutch, in spite of their valour, collapsed after only four days of fighting, her world changed forever. Her family were no longer minor gentry. They were an occupied people, and as such were obliged to let German officers live in their home.

And of course, many of the minions of Seyss-Inquart, *Reichskommissar* of the Netherlands, were young men, some not much older than her nineteen years. That Bertha, the squire's daughter used to having her own way, would fall for one of them was almost a foregone conclusion. So were the assignations in cellars and fields. So, sadly, were the pregnancy and her father's predictable, but necessarily muted, outrage.

When the Germans were finally chased out, Bertha had a small son, nearly three, by Klaus Kellerman, who promised to return, but who never did.

With her parents dead, her father of repressed rage, her mother of grief, humiliation and despair, a small son on her hands and the stony hostility of a whole region looming over her, Bertha felt she had no choice her but to marry the first halfway suitable suitor: a former member of one of the Dutch resistance organisations, himself the son of wealthy farmers, who had lost an arm in the war and who kindly condescended to ally himself with the whore of the Germans and adopt her son.

It is hard to be a fallen woman in a small place.

They sold what remained of her father's estate and she moved to The Hague. They built a substantial construction empire with the money from their family legacies. Her wartime indiscretion was gradually forgotten in the new setting and the reconstruction work that followed the war.

Then came the sixties, with their new and addictive temptations, and her son took the new doctrine of freedom very much to heart. He died of an overdose at twenty-five. A rare cancer took her husband with terrifying brutality not two years later. Bertha was on her own again. But she had good business sense, experience and a peasant's cunning, and now she had nothing else to live for, she lived for the business.

When her bones began to suggest that she slow down somewhat, she retained the services of an excellent manager and decided to travel and see the world. She went on cruises, visited museums she had dreamed of seeing in her youth, went to Luxor and rode a camel, a very tame animal, she said, with an expression of permanent disdain, and went to Hawaii and wore a flower necklace. She wintered in Florida and, for a while, played the role of blue-rinsed, moneyed matronhood. Having explored the world and discovered new ways to have stomach upsets, it seemed pointless, anticlimactic to retire to a city where everyone she knew was dying or had gone away. But she did not feel like moving again, and resigned herself to her loneliness.

"I go out most days because I fear I will start talking to the walls soon if I do not!"

The tall African girl with the blank, pretty face and the sad eyes had intrigued Bertha first because she was a new kind of person. She was like a story written in a new style, and Bertha wanted to read her. She heard about Martha growing up in a small town with a strong Catholic missionary presence, school, the banal milestones in any young girl's life. Of love Martha was reticent, but when Big Bertha told of her experience with the German, it seemed rather small not to tell her about the King of Rats.

Life went on. Cornelius was there, always present when she wanted him, never intrusive. Their relationship had grown as far as it would ever go and though they both recognized this, it was never discussed. Her studies at the ISS were more than satisfactory. It was indeed a pleasure to study in a new environment, a far cry from the university back home, from the crowded lecture halls and dusty windowpanes, when there were any, same-plot sex scandals and outdated textbooks. Here the attitude was different, the faculty seemed actually interested in seeing you make something of yourself, rather than showing you how much more they knew than you would ever know.

They also did not trade sex for marks or imply that they would be doing you a favour if they slept with you.

12

O ne afternoon about eighteen months into her stay, on returning to her room to change for an evening with Cornelius, she found a telephone message slip under her door. Bertha had been taken to hospital. She had fallen down the stairs.

Martha, dropped her bulky schoolbag, pounded down the stairs and rushed out again, calling Cornelius on her cell phone.

On the bus to the Bronovo hospital, she sat staring sightlessly out of the window, her mind busy.

In spite of the age difference, she and the old woman had forged a real friendship based on affinities other than age. When they had met, she had needed to compare notes with another woman, someone who was not constrained by propriety and empty moral generalisations. Someone who knew what temptation was. Someone who understood why she agonized over what was to others a mere peccadillo, a fellow sinner who could help her come to terms with the new person this experience had revealed her to be. Bertha had been all that, and more. They were women who had sinned against themselves, broken their own rules. She had felt closeness to this fat white woman with the crinkly eyes that she would never feel towards her own mother. Her mother was forever buried in thrift-and-loan initiatives and church groups, petrified in her rigid, small-town mentality, a buttress and willing victim of the tyranny spawned by society's superficial, do-but-do-not-be-caught-doing morality, a disciple of conformity, a prisoner of her respectability.

Her mother would have seen any sexual deviation (and to her, wanting the wrong man was deviant behaviour of the worst kind) in terms of a loss of marriageability. To her, a woman came to this world to do two things: 1) bear children 2) be a good wife. All other ambitions were perversions. Her sole remaining aspiration was to see her daughter married in her twenties, and she would have had a conniption if she had heard that her daughter had jeopardized her place in decent-woman heaven by allowing herself to be pawed by a man not much younger than her father.

Most of her classmates and halfway friends back home approached relationships with a combination of pragmatism and do-but-do-not-be-caught-doing morality. It was all right to sleep with a married man because he helped with the rent. You could also have a young man on the side to be in love with. He was the one who made you cry; he was the one who hurt you, and he was the one you would marry and for whom you would bear children.

So Martha confided in two people of another race, another time and place, people she could related to across the chasm of colour and culture, and they formed a bond stronger than any mere accident of birth or geography.

At the hospital, they made her wait half an hour and then only let her see Bertha for a few moments. Bertha was groggy with sedatives, but still awake enough to grasp Martha's hand with her own.

"Is the pain very bad?"

"Not too much. Do not worry. I will be home soon."

A nurse came in and signalled that it was time to leave.

13

Big Bertha was in the hospital for three weeks, and when she came back home, she was thinner, sadder, and somehow smaller. The vital, twinkle-eyed woman Martha had known had been replaced by a shapeless lump of clothes with dull, filmed-over old person's eyes. Her skin hung about her bones in folds, as if her diminished soul was floundering weakly about in a worn-out, hand-me-down casing.

Martha decided to invite herself to Bertha's house. The old woman needed company. Commuting to the ISS would be a drag, but the city had an excellent public transport system. Several times, Martha caught the old woman looking at her with a strange, searching gaze. She talked little and spent less time outdoors. There were no more walks round the city. Only later would she understand that Big Bertha had commenced system shutdown. Somehow, she had lost interest in life. And some men visited her twice while Martha was there, business types in suits. Once a big Audi came and picked her up.

The end came quietly. One evening, Marijke, Bertha's maid, had gone into her mistress's room to tidy up and turn the bed down for the night. She found the old woman slumped in her chair by the window. She called the police and the ambulance services and when they came, she was taken to the kitchen and allowed to have as much tea and hysterics as she liked, which was just fine with her.

After the funeral, at which there were less than twenty people present, everyone trudged to Bertha's house in silence. There was a small collation of cold meats downstairs in the dining room, and a final curtain was drawn tiredly, but inexorably, over one more life. No one from Bertha's family appeared. It seemed that there was no one left. The people there knew nothing, and cared less. It was not strange in this country to have no relatives at one's funeral. Martha thought with nostalgia about the heat and feeling of funerals back home, where people rolled about in the dust and drank too much and coupled frantically in the shadows. She had found it uncivilised; now she found it was more human than this...mere formality. After ten minutes, Martha felt she could no longer bear this cold, polite regret. It seemed somehow callous that the epilogue to a life would be the ingestion of cold, dead animals. It was too morbidly carnivorous.

She wondered why the old woman had let herself die. What was it about the fall that changed her life? Was it that all those she had loved were dead, and with the threat of frailty inherent in advancing age, she had begun to feel that there was no one left to look after her? Had she lost confidence in her ability to look after herself?

Martha escaped to Cornelius's flat where she allowed herself to be consoled in bed. Though she had seized the day, as if to ward off her own mortality, her grief was sharp. It was also short. She soon learned to build her schedule around other interests. She was coming to the end of her course and had to prepare for her return home. She might have found some means of staying on as an illegal alien, but the prospect of dodging around forever without a residence permit was too daunting. And she knew it would be easy to get work back home with one of the more credible NGOs. She began to prepare for her journey back.

One Saturday, Martha, looking out of the window, saw a black Audi drive up to the hostel. She gave it no more thought until the call came that someone wanted to see her. Two men. Martha was intrigued, but not overly curious.

When she went down to the entrance, she found two men who looked like father and son, both rather thick around the middle, the younger one sporting one of the inexplicable orangey tans that some people in this country seemed to like. Her first thought was that the immigration authorities wanted to check up on her. But she had nothing to hide; she did not want to extend her stay.

"Miss Martha Elive?" asked the older one. He pronounced it to rhyme with olive. "I am Peter Heemstra and this is my son and partner, Leenert. We are lawyers. We have some important news to communicate, and we were in this part of town by chance when this was confirmed, so we thought we'd just stop by. There is nothing to worry about, I assure you."

"What is this about?" But they would not tell her. Their offices were in one of the beautiful old buildings on the Prinsengracht. From outside they looked expensive. They were, and discreetly but tastefully furnished in the softest brown leather and dotted with various pieces of antique furniture. Martha was directed to sit in what she judged was the elder Heemstra's office. And that is when, with a cup of coffee in her hand, she was informed that she was the sole beneficiary of the will of one Bertha van der Aa There were still some things to be ironed out, but the late Mrs. van der Aa had instructed that all her assets be converted into cash and the sum deposited in an account created for the purpose. The amount, after inheritance taxes and death duties, was quite enough for the annual budget of any respectable middle-income nation.

The coffee cup trembled in her suddenly nerveless fingers. If she had not put it down quickly, she would have dropped it.

"But why me? Was there no one else?"

Mr Heemstra senior looked faintly amused. Indeed there was no one else, and even if there were, it didn't matter. The last will and testament of the lady in question was clear; he and his son could attest to her soundness of mind when the decision was made, so it was all settled, she was the sole beneficiary of the estate, they were the executors, and it was all perfectly legal, he could assure her.

Martha began to cry. "These past days she was very sad, so quiet, not at all like her old self."

Leenert Heemstra told her that in the course of routine tests following her accident, it had been discovered that Mrs. van der Aa had cancer that was too far advanced to be treated.

"It was just as well that she had the accident, because before then she had left all her property to her son. After he and her husband died, she had not made a new will. The stay in hospital enabled her to dispose of her money as she wished.

"To use an English expression, Miss, do not look a gift horse in the mouth. Mrs. van der Aa had a lot of respect for you.

She felt that you would know what to do with the money if she gave it to you."

"It is true that she asked me once what I would do with a lot of money if I had it and I told her of a dream I had about starting an establishment for women in distress but it is just a dream..."

"Well, now it can be a dream no longer. Go home and make your dream come true. I think Mrs. van der Aa hoped you would do so."

They agreed to meet again on Monday for the formalities. Mr. Heemstra Senior would contact Mrs. van der Aa's stockbroker and convert the assets, which would be transferred to an account in her name. All of that might take a while.

In a daze, Martha somehow found herself in Cornelius's flat without actually remembering how she got there. She remembered how she had come here to be consoled on the day of the funeral; she remembered how quickly she had forgotten the old woman.

Cornelius was not in, but she had the key. She let herself in, lay on the bed and wept her guilt.

She was woken by the sound of a door opening and closing. She sat up. Cornelius came in and tossed his bag onto his desk.

"Ah, what a tiring day. And how are you, God blesh you?"

It was their secret joke. Martha had told him how the Dutch priest in the parish back home always said "blesh you". He had been very amused.

But now, Martha did not smile back. Instead, she began to weep again and told him about the money. He was silent for a long time, his grey eyes thoughtful, fighting a private war with himself. Finally, the better part of him won, and he said:

"Of course you must do as she would have wished, if you are able to. And even if you are not, there are people and organisations that can help with this sort of thing."

"But I feel so guilty about it all. You remember that on the day of the funeral, I came here and..."

"What do you want to do, wear sackcloth? Do you think it would have been better for the money to go to a museum or some distant cousin? Look, the woman has given it to you because she felt that you would do some good with it. Believe me, she had other options, and she was aware of them. She had no obligation to you. If she gave it to you, then she knew what she was doing. Now stop crying and celebrate the fulfilment of your dreams."

"But what if I fail? What if I cannot do as she would have liked and I waste her money?"

"You can only do your best. If you do fail, it cannot be helped. But you cannot refuse to do something merely because you are afraid that you do not have what it takes. You can only find out if you try first. And there is a lot of money indeed, so you can always get a second chance to try again. Don't be so defeatist. If you like, I can help you find someone who will give you some advice on how to start."

"Thank you, but if I have to do something, then I'd better start finding out by myself where to get the help I need. Thank you very much."

"I expect my pay in kind, tears or no tears."

She punched him playfully on the upper arm. "It is strange how talking about things to someone makes them so much easier to handle."

"That's what mouths are for, apart from kissing." He kissed her to illustrate. "And that is what other people are there for, silly. You rely too much on yourself. As a sociologist, you should know better. What is that thing you say in English? Bootmakers' wives are worst shod?"

"Shoemakers, silly yourself." She pushed him onto the bed and sat astride him. "Maybe the best way I can thank her is to show some gratitude of my own to you in a particular way, hmm?"

"Good. You are finally beginning to think. Spread it around."

But while she was unbuttoning his shirt, she felt the old fear steal up. Suppose she failed to satisfy the old woman's last wish? Suppose the lamb was not worthy to take the scroll?

Part Two

14

Martha woke up with a start. Through gummy, half-open eyelids, she could see the fat black flight attendant with the impossible auburn wig swish forward to the front of the aircraft. The sound of the engines had changed; the plane was gearing down for landing.

The attendant began her spiel in a tinny twang: "leddies an' gentelmun," she intoned, "we are now approaching Douala international airport. It is 22.00 hours local tahm..."

Trying to force the post-slumber bad taste back down her throat, Martha wondered why, on a continent of myriad accents, the airline had chosen to hire the one woman with an accent no one could understand. It was the first sign that she was back home, where nothing was ever done for the right reasons. Idly, collecting her stuff, she considered suing the airline for risking her life by hiring attendants who, from all indications, resolutely refused to learn English and always had colds. If one did not understand the security recommendations because their accents were too bad, were those not sufficient grounds for legal action?

The amazing thing was that this was a bilingual country with many hostess-quality, English-speaking women who could do the job just as well. But did they hire them? No, of course not. It would be too logical, too reasonable for an airline that was determined to run itself into the ground. Airlines such as this were overstaffed with lazy, lackadaisical employees with no idea as to how to please their customers, and no inclination to find out. She remembered hearing about one regional airline having over 4000 employees to service and fly seven or so antediluvian planes. Despite warnings of impending bankruptcy, the company was managed in much the same way as it had been done for years. When they were threatened with losing their jobs, the employees squealed and threatened to strike. The same applied to most state-owned companies. Everyone mismanaged and stole to their heart's delight; people hired their girlfriends and the unqualified cousins of their cronies, and then began to whine when privatisation was threatened. To Martha, all those employees deserved what was coming to them, and the thing was to seize the personal assets of those found guilty of mismanagement, and if a person had spent all he had stolen, he should be made to work for nothing till he produced enough to compensate.

Anyway, there was time enough for crusades. Besides she had heard that the airline had just changed hands. Maybe the new management was still learning the ropes.

Right now she had to get on the ground first, and explain to her parents why she would not become the ideal daughter they surely felt they had a right to expect. That was worry enough for now.

The heat was a huge, wet, drawn-out slap, soft and lazy and insidious. As she reached the bottom of the gangway, she could feel sweat trickling between her shoulder blades down her spine. Her shirt gave up its independence, instantly developing a marked aversion to standing on its own threads, clinging to her back like an unsuccessful relative, or a child who hides behind an adult when faced with a barking dog.

In the customs section a lentil-eyed official waded through her things and, finding much to occupy him, settled down happily to give her a hard time. His colleagues soon joined him, their brains dead to every stimulus but the chance to intimidate hapless travellers into parting with some of their foreign currency or goods.

Martha emerged half an hour later, sweating with anger and fear, sans her digital camera, and a hundred Euros poorer. Home sweet home.

She was immediately surrounded by a swarm of predatory porters anxious to carry her stuff and extort outrageous tips. They knew that women travellers were more vulnerable to that sort of intimidation masquerading as solicitude, but Martha wasn't having any. She'd had enough with the customs people. With her new assertiveness, she snapped at the hopefuls hovering around her like a cloud of flies, shoved through the sweating, chattering gaggle, seized a trolley waiting patiently in a corner like a shy boyfriend, and piled her luggage on it. She pushed off, looking for her parents. They had said they would be there with a hired vehicle.

She spied them near the exit, her father looking bewildered and determined not to show it, slightly plumper than she remembered him; his hair, having lost the battle with his face, was retreating with bad grace, leaving behind random, undignified tufts like bushes to be used as cover in a scrubland war. He was wearing his best Nigerian lace up-and-down, a violently embroidered affair of voracious-looking flowers on an incongruous seascape background.

His wife, stout and timid, stood slightly behind him, draped in her newest, wine-coloured Indian wrap (from Saudi Arabia, actually), looking for all the world like a barrel topped with a homely face edging past its prime, her small, deep-set eyes vacant and blinking in slow motion, deadened by the heat and novelty of it all. Airports bewildered her. Later, of course, it would be gratifying to let drop in the neighbourhood common initiative group as casually as possible over the chunky fruit salad: I say, that Douala airport! So noisy! I was there the other week to fetch my daughter, you know, and those porters were so aggressive!

But right now, she had lost her bearings. She just wished she were back home in her homely little kingdom, deciding what to eat tomorrow. Thank God there were men to handle such things; she could never have managed it alone, coming to a strange place to welcome a daughter who would probably be stranger than ever with her airs and her high book learning. Around her people met and hugged; a whole family had come to welcome a prodigal daughter who had finally come home several shades lighter of skin, with a short, balding white husband and his austere-looking father in tow. Mrs Elive shuddered inwardly. God forbid that Martha should do that to them. Such a shameless thing! She could conceive of white people as priests, as nursing sisters, as tourists going up the mountain, as alien beings on television. As husbands, never.

Aha! There she was, looking too thin and wearing those odd clothes, as usual.

Martha waved to them and her father saw her. Mr. Elive scuttled forward and braked sharply in front of the loaded trolley. As the thing was between them, he could not hug the girl. He smiled more in embarrassment than welcome, not knowing how to handle this. He started to wave, then dropped his hand awkwardly, torn between showing his joy and his fear of being over-demonstrative. His wife stole up beside him. She stretched out her hand to touch her daughter but the gap between them was too wide. She smiled with painfully dignified, parochial self-restraint.

"Papa! Mama!"

"Welcome", her father said, not quite meeting Martha's eye. His wife still hovered. Martha cursed the eternal awkwardness of her parents. Why could they not be like everyone else? A normal mother would have charged past that trolley or toppled it unconcernedly, and enfolded her daughter in her arms, uttering cries of joy.

Martha came round the side of the trolley and hugged her mother. They smiled tightly at each other. Her father stood to one side. He was relieved. Pleased, delighted indeed, to see his only child come back from the land of the white man, but public displays were not his thing. He jerked his head at a young man in his twenties.

"Ngalle, come and take these things to the car." And to Martha: "You remember him now? Mola Ikome's third son."

Martha did not remember him. Mola Ikome's unbridled procreative instincts had produced, at last exasperated count, nine unfortunate offspring, each more catatonic than the one before. The less impecunious relatives were supposed to feed this large family. Ngalle, a gangly youth with a chip on his shoulder the size of a full-grown Sapele tree, who had grown sullen and apathetic on a diet of heavy starch, seething resentment of rich relatives and too little meat, had until his name was mentioned, displayed the animation of a zombie. He now sidled forward and wrenched the trolley from Martha's grasp with the surliness of the lesser-born in the presence of hateful higher beings who make them feel inferior. He mumbled a greeting of some sort and propelled the trolley out to the waiting car.

The family trooped out after him into the hot night, fumbling for opening gambits. Mrs. Olive offered some:

"He just came back from prison. He has learned driving. At least he has a job. The others –"

Mr. Elive sighed.

Mrs. Elive's social-critic glands spurted a dose of criticase. She perked up. It was easier to talk about other people than to delve into the reasons for the uneasiness she felt when faced with this self-possessed, restrained young woman.

"M–hmh! I tell you! Nothing, nothing to do. That Messanga, their oldest sister. She got up and went and married a fisherman, she said. What fisherman? Some *bolo*-boy who helps drag canoes onto the beach and gets a few bony *mololo* fish in return. Four children they have, and nothing to eat. She is in my house every week. Auntie this, Auntie that. I just don't know..." She stopped as they reached the car.

They got in, Mr. Elive in front, next to Ngalle, and Martha behind Ngalle. Mrs. Elive sat directly behind her husband.

Martha asked about the neighbours. Her mother settled back. This was her favourite topic. That Elsie, the girl Martha's age next door, she had left her husband again and was back with her parents, five more mouths to feed and how would poor Esther manage with a husband on retirement, she could not imagine. If you see the baby's napkins cloth, enh! Quite *brown*, I tell you.

"Mrs. Ekwen, you know, the mayor's wife, she was just telling me the other day in our CWA meeting that some people just don't know how to bring up children. I am telling you! If you see their backyard, enh, you will not eat that day, I swear. No, I am telling you! And none of her children have gone anywhere, all the boys are drivers, mechanics, that sort of thing –" She paused to draw breath, but her husband, conscious that his nephew driving them was just one of such ne'er do wells, reached quietly around the back of his seat and dug an angry, spatulate thumb into her calf. She gasped and was silent.

Guessing what had happened, Martha smiled in the dark. Thank God for small mercies. At least she would be spared the smug comparisons between herself and the neighbourhood kids as long as Ngalle was with them. Her mother was unable to talk to her own daughter about the things that filled her heart, so she talked about other people.

In any case, the rain obligingly intensified, making further conversation difficult. She and her mother sat, each in her own corner. She could see her father's balding pate in the intermittent glare of passing headlights. Ngalle drove on steadily, busy with his own thoughts, planning in his two hundred-word vocabulary what he would do to the parish priest's plump cook to get the taste of his skinny Johnny-just-come cousin out of his system. Skinny bitch. *He* liked his women well padded.

As they left the coastal plain and began the climb up to the mountain zone, the rain eased off somewhat. Dissecting skills recovered, Mrs. Elive stirred again and cleared her throat nervously, clutching her totally unsuitable midnight-blue sequinned evening bag to her heavy bosom. What to say? Ah, good. The house.

"You will see that we have made some small changes. Your father got Cousin Morris to come and repaint the house. It's true he cheated us, but how man go do? You cannot paint your own house."

She shifted gear in time with the climbing pick-up.

"Am tellin' you. Jealousy in that quarter, enh! The comments that Mammy Esther made over a small matter like paint. I just looked at her and said to myself: you cannot see your own dirty backyard; you only sit there losing weight about other people's progress. Her daughter sits every day on the veranda with untidy hair, cannot even greet you as you pass. Odd woman. None of her children went anywhere. Just sitting there having babies. The boys are all thieves. The last one even went to prison. I cannot imagine -"

"Leave the girls alone to rest. Yah!" broke in Papa brutally.

Mrs. Elive swallowed painfully, the venom searing her throat as it went down. But she could say nothing; her husband had spoken. She could not contradict him in front of his useless nephew. But there were ways to get back at him, as he seemed to have forgotten. There were small ways of getting one's message across. Let him not sit there and think that he would get away with it.

The pickup danced determinedly over the last of the potholes and pulled up in front of their family house, its headlights cutting a swathe through the drizzle. Martha's father, as her mother never tired of mentioning in her soft little voice to her CWA colleagues, had "built", meaning that he owned a house of his own. It was low bungalow with four bedrooms and three toilets - my husband said we should at least have our own private toilet, you know someone visiting can give you a bad disease, she announced blithely to her future visitors. The women had raged inwardly, but had gone to see anyway, and had come away incensed but unable to refute the painful evidence of the Elives' success in acquiring middleclass trappings.

Ngalle carried the luggage into the living room. Then he took his leave, mumbling his thanks as Mr. Elive pressed a banknote discreetly into his cupped palm, away from his wife's sharp eyes, and melted away into the night, heading for the priest's cook's house.

The housegirl, a distant cousin sent from the village a year ago, came in from the back room that had been tagged on to the kitchen for poor relatives, and murmured shyly in greeting to this tall, thin girl who had come to add to her housework, as if she did not have enough trouble with the things Auntie said to her. She was dressed in what were obviously the badly adjusted cast-offs grudgingly handed down by Mrs. Elive. Only Martha answered her greeting. Curtly, Mrs. Elive ordered her to take Martha's luggage to the room.

It was raining still, and Martha's childhood came back to her in a rush of memories: the monotonous drizzle, the cool mist and smell of woodsmoke from less middle-class dwellings, the sound of giant raindrops thunging onto corrugated metal roofs from overhanging branches, the thought of clothes mouldering away in her plywood wardrobe, the cold cement floor (before her mother put in hideous sky-blue carpeting that must have been 10 nanometres thick maximum, so that she could go to her CWA friends and annoy them with sibilant remarks about how the housegirl, her distant cousin sent from the village, had spilled a bucket of water on the carpet – soft but unmistakeable emphasis on *carpet* - in Martha's room: "you cannot imagine I swear my husband just looked at her and she started to cry", and giggle in fond, submissive remembrance of Martha's father's wrath - I am telling you, he looks quiet, but if he is angry, enh! - , looking down at her calloused hands), long holidays with her father sitting in his armchair on a dreary afternoon, reading the parish newsletter and not speaking to her, while she toyed listlessly with a twice-read teenage novel, waiting unenthusiastically for a boring lunch of cocoyams and palm nut soup, waiting for something to relieve the tedium, not understanding the vague yearning for something *more* that she was feeling.

And so Martha came home, to the fussy sitting-cum-dining room with its ageing brown faux-velvet armchairs, its squares of grey carpeting and its fluffy woollen backrests of blue and white, and a varnished bird, badly carved in pale wood, with its beak painted blood-red, frozen incongruously for ever on the lavender-and-brick-red coffee table antimacassar. Nothing had changed. *Plus ça change...*

A special supper had been prepared for her: ripe plantains and sea bass in tomato sauce, which Martha ate with gusto. She had missed the spicy food. Her mother hovered on the sidelines, smiling in modest pleasure at Martha's appetite, fussing over the small details of this special supper and seeing to the stowing of Martha's luggage, rarely sitting down because even though she was a member of the middle classes; she still found it difficult to sit at a table with her husband because in her experience, men ate in the main hut and women ate in the kitchen with the children. Mr Elive, head of the house, munched diligently and proffered nuggets of impersonal knowledge between mouthfuls.

After supper, they went to sit in the living room area, and her parents sat in portly, expectant silence, wanting to be regaled with her adventures in the land of the white man, so they could go and repeat them with just the right degree of offhandedness, he in the Junior Service Club, she in her CWA and common initiative group meetings. They knew that many of the priests in the local parishes were Dutch, so they wanted to hear tales of how the people of these white men they deferred to in almost all matters lived.

In a fit of ill-advised curiosity, the distant-cousin housegirl, having cleared the table, sidled over from the back of the house and perched on one of the dining chairs, sufficiently far, she thought, from the lady of the house not to offend, to hear Martha's account of her life with real white people. But a venomous backward glance from Auntie sent her scurrying back to her den next to the kitchen, to spend one more evening sobbing her frustration into her cheap polyester pillowcase.

A quiet evening in the province.

Martha went to her room and brought out the presents.

Her parents were pleased.

"Weh, thank you-oh!" said Mrs. Elive as she contemplated the heap of sweaters, handbags, shoes and jewellery. The CWA women would faint.

Her father looked at his shoes and ties and grunted. He was glad, but he restrained his enthusiasm. It would not do to display an unmannerly delight in mere articles of clothing before women.

"Must have cost you a lot."

For the housegirl there was a good, thick cable knit sweater.

"That is too expensive for her. I shall send it to my sister in Mile Sixteen," said Mrs. Elive, her thick eyebrows beetling. "Last week she sent us yams –"

"No. I bought it specifically for her."

"Nonono. It's not nice for someone like her to have expensive things. She will begin to expect more. You know how greedy these village girls can be. I send money to her mother every month. These people sit in their huts and expect the world to come to them. They are so lazy, they don't work, won't go to the farm, and yet they want you to come and give them things."

"Let the girl have the thing! She has little enough as it is," said Papa. And the matter was settled. Or so Mr. Elive thought.

Mrs. Elive subsided, but she took a secret vow. She would *see* how that girl would wear that sweater in this house. And her husband would be taught a lesson. Her face took on a look of injured dignity: her superior knowledge had been ignored; poor relations must not be made to feel that they could rise above their station in life. She was quite unaware, or had chosen to forget, that only marriage had saved her from a similar fate.

But she soon forgot to be petulant as she contemplated the array of presents. However, there was just one little matter.

"They did not have Holland wax?"

Martha stifled a sigh of impatience. This woman! "Mama, I don't even know exactly where Holland wax is actually made. I never saw any on sale. I think they have a Vlisco factory somewhere there, but I thought that there was no point in getting you something that you could get here."

Mama did not look convinced, but she decided not to press the matter. It was just like her own daughter to go abroad to a country where they could not sell the things one really liked. In her mind, the really right sort of "abroad" was limited to two countries: Great Britain (which she called Britin) and America; that is where people she knew went when they travelled. The CWA women whose children went to Britin and America were at the upper end of the social scale. Holland she knew the name of because she wore cloth that should have come from there, whatever her daughter said. And with the resilient stubbornness of the truly stupid - what did Mrs. Elive know of manufacture for export - she thought in her heart that her daughter must be lying. But she would say nothing. It wouldn't do to antagonise the girl. There were important things at stake, and she could become uncooperative at the drop of a hat.

The evening dragged on for another half-hour, then her father said with false heartiness, feeling that he had done enough for family togetherness for one evening:

"Time to sleep!" and, seizing his parish council documents as he did every evening, went to his room to wait for his wife to talk to the girl. He hoped it would not take too long. He had told her to save it for tomorrow, but he knew his wife only too well. She wouldn't.

Mama hovered for a while and made a show of straightening the back rests. Obviously there was something she wanted to get off her chest, but Martha would be damned if she asked her. She bid her good night and went to her room.

84

15

In her old room, the luggage was piled neatly in a corner next to the rough table, now covered in a cloth with an incongruous Christmas motif. The sky-blue carpet, pride and joy of her mother, clashed violently with everything. She was irritated to notice that her mother had put on the special sheets for her; the ones with the cotton lace edging that cost 700 CFA Francs a metre. The poky plywood closet had been re-varnished. The sentimental and scholarly junk she had accumulated over the years had been locked into a tin trunk and shoved under the bed. The room smelled of synthetic fabric, new varnish and concealed mildew.

Who did they think she was, royalty? Why were they treating her like a rich relative they did not know very well? It was as if her stay in Europe had erased the fact of her exact origins from their minds and they had to treat her like the visiting parish priest.

Anyway, time for a shower. As she was towelling herself dry, her mother knocked (another disturbing development – since when did her mother start knocking at doors?) and came in diffidently, looking about, waiting to be told how nicely the room had been done up. She averted her eyes from her daughter's naked body. This child just did not know modesty. She did not even move to cover herself.

No compliments were forthcoming. She hung about for a while, tweaking the curtains into place, at a loss for the opening words. She hovered and chattered about small things – the toilet is okay, because I told that child to use the pit latrine behind the house. The way things get damp in the rainy season! Martha waited for her to get into gear. Her mother finally looked at Martha's naked back out of the corner of her eye. She could not remember the last time *she* had stood naked before anyone with the light on. Children these days...

She sighed and finally parked her slope-backed bulk on the edge of the freshly made bed, crossed her ankles, her hands resting in the fold of wrapper between her knees. It was cold in here. She finally began, staring fixedly at a point just beyond her feet, two dark freshwater fish on a fishmonger's slab in the market.

"Martha" (she pronounced it Mattá, with the emphasis on the second syllable, the name itself a question), as you have come like this, it is a good thing. Because now you can settle down and live your life as a woman. It is true that education is a good thing, but you also have to think of what God put you in this world to do as a woman. You have to settle. Since you became a woman" (Martha winced, her stomach tightened – her coming into womanhood had been a source of great upheaval in this household), "we have not really seen you with a boy that we thought was your" –a pause, her voice faltered, but she focused on her left big toe, wiggling it like a caterpillar inching along a branch, and went on: - "friend, a serious friend, and now that you have come back, we feel that you should start thinking about it seriously.

"Your father – well, you know Lawyer Etchu, he has four sons, and the first one just came back from Britin, and his father says they are looking for a wife for him. Your father spoke with him the other day after the parish council meeting, and they say that it is a good thing.

"At my age, at least I should have one grandchild. Only you can give me that. All my friends have at least one. So we feel that you should think about it very seriously. He is a serious boy, very polite. It is true that their mother is dead, but their father brought them up well – so you should think about it very serious– "

"Mama, I am very tired, I need to rest. We will talk about all this tomorrow. I have something to tell you myself."

"Plans?!" Startled, Mama raised her eyes connected brutally with the cold-darkened, thrusting nipples of her daughter's breasts, and hastily moved her gaze to the opposite wall.

"What?" Her voice rose a notch. "You have met someone else? Then why did you not tell us? Who is he? Where are his parents? What tribe - "

"No, I am not talking about - "

"No, because we need to know who he is." A hideous thought crossed her mind, borne on the wings of the family reunion at the airport, the bald white husband. "I hope you have not brought us a white man! Because let me tell you that it will never, never, never work! People will say it is because no one here will have you. Oh Papa God. What will I say? The disgrace. Where will I keep my face?"

"On your neck, where it belongs. Mammy, no one talked about a white man. You are jumping to conclusions, as usual. All I said was that I have plans of my own, and I will tell you about them tomorrow. Period."

"Then if it is not marriage, what can it be, at your age?"

Her daughter sighed. Her mother waited. When Martha did not elaborate, she chose to believe the worst.

"Ey! Let me just tell you now that we will never accept him. Never!" Her voice rose to a squeak.

"Mama, I did not say that I had brought a white man to marry. Be patient. I will tell you in the morning. Now I am too tired. Please try to understand."

Her mother waited for more, but as none was forthcoming, she sighed and rose heavily to her feet, mouth puckered in defeat.

"Okay. My own things are always like this. Always struggling, never resting. Since you cannot tell me - good night now."

At the door, she turned again. "I say, Mattá, what plans do you have that you cannot tell your own mo- "

"I said I will tell you tomorrow. Leave me! I want to sleep, ah!"

"You want to sleep. Sleep. So your mother can stay up all night worrying about what you have to tell her. Sleep then, so that we can be disgraced forever."

Silence.

When she left. Martha shut the door and turned the key. Happy, happy homecoming. She lay on the bed. Outside, small animals quarrelled shrilly with the rain, chirping from their shelters under the broad cocoyam leaves. The rain, unperturbed, droned on. The wind scraped a branch across the roof and the raindrops, dislodged from their perch on the leaves, chorused onto the roof in protest. The house creaked and shifted.

The sheets were cool and starched. Martha turned onto her belly and sighed. Tomorrow would solve its own problems.

She slept.

Her mother did not.

She burst into their bedroom, startling her husband awake from his light semi-erotic doze. He had been hoping for a bit of lights-out fumbling under the downy Arabian blanket to celebrate the girl's return, but a look at his wife's eyebrows (now really just one thick black line across her face) and incandescent eyes told him it was unlikely. Not right now, anyway.

"That child!" spat the object of his desires, throwing a wrapper around her shoulders and wrestling with her brassiere, thick straps snapping. She pulled her high-necked nightie on over her head and pulled down the wrapper in one fluid movement. No part of her body above the calf showed at any one time during the whole exercise. Mr. Elive had watched her do this all through their marriage, and the wrapper had fallen off only once. She had been weak with malaria then.

She turned around and he let his breath out in disappointment. Nothing. The damn night-dress was buttoned to the throat. She marched to her side of the bad and climbed in.

"Can you imagine that I tried to tell her about Justice Etchu's son and Madam said she was tired. Had plans of her own, she said, Queen Mattá."

"Well I told you to wait a little."

"You said nothing! You are the one who said we should strike while the iron was hot! You and you daughter will kill me in this house." She pulled the blanket angrily about her rounded shoulders and turned her back to him.

"Tomorrow is another day." His hand, obeying its own instincts more than common sense, crept across to touch the roll of flesh in her side. She shook him off like an insect, and managed to grind her elbow into his ribs for good measure.

He stifled an unmanly gasp and retreated to his side of the bed, his hand trailing like a shocked snail that is hurt but cannot hurry away from danger.

Outside the rain continued, oblivious.

88

16

Next morning, breakfast was fraught. Apprehension hovered over the omelette. Mr. Elive made a show of tucking into his Quaker Oats, but his heart was not in it. What his wife had related to him as they lay on their spring mattress bought with the interest on their credit union capital had worried him. The girl was headstrong; if she refused to consider the Etchu boy, it would be very awkward. He had practically accepted. All was settled and he had not anticipated any real objection on her part. In her late twenties, a woman did not have that many options available.

Martha forced herself to swallow her eggs (she was not a breakfast person, a fact her mother seemed to have forgotten) and, her plate cleared, she threw down the gauntlet. She told them about her inheritance and the woman who left it to her.

"Well! That is good! There is no problem. You can give the money to your husband and he can help you manage it. No problem at all. It will even help things. The boy is a doctor, and he can use it to start his own private clinic." Mr. Elive was so relieved he even looked her in the eyes as he smiled at her. His wife had exaggerated as usual. Nothing there.

"No, you don't understand. I mean that I want to do something else." She explained her dream to them. They listened with the air of people whose worst nightmare was unfolding before their very wide-awake eyes. Her mother began to rock back and forth on her chair like someone in a trance.

"What!!" spluttered her father, spraying oats all over the breakfast things.

"I told you," began his wife.

"Shut up and let me handle this," he snarled, the refusal to perform certain nocturnal ministrations still rankling.

"So now you say you want to use all that money and open a school for women. What is wrong with our own schools?"

"It is not really a school. More like a capacity-building establishment."

"Capacity building is what? Give the money to Monsignor Etta. The church does a lot of charity work. That will be very good. You will make a good name for yourself, enh?" Yes, that was a good idea. He was yet to see the woman who did not want people to think well of her. No problem here. Show him the woman he could not manage!

"No, you do not understand. I won't marry that guy. I do not know him. I do not even know that I would like him if I saw him. I am not sure that I could love him."

"Oh, I knew it! I just knew. Bad luck. Why me oh Papa God why *me*?" Mrs. Elive opened her deep-set eyes and gazed tearfully at her daughter. "I say enh Mattá, what have we not given you that you should turn against us like this? What will my friends say?" Her heavy chest juddered with warring emotions.

"Wait! I did not say that I would never marry. Just that it is not my priority now. I want to fulfil my dream first, but that does not exclude marrying someone if I truly love him."

"Love?" shouted her father, jowls trembling. "What has love got to do with it? We are telling you about marriage and you sit there talking nonsense about love and throwing away good money. When I married your mother, there was no talk of love. My paternal uncle just called me and told me a wife had been found for me. And I accepted. I had not even seen her yet! She came from a good family, which is the important thing! We have been married twenty-eight years! And you come here talking nonsense about love. What love? Someone gives you money and all you want to do is give it to some stupid prostitutes! You leave your family here and you begin to think of other people!"

His voice faded with the rage of it, and he gesticulated wildly, unable to speak.

Mrs. Elive, now that her husband had lost his self-control, regained hers and decided to intervene before her husband had a stroke.

"At least meet the boy. You will like him. He is a doctor."

90

"Shhhp!" hissed her husband, finding his voice again. "I hsaid hshut hup!"

"No, I did not mean that I would not do anything for my loved ones. There is a lot of money. Even if I gave it all to you, you would not be able to spend it even if you lived up to the age of three hundred. No, there will be some for my family. And some for me. But I just want to do something good for people I feel need help."

"Then why don't you give it to the parish?" He spoke with forced restraint, glaring at his wife, who had opened her mouth to speak. "Priests are there to serve the faithful. They know best how to handle these things. They have experience in charity work."

"No. Papa, I am very sorry, Mama, that I am causing you distress. But I have looked at my life as you want it to be, and I find that there is something I still need to do. There has to be more to life than that. The money was given to me as an act of love. That white woman trusted me with a mission. I cannot now keep it for myself alone. I have to do something worthwhile with it. I have to do something with my life. God cannot have placed us on this earth as women just to have children and be married and do as we are told. He cannot have. Because every creature has a way to replicate itself and continue the race. Rats have children. Does it mean that my ambition should be limited to performing the functions that lower forms of life like rodents perform by rote, without thinking? No, I have thought about all this, and I feel that I have something more important to do on this earth than just procreation. Anyone can do that. Most people do it without really trying. It is basically mindless. And marriage as you see it is a kind of bondage to one man, to do his bidding: I know you mean well, but that will reduce my life to a mere echo of someone else's voice, a mere compliance with rules that some one else has fixed for me, and I *cannot* do that. I cannot limit myself because you say I should. I want to have hopes and dreams that are my own. I want to live my own life! I cannot fit into the mould that you have cast for me.

"I know you mean well. But I cannot live like that. I cannot live in a world of restrictions that are set for me by people who do not care what is going on in my head. Society has determined that women have to play a role within boundaries. It is not the role for me. I cannot in all conscience consent to limit my experience to the narrow confines of someone else's imagination. I want to strike out. If I make any mistakes, I want them to be mine, not someone else's. I want to be free to chart my own course.

"I know you love me, and that all you want is the best possible life for me. But your best is not my best. Let me find mine. Let me walk my own road. If I stumble and fall, let it be because I was not looking where I was going. Let it not be because someone pushed me. I know you are disappointed. But I have to go on. I only hope we can go on together as a family. But if not, so be it."

By this time she was crying, and her father's eyes were wet, though it was not clear whether it was from anger or empathy.

He tried to speak but something clicked in his throat and he remained silent. This was beyond the realm of his experience or imagination. This daughter he did not pretend to understand. She did not respond to discipline. She did not respond to talk. He thought of beating her. His cousin always said that women responded best to beating, but something in the way his daughter spoke smacked of rock-hard conviction that would not be dislodged by intimidation. She sounded like one of those born-again people, such was her fervour. And he knew that it was next to impossible to pluck people from the grasp of their own delusions. Time would tell. Let her have her day. In a couple of years she would come back. For he had no doubt in his heart that this crazy project of hers would fail. What kind of idea was that? He would have laughed if there were not so much money involved. He could barely begin to imagine it. So much money.

If only the girl had come to him and said, "Papa, here is the money, tell me how we can use it"! Then he would have decided how much to leave with her, how much was to stay in the family and how much would go to the parish priest. But this!

The money was also uppermost in Mama's mind. The things she would have done! But now she saw the glorious provincial triumph marching inexorably out of her life like silhouettes on a distant cinema screen. Marriage with the Etchu boy was a lost cause. The social problems this would cause she could already imagine. Her chest heaved, she longed to scream, but feeling blocked her throat. She wept instead, rat-squeaks of grief and thwarted ambition. Here was a woman who had lived vicariously, resting on her husband's laurels, basking in the warm glow of her daughter's academic success. And now the final triumph had turned to powdery ash before her very eyes. What would she not have done with that money!

"Mother, don't cry."

"Why should I not cry? Why not? We spend all our money on you, deprive ourselves to send you to university, and you come here talking some white man nonsense about money that should belong to us and giving it to loose, free women, sluts! - "

"Ah, I see. Not to worry, Mother. There is a lot of money. I forgot to tell you that you will never want for anything for the rest of your life. I will settle some of the money on you. But somehow I did not think that it would come to this, the obsession with money." She quoted a sum that Mama did not know could actually be imagined, much less owned by a human being.

"Enh?" said Mrs. Elive, her mouth open. Her father came back from his bitter waking nightmare with the speed of a meteor.

"What? Wha – what?

"I said some of the money is yours. I did not mean that I would use all of it for my project."

"And you say you will give us how much?" Head tilted like a bird.

She told him.

The discussion was less acrimonious after that. Her mother dried her tears. Her father finished wiping the porridge off his face. They told her they still wanted to see her married. She could choose whatever man she wanted. But she should marry and have children. Every woman need a child to be her best friend as you and I are friends, her mother wanted to say. But something about the look in her daughter's eye caused her to stop in mid-sentence.

The breakfast meeting ended on a moneyed truce. But something had flown out of the house, never to return.

Part Three

17

[EXCERPT FROM THE WEEKLY CORRESPONDENT]

Interview with Martha Elive, Founder of the Women's House

WC: What exactly is this edifice?

ME: This is a place of solace and self-fulfilment for women. It was created to provide women with more choices than they have had so far.

WC: So this is for the empowerment of women?

ME I dislike catchwords. It seems...trite and somewhat hypocritical to reduce the struggle of fully half of the human race to a blithe, fashionable concept coined by a combination of briefcase NGOs, meddlesome and ineffectual do-gooders and so-called development partners. As I said, the aim is to provide women with more options concerning the direction their lives take. I want them to be able to influence their future. I want them to think and act like mistresses of their own fate.

WC: So they do not have that power now?

ME: I do not think so.

WC: How was this project born? How did you organise funding?

ME: This is my idea, my vision, and the money was given to me by a philanthropist who is now deceased. Honest money, I should emphasise.

WC: Concretely. What do you aim to do? What are the projected activities?

ME: Education, Retraining and Support. Education will be provided to women whose schooling was ignored or interrupted. Retraining will be given to those who wish to upgrade or diversify their skills. Lastly, support will involve assisting women who, for various reasons, have come up against obstacles to self-fulfilment and need help to tide them over a bad patch. Therefore, as you realise, the overall aim is to give women a chance to reinvent themselves, both socially and mentally.

WC: So, in fact, you aim to empower them to make choices and implement these choices.

ME: If you insist on using the term, yes that is it, in short.

WC: How are you going to implement this?

ME: I cannot go into detail as we are just beginning. The method will depend on the obstacles we face, on the situations that arise. There are no hard and fast rules. However, I am sure that there is a need to be fulfilled, and we are here to fulfil that need.

WC: Who are "we"?

ME: Time will tell.

18

When the narrow-faced reporter left, Martha summoned her personal assistant on the intercom.

"Hortense, *tu peux venir une minute?*"

A minute later, Hortense bustled in. She was short and dark, with a compact weightiness to her, a bust of epic proportions and short, thin legs whose upper calf muscles were perched high up, close to her knee, looking small and hard and incongruous like tennis balls buried in flesh. Martha had put an anonymous ad in the papers for a personal assistant with a good command of French and English, along with the rest of the usual skills. Hortense had just left the graduate school attached to the city's university. She looked good on paper, and Martha hired her after a very brief interview.

"Tell all the new department heads – are they all around?"

"Yes, only Mrs. Morton went out, but she should be back by now."

"Alright, meeting in ten minutes. In my office."

Martha rose from her huge desk and went to the east window of her aerie, as she called it to herself, where she had her private office and living quarters. The harsh hot sunlight glared down at a featureless, boggy plain clogged with the green and brown of swamp vegetation. The centre was located just near Bekoko Junction, away from town, almost at the crossroads between Anglophone and Francophone Cameroon.

She opened the French windows and stepped out onto her terrace. The air shimmered with malevolent heat, producing waves of thermal energy that were almost visible out of the corner of one's eye. She could feel the sun on the sliver of bare scalp where her hair was parted. Swamp birds called lethargically to one another, describing large, lazy circles in the mid-morning heat. From the other side, the front near the highway, she could hear the intermittent, angry-bee zing of small vehicles in a hurry, and the laboured, choking roar of big diesel engines in need of maintenance.

Mistress of all I survey.

It had been a hectic two years.

Events had progressed inexorably, interspersed with the predictable bottlenecks: the land purchase, the building permits, the snide contractors, the cheating foremen, the lackadaisical workmen, probing, corrupt local officials, the cement shortages - the alphabet soup of greed and corruption any entrepreneur had to face - but she had triumphed over all that. Finally the buildings were ready. It had taken a lot more time than she had initially planned, because of what was described as her "refusal to understand". She had built her complex without conceding a single bribe or kickback, all four levels of it, if one counted the basement and her aerie perched on top of the central section, poking defiantly up at the sky, like a show-off pupil drawing attention to himself in a class of mediocre scholars. The stage was set. All she needed now were the actors. She heard voices in the anteroom and went in to chair her meeting.

They were there, all five of them, her lieutenants, her council of war, she thought, and wondered why she was thinking in such martial terms.

But it was a war. When people found out what exactly she was up to, it would definitely be war. But she was ready for that. There was nothing in the law to prohibit her from doing anything along these lines, but that would not stop them trying to stop her. It had never stopped anyone in this country, she thought, as she surveyed her team.

She would fight back. Or else life for many women would be like having the feeling that you were going to sneeze, and waiting forever for a sneeze that never came. It would be a life of annoyed perpetual expectation. She was convinced that a lot of the dissatisfaction that caused women to turn on each other was similar to what happened when people had to live in cramped quarters with no space for turning. It became every woman for herself and everyone snapping and nipping at her neighbour.

It was all caused by men. They were like sadistic zookeepers; they put animals together in a narrow cage with no

99

freedom and watched them tear each other to pieces. Then they told each other that these animals would never really rise to a higher plane because they were basically bestial, and they felt superior. She was going to break open the cage and let the animals out to stretch and gambol in the sun. It would not be easy, especially when the animals had been used to living in cramped spaces and were afraid to stretch. It was living below deck in a slave ship, and then being taken out to see the sun and the prospect of escape and freedom. The cramp of confinement would take a while to wear off.

"All seems to be going well. We will be accepting our first residents in three days. All that can be done in a material sense has been done. Now I am afraid I must preach a little.

"I will tell you a story. The other day I was angry with someone. One of those city officials you know so well. He had tried to rid me of some money that I was anxious to keep. I looked at this man, this little upstart in his badly cut suit, with his greedy eyes, and I thought to myself: I can destroy him if I want. I can ruin his career. I toyed with the idea for a while, as he defended himself. Then I thought: I can do it if I want to.

"But I won't.

"And that, for me, is the definition of true power. It comes when you have an option that you decide not to exercise, not because of outside influence, but because of self-restraint. Real power is born of self-restraint. And that is what I want you to tell the women who are coming here on Monday. I want you to help them acquire the ability and the means to make choices. In the process, you will all have considerable power and influence: I want you to use it with restraint.

"Many of these women are stupid. Let's face facts. Much of humanity is stupid. But it is not the kind stupidity that cannot be changed. This is because these women are not actually stupid. They are just ignorant. The reason you women are on this team is that you are anything but ignorant. At least I hope so. So please do not look down on these women and make them feel more inferior than they already feel. Be their friends, not their superiors. Help them to break those chains that our society has placed on them.

"Shine by your commitment. I do not need to tell you that there are wolves out there just praying for us to fail so that they can say that women are not good for anything. It is our duty in this centre to prove to these people that we are not what they think we are, that we can be more than what they are determined to reduce us to. So we have to present a united front. I imagine that there will be disagreements on policy and suchlike, but I am asking you now to keep all disagreements within this centre amongst us. If they come out, you know what they will say.

"So let me formally welcome you to this project of mine. Not mine, as such; it is *our* project. I do not for one moment imagine it will be easy, but I am sure that together we will triumph."

There was silence. The women looked back at her with what she hoped was agreement and a determination to succeed.

"And now, let us move on to other matters. We will proceed according to department.

"Administration, how are things?"

Administration was Gladys Morton.

She smoothed back hair that was already so severely pulled back that it forcibly arched her eyebrows, lending her an air of permanent, haughty surprise. She was in her early forties, and always dressed in conservative business suits. She was not particularly open or friendly, but she was highly competent, a graduate of the Wharton Business School. When Martha had interviewed her for the job, all she would reveal was that she was born and had studied in the U.S., had started working there and married an American. The marriage had not worked and she had decided to return to her roots. And she wanted to do something for her sisters.

"Everything is set from my end. We got all the supplies in and Mrs. Ngallah says the stationery guy will be delivering at two. She's just been to see him. No other problems, at least none that I can see."

"Logistics?"

Logistics was Mrs. Ngallah. She was, in her early forties too, the typical successful village girl reinvented into city matron, who later became the typical abandoned wife, moaning

101

and accepting sympathy for two years until she decided that choirs and Sunday afternoon tribal meetings were not enough, and opened a small business with what she had managed to salvage from her broken marriage. The business had carved a rather cosy little niche for itself. Martha had met her at a mostly middle-aged party thrown by some man in the ports authority who had just been promoted.

At the party, the stereo was booming out a hot Bikutsi dance number with frenzied drumming and skilfully arranged xylophone sequences. The babbling of the chorus seemed incoherent to her, but then they were not singing in the language of her tribe. From time to time, the lead singer delivered declarations in a hoarse, breathy staccato of French and Ewondo which she was told described in graphic detail what he would do to a certain unnamed female of his acquaintance when he finally caught up with her. The male dancers grinned and their mouths moved in inaudible comment on his declarations, moving their bodies in increasingly novel ways as the drink got to them. The wives shuddered and thrilled to the risqué language, pretending to be shocked, while some of the single women who were not otherwise occupied laughed uproariously, causing heads to turn in curiosity and turn away again in superior moral disgust.

Martha prided herself on not being a good dancer. There was little in her view that was ennobling about gyrating one's hips and hopping about in a way that seemed somehow to have an atavistic connection to dancing apes. That is not how she wished to show herself. She was also afraid that she would be the object of amusement if she tried to dance and missed the complicated steps. It was better to wait for something more sedate, and in any case, with whom would she dance? For years now, the local music industry had been invaded by the throbbing beat and xylophone virtuosity of the Bikutsi, which was the music of the ethnic group that held the country's presidency. She admitted that some of it was stirring indeed. But a lot of it was just poorly-arranged semi-pornographic noise by people who sang only because production was easier when your tribesman was in power. The increasingly overt sexual references in this and other music did not seem to unduly

102

concern a government whose catchphrase, at least in the early days, had been rigour and moralisation. There seemed little that was rigorous in a government that often appointed (and reappointed) as government ministers people who had been accused of corruption. What made it pathetic was that the very people who bemoaned the chronic corruption in government circles were here at this party, hobnobbing with the great and not-so-good, shelving criticism for a piece of the action when it suited them.

She noticed that some of the dancers had withdrawn from the floor the moment the Bikutsi number started. These were the sympathisers of the fractious opposition who deeply resented the musical hegemony that the government sympathisers had tried (and failed) to impose. Thus the musical scene was dominated by Bikutsi and the more universal Makossa beat, each with its own ardent adherents, each claiming artistic superiority.

She was not interested in any of that. Individual tastes would ultimately prevail. In any case, both types of music were guilty of using scantily-clad girls in their videos. She wondered whether these dancing girls were aware that they were being exploited. It did not seem to strike them as odd that the singers they danced for were themselves covered with complete, if gaudy and tasteless, clothing while they capered about on stage with their navels in the air. The vulgar, strident nonsense of it bored her in the extreme. She herself was more inclined to pieces that stood the test of time.

Martha was prowling along the edge of the dance floor, conducting an inventory of the men out of habit. There were the usual middle-aged husbands, some with incipient paunches and others with fully-grown basketball bellies. They all looked married, and Martha could see their wives watching them out of the corners of their eyes. She did not want a disgraceful scene, so she steered clear of those who seemed inclined to make an approach in her direction. The more experienced ones studied the women from under lowered lids, or settled their gaze on her accidentally on purpose as they scanned the room. She put on her most forbidding expression. She was about to embark on a huge project. Now was not the time to alienate that half of the population that was likely to support her by starting an affair with someone's husband.

There were men whom she detected to be single by the swarm of what she called the Clingfilm girls that seemed glued to them. She surmised that these were the society husband-hunters. The competition amongst these girls was ferocious. Boyfriends were "seized" from the unwary all the time, so one had to be vigilant. It did not make for sisterly unity among these single women who, with all their degrees and successful businesses, would always feel insecure about their status because they had not been married yet. They lived in a state of armed truce with the wives: they exchanged the usual social pleasantries, but things were apt to degenerate into outright war between the married and the single women when a careless husband allowed himself to be drawn into the smothering grip of the Clingfilm girls. It was well known that if he was young or rich enough, and sometimes when he was neither, a woman's husband could be easy prey for these unprincipled harpies.

As she skirted the dance floor, Fanta in hand, she overhead one of the society matrons declaiming in a loud voice that easily dominated the music. She was frankly fat, and was at present surrounded by a gaggle of youngish wives who were listening to her tirade with expressions that ranged from rapt to merely bored. She was explaining to a young wife who seemed to be in some sort of in-law trouble that the thing was to stop pretending.

"If you feel that there is something you do not like about the way your in-laws are behaving, say so. If you hear that one of your in-laws has said something, go up to them and say: sister, I hear that you said such and such a thing. Now if you did not say it, then I am sorry for accusing you wrongly. If you did, then this is what I think of in-laws who go sneaking about and saying unkind things about their brother's wives. And tell her! Because if you keep pretending that everything is all right, they will walk all over you. Stop trying to play the decent wife and show them who you are. They are determined to dislike you whatever you do, nobody knows why, but that is how in-laws are. So you might as well be hanged for a sheep as for a lamb. Work with the ones that want to work with you and hate the ones that hate you. Marriage is not a debt that you must pay all your life. Tell these people that you owe them nothing. They think that by marrying you, their brother has saved you from a life of misery and emptiness, but prove to them that your contribution to their brother's happiness is not something to be underrated. Stop trying to please people. It never works. As long as your conscience is clear, you have nothing to fear. You have to be firm with your in-laws. I used to be like you, but suffering opened my eyes. You hear?"

Intrigued, Martha had insinuated herself into the next conversation the woman began, and that was the beginning of their collaboration. She was a veritable tower of strength; she could shame all her absentee husband's influential friends into pulling strings and helping her get things done. She knew everyone, had everyone's history at her fingertips, and she was worldly wise. Later, when Martha's naïve enthusiasm threatened to get the better of her project, she was the one who stepped in and righted things. She was invaluable. Martha liked her midwife-explaining-the-facts-of-life-to-rural-women frankness; she would be just right for the motivational talks and the social liaison work.

Now at the meeting, Mrs. Ngallah blinked her razor-sharp eyes at Martha and assured her that all was under control. "We have some minor things to fine-tune, but nothing I cannot solve."

"I doubt that there's anything you cannot solve, Mrs Ngallah"

Everyone laughed, except for the engineer, who scowled and slumped down lower in her chair. She was big and solid, and almost entirely waistless, with short dreadlocks and a round, pimply, dark face. A lethal combination of tactlessness and assertiveness, Grace had come to them from the National Polytechnic, where she had managed to antagonise everyone except the gateman, and then only because she never spoke to him anyway. With her charmless, uncompromising manner, she was a nightmare to the almost exclusively male teaching staff, who were not used to working with females who did not care about what they looked like to men, going about in wrinkled trousers and dog-eared tee-shirts, and who contradicted the Dean at staff meetings.

Worse, she was good, very good. She might have fared better if she had smiled and simpered and cast her eyes bashfully down when the Dean was talking to her, if her demeanour had let her male colleagues understand that she was a genius, true, but only a female. Then they would have accepted her, knowing that she herself knew that she was tainted by nature, and that she was not to think that her brains were any reason for her to think that she was equal to, or God forbid, even better than they were.

They would have been satisfied if her keen intelligence had seemed to have survived in spite of her being female, but she was not apologetic about her intelligence. She was, in fact, unutterably graceless about it: she was not the sort to suffer fools gladly. She had lasted all of two years, and was about to be thrown out on some pretext or other when Martha got hold of her.

When Martha turned to her for her own report, she said: "Nothing to report. Any problems, I'll let you know." No more. There was a small, embarrassed silence. She had been much too abrupt.

The women gathered there, though they were highly educated and aware that this new task was about breaking barriers, still thought with the reflexes of their past experience. So they felt that women's gatherings were supposed to be friendly affairs where the acrimony, though veiled with feminine sweetness, was no less present. Such indifference to conventional behaviour baffled them.

Martha was not worried about the conventional behaviour; at least that is what she told herself. She was more concerned with how this woman would fit into a team if she did not communicate. She had hired her on the basis of her impressive qualifications and had told herself that the woman's personality really did not count as long as she was good at her job (and was secretly pleased with herself for her objectiveness). She was not there to share her bedroom with anyone; she was there to do a job, and if the person who was qualified to do the job was rather short on socialising skills, then so be it. Personal likes did not come into it at all. And whatever they said, everyone admitted that Grace, the Mechanical Woman (as Mrs. Ngallah had dubbed her), was a genius.

This reasoning notwithstanding, Martha felt her stomach tighten. She hated difficult people who refused to let things run nice and smooth, and she hoped it would not come to a situation where she would be forced to arbitrate, or sack someone. She would really hate to do that. She had realised about herself that she was able to be tough and decisive when the object of her toughness was not looking her in the eye and preparing to cause a scene. She hoped that this woman would not give her trouble.

Which left the indoors lady, as she was called. She was the daintiest little hothouse flower, petite and very fair, with big, old-fashioned glasses and frilly little calf-length dresses. She also had the deftest pair of hands that money could buy, and she was giving them for practically nothing. Perplexed and trying not to show it, Martha had wanted to know why she insisted on working for so little, considering what her experience abroad would have earned her elsewhere.

"My father was a white man", she was told in a soft, ladylike voice that reminded Martha of pastels and lavender. "I was the result of a union that was frowned upon by everyone. When my father died, my mother, unable to face her relatives, went to live in England, since she had acquired citizenship through her marriage. When she got there, no one accepted her either. So I was brought up with a feeling of not belonging to any world. I was also left a great deal of money, to the fury of my white cousins and the dismay of my black ones. So I tried living it up for a while, but I got tired of the permanent excitement and decided to come back here and find my roots. The rest you know."

She was in charge of the catering and hospitality department. "Everything is set for business on Monday," she said. "I have all my supplies, and the fires only wait to be lit in the kitchens."

"Alright! Good. Everything seems to be hunky-dory. Any comments? I need not add that we should be as proactive as possible in our management. This is not the kind of management structure where there is one big boss, who comes and tells everyone what to do and they do it. This is not one of our venerable political parties. I expect us to run this thing together. So, let fly."

No one felt like letting fly, it seemed. So the meeting ended with Martha feeling that she had missed something about how to conduct high-power meetings. She really was not much good at that sort of thing, she had to admit. If anyone had told her that there was nothing to say during the meeting because she had taken care of all potential problems, she would not have believed them. If Ophelia had been here, she would have known how to infuse them with her fervour. Fervour was Ophelia's stock-in-trade.

19

Martha had met Ophelia at the same party where she had met Mrs. Ngallah. After their conversation, which had ended with an invitation from Martha to visit the Women's House, Martha had continued her solitary prowl on the edges of the excitement. She saw, standing near to one of the huge speakers, but seeming oblivious to the noise, a woman in her early thirties who seemed as out of it as she was. Even in the smoke-filled room, Martha noticed that her eyes were unusually bright, radiating a hard intelligence tinged with a kind of streetwise watchfulness. Martha had sometimes seen that look on domestic animals that were used to dodging blows. She was wearing a black lace dress that did not cover her knees. Her legs were slim and muscled. Her face was triangular, with a crop of adult acne that had created a landscape of small black scars along its edges, where her beard and moustache would have been. Her complexion was darkish, her skin rather dull.

She had a tawny drink in her hand, which she sipped from time to time, but she did not look as if she was enjoying the drink or anything else. Martha thought of walking over and engaging her in conversation, but their eyes met and the woman scowled at her, and Martha looked away.

After a while, Martha began feeling peckish, so she moved towards the buffet, hoping to get a late-night snack before heading home. As she was nearing the buffet, there was some commotion on the far edge of the dance floor. There was a man held in the unrelenting grip of another man and what seemed to be his own wife and they were leading him away from a woman in a tight red dress who stood as if petrified in shame. The man who was being dragged away strained against the grip of his captors, visibly intent on going back to the woman in the red dress. Focussed on the scene, Martha was not looking where she was going and bumped into someone. She turned in time to see the woman in the black lace dress shying back from her, a spilling glass of beer in her hand, her eyes murderous slits.

"Oh, sorry! Martha exclaimed in confusion. "Oh my God."

"Oh your God indeed. Oh my dress, you mean. See my little black number drowned in beer!

She had a high, educated, precise voice, with a humorous undertone that belied the look in her eyes, which did not smile as she surveyed Martha coldly from head to foot. Martha squirmed inwardly under her scrutiny.

"I hope the damage is not irreversible. I could pay for the — "

"That will be necessary, but I shall pay for it myself. My mother told me never to take money from strangers. Or not. Pay for it, I mean. It was a rusty ole thing in any case," she added, dabbing at the wet patch on her thigh with a tissue.

She looked up, her luminous eyes penetrating. "I don't think we have met before. Or have we? I do tend to go around in a beery fog at these functions."

"No, I don't think we have met." Seizing the day, Martha introduced herself.

"A gleam of recognition has just lit up mine expressive eyes, I trow. Ah! So you are the intrepid taboo-buster, enh? Hm! Maybe the little black number is not that important. A dress is, after all, only a dress. Nice meeting you. At last. You are rather elusive."

"You have the advantage over me. What may I call you?"

"Don't call me, I'll call you." She laughed loudly, a high cackle. Some of the sedate matrons murmuring together in a corner looked at her out of the sides of their eyes and leaned closer together to dissect her in discretion.

The woman was oblivious, Martha noted. She wondered how many drinks she had had.

"Five."

"What?"

"Five drinks, each different from the preceding one. I could see the question in thine roving eye. I was saying…that is the story of my life. They never call again. But when they call, they call me Ophelia, or Ophie, if they like me. Many don't. So here's Ophelia Taboko at your service, beck or call. I teach comparative literature in Anglo-Sax."

"Anglo-Sax?"

"The University, Milady. Where have you been?"

She put down her glass on the ruffled satin tablecloth of the buffet, where it promptly keeled over and spilled the remaining beer.

"No problem," she said, staying Martha's hand as she moved towards the glass. "Madam Hostess will deal with it efficiently, or else her six housemaids will. More important, I am interested in you. As Chief Zebrudaya said to Bewitch Bankrovitch, 'dis are very good bizness, an' I am intress.'"

"You would like to join the teaching staff?" asked Martha, who already visualised rousing literature classes with this woman.

"Nope, no offence intended, but crusades are not my glass of beer. However, crusaders are. They are a species of person that intrigues me no end. So, what are you crusading against? You hate guys, is that it? You prefer to smell the bad breath of a woman when you wake up in the morning?"

"Gracious! No. I don't hate guys; actually, one of the problems in my life is that I do not seem to know how not to like them. I have nothing against lesbians, really, but I am, often to my great distress, heterosexual. I suspect it will be the death of me."

"Why?"

"Men hurt, and they occupy your life to the exclusion of most other things."

"Ha. My view, sorry to disagree, is that whatever occupies your mind at any time is what should be there. I don't fight it. I'm a wallower, you see. No self-control at all." She waved the subject away. "Enough of the psychobabble in any case. I have to go home and sleep off the beer; I do not currently own a car, and I am more than slightly drunk, as you may have surmised from my demeanour." She stared at Martha. "Like beer?"

"'Fraid not."

"Never fear. Pity, though. Don't know what you are missing. Beer is the great soporific, the great deadener of throbbing nerve-ends, the nectar that passeth all misery."

"I know. I once found out its potency to my upchucking discomfort."

Ophelia laughed. "I guess our generation has tried everything and found it wanting. At least we know where we stand on a lot of issues, do we not? You own a car, I believe?"

"Yes. Can give you a lift."

"Much obleeged. Mine jalopy, were I in a position to drive it, would still not do the job as it has been in a garage for the past four weeks. I am not inclined to move it for the time being." She belched softly, a faint whistle of air between her teeth. "Sorry."

They walked out to the car. On the drive home, Martha was quiet, concentrating on her driving. Ophelia soon dozed off. Martha was wondering whether this woman was a habitual drunk. Some of the women she knew drank to drown their feeling of displacement in a society that had not yet found a suitable status for them.

When they got to her junction, the woman sat up as if on cue.

"There. Near the water tower. I'm staying up there with the current interest. Second and last floor. Wasn't much company, was I? Not very compos mentis these days, so I'm trying to soothe my fevered brain with drink. Have had a bad week marking the scripts of creatures that I can only describe as *Morlocks*. Children are getting increasingly stupid these days. Don't know if it's TV or what. Hear what some kid wrote in an essay on neo-colonialism: 'we have resources, that people come in and tap the resources and go them away' That's a university kid. I don't know why I ever agreed to become a teacher."

"Well, the decay is everywhere. Have you listened to their parents? How else can you expect the sons of people who are too busy stealing to have a family life to perform?"

They sat in silence for a while. The Ophelia stirred.

"Well, let me go. Mustn't get maudlin on you. You free on Monday?"

"Yes, in the afternoon."

112

"I might come and have a look-see at your outfit on my way back from Anglo-Sax. That okay?"

"Should be. But if not, will call and tell you." They exchanged numbers.

By the following week, Ophelia had visited and met the rest of the senior staff. At the end of her tour, she had allowed herself to be persuaded to give what she called "suffragettist rant-and-raves with a little literary appreciation thrown in" on a fortnightly basis. Martha liked her odd speech and quirky sense of humour. She called the Mechanical Woman the "waistless horror".

"Leave her alone. You yourself are not perfect." They were relaxing in Martha's private quarters after a staff meeting.

"So what. My slim waist was the toast of the campus in my day. But look at that girl. Who says that women with brains should go around looking and smelling like a sack of rain-soaked smoked fish? Even though men think the world grew out of their turds and that they are the authors and finishers of our faith, they still go out of their way to be attractive to us. They wear nice suits. They like sleeping with us; they just don't want us to be in control."

"What has that got to do with Grace?"

"I am famous for my non sequiturs. But what I was trying to say is that your principles should not be expressed in terms of your physical appearance. Even if she dresses like that, will it add or detract from what she is? What has what she got in her head to do with how she dresses? She opens her mouth and people know who she is!"

"I suspect she is using the same line of reasoning to justify her shabby clothes."

"Granted. It works both ways. But a person should do their best to be attractive, or at least neat. And I suspect that her clothes are not an expression of her intellectual independence. She is just plain sloppy, if you ask me."

"I do not."

"Shut up, damn you. I am the university lecturer here."

"Fine. But you will admit that she and the others have a lot of good ideas, even if you hogged the floor most of the time."

113

"I'm the one teaching comparative literature here, so I'm best qualified to hold forth on feminism in literature and elsewhere. I've read all the books on the subject."

"Alright. But it was great to talk about it all the same."

"Yeah. The booze was sublime. Never tasted Cherry Marnier before."

Martha fell silent, remembering the meeting.

She had invited all the senior staff, plus a few other women to a pre-commencement get-together, and the discussion had turned to women and writing. Ophelia had been in her element.

"You know, there was a woman, Margaret Cavendish, who described my mother's life exactly: 'we live like bats or owls, labour like beasts and die like worms'. My mother is mired in drudgery. Even when I have been able to support her, she had been unable to stop working and relax a little."

"Most mothers are not able to stop working," said Prudentia Ngallah. "I think they feel guilty about sitting there doing nothing, as if they would cease to have a worthwhile existence if they did not work."

"It has always been like that," Ophelia said. "As Mary Cavendish said,

'wife and servant are the same
but only differ in the name'."

"But do they have a choice?" cut in Martha. "Has anyone told them that life can be different? I don't think so, not on this continent."

"Well, elsewhere, women have been writing about it," said Ophie. "My best woman among those early crusaders is Mary Wollstonecraft. She was a great woman."

"She wrote Frankenstein, didn't she?" asked Prudentia.

"Oh ye of little learning. That was her daughter, Mary Wollstonecraft *Shelley*. This one was the mother. She said that self-improvement for women must be at the expense of the 'illegitimate power' that women obtain by degrading themselves into objects of admiration. She called it the 'arbitrary power of beauty'."

"Right. Couldn't agree more." It was Grace. Martha and the others looked at her in mild surprise. She had marched in, plopped onto an armchair and had not spoken since. "The power that beauty confers is transient at best. To base one's sense of achievement on what it will bring you is a kind of suicide. I think a strong character is more important. It will get you where you want to go, however you look. Beauty as a weapon is used only at the expense of self-respect." Her face twisted. "Men. If only one could live without them. If the world could be totally free of them! Exterminate all the brutes, as Kurtz said." She slapped the flat of her hand on the armchair and fell silent, her face a mask of anger.

There was a small pause, and then Ophelia stepped in, laughing. "Well! And I thought I was radical. But exasperating as they can be, the brutes are not all evil. John Stuart Mill, for instance, did what he could."

"How many Stuart Mills do you know in this country?" countered Grace.

"None, admittedly. But do not forget that we are not a nation of writers. People think and live things that they may never put on paper. We have silent supporters among the menfolk.

"True, Grace," added Prudentia. "Not all men are rotten."

"If you have met some good ones, good for you. In my experience, there are no exceptions. In fact, there are few exceptions anywhere, among male or female. I think we are doomed as a country. Everyone is so stupid, so wrapped up in stealing and making money and getting connections to those in power. I have never seen greed on such a scale. Even the women steal from each other. And the ignorance!"

"You know, I am tempted to share your despair," said Gladys Morton, who had been silent until then. "I visited a couple the other day, and I discovered that even among educated people, the ignorance is appalling. I mean this man and his wife, both educated abroad, firmly believe that making a baby wear yellow clothes will give it jaundice. How can you account for deliberate ignorance at such a level?"

"Gladys me dear," said Ophelia, "out here it is called tradition and custom and it is venerated. It is not called a refusal to think."

"But these people have been through university!"

"The university has not been through them. They did not acquire an *eddycayshun*. They only have certificates."

Gladys smiled fleetingly. "Another thing I noticed is that the nursing mother absolutely revels in the pain of childbirth. It is as if the pain was a rite of passage to a higher plane."

Martha said: "When I was in high school, I nearly got lynched one day because I told my female classmates that I would avoid the pain of childbirth, and get disposable diapers, if I could. They nearly killed me. They said you couldn't love your child if you did not suffer to bring him into the world. I asked them why they thought that women had to suffer to be worthy. They did not have any answers. It just was *so*. I asked them whether, if a woman was unconscious while giving birth and did not feel the pain, she would love her baby less. They told me that even if she had a caesarean, she would still feel post operative discomfort and that was enough to make her a member of the sorority of pain."

Grace said: "In any case, childbirth is not for me. I can't stand children."

"What!" Prudentia started violently. Grace faced her without flinching.

"I will never have children. They get on my nerves. People forget that when a baby is born, he is just an animal. He has to be civilised by his parents. I do not have the patience to break in young animals. And I do not have the heart to bring children into a world like ours. I think if many women faced facts, they would admit that childbirth is a messy business with endless work and little reward. I do not understand how a society can advocate birth control in one breath and castigate those who practice it in another."

"But if your parents had thought like that, you would not exist."

"My parents were having a good time, of which I was the by-product. I owe them nothing for being born. So, I have decided that since I can control that part of my life, I will not be burdened with children. Period."

Prudentia made as if to speak, but she caught a warning glance from Martha in mid-air and fell silent. Martha changed tack.

"Well, one of the reasons we are here this evening is that we have to try and define what we are trying to do in this House.

"The process we are about to begin is a kind of creation. But we are going about it backwards. You start things with a frame, before you add flesh. We already have the flesh, that is, the women who will come to us, but they do not have a backbone. If you want to build a house, you start with the foundation and stuff like that, before you add the accessories. We have instead the trimmings, to which we must add a frame. These women are like a bag of flesh with no bones. That is why we have to give them a spine so they can stand on their own. You have to fit the bones right so that the body works. You will probably get it wrong sometimes, and create deformities, but a deformed backbone is better than no backbone at all. You have to bear that in mind."

"That is clear enough, I suppose," said Gladys, "But do you have an ideology?"

"Nope. In this business, an ideology is difficult to express. But my aim is that women have to exceed their perceived limits and acquire power over their own bodies."

"Yes," said Ophelia. "But what do you base that on."

"Elucidate."

"What brand of feminism are you peddling? All we are stating here has been thought about and died for by women before us."

"To be frank, I'm not much into theory. I am for a practical approach."

"I think you're an old-fashioned feminist, in the sense that neither you nor the women you wish to work for have ever been exposed to feminism before, so you will begin where white women began. There are now post-feminists, in case you have not heard. We are still at the level of Wollstonecraft and the early crusaders."

"Wollstonecraft had an ideology?"

117

"Oh dear! Does no one ever read? She was a theorist. I have a few books on her you should read. But in a way, you are lucky. To start your project in this country now means that you do have to throw yourself under a moving vehicle, as some did. Women already have the right to vote. That the politics are rotten is another matter. The groundwork has already been dealt with."

"True, but only partly so. Those women fought in a different context from ours. Victorian ladies just sat around and fainted, and were in my view rightly held in contempt by their menfolk for their unproductiveness. Our women slave in the homes and fields and are still held in contempt. The white women were protesting against the enforced uselessness of women. I am protesting against their unacknowledged usefulness, and I want to make sure that those who can be useful to themselves can do so in peace and keep the profits for themselves. I want to make sure that even if their usefulness is not acknowledged, they can be independent enough not to care. We have to lay down the basic tenets - "

"Basic tenet can only be valid if they are common to all women on the globe. At whatever stage the struggle is, it is the same struggle everywhere."

"That cannot be. Women live in different cultures. How are we going to reconcile all these cultures? Even religions are different. See how people fight about them."

"The wars you refer to are not wars of religion. They are wars of economics, waged by the clever, strong and unscrupulous over the weak and unscrupulous, and occasionally vice versa. What I am saying is that the Universal Declaration of Human Rights applies to people of all cultures. The rights of women should be universal enough to apply to all cultures as well."

They had gone on debating the development of a universal ideology for some time. When the other women left, Martha and Ophelia continued.

Now, Martha said in response to Ophelia's praise of Cherry Marnier: "Shut up, you drunk. But you may be right to some extent on the ideology business. However, we have to start somewhere. We cannot fight at the same pace as white women, who can already sue for sexual harassment."

"True. Think about it some more. And think about men."

"That is all I ever seem to do."

"Yes, they *do* have their uses. Any way, I think that I would rather let my beauty 'goad a man to think of toads' as Christina Rossetti said, than to be a submissive angel without fulfilment of any kind except childbirth. To quote another woman, Sarah Grimke, 'whatsoever it is morally right for a man to do, it is morally right for a woman to do'. I will even go further to say that even if it is not morally right, as most things are, I want the right to do it. If sin is profitable, I want to sin too. Why should I be a Madonna and be pure and forgiving while men have all the fun? I don't want to go to heaven. I want to be worthy and fulfilled.

"One of the words I resent most in this world when used in relation to women is 'must'. Women must do this, women must do that. I have decided that I *'must'* not. I will *not* be governed by the musts of other people. That word is the most pernicious influence in our lives."

"Too true. Yes. I aim to eliminate the 'musts' as well. Women should not be confined by obligation to menial, unthinking, safe things like cooking."

"Cooking is not safe. Cooking is anything but safe. It is dangerous work. You can be roasted by an ember or fried by hot oil. You can be cooked by scalding water. A knife can sever an artery or a large vein, you can drop a grindstone on your toes and break them, and you can be killed by a gas explosion. You can be beaten up by your husband if, in spite of risking all this to cook for him, the result is not to his liking. It is not safe at all. Anyway, to return to men. How do you see them in all this?"

Martha thought hard. At last she looked up.

"Let me put it this way. My room in the university had a varnished brown ceiling with boards of alternating length. I used to lie down and imagine that the whorls of the wood were deliberate shapes. Over time, I came to see the shape of a man spread out over six rows of board. His chest was long and thick, but shapeless. He was in profile, you see. His head tilted forward like an anxious old man, and there was the suggestion of something slow and simian about his lower jaw. But that is all there is to his head because the board stops at the cheekbone, and above that, the next board dissolves into graceful zigzags of the kind of meaninglessness that only nature can produce and still make beautiful. His belly is lean, his arms are too short. A board obliterates where his groin would have been. His legs end at mid-calf.

"To me, that is how men are. Their brains do not interest me because I can think for myself, and I have not been able to fathom the power that their groins have over me. But both imprison me, and both terrify me. And I do not understand them."

"Powerful. Perhaps you had better write the book," muttered Ophelia.

"What book?"

"Never mind. Continue."

"Another thing I do not understand about men is that they believe devotion to them is an all-or-nothing business. Being even slightly pro-woman is interpreted as being automatically anti-male. Why do they assume that if you want women to be comfortable, you must hate men?"

"Because what you want is what they have and do not wish to share. The power over you is their greatest wealth, and you want that. These people have you to look after the small details while the go ahead and invent things and get mentioned in history books after they are dead, and you want that too? They are bound to fight you."

"But that is not all I want. If they could just acknowledge that the small details, and taking care of them, are often just as important, and sometimes even more so, than their grand plans, then I should be more tolerant of their megalomania. But they denigrate all that is women's work, and they pay less for it. So we will move in and do men's work, because we can. And maybe that way we will get respect."

"You are going to start a war."

"What you cannot get by peaceful means, you must get with war."

"Brave words spoken bravely. But can you hold out to the end?"

120

"To be frank, I do not know, and I am scared to death. But I am willing to try. I promised."

"That's all very noble and moral and all that, but have you found that with all these high and forward-looking notions of equality, your own emotional reactions are firmly rooted in this place and time? How will you handle it in the women under your care?"

Martha only spread her hands in reply.

"You know, you are aware that men can be terribly exploitative of your vulnerability, but you will still love them with total abandon. You still will, even when you are smarter, want them to be your master; you want to lose yourself in them. And from time to time, more often than you care to admit, you hear the treacherous tinkle of wedding bells. I call them cowbells."

"I know that emotional dependence is going to be hard to deal with, but I'll start with the material dependence. I cannot attack on all fronts."

"Good. If you know that, you'll fare better. Many women will move on to the next stage once they have their own money. But it won't be easy. I forget which of those female sages said this, but I remember she said something like, if a man and a woman are to become one through wedlock, the one they become is the man. That is the link you have to break."

Martha sighed and stifled a small yawn. It had been a long day.

"I see you are getting tired.'

"I ought to sleep."

"Me too." They rose and moved to their bedrooms.

20

Monday morning. Lying in bed the on the morning of the opening day, Martha wondered whether to pray to God for success or not. After the constricting religious observances of school and home, Martha had rebelled against, and subsequently ignored, God. Then she had gone through a period of tentative, pain-induced spirituality during the business with the King of Rats. That had been followed by a gradual relaxation into wary indifference to organised religion, though she still prayed occasionally.

God as a concept, not as the invisible head honcho of a worldly organisation, was always at the back of her mind, but she did not talk to Him often. Mostly, it was just laziness. But sometimes she was afraid to. She had a theory that God was like an exacting parent. His children were to be seen and not heard. Bring yourself to His notice and He might ask something of you that you were not ready to give. So she tried to live beneath His radar sensors, so to speak.

God also had a unique sense of humour. His jokes were expensive, and it was best not to risk becoming the butt of one by drawing attention to oneself.

Sometimes she was tempted to talk to Him. Her method of communicating with him was like a child who has broken something and prefers to leave a note on her father's table, dashing off to school before she can be questioned. The child could never be sure if or when his father would see the note. So she prayed when she felt the need, but she was never sure whether God was listening or not. This morning she felt she ought to pray because she was embarking on an adventure and she needed all the help she could get.

So, before the ceremony, she left God a note, a brief blip on a radar screen, soon gone.

She prayed for the success of her project, a truncated Morning Offering, with selfish bits thrown in. She did not know what He would think of it. All these things in the bible about women being obedient and all that. Part of her was dismissive of all that nonsense as having been inserted by men desirous of using religion to keep women under the yoke forever. Another part was not so sure. If he had actually said those things, He might think the she was challenging His authority.

But, she said to herself, when she died, she would explain to Him what it was that she had tried to do. If He was as good as they said He was, He would understand.

While waiting for the day of reckoning, she had a refuge to run, a dream to make work.

When she got downstairs, Hortense was staffing the front office in orangey-pink check.

"*Bonjour Madame.*"

"I'll accept your greeting when you decide to call me Martha." She flapped the wad of papers she was carrying at her assistant, who pretended to be terrified. They both laughed.

"*Alors, quoi de neuf?*"

"Well, nothing, everyone is settling in nicely. We will have the immersion session this morning in the Hall. Mrs. Ngallah is eager to start. You would think with all the running around she did yesterday that she would be tired. But not at all."

"We have a real jewel in that woman. We start at nine, right? Okay, that gives me twenty-eight minutes. Buzz me five minutes before time. See you!"

The first crop was seated, all restive, muted coughs and anxious hairstyles, in the auditorium. The auditorium was fan-shaped and had a high, domed ceiling with white-on-gold moulding, and plush red seats arranged in six rows that radiated outwards from the central dais, like in a university amphitheatre. The floor was made of black and white tiles. There were long windows on the right side of the fan, but these were closed because of the air conditioning. Some of the women shivered in the unaccustomed chill. They sat, each in her own silence, though some murmured to each other about the opulence of the room. Attitudes ranged from jaded expectancy (for those who, having dined on promises all their lives and found them unsatisfactory fare, were still unable to resist hoping for more) to fervent hope for deliverance. Some people were there for their own unrelated reasons: an outing, a chance of getting free food, or just a place to sit down, away from the sun.

Martha came in from the soundproofed door at the back of the stage. Dressed in a simple, straight-cut pale blue dress with short sleeves and wearing no makeup, she was followed by her senior staff, as Mrs. Ngallah had decided to call them. Martha had told them last evening: "Let's not get, dressed to kill. We are not here to kill anyone or show them how well-furnished our wardrobes are, so let's just wear something easy, with as little makeup as possible. We have to look non-threatening to them or else we will drive a wedge between them and us and things will not start well."

So they all wore casual dress, though the mechanical woman had rather overdone it in faded, elastic-waisted black trousers and a dog-eared olive green tee-shirt. They had also agreed not to sit down behind a table. Instead, the table had been pushed to the back of the stage and they had decided that anyone who got tired could lean against it, or sit off to the side at most.

When they came in, Martha walked to the edge of the rostrum, waited for silence and began. She welcomed them, introduced the staff, and went on to the meat of the speech.

"The world as it is today is controlled basically by a lot of white men who have most of the money. Not everyone will admit this, but it is true. Even in their world, developed as it is, the women are allowed to go only so far." She indicated an imaginary point in the air in front of her. "No further. Some of you will have heard of the glass ceiling and other privations white women have suffered and still suffer. You know that some of them died trying to obtain the right to vote.

"But you, you are not even white. You are black, which means that in addition to facing the problems that white women face, you also have to face the eternal problem of racism. You are black in a world run by white men, some of whom still publicly declare that you are just apes which can talk.

"So, you are first, women, then to make it worse, you are *black* women.

"Next, you are Africans. Black African women. We all know what our cultures tell us about the role of women. We have clearly defined roles. You do this, I do that , and if you do not, you get punished. Some people tend to glorify the idea of African culture and so on and so forth, but my personal view is that anything that causes any segment of a society to lose some privilege to the benefit of another segment should be scrapped. Period. But let us return to our analysis.

"So you are Black African women, many of whom live in repressive cultures.

"Then add the fact that, to say the least, democracy is not well established on this continent, not to talk of our esteemed fatherland.

"That means you are Black African women living in backward cultures and under a repressive political regime.

"Consider your economic power. For many of you, it is non-existent. Few of you can earn a decent living even if you were free to do so. You are not trained for it.

"Then add to that your lack of political power. My personal view is that we will have come a long way when we will have a woman as minister of finance or of the interior. In any case, don't count on it happening anytime soon.

"So you are poor, marginalised Black African women living under a repressive regime in a culture that accepts female subjugation as a given.

"Last but most, many people, including some of you yourselves, think you are fundamentally limited up here," she tapped her temple, "and that all you can do is keep house and make babies and let the men do the thinking.

"You bear all this weight.

"Some of you will wonder why you should bother to get up in the mornings, the way things are stacked against you. Why not just pull the sheets over your head and refuse to speak to anyone? Why make any effort at all?

"Indeed, why should you?

"I will tell you why.

"First, because all those things that people think about you will only be true if you allow them to be so. You have to start living for yourself, not for the people who dominate you.

"If you refuse to improve yourself because you think the task too difficult, then you will prove them right. If you allow

125

your life to be a failure because you are living according to their rules, it is your failure, not theirs. *They* are all right. They have their world ordered just the way they would like it to be.

"Second, because there is hope. Boundless hope. You bear within you the seeds of your own regeneration. All you need is fertile soil. We are here to provide it.

"So the message here is, you can change your lives. And we are here to help you.

"We know who is responsible for all this. The men, isn't it? They have trodden you underfoot, they have curtailed your rights, they have humiliated you. Right?

"Right. And wrong.

"Wrong. Because they have done so with the power you gave them. Some of you help them. Who give the widow the hardest time during her husband's funeral? Is it her male in-laws? No! It is her sisters-in-law and her husband's aunts and female cousins.

"And why does the widow let them give her a hard time? Because she thinks that it is her lot as a woman to endure some kinds of suffering, and that it is her duty to inflict it on her fellow-woman when it seems to be required.

"You have abdicated power over your own lives. You help maintain the status quo that deprives you of that power. Worst of all is your ignorance about the extent of your abilities and the choices open to you.

"So you see, the problem has three faces: what men have done to you, what you have done to yourselves, and what you do not know.

"Ignorance breeds fear. Fear breeds hatred. When a man marries two women and each of them is afraid that he might love the other more than her, what happens? Hatred, poisoning, visits to the witch doctor.

"Ignorance is our devil here. We must overcome him. That is why I created this place. To help you by overcoming your ignorance and give you the tools with which to shape your own lives. I have some women here who will help you do that. Each of them will talk to you about how things will be organised here.

126

"My last word to you is, never seek to follow the rules because it will make you look good. Let me tell you: goodness can kill you. If you want to be good to your husband and bear him many children when the doctor has told you to stop, you can die in childbirth or before. If your husband beats you and you do not want to reveal to anyone that he is less than a perfect husband, then one day he will slap you, and you will crack your head against a table edge and you will go to heaven sooner than you thought.

"If the rules suit you, fine. Go along with them. But if they do not, then do not be afraid to be the exception, if that is what your conscience tells you. Now, there are some people who do not have consciences, but that is another matter altogether. There are men out there with no conscience, but they are entitled to things some of you will never have till you die.

"Remember, we are declaring a war here. But it is not against men. They have enough wars to occupy them without our adding to the number. They love war, even if they pretend not to.

"Our own war is different. It is against ignorance. Because your subjugation, voluntary or otherwise, is the cause of your ignorance. And your ignorance is in turn the cause of your subjugation.

"Someone said knowledge is power. Someone else said the truth shall set you free. Seek the truth. It will be a long process. It will be difficult to unlearn some of the habits that have been inculcated into you from birth. We will all die without unlearning *all* of those things. But we will unlearn *some*. And that is how we will teach our girl children, and so on and so forth down the generations till we have conquered our enemy, ignorance and his son fear.

"I will leave you with that for now, but over the next few months, we will hear more about this new adventure that we will experience together. This is our child, yours and mine. It is our duty to nurture it. Thank you."

21

For Alice, the woman's words washed over her like a cold evening shower after a hot day tending cocoyam plants in the sun. She was so moved, she had trouble breathing. Her tired, much-sucked breast swelled and heaved with hope for something she had thought to be forever beyond her reach.

In Alice's muddled world of thwarted hopes and desire gone sour, in the sea of minor disappointments that added up, and resulted in a failed life, someone *knew*. Someone had the key to the cell of perpetual limitations whose inmates nursed their private aspirations like old wounds that refused to heal. Someone understood the debilitating dissatisfaction of being a poor wife in a marriage where romance had died young, where money was scarce and bad temper abundant.

It was like a picture of that saint, Sebastian, wasn't it, tied to a tree and being stoned, only in her story someone came and rescued him.

The tears stung her eyes, making her lids twitch. She blinked them away absently; a long acquaintance with tears had taught her to ignore them.

When the slim woman finished talking, a fat one took over and began to explain other things, but Alice was already far away in the house she had left in the pale grey dawn. The little house had a bedroom on either side of the parlour. A door in the back wall led to the outdoor kitchen and bathroom, connected to the house by a short, covered corridor.

The parlour wash furnished with semi-upholstered armchairs in scratchy greenish-yellow nylon fabric, brought home one exuberant evening by Herbert. A table leaned against the front wall, beneath the window. It served as general parking area for objects whose use in the household could never be adequately determined, but which seemed too important to throw away. The walls were covered with garish representations of Jesus either as a man holding his bleeding heart in his hand, blue-eyed and incredibly handsome, or as a plump babe in the

Madonna's loving arms, and a calendar bearing the pictures of Herbert's tribal elite.

It was mid-morning now, and her mother-in law would be sitting on a kitchen stool out on the veranda no wider than a wrapper of the Clerks' Quarters house, spreading her ill will out in the sun to dry, like the piss-soaked mattress of Alice's toddlers, preparing it for re-use. Alice's little boys would be rooting about in the dust or playing with their "cars", empty condensed-milk tins with sturdy wire axles tied to a dried elephant grass stalk, driving them around on the scabrous grass in front of the house, instead of going to playschool like other small boys.

And if she had not committed this monumental act of rebellion, letting her head, rather than the traitor between her legs, make the decision for her – taking her pathetic savings, squashed unproductively in the knotted edge of a handkerchief hidden under the pile of musty bric à brac on the currently idle baby's cot, money stealthily, patiently shaved off the volatile block of housekeeping money when it came her way – if she had not taken the money to pay for a trip to a city only an hour's drive away, but so divorced from her existence that it might as well have been on the moon, if she had not stumbled through the morning mist to Bongo Square and onto a bus already full to bursting with foul-breathed, mumbling market women, she would have been busy in the lopsided makeshift kitchen behind the house, trying to coax a flame from damp, unwilling firewood to cook another uninspiring lunch in time for Herbert's return from work.

But here she was, in an air-conditioned hall with plush red chairs, not fully recovered from the shock of her own temerity. The decision to leave seemed to her to have been taken in a matter of hours, but she realised that it had always been there, embryonic, creeping silently around her subconscious, never acknowledged, like an illegitimate child in a patriarchy, never concrete until it was delivered by an announcement she heard by chance on the radio, slipped in between the obituaries and the six p.m. news.

And so she had risen silently from beside her sleeping husband, felt around under the junk till her fingers closed around the scrunched-up notes in the handkerchief, sharp points digging unnoticed into her palm.

She eased open the back door and slipped out, a girl cultured in the witches' brew of ignorance unaware of itself, rampant adolescent hormones and absent ambition: the girl in an evening stenography school who allowed herself to be fondled behind hedges on misty evenings instead of going back home after school, by a boy from a technical school down the road. She got pregnant, of course. It happened eight hours after a particularly gratifying frolic behind a hedgerow in the Government Residential Area.

Her parents, when they found out, were suitably indignant, but not too much to hasten to rope in the young blade who could not keep it in his trousers. The young blade hadn't objected too much; indeed, he was quite content to leave school and find a job so he could continue certain pleasurable activities in a real bed, according to recognised standards, rather than on fresh-cut grass with the sheared stalks pricking his knees and elbows.

Alice's father could not in any case afford the luxury of thinking of his daughter as the innocent maiden defiled by a lecherous young he-goat. If she married the boy, it would be one less mouth to feed. The marriage was performed with a minimum of fuss.

Once a more comfortable bed was purchased, Herbert applied himself with gusto to the task at hand, pregnancy not interfering with his athletic inclinations. Alice sank into the sea of unformed hopes, letting her body take over the steering of her life. In six years she was pregnant four times. Thereafter, her body followed the cruelly charted course of her life, bobbing lazily in the mud-thick river of much-indulged basic needs, carried willy-nilly to a beach littered with the bones of tired marriages and the sightless, mud-filled eyes of drowned hope.

Herbert found a job in a factory; she had vague ideas about having the children and returning to school. But Herbert's mother did not see things quite like that.

This tough, abrupt, sour woman, aged beyond her years with hauling heavy baskets on her back to the food market, just so she could pay her son's school fees after his father's early death (some said of repeated lashings with her bullwhip tongue), had had other plans for her son. But the fool had fallen into the sticky clutches of that snail-like creature and her lazy parents. Even the grandchild was no consolation. When the second pregnancy turned into a miscarriage, she abandoned her farms and moved in with her son. After all now he had a job, he could support her for a change. She had to help the inexperienced couple "find out" from a witch doctor what had caused the abortion. Probably the bad blood from the girl's side of the family, but it could be witchcraft.

She arrived, pinchfaced and unsmiling, and in the time it would have taken her to sow an acre of corn, the wife, feeling empty and unfulfilled for having gone through four months of a pregnancy with nothing but pain to show for it, was reduced to a timorous workhorse with permanent backache.

First it was the cooking. Next it was the housekeeping. And then it was her. She was lazy, rude, disrespectful, a neglectful mother, a useless burden.

Alice grew desperate and listless. For the first time, she kept her knees together at night, despite Herbert's attempts to pry them apart. Their bed had a tendency to creak and Alice was terrified of what the old crone would say if she heard any rhythmic noises from their room. Hers was just across the parlour, where she slept with the children. Herbert was upset. She blurted out that his mother was cramping her style, in these as in other matters.

She got her first beating then. In the morning, her mother-in-law walked with a spring in her step and a gleam in her eye. Things were coming right at last. Herbert had slapped Alice so hard that she had hit her cheekbone on the knob of the bedpost, and his mother spent the next morning leaning on the backdoor jamb, taking in the view of that beautiful bruise.

Yes, things were right at last.

Alice understood the futility of swimming against the current. Her parents did not want to hear about her problems. Marriage, said her father sanctimoniously, was for better and for worse. Her mother was blunt.

"You act as if you never saw your father beating me. As he said, it is for better and for worse. That is how the world is.

Men can do what they want. It is their better, and our worse. That is how life is. You must respect your husband and give him what he wants. You remember that your father's mother lived here till she died, damn her. Marriage is like that. Go back and keep quiet. You know we cannot take you back. See how we struggle with your brothers and sisters."

Alice went back to her house and let the current take over. She had another baby, conceived in bitter apathy below and grunting, invasive indifference above. Her body slackened. When the fourth pregnancy happened, it just let go and the child oozed out, soaked her clothing, and was gone.

Her mother-in-law stayed on. Alice had by now lost interest in most things; even the children kindled but a tiny spark of love that was soon snuffed out by her misery. She had begun to feel that her boys were the chains that bound her to this unsatisfactory marriage.

Herbert, too, lost interest in everything matrimonial, except beating her and complaining about the food. At night, Alice dreamed of escape, but in the morning air, her dreams blended into the mist and faded away with the sunlight.

Then came the announcement, like a canoe round a bend in the lonely river where she was about to drown, and Alice decided to start swimming again. She stood still and listened, her thoughts spiralling up, up and away. She did not even notice her mother-in-law glaring at her from the doorway. She spent the rest of the evening in a daze, planning and hoping and praying. The night passed quiet and white. And in the morning, a new woman rose like a phantom and left her husband and children, took up her savings, all twelve thousand francs of them, and walked. She got onto the market bus to the big city. The old viper could keep the children for now, but one day she would come back for them.

As for her husband, she just did not know.

The first day at the House was for looking around and getting used to the surroundings. The next day was registration. When the woman who helped with the forms asked her whether she was married or had children, she said no. She did not quite know whether having a family would cause her to be sent away, but she did not want to risk it. All she knew was that she had been saved from drowning in the sea of despair, and she would stay on this canoe until it took her to clement shores. She would not go back to that house as she was now. She would become a secretary or die trying.

22

A dozen or so rows ahead of Alice, Maggie sat chewing slowly on her three day old gum of jackfruit sap, and watched the clean, rich women up there. She did not really understand what the woman was saying and she did not much care. It was just nice and cool in here, away from the sun and the mosquitoes. Maggie had never heard of air conditioning. She had, in fact, never heard of most things. She had seen a bath once, in somebody's house, but the other children called it a swimming pool.

She had just been dumped here, riding on the crest of someone else's changing will.

The fifth of nine children sired at irregular, sweaty intervals of drunken sex by a plantation labourer and his used-up wife, she had only stood out in the rabble of snivelling, scab-picking, scrabbling siblings, whom constant need had rendered acutely selfish, because of her silence. It stood between her and all the futile sound and fury of her environment. Wrapped in the silence, it was as if she did not exist. No one noticed her, and consequently, no one could hurt her.

She was a large, soft, dark brown baby who cried little and talked late. No one really noticed her in the house; she sat placidly in her own urine and excrement, and studied her grubby, pudgy little fingers. When she was fed, she ate. When she was not, she fell asleep on the bare cement veranda. Her father came in at night, drunk on illegal *afaw-faw* gin, his breath alone fit to power a rocket, stepped over the children on his way to bed and beat her mother, more often than not.

Some days he came in a mellower mood, having imbibed only grainy corn beer, and threw his wasted frame on his wife's large, soft belly, and pushed his half-erect member, dully and blindly seeking, into her, letting his sluggish seed find its way up the dark, dull, flaccid canal to do or die. Most of it died, of course. But sometimes it met its quickening conclusion, and became someone else.

Pregnant or not, her mother rose before dawn and soon one could hear the hollow rumble of the pestle in the mortar, grinding the beans for her fried bean cakes. Then, if she had time, she performed her abbreviated ablutions, and if she hadn't, didn't, put on her blouse and wrapper, rancid with the old smell of sour breast milk, and went to ply her breakfast trade. One could hear her voice fading into the morning mist, made porous by the rays of the sun rising behind the school buildings:

"Fine-fine accra beans for sell! Thro'way, thro'way!"

Her father rose at five with the labourer's bell and went to the morning line-up to be told what stretch of banana plantation he would clear that day.

Later, the children rose from their piss-soaked pallets spread in the parlour of their home, which was a crowded single room divided in two by a grimy, seamy curtain of indeterminate age and colour. There was a government school near the labourers' camp, and as soon as they could walk up the hill, they all went there, barefoot, eyes gummy with myriad infections. A perpetual smell of ammonia, stale food and body juices clung to them, but no one noticed because all the schoolchildren smelled like that.

When Maggie was old enough to shoo away the dogs that came to eat her excrement in the shade of the banana trees, she took her slate, a piece of ceiling board painted black, under her arm and drifted up the hill to school. There she was kicked and pinched and beaten by the class bullies, who outnumbered the non-bullies; her arm-board was chipped and scraped and once, when she dug up a cricket for her mid-morning snack, a boy came and seized it from her, and ate it alive, limb by kicking limb, while she watched dumbly.

In the tight, airless classroom she answered no queries, never participated in the game of hands shooting up in the air, index fingers pointing upwards, middle fingers and thumbs snapping excitedly: "I, Miss! I, Miss!" to say that two times three was six. She waited for school to be over so she could go into the forest and pick up bush plums (or blacking-tongue, as they were called, for the colour they gave your tongue) to supplement her cornmeal and melonseed sauce lunch.

One day, she did not go to school because her head hurt and her throat felt raw and dry; her breath was sour with the hot stench of fever. She was ill for weeks, and a rash came out all over her body. When she felt better, her skin peeled, and she amused herself by sitting on the veranda and peeling off the filmy wisps of dead white skin.

There seemed not to be any point in going back to school after that, so she did not. She stayed at home and watched ant lions dig their conical pits in the dust along the wall of the house, below the eaves. She gathered the little woody grains that rained from the rotting wall and pretended that they were rice (a luxury seen only at Christmas), and she played house alone with tin cans, making orange-coloured sauce with ground avocado seed to accompany her "rice".

Her mother, she of the big, sweaty face, flabby upper arms, unspeakable smalls and the stomach the jiggled as she walked, finally noticed that her slow, silent daughter was no longer going to school. She co-opted her into the bean-cake trade immediately. Maggie was sent out with a tray on her head and told to cry: "Fine-fine accra beans! Five francs you chop you full-up!"

She did nothing of the sort. It was not in her nature to draw attention to herself.

Instead, she stood in a corner of the single unpaved street, scratching the back of her left leg with the big toe of her right foot, picking her nose, and let the flies have their breakfast off the tray. Some of her cakes were stolen by tall, bad boys. Then a fight broke out over a ball of unprocessed rubber string wrapped around a core of plastic wrapping, and the rest of the cakes were knocked down and fought over and trampled underfoot. The enamelled tray was bent out of shape; she carried it home under her arm.

She was thirsty.

Her mother wept and cursed her in broken Pidgin English, and slapped her on the back with her thick short hands, and called her useless. Maggie covered her head with her pudgy little hands and waited for the storm to pass.

Then she drank some water.

Thereafter she sat in the dust and watched the ant lions, or went to the camp pump to watch the ducks hunt for bits of edible dirt and worms in the spirogyra-lined runnels of dirty water: chuck-chuck-suck-suck, with their long, spatulate beaks. Or she twirled the spokes of her father's bicycle and mended it when it was broken.

One of her brothers grew up, went to town, and became a taxi driver. Another also grew up and went to prison. A third was dismissed from school for sharpening a stick and pushing it through both of a (former) friend's cheeks. One of the girls went to work in a plantation field assistant's house as a house cleaner. Another got pregnant at fourteen and went away to God knows where.

Maggie shuffled apathetically into adolescence. Her convict brother came back home, bitter and twisted beyond reason or humanity, and fondled her in secret places. It was pleasant and painful all at once. She let him. There was no reason she could think of not to. Whenever the house was empty of all but the two of them, he pushed her into the "bedroom" whose only furniture was the filthy, prickly straw mattress teeming with bedbugs that was her parents' mating field. There he mounted her and ground roughly past her hymen, and mauled and breathed and muttered foul things in her ear, and sucked and bit at her neck, stiffened in release and rushed blindly out to peek through the curtain for potential voyeurs, his eyes dull and shifty in the fetid half-light. When he went away with a final, backward glance, her body was hers again; she pushed down her dress and went to sit outside on a stool, the wet between her legs running down stickily to dry and flake between her thighs.

She did not become pregnant.

Time passed. Her mother grew flabbier, her father thinner and more incoherent in his drunken anger, and all her younger siblings ran away or were pressed into service. Her convict brother was shot and killed trying to rob the Area Manager's chicken coop. Maggie was vaguely relieved, but otherwise unaffected. That same day, her father dropped dead of cirrhosis of the liver. The company paid for two plain coffins and asked her mother to vacate the house within a month.

Maggie and her mother went to live with a second cousin, also widowed, in a farming village behind the banana plantations. With them came the old bicycle, which Maggie, unnoticed by anyone, had succeeded in keeping alive.

In her aunt's house, farming was a full-time activity. She went to the farm when everyone went and returned when they did. In the evenings, she mended things and slapped at the mosquitoes. Her mother rented out the bicycle to the villagers, and that brought in some money. Maggie made kerosene lamps from old tins, with wicks of plaited rags, and took them to the market. Her mother kept the money. She did not mind. She liked to fix things. Money did not interest her.

Her aunt's only child, Florence, a thin, avid little thing with strong, sudden impulses, tried to make friends with the big, slow girl with the deft hands, and could never tell whether she had succeeded or not. Maggie followed her around and looked where she pointed, but she said little.

Flo heard the announcement on the evening news and thought she might just go and find out what it was all about. There could be men present who would deliver her from this rural backwater where all the men went away or died young and nothing ever happened.

She badgered her mother and her aunt for the bus fare to the city. But the market was flooded with cocoyams; prices had plummeted and life was hard, so the women refused.

Florence waited till the older women had left for the farm and stole the money from the rusty cigarette tin her mother hid in a basket hanging on a nail behind the door.

She walked to the market town, followed by Maggie, who had cut her finger and could not work on the farm that day.

They arrived in the evening and spent the night in the room of one of Florence's market-day beaux. He had posters of Michael Jackson on the wall and his clothes hung neatly from a rope tied diagonally across the angle formed by two walls. Maggie slept on the bare floor while Flo and her beau of circumstance coiled and writhed around each other on the narrow metal cot, like warring snakes.

Early in the morning, they took the mini-bus to the big city. On the bus, Flo sat next to a young trader going to the city

138

to replenish his stock. At the end of the one-hour trip, they were fast friends, especially as Flo had encouraged the *entente cordiale* with stealthy but close attention to his secret parts by way of his capacious trouser pocket. The radio announcement was becoming increasingly irrelevant in the face of the power she held in her hand.

So, when they got to the Women's House gates, she told Maggie to jump down and go to those big gates over there.

"I am going to town. I will come and meet you here later."

And thus, she rode out of Maggie's immediate future, her hand in the trouser pocket of the excitable trader.

Maggie shambled up the scrubby wasteland to the road that led to the big green gates. She saw other women and girls walking up towards a big, big yellow house, the biggest she had ever seen. She followed them and found a seat in a big room, where there were many women, some talking, some silent and watchful.

Much of what was said she did not comprehend, but she knew that this was her new home. If they would let her touch and fix things, fine. She liked to make broken things work again. She liked pieces of things working in tandem to make things happen.

At the end of the talking, they all walked around. That is how Maggie came to the workshops.

23

Right up in the front row, on the right side, sitting on the last seat before the central aisle, wearing a slightly passé red jacket over an exuberantly flowered drop-waisted polyester frock, her stringy feet encased in red shoes from whose bone-like spiky heels the fake leather had peeled back in revulsion, was Vera.

She understood all that was being said. Oh yes indeedy! This was the beginning of the new life she was going to live! She would show them all. Those rich girls from their rich-man mission schools, with their student trunks full of chocolate and corn flakes, with their talk of white man cookery and Miss this and Sister that, while her father cut their parents' lawns with a machete, ruining his back forever. She would show them who was who. This was her chance.

She already knew what she wanted: everything. All of it. And if one of those damfool rich bitches up there had gone the way of rotten eggs and was throwing her money at the crowd, who was she, daughter of a yardman, to refuse?

When the Department Heads were introduced, she decided there and then that she would go into Home Skills with that doll-like woman who was so cute she looked like candy waiting to be sucked, and learn all her tricks, know all the rules, surpass the rich bitches, beat them at their own game, those who would not recognise the yardman's daughter and accept her into their group. One day she would rule them all.

During the tour of the premises, she shoved past them all, the scaredy-cat, snivelling, spineless little sluts with the beaten-dog look down pat, as if they'd practiced in front of a mirror, the village idiots, the eternal exam-failers (she always passed hers, there was just not enough money for her to continue), the lean and hungry, the herd animals, the plainly desperate, the merely curious, a bunch of failures all.

★ ★ ★

Of the three hundred or so women who turned up on opening day, one hundred and twenty eight finally stayed. Some were not interested; they had just come for the show and the free food. Some went back to obtain permission to return, and it was not granted. Some meant to return, but were too busy or too scared to risk change.

Alice climbed into her new bed with the peach-coloured sheets to rest awhile, and wondered whether her children had been fed.

Maggie got onto hers and fell asleep immediately.

Vera put her bag in the closet and went out to study the terrain. One had to know exactly where one was.

24

Maggie woke up a little before six the next morning. For a moment, she did not know where she was. It felt like a big, warm place with machines humming benevolently in the background. Then she remembered.

The big house. She relaxed and lay back in her soft new bed, just for her, all alone, in her own room. Slowly, her eyes got used to the semi-darkness. There were waking-up noises on the other side of the door that led out to the parlour. She decided to lie down for a little longer. She had discovered that although being around people did not really bother her, she preferred being alone. She mulled over the previous day.

In the afternoon, they had gone round the whole house. Inside the house, there were many other houses, big ones and small ones. There was a room full of sewing machines. There was another one full of things like white TVs. They were called computers, said the woman who was taking them round, for writing and drawing things. Then there was a big, big, kitchen with shiny things in it all neat and clean.

And then there was a room of machines. Machines of every sort, thrumming and murmuring and humming. Margaret knew then that she had come home.

There were other rooms for other things, but the machine room was best. She had trailed reluctantly after the group of women, her mind back in the workshop. It was as if the machines spoke to her, beckoning, asking her to stay and stroke them, and make them move slowly and gracefully, or fast, whirring and whining. She could not wait to try.

After that, the rest of the tour was irrelevant for her. There was a swimming pool, a real one, not the big, oval enamelled basin she remembered in the area manager's bathroom. And there were fields for playing and some of concrete with white lines and nets hanging from poles, round at the back.

They were led back to their houses. In each house, there was a big parlour with a television and a kitchen. The bedrooms led off the parlour, eight of them, and there was a toilet and shower for every two rooms. She had seen that sort of toilet, but she had never used one. Once, one of her sisters had taken her to the house where she worked. She had refused to sit on the toilet, not feeling like a pee, but her sister had pulled down her panties and urinated noisily into the bowl, smiling up at her all the time, and pulled the chain to wash it away.

She felt like using it now. She went in there, but there was no chain to pull. She came out to the parlour to meet the other girls, who were chattering excitedly about the wonderful things they had seen.

"Ah wan' piss," she said.

The voices ceased, mouths open.

"Go to your toilet, *nah!*"

"No chain."

Pause. They looked at her in silence. Then one of the girls came forward.

"You and I share the same bathroom. Come, I will show you how it works."

As the door closed, someone sniggered.

"Mama! I will see everything before I die."

"Can you imagine? Where d'you think she comes from?"

"Probably a labourer's camp. They live like dogs there."

"Don't say that. It's not nice. It's not her fault that she does not know."

"Oh-oh!" said the sniggerer. "Man no go talk again?! Is this not supposed to be a place where you can feel free? This is not your house. It is not mine either, it is nobody's house, and so no one can tell me what to say."

"But think of the people you hurt when you speak. The Founder said that women are their own worst enemies sometimes; I think that we should learn our lessons and try to practice in small ways. We can start today."

"Born-again," muttered the sniggerer under her breath, looking about for support. But the others looked away. They did not want battle lines drawn so early in the game.

There was the muted sound of water running through pipes, and Margaret and her roommate emerged.

After that, it was time to eat. She ate. There was plenty of food. Around her, people were jostling, testing the waters, forming alliances, appraising roommates, and comparing clothes. She ate, and afterwards went back up the stairs to her room. She felt the curtains, she opened the wardrobe, she looked in the drawer of the table, she sat in the chair.

She went into the bathroom and sniffed at the soap in the dish It smelled like perfume. There was a small cupboard above the mirror. Inside were washing powder and other things the use of which she could not determine. They all smelled nice. There was no small-size swimming pool, but there was a shower behind a plastic curtain with flowers printed on it.

It was all beautiful. She wondered where Florence was; she would have liked this place. She liked fine things.

Maggie remembered her mother. A frown creased her placid face. Mother wouldn't like it if she did not go back home. But she wouldn't anyway. No reason to. And when Flo went back home, she would tell them where she was.

She went back into the room and lay on the bed, ankles crossed, hands linked beneath her head.

25

In the afternoon, the women went to a smaller hall for another session.

Vera was fed and rested, her immediate future was foreseeable, and what she saw was as delicious as coconut rice.

The seats had been arranged in a circle with a space in the centre, where Mrs. Ngallah strode about on her thick, powerful legs. A memory flitted across Vera's mind of a biology class in which their teacher said that the grasshopper had powerful hind legs. How could such a puny thing, which allowed itself to be fried and eaten, be considered powerful? The teacher, a rare good one, explained about how things could be relative to one another. Vera smiled to herself, remembering.

In the hall, there was the usual cough and shuffle. There were a lot less women than the previous day. That was alright with Vera. It meant that there would be more money to go round.

"Good afternoon women."

"Good aaaaaaafternoon, Madam," chorused the women, in pure schoolgirlese.

"Good afternoon. Is everyone comfortable?"

"Yeeeeeeees Madam."

"Is that all you can do? Say it loud and with feeling! You have come to a good place, so show your happiness!"

"YEEEEEEEEEEES MADAAAAAAM!!!"

"Good. Today we want to welcome you all once more to this new place of ours. We have dreamed about it for long – very long. And today our dream has come true. But this is only the beginning.

"The future of this place depends on you. You will be our advertisement to the country. And the world."

Oh yes, thought Vera, an advertisement is certainly what I will be, but only for myself, you fat idiot.

"Many of you have come from afar. It has been a long journey to this place. For others, the journey may not have been very long, but the process of getting here was no less difficult. But though you have arrived at your destination today, all of you are travellers in a sense. All human beings are travellers, but as women in this context, you travel across a different landscape. You are like travellers who have been thrown off a bus on a lonely highway. You have a lot of baggage, and there is no one in sight to help you. The few vehicles which pass you refuse to stop.

"You have a choice. You can give in to despair and wait for nightfall and marauding animals, or you can carry your bags on your back and begin the long trudge back to civilisation. In your baggage you will have non-essential items, excess baggage, things you do not really need. You should remove them and throw them away. They will only slow you down.

"Do you know what excess baggage is? Someone give me an example."

"Doing only what other people tell you to do," piped up a slim, fair girl with neat braids called Lawino, who, with her clean good looks and easy confidence, seemed set to be the resident *wunderkind*. She set Vera's teeth on edge already. She hated goody-two-shoes like her. She would be the sort that hogged the limelight and made the teachers like her. She sounded like the sort who would always speak up before you had the time to marshal your thoughts.

"In a way, yes," said Mrs. Ngallah, the Adipose Wonder, that mass of animated blubber, "but not quite. If what people tell you to do is good for you and makes you happy, then you must follow their advice by all means. But if it is not good for you, then don't, whatever they say. Excess baggage is all those things that you were told not to do, or those things you were told you must do, but which make you unhappy. For example, those of you who have been married and widowed know how hard your in-laws can be when it comes to funeral observances. Telling you, for instance, that you may not sleep or wash until your husband is buried is nonsense. Logically you know that if someone says: 'If you sleep when he is not yet buried he will come to you in your dreams and make love to you, and then you

146

will surely die', that person is lying, because when have you ever heard that such a thing happened? But do you allow yourself to even *think* that it may not be true? No. You are too scared of the in-laws.

"But look at it this way. How many in-laws look after your children after their brother's death? Very few. So doing as they say is excess baggage, because if you carry it, it does not help you to live better, and even if it helps you to live better, it makes you subservient to the wishes of someone else, which is never good, because another person's wishes cannot always be in your best interests. It is even less good when you are economically independent and do not need their help. Do you see?

"Excess baggage, in our case, means seeking approval that will not help improve your life from people who are not qualified to give it anyway. You must set aside meaningless or frankly harmful practices and make your own rules as you go along, depending on your experience. Some of those old rules were useful at one time. It is up to you, and you alone, to decide which ones you will respect, and which ones you will discard. In other words, you have to decide during your long trek home, under which tree you will rest, and whether you may eat of its fruit. Some fruits will give you strength. Others will poison you. You have to learn not to be lured by the poisoned fruit of superficial comforts which cover the underlying evil or injustice."

Vera disagreed. It was those superficial comforts that made all the difference. She would marry all her husband's brothers in turn after he died if it meant having an indoor toilet, and not going out to the latrine to do a perilous balancing act on a rainy night over a smelly, gaping hole. She would stick like a leech to whomsoever would help her along the road, but when she arrived, then they would know her, by God! But it was time to earn some points here. She spoke up.

"Please Madam," she said in a sweet voice, "what if the fruit you refer to is religion, which tells you to do this or that thing? I mean, some religions have some very strict rules about how women should behave."

"Good point. Very good point."

Vera glowed. You will *know* me, she thought.

"It is true that some religions are very strict about certain things. But if there is one thing the modern world shows us, it is that religion is a matter of conscience. Let me tell you a story of how religion can be bad for you. Who here has heard of the Taliban?"

Before Vera could react, Lawino's skinny arm was waving in the air. The Adipose Wonder smiled and nodded at her.

"They are Muslim students who took over Afghanistan."

"Excellent. So what did they do? Someone else now," said Mrs. Ngallah as Lawino's hand shot up again.

Got you this time, said Vera to herself as her hand went up with the speed of a meteor.

"They limited the movements of women."

"Right. They limited the movements of women. Women could not go out unless they were accompanied by a close male relative. They could not consult a male doctor. And you know what? Women could no longer exercise any profession out of the home. They could not teach or be lawyers or accountants or doctors. And if there can be no women doctors and women are not allowed to consult male doctors, what happens to women when they are ill? They die, of course, or live with the disease.

"And the Taliban did all this in the name of religion. If you disobeyed, you could be hanged. Do you think that is a good way to observe your religion?"

The girls looked around at one another, shocked.

"Yes, girls, that is what I mean. If a religion restricts you to an extent where your life is in danger, why should you follow it? You see? You must decide what you will be easy with in your own mind, as long as you hurt no one, of course - "

Vera put up her hand again.

"Sometimes, if you want to do what you feel is good for you, you cannot avoid hurting people, or making them angry. So how do you know when to give in and when to tread on people's toes?"

"That is what you are here for. The aim of these discussions is to help you make difficult decisions, like those concerning religion. Any aspect of culture or religion that prevents you from feeling fulfilled should be set aside. There is the will of God, which many people claim to know, and there is the will of man, which often masquerades as religion. As you know, human beings are not perfect, and even where there is goodwill, there are blanks in the messages purportedly received from God. Remember this: you and the Pope are equal in the sight of God. The Bible says so. If he can pray for guidance, so can you. But the Pope is not you, the Imam, the Mullah, the Pastor are not you. You are the one who knows where the shoe pinches. So you must take the ultimate decision.

"So, as I was saying, our role here is to make you aware that you are entitled to make decisions about the things that affect you, and then we will help you acquire some basic principles on which to base your judgements. We will also help you acquire the means to make such decisions. By this I mean that, for example, if you refuse to marry your dead husband's brother, and your family casts you out because they are too poor or too scared of going against tradition, you should be able to look after yourself. So an important part of this program is economic viability.

"You should not take a decision that is likely to affect the rest of your life based on whether you will eat tomorrow or not.

"Which brings me to yet another point. You all know what a prostitute is. A person who goes with men for money. This is money that she uses for rent, food and clothes. What is the difference between what she does and a woman staying in a marriage or a relationship for the money? In a marriage you have a man who pays your rent and gives you the money to buy food. In return you sleep with him and you keep his house. Some people will tell me that there is also love in a marriage. I reply that when the husband loses his job, that is when you know how far that kind of love goes. It is all the same thing. The prostitute is simply less hypocritical about what she does.

"So there are two kinds of prostitution: the one everyone condemns and the one everyone accepts as normal. Do not fall into the trap. I have walked on that particular road, I sat in the shade of that tree, and I ate its fruit. And I can tell you, the day I knew what I really was, I was shocked. But I decided to change, and here I am. I am not the happiest woman in the world, but I

149

belong to myself, and that is the ultimate triumph. Let no one deceive you about being accepted in society or being the wife of someone important. An important man is important because of the work he does. You too should work to earn importance that is truly yours, and not borrowed.

"Do not be fooled into thinking that if society says something is right, then it is. At one time in India, for example, they used to burn widows when their husbands died. Who has read *Round the World in Eighty Days* by Jules Verne? Quite a few of you, I see. You remember the story of Aouda, the woman Phileas Fogg saved from burning. Closer to home, some old chiefs were buried with their households, their wives and slaves and livestock. Everyone accepted it. But it was wrong.

"You all know about slavery and the slave trade. The slave trade was conducted for profit by powers that claimed to belong to the Christian world. See what I told you about religion? Human beings set aside religion when it is convenient for them to do so. Although the main reason for stopping slavery was economics, it was also stopped because some people came to their senses and finally refused to playing by the rules of that time. Someone asked questions about an existing situation. They broke the rules. And they were right to do so.

"I must repeat that even when you feel that the people who make the rules are very important and always right, you must still ask questions. You have all head of Aristotle? Well, such a wise man, and he believed that goats breathed through their ears! Hundreds of years ago, the Catholic Church believed that the world was flat and punished people who said it was not."

There was general laughter, in which Vera did not join. Sniggering asses. This was stuff you learned in Form One and Form Two. Why were they acting as if this session was the Epiphany?

"So!" Mrs. Ngallah said after the laughter had died down. "I said in the beginning that your life is the road you have to travel. And whatever you are told, this is a road you have to travel alone. When you see that cars do not stop to pick you up, you will be angry, right? But you did not buy those cars and you do not fuel them. If you need a car, buy yours. Then no

150

one can throw you off a bus. And when you feel angry, use that anger as fuel. Channel your rage to make you walk faster. Do not let it destroy you.

"Most important, do not let it destroy other people.

"The thought for today is therefore: the world is always changing. There is no reason why you, too, may not be an agent of that change."

In other words, thought Vera, everything is relative. Mosquitoes are small, but they can kill you. Do not mind if you are a mosquito. You too, are important. You can participate in population control.

After the class, the girls went out into the grounds, huddling in groups and talking animatedly about what they had heard. Vera noticed that Lawino walked alone, smiling to herself. She decided to sound out the competition.

She caught up with Lawino as she stood smiling, it seemed, at a bed of orange lilies.

"Hello, my name is Vera. What's yours?"

Lawino looked up and smiled at her, looking straight into her eyes. It made Vera the tiniest bit uncomfortable. "Mine is Lawino?"

They stared at the flowers together in silence for a while. Then:

"Where do you come from, Lawino. How did you get here?"

"Well, it's a long story, but to summarize, I am an orphan. I lived with some very nice people, or so I thought, who took me in when a landslide hit our house and killed my parents and my little brother.

"All was well until about a year ago, the cook attacked me – sexually. When my auntie, well that is how I used to call her – found out, she said that I had led the cook on and that it was all my fault. She had two girls of her own and she told me that the cook had not attacked her own children because her children knew how to put the cook in his place. I think it was because I was doing so much better at school than her own children. After that, she asked me to leave my room in the main house and share a bed with the housegirl in the servants' quarters. She took me out of school and set me doing housework with no pay. Then the cook started coming to our room. He would bribe the housegirl to let him come in, and he would cover my mouth with his hand and rape me." She looked frankly into Vera's eyes as she said this, showing no shame.

"He was very strong, and there is nothing I could do. I could not go back to the main house and complain to my auntie, because she wouldn't believe me. Then one day I was listening to the radio while working in the kitchen. I heard the announcement and I came straight here." She stopped and smiled at Vera. "That is my story. I do not think it is very interesting or unique, but there it is. Now you tell me yours."

Vera thought quickly. The truth was absolutely out of the question. This girl was one of those pure types who would not understand. She should have given in gracefully to the cook and improved her meals. They could even have worked out an arrangement to sell some of the food supplies to outsiders. What a fool! She remembered a story of incest that had been whispered in class and decided to embellish on that.

"Well, my story does not differ greatly from yours. But in my case, it was my father." She allowed her voice to break at this point. "He – he used to come to my room, and did terrible things to me!"

"Oh you poor thing." Lawino put her hand on Vera's forearm and squeezed her in a bid to comfort her. "But I guess that is over now. I believe Mrs. Ngallah said that a psychologist would be coming here to help us deal with these things. So I guess we'll get over it. Did your mother know?"

"I think she suspected, because she began to treat me like a rival."

"Awww! Anyway, we have come to a safe place. There is no need to worry any longer."

"So what class were you in when you left?"

"University. First year."

Ah, that explains it, said Vera to herself.

A bell rang.

Lawino said: "I think that must be suppertime, don't you? "We'd better go in. I'm a little hungry. It's been an interesting day."

26

A t the end of the day, the women and staff all went to their various units and homes, Mrs. Ngallah to her house in the city, and the rest to the staff quarters, which were situated on the east side of the main building of the House and separated from it by a high hibiscus hedge. Martha was alone in her apartments in the aerie. She ate a late lunch and went to sit out on her small balcony, looking at the indifferent landscape and sipping a gin fizz. The sun went down in a blaze of colour, and the sky, its warmth withdrawn, subsided sullenly into darkness, with a multitude of hues that reminded Martha of a fading bruise. At seven, she called her parent's house.

Her mother answered.

"How is Papa?"

"Fine," she said, and her manner said: as if you didn't know what you have done to him, you wicked girl.

Beyond that stage, conversation was difficult. Mama usually told her about the latest household appliance they had bought with their new money, and then faded into heavy silence. Martha told her that she had called to tell them that the House had formally opened on Monday, so they would know and be careful what they said.

"We heard", said her mother with tired hostility. "I will tell your father you called."

Martha hung up feeling frustrated. They had never forgiven her for not being their nice ordinary *married* daughter, instead of traipsing about trying to sow discord. Her father was getting the worst of it, if her mother's moaning were to be believed. Already, Justice Etchu was publicly critical of Mr. Elive's inability to manage his daughter. It made him seem weak in the eyes of his friends. What matter that they could now buy all of Etchu's worldly good and not even notice, if they could not be proud of their sole offspring as well?

153

Martha had moved out soon after the fateful breakfast. For a week following that event, her mother had gone round the house sniffling and singing traditional wake-keeping songs in a quavering falsetto that often dwindled to a hoarse squeak as she heroically suppressed the sorrow welling up in her heart, determinedly going about the housework as if to say to her daughter: Look! Setback or no setback, I at least know my duty, even if some people don't!

Her father had taken to coming home late, as if he wanted to avoid her as much as possible. The crisis had revealed in him certain symptoms reminiscent of a dog with post-traumatic stress disorder: he had a perpetual, flinching look about him, he snapped at everyone, and he forgot where his parish books were. When, on the last day of her stay at home, she came to breakfast in the morning and put a passbook on the cross-stitched tablecloth near his left hand, he had given her a brief, baleful look before returning to his porridge. He did not look up when she explained that this was the joint account she had opened for him and her mother.

"I have opened an account for you both, this is the passbook. The money is yours to spend as you see fit."

He still did not look up. Mama craned her neck over the faded plastic flowers to look at the passbook. She would have liked to see it, as she had never owned a bank account before in her own name, but the way Papa was scowling, she might be risking her life if she tried. So she held her peace, and watched her daughter squirm. She would not speak up for the girl, no, never, not with all the distress she had caused them. The money would come in handy, of course, no denying that, but they had earned it. Who sent her to school, after all? But the big thing was, how would she explain to her friends who had sons that her daughter was not on the market? That the wayward girl had decided she wanted to spend a huge fortune on "free girls" and women who refused to behave like women? They would use the money, of course she would see to it; there were, after all, ways of convincing Papa, though she had not travelled down that road for a while now. But nothing would ever make her forgive this child for what she was doing to them.

In the face of her parents' accusing silence, Martha carried her things out to the car she had just bought. Patience, the housegirl, slunk around the corner of the house to say goodbye. Martha gave her more pocket money than the girl had ever dared to dream of, and her phone number as well. "Call me if you feel you want to do something apart from keeping house for my parents. You deserve a chance to improve your life. I want to start a centre to help women help themselves, so if one day you want to come and see me, feel perfectly free."

The girl took the card, eyes glowing in grateful hope. She had sensed that there was something the matter at home, but since no one ever told her anything, she really could not tell what it was. She had only found out the other day when she met Justice Etchu's housegirl, Stella, in the market. The other girl had overhead the justice telling his son: "That foolish nurse cannot control his daughter. I think we should consider one of the Matike girls."

The son had not sounded too keen. Apparently, he had quite set his heart on the Elive girl. The Etchu housegirl drew Patience to one side and confided that she thought she herself had a fighting chance with the son. Wide-eyed, Patience listened to a blow-by-blow account of how the young doctor had given her quite a rub-and-squeeze the other day as she was coming out of the kitchen. If he liked her, said Stella the housegirl, then she could work her charms on him. Her mother would take her to a woman who cooked good medicine. After all, what did that thin Elive girl have that she did not have? They were both women, and no woman could claim that she had anything that other women did not. All women were the same, education meant nothing. All these high and mighty women who acted as if they shat cake, they had the same business between their legs, they had periods, they farted, even if they pretended that they didn't.

"So if you wan' be weak-weak, na you know. Woman no suppose for suffer for this groun' if I know whati for do. Man wey i slack, na i know" (if you want to be pliant, that's your business. No woman who knows what to do with her charms should suffer), she told a shocked Patience, whose exposure to matters sexual was non-existent.

155

Having got the call over and done with, Martha moved back indoors and turned on the TV. Nothing there but the usual harsh colours of government TV, with its low-budget documentaries and the occasional home-grown soap opera with alternately wooden and strident actors. She had not had time to have the cable connection from downstairs extended up here. It was all very well to say *"consommez camerounais"*, but if the *camerounais* was not *consommable*, there was no reason to ram poor quality products down people's throats. There was room for improvement, and it should be taken up by all means.

Now that the day's business was over and done with, the problem of living through the night had to be dealt with. Even as a girl, she had never been particularly gregarious, preferring her own company to the tittle-tattle of her girlfriends. She could, of course drive out to the city and meet some people her age, but it was the same endless round of bars or restaurants, the same meaningless pursuits, the same dull, rote-like lust, the same yuppie types who were convinced that any female over twenty-five who was not accounted for was on the prowl for a husband and so had to be made to do the groundwork. In her case it was particularly difficult because now she was known to have some money. Her being in the news and her brand-new German car attested to that.

Thus, when they saw her drive up, people usually pretended to ignore her, became too deferential (in the case of those eternally impecunious hangers-on who hovered on the fringes of any barroom group outing), or glance at her with easy, dismissive hostility, in the case of those up-and-coming young banking execs trying to show that they could have any woman for the asking – the woman's asking, that is. They waited for her to ask, and when she did not, they were puzzled and angry, and even more determined to take her down a peg or two. So in the end a great many of her outings degenerated into undeclared tugs-of-war. She would be in a group of eight or ten people, and half of them would not speak to her. And usually the girls who came along on such outings were not of a sort that she could relate to. They were dressed in the regulation low-waist figure-hugging trousers and anxious to keep their men. Single women with money and closed faces were a nightmare to be avoided at all costs. In the meantime, the men were trying to prove, by ignoring her, that she was nothing extra, while she was trying to indicate, with her glass of wine rotating idly between her fingers, that they were beneath her notice, which indeed they were, as they had started the silent war. But that still left the issue of her desires to be dealt with. And deal with them she did, after a fashion.

Because in this milieu of stuck-up male pride and predatory females, she still managed to find someone who seemed at least halfway decent, in her view. He was Charles, one of the innumerable city council members she was expected to cosy up to in order to obtain a building permit. Many of the council members she had to meet believed in being lobbied while one was prone, with nether members obligingly parted for maximum effect. Usually the moment allusions to any such arrangement were made, she made veiled references to lawyers and people of similar persuasion, or got Mrs. Ngallah to call and browbeat someone into helping the city official unravel his tangled priorities.

But this one, he hadn't indicated, by word or deed, or the absence thereof, that he required any lobbying of the Adam and Eve kind. Charles was in his mid-thirties, slightly plump, with a receding hairline. His complexion was very fair, and he had the slightly curly hair that told of female ancestors raped or kept as concubines by colonial masters. After a late meeting one Friday, he invited her to dinner at one of the city's more expensive restaurants. Not having anything planned for that day, and beginning to feel the all too familiar ache in her loins, she accepted. Over the course of the next month or so, they circled each other before the kill. He was charming, urbane, and knowledgeable about his job and a great deal more besides. They had, she discovered, the same tastes in music. The last man she had bedded was Cornelius, and Cornelius, after all, was a steadily dimming memory. This man sounded a lot less stupid than the usual local politician, and he was *here*.

He was a rather busy man, who suited her just fine, or so she told herself. She felt that with all the things she would be called upon to handle in the subsequent few months, it might be a bit difficult to conduct a full-contact relationship. So they

157

usually had dinner on Fridays and went on to his house or her apartment to spend the evening, and very frequently the whole night.

In the beginning, she was not too keen on finding out details about him; she was just not interested. It was not a lifetime commitment she was after. She just needed someone to overhaul the old juice ducts from time to time. Of course, she asked him whether he was married or otherwise attached, and he said that he had been engaged to one woman for five years but that had not worked out. She did not inquire further. After all, she told herself, she was not in a position to demand of him the time and energy that a close relationship would require, and so if she did not act too interested, he would not get too involved. After a while, however, she began to feel more than mild curiosity about him. Who were his family, where he had grown up, that sort of thing. And she wondered why his engagement had broken up.

But there she met a blank wall. Even in the mellow glow of post-coital relaxation, he remained strangely unforthcoming about his emotional past. Martha was at first idly curious, then really intrigued. He was as polite as ever, but he would not discuss anything about his past. Martha knew she could ask any of her former classmates in the city's social butterfly brigade, but she hesitated to do that. If you asked about a single man, people inevitably put two and two together to make at least nine, and she had a strong aversion to having her sex life discussed after choir practice or at the hairdresser's. She never really bold enough to ask him outright if there was something he was hiding; she just sent out feelers from time to time. After about six months of this cat and mouse game, she decided to take the bull by the horns.

It turned out to be one more story of betrayed trust and broken hearts, only this time, the girl had done the breaking. Apparently, all was going well between them, and the girl had not indicated in any way that there was something lacking in the relationship. One evening, his car having broken down, he took a communal taxi home. They had arranged to spend the whole evening together, and after the gruelling day and the trouble

158

with the car, all he was looking forward to was a shower and some R&R of the more active kind.

About halfway home, the driver paused to pick up a fare. It was a couple, standing close, obviously reluctant to separate. He heard the girl say, "I have to go now, he is waiting for me," and his heart lurched. Because it was his fiancée and the way she was looking at the guy, there was no doubt about what sort of relationship they had. Even more damning, they were standing outside a seedy hotel well known for abbreviated stays and furtive departures. The girl tore herself away from her lover and got into the cab. As he was sitting in front, she could not tell who the other passenger was, and she sank back onto the seat with a relaxed sigh. He kept silent on the front seat, his heart thudding. When they got to his junction, he silently handed over the fare to the cabbie and stepped out. She got out too, paid her fare, turned around to leave and there he was. He said nothing. She followed him home and stumbled through a tearful explanation. It was temptation, she did not know what had happened to her, etc. He was quiet, but implacable. It was over. She went and got her family to come and plead, to no avail. Finally, tired of the hassle, he moved house and told the guard at the gate in his office not to let her in on any pretext. Then he settled down to lick his wounds.

Thus encouraged, Martha told him about the King of Rats. He listened in silence and said at the end: "So you too are one of the walking wounded." That was all. Now she knew what had hurt him and that he prized fidelity, but sometimes she wondered what he was really thinking. Oh, he talked about work and suchlike, but since they were both busy people, they did not spend more than two days a week together at the most and then only the evenings. She knew he went to church, he was Presbyterian , but that was all. He was an amusing companion and a satisfying lover, and best of all, he was cultured, but that was it. After the story of his fiancée, he never told her anything about himself. It was as if, without actually stating it, he was placing a limit on the degree of intimacy he would allow himself to be drawn into.

As time went on, Martha began to find it galling. Love was so calculated among adults her age. As a woman edging inexorably past the age considered suitable for marriage and safe childbirth, she was coming to realise that with age, the insouciant sentimentalism of late adolescence was left behind forever. Everyone who was still single had been hurt at least once, and unless they were arrant fools, had learned to keep their hearts safe from, unpleasant jolts. Martha admitted to herself that she had become a past master at the sex-without-intimacy game, but she yearned for the freedom to love that she had enjoyed with Tom so far back in the past that it seemed to have been in another life. The price of losing one's innocence seemed inordinately high.

What was the point, really, of being only half alive, because that is what this conditional sort of love to her was? When Tom had left her a lifetime ago, and when the Rat had discarded her like stale leftovers, she had yearned for self-possession. But now, with time, she had learned to keep her feelings in check, learned too well for comfort. She wanted to give herself up, to sink into a relationship, a total suspension of ego.

But she realised that she no longer could. Ultimately, if she were honest with herself, she had to admit that what she wanted was for Charles to utterly lose control; she wanted that heady power that comes from knowing that you have another human being completely in your power. But he was too contained for that. Perhaps if he had given up first, she would have thawed and taken the risk of allowing herself to fall madly in love. But she was too busy, and the tack she had decided her life would take did not allow her to make concessions when it came to men. The game here was: eat or be eaten with relish.

When she saw him for the first time, she had felt somehow that he had the blank eyes of a liar, but since the world was not perfect, and in any case, she was not looking for a saint, so who was she to make demands? But now she had decided that she would like to like him more, and he was playing by the unspoken original rules. It was very frustrating; it was a trap she had walked into with her eyes open, but in the interests of self-preservation, she did not see what else she could have done.

Such as it was, however, the relationship could have been worse. She got good, clean sex once or twice a week, the guy was fastidious about his appearance and personal hygiene, and he was single. That was more than many women could hope for. She did not want wailing violins and impassioned declarations. Well, she wanted them, but she could settle for less.

This evening, she was alone because he was out of town. Instead of brooding about his aloofness, she could watch a movie or go over the finishing touches for the rest of the week.

As she rose to replenish her drink, the phone rang.

"Yoo-hoo! All hail to the giant-killer, Martha-Martha! So what are we up to, this fine evening of the Lord our inestimable and unknowable God?"

"Have you been drinking, you idiot?"

"Nope. Just shoved a hot iron rod up the Dean's tight arse. I am in my office, and I can see him running around on the lawn and screaming."

"What have you gone and done again?"

"Just tole dis ole boy that I wouldnae take on any more courses for colleagues who have obtained fellowships that should by right belong to me."

Martha laughed, and Ophie's old-witch cackle screeched down the line.

"So. Wazzup you wilting wallflower?"

"Nothing. Just sitting here counting my blessings."

"And where is David, dear Bathsheba?"

"Out of town on business."

"Good. I am coming over. The current sex interest left in a huff because I told him brown lines in his underwear are just not cool these days. He did not like my lecture on the proper use of toilet paper, so he upped and gone. Tell me, why should I spend half my life in school only to meet a guy who just came down from de tree? Anyway, he can go to hell. I should be there in an hour or so."

"No classes tomorrow?"

"Nope. And I am supposed to do the keynote address at your place, remember?"

161

"Ah yes. Good! So you can spend the night here and you'll do the lecture tomorrow."

Ophelia arrived driving her old bottle-green Honda.

"How's the car behaving?" Martha asked, to tease her.

"Yes, ask me how my car is behaving, you rich bitch. No worry; your sins shall find you out one day and you will give painful account to the people of this nation."

They laughed together as they went indoors.

"How is Prudie-woodie Ngallah, the big tank engine who could?"

"A godsend, believe me. She gave her first talk today and it was a success from all indications."

"I was talking to someone today who knows her rather well," Ophie said as she headed straight for the bar. "She seems to have had a really hard time with her hubby."

"What happened?"

"Wait. Let me sit down on your nice leather armchair and sip your expensive vermouth, me dear. The closest I've come to a decent thing like this inside this week has been some watered-down, bottled-in-Cameroon, pissy nonsense the brown-trail-in-drawers wonder offered me yesterday at his club." When she settled down, she said:

"So! Where was my esteemed self in the narrative? Okay, engines revving up. I hear she was married to one of the guys that worked with that rich contractor from up the hills. I forget his name. So, he goes back to the village and gets this young girl who has just had her GCE Advanced level. Not so? So indeed. Husband brings her down to the coast and rapidly bears two children by her, so rapidly indeed that it is suspected that the children were only eighteen hours apart."

"Twins, then?"

"Who said anything about twins? If I wanted to say twins, I would have said so. I am the one who teaches literature, not you. If you hadn't caught the do-good bug, you would be camped out in the wilderness somewhere, studying the mating etiquette as expressed in the gathering of palm nuts among the Furonclemabulatvalhalla people of the Upper Krumunjang Valley or some nonsense, so shut up and listen.

162

"Good. I like people who can be disciplined," she said in response Martha's shout of laughter.

"As I was saying, using a well-known literary device called exaggeration for effect, she bore him two daughters in quick succession, delectable little creatures, even if they mewled a little as babies tend to do...hohoho, don't tell me I wasn't there to hear them. Babies *mewl*. It is one of their less endearing qualities.

"Well, Monsieur the big-gun-in-construction tries for a son, but his wife's loins were feeling that they had been overworked and needed a teensy weensy rest, so they refused to oblige Monsieur, who, in his frustration, tried to beat the boy children out of docile little wifey."

"You know, somehow I have trouble seeing the Prudentia Ngallah I know in a situation like that."

"Do not forget that she was young and impressionable, and where she comes from, women should have sons to carry the husband's family name. Their own name, or rather their father's name, dies with them if they have no brothers. Plus, women were taught, and are still taught, to submit.

"To continue, hopefully with no further interruption, one of her more enlightened uncles hears that someone is using his niece as a punching bag, so he marches down to the coast with a rusty ceremonial sword and attempts to decapitate the husband. The latter, quickly understanding the language of violence, apologises to a full gathering of dowry-crunching uncles and promises to keep on the straight and narrow henceforth, and let nature take its course. He also agrees that Madam should go to university, as he had promised prior to the marriage. So the boy-making is shelved for a while and Prudie the punching bag travels to distant climes to study things that are now shamelessly exploited by your naughty self.

"Her husband visits her once or twice, but you know that those spot checks on the reproductive apparatus rarely yield babes of any sex.

"When she returns, degree and graduation gown billowing in the wind, it is to find her place in the marital playground usurped by a comely, buxom wench who is not averse to punches, and who can and has produced male heirs in triplicate, thus complicating the succession business no end, but we'll save the fratricide for another day. Too much violence already.

"Anyway, Prudie the tank engine wails out loud and calls on her uncles. But they point in silence to the marriage certificate, which states that this is Polygamy, a kingdom in which the man rules and in which he can have as many wives as he can possibly screw to ensure that his spawn spreads far and wide and he is remembered for his great deeds; where the women wait their turn, and at least two people know when you have sex with your husband. Thus Prudie learns that she's been sold down the river by her own kin.

"With her shiny new degree, she settles down in a bungalow hubby has built for her. But he does not come there. The thighs of the new wife are smoother and firmer than Prudie's and she does not talk back when talked to. Most of all, she does not have degrees to goad him with.

"Prudie grows as thin as she can, which is not much. Then she calls his friends and tries to talk them into talking *him* out of this new arrangement. Hubby is adamant. He has his sons. She goes to the Pastor for succour, but hubby's generous contribution during Harvest Thanksgiving causes the Pastor to develop milk-white casts in both eyes that blind him to injustice, which casts he removes and places on the lectern before him, right next to the bible, whenever he preaches the Gospel of Our Lord the Great JayCee, in particular the parts about doing unto others, etcetera. When he sees Prudie bearing down on him after the service to ask if he has made any headway in convincing her husband to get back on the straight and narrow, he puts his casts back on.

"Prudie contemplates other dark things, and acts, ill-advisedly, on some of them. She marches, for example, in a rage to hubby's new house in his absence and beats wifey black and purple. But wifey is a sturdy peasant girl with the healing capacity of a Hollywood mutant, and this has little impact.

"She becomes the laughing-stock. She herself is decidedly unamused, but no matter. She thinks hard and long, and decides that she will not be saddled with any little girls. Their father and his new wife will raise them, and she will move on to something else. Then she will go back and take her girls when she has enough money. She lifts said little girls, one under each muscled arm, and dumps them on gaudy blue fake Persian rug of esteemed male parent. The male parent is not impressed, but Prudie threatens him and the new wife, who is beginning to stir, with dire consequences if they do not do as she asks. They subside and do as she asks.

"She can visit her children whenever she wants. You know the rest, I guess. She opens a business of some sort and goes about telling wives to kill their husbands in their sleep or some such revolutionary thing, and then she meets you. End of story. I need another drink. Want one?"

Ophie got up and moved to the bar again.

"I see why she always knows what she is talking about. But for one who can be garrulous at times, she is noticeably reticent about her own story."

"She'll probably tell it to you one day accompanied by sobs, violins and a stiff drink. Like mine." She gulped down at least half of her drink.

"Ahhhhh. I feel that one right where the nerves had knotted around my shoulders. Almost orgasmic. Talking of which, how do you and Charles do in that department?"

"Anh-anh, Ophie! I am a shrinking violet in that department oh! I don't want to talk about it."

"Why? It's healthy. Let's compare notes. You might be missing something."

"Then I don't need it, I guess."

"Oh, go away you boarding school nitwit."

"You know, you and Nora would do rather fine together. You have the same mindset."

"Nora who?"

Martha told her. Ophie was silent for a while. Then she said:

"I guess I ought to tell you that Brown Trail is her husband, and I am not real popular with Nora right now."

"Weh, Ophie! You said no more married men. We agreed that they were destructive."

"Yes, only if you love them. I don't love Brown Trail, but he gives good head. And he doesnae want me for keeps, which I think is rather sweet of him." She kept the bantering tone, but her eyes were no longer on Martha's face. She threw the rest of her drink into the back of her throat, stiffened, and then shuddered, blinking rapidly. When she glanced at Martha, her eyes were rather shiny, but Martha could not tell if it was the drink or the beginnings of tears.

She turned away and waved goodnight to Martha without speaking.

Martha lay on the sofa for a while, thinking about what Ophie had told her. Then she got up and went to her workstation, which was hidden behind a lacquered Chinese screen, and worked awhile on the computer. Then she shut down and headed to her room, which was reached by a spiral staircase of wrought iron painted white, as finely wrought as filigreed lace. Right next to that was a door made of the highly-polished Bubinga wood she had used for all her doors and windows up in the aerie. It led to the guest room.

As she was heading up the stairs, the door opened and Ophie peeked out.

"Come in here, girl. Why were you sneaking past my door like a teenager who is out late?"

Martha smiled to herself and went in. Ophelia went back between the sheets.

"You know, I am a university professor and this is the first time I've slept between silk sheets. I am almost afraid to fart in them." She patted the bed next to her. "Come sit." Her eyes were luminous in the semi-darkness.

"Now. I guess I ought to tell you about Nora's husband and me. Do not please interrupt. That sort of thing does not go down well with me.

"Anyway, I would like to lie that I fell for the old trick where he tells you that he is not married and you find out later that he is. I did not. He is married, though not as firmly as you may have been led to believe. Nora moved out last week because she discovered something suspicious about the babysitter's waistline and upon investigation, it was revealed that the girl was with child. The girl refused to name the culprit with the fertile seed, so Nora chose to believe the worst and declared that it was Brown Trail. She packed her things and is now living in a two-room plank house in Molyko. So Trailer has more or less moved in with me. No, no, not literally; he just spends a lot of time at my place. So there it is. And before you come all over moral with me, remember that unlike you, I did not go to an expensive boarding school run by white women. I went to a government school and I bribed the discipline master fifty francs when I did not want to cut grass.

"And let me tell you that I am just making do with what is available. A girl has got to have orgasms from time to time. You might be surprised, but there are educated men our age out there who do not know that women are supposed to enjoy sex too. So when I see one who actually gives head...I do not hesitate. Husband or no. A girl must fuck for chrissakes. I just want to tell you that this is what I have decided to do. I have tried being nice and moral like you, but it does not suit my appetites. And let me tell you something. If you try to run this place according to your own stringent rules of morality, you might find that most of your women have gone quietly back home to be downtrodden. You have to try not to be shocked by some of the things they will have done. You may even have a baby-killer or two here, so you better start thinking about how you will deal with that when it comes.

"Let me tell you these things because no one else will tell you. Another thing is that you should not believe all these women with sad pasts who have come here to help you. You have just realised from what I told you about Prudentia that at least part of the reason she is here is that you pay well and that she needs to set by some money so she can send her girls to good schools, so that they will be more powerful than the men who would enslave them. You did not know that before, so you need to factor that in when you consider how she may be trusted with funds.

"But I really wish to emphasize the morality thing. Do not be too hard on them. Part of the reason you feel that they should have such high standards is that you yourself were not really exposed to the nitty-gritty of poverty. Your parents were not wealthy, but they could pay your school fees, so you never went with a man you hated just for the money to pay your fees. I did. Sometimes the price of freedom is very high. It is either be squeamish and not go to school and be condemned to sleep with people of his ilk for the rest of your life or to seize the chance and climb out of a hole you might well die in otherwise. It is the case of a drowning woman clutching at straws. I will be talking about this in my lecture tomorrow, so let this serve as advance warning.

"Please do not be upset that I am poking my nose into the organisation of an institution that I refused to work for full-time. I only want to help. I like teaching at the university; working anywhere else will kill me, and worse, kill my career prospects.

"Now, go away before I begin to cry with a sense of my own goodness in giving you due warning. Don't say anything, please. If I have overstepped the mark, then I am sorry. But if I have not, go and ruminate in your own room and don't ogle my sheets like that!" Her voice rose.

Martha stood up and seized the spare pillow, and beat her with it.

"You talk far too much, but good thing for you, you occasionally talk some sense. I will examine the matter you have placed before me, and then we will see in the morning for breakfast, which, this time, will *not* be a glass of beer. How your numerous boyfriends can stand you breath is beyond me."

"I give them a lot more. Now go away."

"*Sharrap*, idiot, this is my house, Go build yours if it hurts you."

Martha went off to bed, heart considerably lighter about her enterprise. With friends like this, how could she fail?

27

Ophelia's talk was at eleven the next morning, "to give me time to recover from my hangover".

The girls were gathered in the auditorium, having finished their regular classes for the morning. Vera was interested in this new bird they were bringing here to show them. What would be her own approach, she wondered. Things would begin to pall soon, if nothing interesting happened. She had not come here for pep talk designed for idiots; she had come here to *get the power*.

Maggie was ruminating contentedly on the internal combustion engine they had been looking at this morning in the workshop. She did not know its name, but she would soon know how it worked.

Alice was still savouring the pleasure of sleeping on clean cotton sheets that were washed by someone else, and the novelty of learning how to use a computer.

Ophelia came in promptly at eleven o'clock, eyes dark and bright as onyx, showing no ill-effects from her drinking the night before.

"Now girls, good morning. I command the morning here so you all sit up and listen. Now, we will do a leetle exercise here. Everyone will stand up and tell me what their name is and how they came here, hm? We'll start with the first row. You!"

Vera stood up. "My name is Vera. I am twenty years old. I came here because my father used to come to my room at night and make love to me."

Ophelia tsk-tsked. "Next."

My name is Lawino. I am eighteen years old. I came here because the cook in the house where I lived raped me, and my aunt thought that I had brought it on myself, and reduced me to unpaid servant status."

"My name is Yvette. I was married off by my parents at fourteen to a very old man. I did not like him, but he gave my

169

parents a lot of money. I ran away as soon as I could, leaving four children behind."

"My name is Hannah. I am a widow. I ran away because my husband's small brother wanted to take me as his wife after my husband died."

"My name is Gladys. I am thirty-five years old. I live, lived in my village with my three children. Life is hard there, so I came to learn a trade so I can feed myself and my children."

"My name is Evelyne. I was a secretary in a company. My boss refused that I should not learn computer and so when I heard that you can live here and learn computer for free, I came."

"Maggie. I come out for, I come from camp."

"My name is Alice. I got pregnant before finishing school and I married the man. Then his mother came to live with us and he and his mother maltreated me, so I ran away."

"My name is Dorothy...

At the end of this, Ophie took the floor again. "Now, everyone has told their story. My name is Ophelia. I am a teacher in the university. My father was an office messenger in the colonial administration. He married a first wife, who bore him no children. They lived together for a long time. Then when he retired, he began to be afraid that he would die without leaving an heir, so he married another wife. That was my mother. He had eight children, of which I am the third.

"Of course, since his pension was very small, and he did not like to farm, there was never enough to eat. My mother and my stepmother, who loved us very much, worked their fingers to the bone in petty trading while my father drank palm wine with his friends. Of the eight children, five succeeded in getting their A Levels at least. I went furthest. Among my siblings, there is one, the second boy, who refused to go to school and became a layabout. All he does now is go from house to house asking people to give him money, and hating them when they do not. I have told him not to darken my doorway again, but that is another story. I want to tell you how I became a university teacher.

"Primary school was not expensive in those days. In some places, it was actually free, not like today when

170

government tells you it is free and the headmaster takes bribes for admitting a six-year old to class one. In secondary school, I had a government scholarship till form five. My problems began when I went to high school. I had lost my scholarship, and my mother and stepmother were hard put to it to send the other children to school and provide my school needs as well. Plus my no-good brother had begun to steal about the house. You know that sort of child. He will sell the radio, his mother's wrappers, anything. Once he stole the school fees of four of us children and spent it in one week.

"I had to go to school, because I felt that the only way to survive this life was to get out and help my siblings to get out as well. There was a rich man in town. He was married, but he had many girlfriends and concubines, and he was always looking for more to sleep with. He treated his women very badly because he knew that he could replace them whenever he got tired of them. I arranged to be noticed by him and very soon, we were having a relationship.

"I moved out of the house and he set me up in a nice room with a gas cooker and so on and so forth. More important, he bought all my books and gave me money for my taxi fare to school. I did as he asked; when he insulted me, I did not talk back. I was his slave. But I finished high school and went on to university. My mother and stepmother were beside themselves with joy. They knew I was sleeping with that rich trader, but they had encouraged me because they understood that I should not end up like them, working hard every day of their lives with little or no possibility that it would ever end.

"When I passed my exam, my father did not say anything. But when he heard that I wanted to go on to university, he was very angry. He said that I was depriving him of a dowry and a son-in-law who would buy him things. He threw his snuffbox at me and called me many bad names.

"In any case, I went on to university. At the time, there were bursaries, so one could manage on that. There was no need to sleep with men any more. That is how I stopped being a prostitute and became a serious woman.

"So, from your stories and mine, several things can be learned. And that is what I will base my talk on."

171

She went to the board and wrote out a list of points for discussion:

1. Making your body work for you.
2. Acquiring control over your life.
3. Dealing with parasites.

"Those are the main things that we will develop this afternoon. Does anyone have anything to add? So, we start with point one. How do you make your body work for you?"

A hand went up.

"Work."

"Yes physical labour. Getting a job. Farming. Even housework, though I personally hate it. But what I mean is, using your body to get on in the world. Right? I mean doing what I did with the rich trader who treated me like shit but paid my school fees.

"I know that many of you think that is prostitution. I suspect that is what they tell you here. They are mostly right. But what if you have no other options? Our country does not have many of the kind of philanthropists who will sponsor large numbers of women through school. We are still too young as a nation, I think. The few scholarships go to the smartest students. What if you are not smart, what if you are stupid, and female? You should not get along in this world? The world is made up of mostly stupid people anyway, many of them male. Most of them, in fact. But male idiots have more opportunities than female idiots.

"Be stupid if you cannot help it, but acquire some cunning and an ability to plan. Get a rich boyfriend and flatter him into making him do what you want. One of the few good things in this world is that men are vulnerable to flattery. And forget about morality. A man who sleeps with you and pays you is no better than you are. But do not spend the money he gives you on clothes and the like. Buy land. Open a savings account. Start a small business. Go to school. Take your mother to hospital when she is ill. Do something.

"If you do not, then you deserve all the bad things that happen to you as a woman. If you have to sell yourself, then make the degradation worthwhile."

A woman said: "But if people know that you are a free girl and you go with men for money, they do not respect you and no one will marry you."

"Who said that? Some of my most promiscuous friends are married. It is funny that Pidgin English calls unmarried women "free", and with such contempt. This is the only time, I think, that freedom is frowned upon. If you are called free in derision, make your freedom work for you. Do not worry about it. The married women who are not "free" and spend their time calling you names are no better than you are. Many of them are just kept women, like you. But you have the advantage that you can get out when you feel like it, whereas they are trapped. They may not admit it even to themselves, but the lack of freedom is what makes them so critical. And they are afraid that you will snatch their husbands, so they have to convince themselves and each other that you are unscrupulous. They know deep within them that they do not have much to interest a man. They know that ultimately, you are all in the same business. So they are afraid of you.

What annoys me about them is that you see a perfectly normal girl who, once she gets married, acts as if she passed a difficult exam to get where she is; as if being married sets her apart from other women. She is not. I personally wouldn't marry anyone even if a cash bonus were attached to the deal."

"Please Miss, but you can make your body work for you in a marriage too."

"Yes. That is what I have been saying. But the thing is that you will begin to think that you are respectable and refuse to admit that what you are doing is a form of prostitution. And your husband might not want you to be too successful or independent. He will begin to humiliate you to show you who is boss. My point is that within marriage, your self-development is limited by the goodness of your husband."

"But if you love each other?"

"That is not something I have ever felt or believed in. But I am told that it can change things. I am in any case referring to marriages of interest, and the power structure that links men and women. The love business is more complicated. But frankly. To me, happily and married are mutually exclusive concepts, in

173

any case for women, because you can never claim to be happy when your wishes are subordinate to those of someone who does not respect you. Being happily married in Africa still entails too much sacrifice on the woman's part, in my view. Things are changing, but not as fast as they should. You have to obey your husband, please his relatives, his friends, and the society. That's a tall order for me. But if you are single, you can do what you want. People may speculate about your sexual activities, but you know that they are hypocrites, and you think no more of them than they do of you.

"There are a few really happy marriages where the spouses are equal and recognise it. That is not my province. I am here to talk about things that do not work. If they worked for you, you would not be here. Any more questions?"

The discussion raged far into the afternoon.

28

Clad in a frilly little pink-and-pale-blue apron over a pink short-sleeved gingham dress, both of which she had made herself, Vera was in the home skills lab. She had just removed some small cakes from the oven in preparation for making the butterfly cakes that would be served after this afternoon's session.

She stepped back and looked admiringly at her handiwork. She had come a long way from the two-rooms-and parlour shack of a yardman. She could sew, embroider, and decorate like the best of those toffee-nosed boarding-school ninnies.

She had channelled her rage rather well, she thought. She had tried to get into the good books of Prudentia, that fat motormouth cow in her stupid Indonesian ready-made suits and loud African outfits. She had wanted to *adopt* her like a pet and learn all her pillar-of-society tricks. But the woman had shrewdly elected to avoid any closeness with any one woman to the exclusion of others. Mrs. Ngallah had noticed Vera sniffing about like a rat on the prowl and decided to keep her at arm's length. There was something contrived about the girl.

Vera hated her now; she represented the society matrons who called you my dear in insincerity and condescension, and asked you to help with the cooking when they were hosting a village meeting, but not when they were expecting the governor of the province. Their sharp eyes cut through your clothes to see the desperate little thing beneath, the avid little daughter of the yardman who must be used but kept at bay, lest she corrupt their soft-limbed, brainless kids, those women in their grand old cars.

It was not that the Ngallah woman was snooty; it was just that she looked like those women; even thought she did not *really* act like them; she had their mannerisms.

But, as she spread cream on the cakes, Vera told herself that she had hit pay dirt with the home skills woman. Malleable little doll! Vera had assiduously imitated her speech patterns and faint foreign accent, to the amusement of the other women. Success in that particular department was somewhat limited, true, but she was working on it. She had gone quite far on her own personal road.

And her antics with language had finally driven Lawino away. Vera was angered by the obvious disapproval of the girl, but it was infinitely better to be all by herself to arrange things the way she wished, without worrying about staying in the good books of some sanctimonious wallflower.

Then there was that firebrand woman who hated marriage. Ophelia. What she said made some sense, but she did not look as if she was happy being single. Her clothes were always just the wrong side of fashionable, and her car was rusty. A successful single woman ought to smell of expensive perfume and project a polished picture of poise and self-fulfilment, but this one looked as if she quarrelled with evil spirits at night. Independence was fine, but a well-fed bird in a cage was better off than a hungry one in the bush. But they whispered in the dormitories that she was renowned for her bedmatics.

If someone were stupid enough to ask her, Vera, to marry him, she would grab him. If he had enough money and could be controlled, of course. No point otherwise.

She had tried to get close to Ophie to obtain a few tips, especially on matters sexual, but those black eyes had stared at her, and Ophelia had said: "Sorry, I am not good with lame ducks under my wing, okay? I am barely able to fly alone, as it is." Skinny, down-at-heel bitch.

She licked a bit of cream off her finger, wiped her hands on her apron and stepped back to admire her handiwork again. Good. The jenny asses would be olive with envy. She was by far the best student in the Home Skills Department.

"Hello! Why are you all alone?"

Vera whirled round. The Founder was standing in the doorway, looking in at her, with that we-are-all-equal–and-I-want-to-help smile that made Vera want to reach for the meat knife and rearrange her idiot face. Instead, she smoothed down her apron and smiled engagingly.

"Good afternoon Miss."

A subservient giggle escaped her, to her dismay. Her mother used to say that she laughed like a dumb girl whose breasts were being fondled. It was never clear where her mother, who was anything but dumb and looked upon people with disabilities of any kind as unnatural beings to be avoided at all cost, got this piece of intelligence. There were not, to Vera's knowledge, adolescent females with speech impediments willing to be experimented upon by yardmen's wives.

"The others went for afternoon sports, but I decided to bake something for this evening's discussion."

"I see." Martha walked away and Vera scurried to the doorway to watch her leave. She looked too thin; like a bit of wire twisted around inside a dress. Vera still marvelled at the stupidity of the woman. Taking all that money and wasting it on misfits and underachievers! She herself knew what she would have done with the money if it were hers.

She finished preparing the trays and covered everything nice and neat. She took off her apron and went up to the living quarters to change and wash off the sweat. Wouldn't do to go and face the hordes shiny-faced and stinking of sweat. Despite what they tried to teach one here, appearance *was* everything.

Humming under her breath, she unbuttoned her dress and went to the bathroom, which she shared with a colourless, timid idiot called Laura, who did as she was told. She was so very malleable that Vera had decided that women like her were born with special handles on their brains. Laura's kind had their uses, of course, like keeping house and having babies. Or washing the bathroom. Which was another reason she found Martha's idea of reform stupid. She *had* to know that some women were and would always be sluttish vessels, neither knowing nor caring what was put into them. She herself had been a vessel only once, but that had soon been taken care of.

In the local government high school, she had set her sights on the young history teacher, fresh out of university. Nothing earth-shaking, just someone to help buy the textbooks and provide some extra pocket money. Unfortunately, she had become pregnant. The young teacher had panicked and put an end to the affair. Vera told him she would reveal it all if he did not help pay for an abortion. She had got quite enough out of him to pay for three abortions and enough left over to go to the hairdresser's, he was that scared. She decided that going to the hospital was a waste of good money. She drank parsley juice for a whole week. Nothing happened. She made vile herbal concoctions. Nothing. So she went to the bedroom when no one was there and experimented with a knitting needle. By the time she was through, her womb was skewered like the hairdo of the Japanese woman on the calendar hanging in the parlour. She passed out.

Her mother found out, and matter-of-factly cleaned up the mess and put her daughter to bed. There was no talk of going to hospital. Vera, when she came to, did not mention the lecturer or the money. Her mother got her some yellow tablets from the medicine peddler and that was that. She stayed away from school for a fortnight.

It occurred to her that she might never have children again. The thought did not bother her. Who wanted to have dependants when the future was so uncertain? She had enough against her without adding some snivelling, coughing, snot-nosed liability to the crowd. The maternal fulfilment thing was not for her.

29

The session that afternoon was rather special, because it was to be conducted by the most recent of the guest speakers. Vera liked Ophelia in spite of her unfashionable clothes and her rough edges because she did not seem to be afraid of anything, and she told it like it was. Unfortunately, the speaker for this day was another mealy-mouthed visitor from abroad.

"Let me introduce our guest speaker for this afternoon. This is Dr. Adeline Smyth-Burton. She is a Lecturer in a university in America, but she grew up here. Adeline has kindly agreed to take time off her very busy schedule to talk to us today. Thank you for coming."

"Well well well. Do not be frightened by my name. I am just a girl from Downbeach Victoria. And don't mind the doctor nonsense either. Call me Adeline. I shall try to keep things as simple as possible because Prudentia has been scolding me in the office about my tendency to get carried away. We were at school together, and she's always been a bully." The women laughed.

"So. I will start with a series of quotations." She put up the quotations, written in large print, on the board.

"Let's start with this one. 'A woman must expire with shame at the mere thought of being a woman.' Any idea who said that? Prudentia, I am not asking you, so do not try to show off." There was general laughter. "Anyone know who said that? No? Well I am sorry for the Catholics in here. It is attributed to Saint Clement of Alexandria. Makes you wonder how they choose people to canonize, doesn't it. A man hates fully half of the human race and he is made a saint. Let's look at the next one."

"Anyone read *Lorna Doone* here? By R. D. Blackmore." A few hands went up. "Good. You may or may not have noticed this next one. The main character says at one point: 'a horse, like a woman, lacks, and is better without, self reliance'. It means that you women cannot look after yourselves and you had better not try. And I personally find horses to be grossly overrated animals, so the comparison is particularly insulting for me.

"Let me give you something from a woman this time. This is from Reay Tannahill. In one of her historical novels, *Fatal Majesty*, a woman is rebuking a man for the way he and others have been treating the sovereign, the Queen, that is. She says: 'You give her nothing to do but sign documents and smile, and be charming; to show herself as a beautiful, graceful figurehead. You deprive her of her reason for existing. If you go on as you are doing, you may find her taking things into her own hands, simply to save her sanity.' That ring a bell with you ladies?"

"Yeees Doctor."

"No no, look, forget the doctor thing. And if you chorus answers like a flock of sheep, then you deserve what is happening to you.

"There are many more quotations like this. I have prepared a list that Prudentia the tank engine will copy and distribute to you later. If you ever have any doubts about what these people think of you, then read what they say about you. My reaction these days when a man tells me to do something for him that I do not like is: 'life is hard enough my brother. Why should I make it easier for you if it will make it harder for me?'

"But you must have realised that 1) men do not think that you have a hard time. You hear them say: money hard, but woman no know, right? And 2) even when they think it is hard on you, they feel that you deserve it because you are lesser beings or you gave the apple to Adam and brought sin into the world or some such nonsense. Nobody wonders why the man whom God first created would be so stupid as to eat a fruit from a tree he has been told not to touch. He is in direct communication with God, and he wants apples. And talking of God, my view is that he was created by men in their own image instead of the other way round, as they claim. That is why he is a jealous God. He says so himself. More on that later.

"I suspect this is going to be a disorganised lecture because I feel very strongly about some of the things I will talk about. But bear with me, okay? The important thing is, know that men do not think of you as equals. You know that. You are some kind of subordinates. And they do not like it if subordinates like you begin to get above themselves. If you are convinced that someone is inferior, you do not like them to prove you wrong. And you are afraid if they start doing unexpected things because you do not know what it might bring. So you are careful to see that they do not do new things. That is the main part of the problem. Men believe that women exist solely as torches to light up the deeds of men. Note that I do not say *some men*. Because when they condemn us, they do not say: *some women*. All women are the same to them. All men must be the same to you. When you find an exception, tell him that he is an exception to the general rule that men are wicked and selfish.

"You can love them if you are so inclined. I have loved a few myself, with varying results. But never trust them. Never give them power over you. Because all men are the same. They live on power, and that power is exercised over you.

"How do you function in a society that believes that you are good only for housework and childbearing and is not prepared to let you prove otherwise? First by putting money in your pocket, and in such a way that it cannot be taken from you. That is by learning a trade so you can earn your own money. Power is basically economic. If you pay your own rent, no one can come into your house and tell you what to do unless you let him. So don't. And get your mind organised about who you really are. I guess Prudentia and others have been telling you all about that, so I won't dwell on it.

"It is possible that when you have done something with yourself, you will become unpalatable, that thing they call a frustrated woman, who cannot get a man to marry her, but who, I tell you from experience, makes a delightful mistress. Many of us are so-called frustrated women. But be happily frustrated. Wallow in it. Have fun.

And remember that some of your fellow women who are so quick to cast the first stone are afraid to face the fact that they took the first exit they came to on the difficult road of life. They have not been tried and tested in battle as you have. They have not proven their mettle. Their lives are safe, they have a roof over their heads, paid for by someone else, a man to protect

181

them. They have not been out in the wild. Some of you have. Some of you are getting there. Those of you who have been out there have survived. You have depended on yourselves, which is something they have not had the courage to do. You have come here to the disapproval of many of your families so that you may change something about your lives. If you die right now, your life will have been a success because you dared to break the chains of slavery that have been wrapped around your feet for ages.

"There are women who prefer to work within the status quo. Who prefer to wield power from the background. But when their men succeed because of their efforts and they go on television and receive prizes, do you see the wife getting a medal? No. She stays at home and prepares to receive their guests or she presents him with a bouquet of flowers for something that she contributed to. There are also women, we have to admit, who have accepted their status of institutional idiot and have no wish to change it, because they can avoid hard work by hiding behind their weaknesses.

"Oh, they will tell you: 'we have given birth', and so on. Tell them rats do it too, and no one gives them a medal for that, and they do it with a lot less fuss. They will say: we can manage a family and please in-laws. Tell them that endless laundry and taking advice from a lot of retarded strangers who know you little and like you less is not your idea of personal achievement. Tell them that they have sold their self-respect for a roof over their heads at someone else's expense. And when a person pays for you to stay alive, he does not respect you. They will tell you how, when the husband is away, they are the ones who keep the home going.

"Tell them that you have to keep your home going all the time, whether or not you have a man in your life. In your kind of guard duty, there is no relief. You have to make all the difficult decisions yourself. When you hire workmen for a job, they charge you more because they feel women are stupid and can be cheated any time, and that a guy is surely giving you the money anyway, and that as men, they are entitled to take some of it back.

"Tell those smug housewives to get a life. Say to them: go and get a job, earn some money. Then come back and tell me how you feel when your husband or your family keeps acting as if what you have sweated to earn is theirs by right.

"I can tell you one thing. When they earn money, they will begin to feel proprietary about it, and they will understand why their husbands are grumpy about giving it out for clothes and the like.

"You notice that I am rather hard on married women. Those of you who are married should not feel bad. It is a *type* of married woman that I mean. I know many responsible married women. I have been one myself, but my husband had the grace to expire early, before I killed him myself. What annoys me about some married women is the way they act as if it is an achievement to be married, to have caught the eye of some man, and that those who are single are failures of some sort, because they have not caught a man. They feel superior to single women, these eternal consumers."

Prudentia moved forward and whispered into her ear.

"I am told that this has been discussed before, but I will go on with what I wanted to say because the point cannot be over-emphasized. This marriage business is very tricky. We need to talk about it, because most, if not all of you, probably think that it is necessary.

"The kind of married women I am talking about are like a sapling that grows in the shadow of a big tree. It is sheltered from the rain and wind. But it is also deprived of much sunlight, and it will grow pale and thin. The only way for it to grow well is to trim some of the branches of the big tree so they can both get some light. As the French say, with their typical obsession with food, you cannot make an omelette without breaking eggs. The problem is that some people question the need to make an omelette in the first place. People who think like that are your enemies. You must stamp them out.

"Think of this business as two people standing side by side in a tight space. One person steps on the other's toes and does not care. His own comfort precludes all other considerations. His neighbour says: sorry to disturb, but you are standing on my toes. He might apologise and move. On the other hand, he might ask his neighbour to shut up. The question is, if he will not move, what should the neighbour do? He can continue to suffer in silence, or he can shove the intruding neighbour off. That is the decision you have to make. And that is what makes you either a mere vessel or a person in your own right.

"When you clamour for your lives to change, some men will say, but you women are so full of sin, you must be protected from yourselves and prevented from doing harm to other people. Tell them not to forget the hurt that men have caused to men and women alike over the ages. Is that a reason for curtailing their right to self-fulfilment? I am not saying nothing should be done to criminals, mind. I am talking about the hurt caused to women because they are women and are seen to either deserve it or not be capable of the kind of refined pain men feel. Think of fidelity. Men take it very badly when they are cuckolded. Women are not supposed to take it too badly because they are not believed to feel the kind of pain men feel in when their wife or girlfriend cheats on them, or they are supposed to be able to handle it because men are 'like that'. I recommend that you too be 'like that' in a way of your own, and see how they like it.

"Throughout your life you will meet many women who have degenerated into a kind of farm animal. Is it the cause of the way men treat them, or is it a result? Ask yourselves that. Remember that you invite punishment by acting as if you deserve it. Moreover, remember that whatever they say, you are all different. You are individuals.

"Now, about God. As I said before, God did not create man. Man wanted to explain where he came from, so he created God. I am not saying that there is no God. If there is one, I have not met him, but I think he is there somewhere. I'll tell you one thing. God was made by men, so he is male. For you Catholics, he can only have male priests, based on some drivel that the fanatical 'saint' Paul spouted about women not preaching. What do you want with a God who thinks you are second-class citizens, who thinks that having your period makes you unclean, or who feels that you may not give devote your lives to his service in a particular way because you are women? He

184

sounds suspiciously like a narrow-minded person. My personal view on this is that there is a God, but He is not the Guy they say He is, people are taking His name in vain to pander to their own egos, and He is too busy to come and clear up the matter of His identity once and for all. This means that many people have different ideas about God, the Great Spirit, Allah, Manito, Vishnu, Maike, Nyambe, Obase, whatever they choose to call Him. They even kill each other over it, believe it or not.

"Now, if no one has seen the Guy and talked to Him, then how can anyone say that they know Him? How can they direct your lives on the basis of what they decide He says they should do? And how can you let them? Most of all, why is it that the male theologians of this world have somehow never been able to agree on just what God wants, and they keep brainwashing the sons born of women to go and give up their lives in his service? And why are they unable to agree on just what or who He is, or what rules one should follow in His worship? Don't you think that, if they knew anything about God at all, they would agree on what he wants for humankind? One of His self-styled disciples said: we are all equal in the sight of God. So you too, being equal to his priests, can be priests. If they do not let you, then find a mode of worship that allows you to serve God in the way you want. I see religion as one great experiment. Go out and experiment!

"Now, I think I have covered the basics of my talk, so I'll give some time over to questions, after a short break. Prue, you said there were refreshments. I haven't had lunch."

30

In another unit, Maggie sat alone watching a superman movie. She had not gone to the discussion today because all those things bored her. All she liked was to stay in the workshop with Grace and work on the engines with the smell of engine oil hanging over everything.

She liked movies with unusual things happening, like strong men who flew. It did not bother her to be alone. She liked it. Most people here were kind and left her alone. She loved this place.

Here, you could forget the other, not so nice things that had happened before. There was no rooting about under cocoyam plants and slapping at mosquitoes and discovering grey slugs under the leaves. There were no maize leaves with their wicked, razor-sharp edges to slice thinly into your unwary flesh. Here was clean. And the workshop was heaven.

Grace was a taciturn woman. That suited Maggie just fine, though the other women complained of her bad temper. Maggie did not learn to speak much, but she learned, with a sure and amazing instinct, the inner workings of a car, the little foibles of a lawn mower; she learned to talk to the machines and show them who was the mistress. Here, there were no bean-cakes to sell. She hated bean-cakes. She talked to the machines and they bent themselves to her firm but gentle will.

In the beginning, they had taken her to a room full of people who asked her questions and wrote things down whether she answered or not, and looked at her in a strange way. Then they had taken her to a schoolroom with some other girls, and every day for many weeks she had learnt again to read and write. The psychiatrists bewildered her, but the schoolwork did not. Nobody ate your chalk here. There was no chalk here in any case, only pens and pencils.

And afterwards you could go and eat something or drink some fruit juice, or just lie on your bed and do nothing, or borrow a technical manual from the library and read about machines. If you were not tired, you could go on doing the things you liked for as long as you liked. And sometimes you got paid for them.

She had a tidy sum already saved with the bursar. She did not use it for anything more than replenishing her stock of chewing gum. One day, she would open her own workshop.

She sighed happily and sipped her fruit juice.

Part Four

31

Alice missed the children. Some nights, unable to sleep, she would wonder how they were doing. Tommy should be in class two now. Were they ill? Did the old woman irrigate their colons regularly, were they taking their vaccines?

Well she was here, and she had what she wanted, she could work with a computer. And she made money, because a percentage of all money earned from freelance work went into her account with the bursar. She had her little book to prove it.

The worst part of all the misery was that she now realised that she had been partly responsible for the things that had happened to her. It was true that she was a product of the environment in which she had grown up, with all its constraints, but the way they explained it to them here, you become what you are by the choices you make.

If she had chosen to explain to Herbert early on that she would not like to have his mother in the house when they were just getting to know each other, then perhaps all this would have been avoided.

If she had refused to knuckle under and stood up to her mother-in-law from the start, the woman might have taken fright and retreated to her hut and her farms. She should have welcomed her, but not sought or listened to her advice about how to run the house.

It is true that there were difficult mothers-in-law, and that Herbert was blind to his mother's faults, but so were many other men, and their wives had not run away. They had stayed and solved the problem. One girl who had come to learn secretarial skills had told of a mother-in-law who decided that the meals she cooked for her husband were too dainty, and decided to make something more filling every time he came home for lunch. The girl had spoken to her husband wisely and gently, with tact. It had taken some time, but one day he had told his mother that he preferred his wife's cooking. The mother-in-law had wept and prayed aloud and sung church songs, but she had left her alone after that.

She, Alice, should have spoken back when insulted or, like another woman did, taken the initiative and criticised her mother-in-law obliquely in her husband's absence till the mother-in-law lost patience and insulted her in her husband's presence. Whereupon she had staged a scene and thus had the older woman evicted.

She might have told the woman she was only a visitor, and asked her to behave like one and know when to leave.

But in pretending to be the good, kind, docile little *hausfrau* prescribed by tradition, she had handed the old hag power over her on a silver platter. And then she had run away. Who would listen to her now? She had lost her husband and her children and something told her that the fact that she had concealed her past from the people here would come back to haunt her.

Also, she could have gone to post-partum clinic and taken advice on contraception. In the dispensary, there were discreet birth control options available at no cost. But she had done nothing in her anxiety to please. Giving her husband sons to carry on the family name, and pleasing the mother-in-law. She could have had one child to begin with, and then gone back to school. Now here she was, earning money and no one to spend it on.

She wanted her sons back. Somehow she had to find the courage and go back to reclaim her offspring. She had played right into the old hag's hands. The woman now had her son back to herself, and two healthy grandsons too.

She had been too soft with Herbert and he had stopped respecting her, if he had ever started. Men were creatures of paradox. They wanted a woman with spirit, but she was not to display it. They respected her in the sense that if she was married, they treated her with a certain degree of deference, while bearing in mind that she belonged in a certain place; she kept the house clean, bore fine children, and only raised her voice to chastise a child. She was modestly dressed. She never contradicted her husband in public, she was a thrifty housewife, and if she worked, she left her professional life outside the door when she came back home. She received his colleagues properly when they came to visit; she sat and smiled even when she would rather be resting. And when there was a crisis, she organised with the skill of a general, and gave her husband the credit.

This was the kind of woman they wanted.

But this is not what they had. They knew that while the wife played the required part in front of the visitors, after they left, he would catch it for not telling her that people were coming in the first place. The real women went to church meetings a great deal of the time only to keep up appearances, they had bad, very bad moods, they spent the housekeeping money on jewellery sometimes; they were in fact, quite contrary a lot of the time. They stopped the playacting when its purpose was accomplished.

This was the kind of woman men settled for, because whatever they claimed in public, they knew that no woman could subsume her personality to that extent without suffering strain of some sort. The older married men knew that the public image was all a charade, but they still preferred to judge potential wives not on their true merits but on the extent to which the women could pretend, when they should have known better. They preferred the myth, even though they lived with a different reality.

It was because of all this unspoken code that the girls who could pretend the best married first. It also helped if they came from families with a good reputation, but it was not essential. For a woman's wealth was her reputation. What she really was did not come into the matter at all. Thus one heard of women who were good, who did all the right things, who were respected by their husband's friends and who enjoyed being called Mrs. So-and-so, because it was the true badge of success for a woman, giving up her own name and taking on another.

Part of the blame, she knew, lay with her husband, who had not noticed that his wife was sinking into despair and apathy. But perhaps his problem was that he believed that good women were subdued creatures by nature, and that his wife was just taking on the normal attributes of responsible wifehood. Perhaps all wives were unhappy, but Alice did not think so.

Some of the women who came to the centre were married and they returned to their marriages to supplement the household income with no problems whatsoever.

Talking with other women here and listening to the lectures, she had come to realise also that most women proceeded by scheming and subterfuge. They had to be discreet and not display their power. Mrs. Ngallah said that an aggressive, enterprising man was regarded with respect, but an aggressive, enterprising woman was looked upon with suspicion. People thought she wanted to be a man.

Herbert, she now realised, was not the best of managers. He ran through his income like you would eat salted peanuts at a boring party. The women here said that on the whole, women were better at managing money than men, but that no one would admit it, sometimes not even the women themselves. She should have taken a closer interest in the money he brought back home, what little there was of it. She realised that she did not even know how much it was, only that it was not enough.

Whatever he was, whatever he had done to her, she knew that it was partly because he himself had not known what to do, and he had not sough advice about it. Some days she wanted him again, very badly, like the early days. But a woman had explained that it was just hormones acting up.

The woman who said that was a hard-bitten case who had been married for fifteen years and swore that there was no such thing as love. It was, she said, a simple matter of your body preparing itself to get pregnant. When you were ovulating, you felt tender and romantic, and you felt you had never loved your man quite as much, and you were ready to forgive everything. It was just the urge to multiply and fill the earth. She suggested that when a man was chatting you up, it was not wise to agree to go with him during your fertile period, first because you might get pregnant, and next because your hormones might be playing tricks on you. The best time for deciding whether you really wanted a man or not was just before or just after your period.

Alice felt that the woman was going a bit far, but it was nice to know why she felt that way sometimes.

But knowing about her body now did not help. She wanted her children, and if the truth be told, she wanted her husband back too. Knowing that women were sneaky and devious because they were forced to be so did not help. She had never been sneaky and devious. She did not want to play a role and be respected by everyone. All she wanted was her children and a decent home, plus a job. Surely it was not too much to ask God for, whatever her mistakes?

Only the lie stood between her and her dream.

She went and booked an appointment to see Mrs. Ngallah.

32

Mrs Ngallah looked at Alice in dismay. I do not need this on top of everything else. I really, most assuredly do not need this particular straw on my back, she thought. I am one camel with serious backache.

Not for the first time, she regretted her role of in-house trouble-shooter.

Martha's dream was turning into Prudentia's nightmare. In the beginning it looked so good. Get in with the modern set, right some wrongs, help some people. (And look good in the process, said a little voice in her head, but she brushed it away angrily.) But here she was, only plugging holes in a sinking boat. Martha, she now realised, was a prophet. But prophets are not practical people. They criticised endlessly and want impossible things to happen, which is why the Israelites threw some down dry wells. They refused to sully their hands with the nitty-gritty. They handled ideals, not burst sewage pipes.

They hired people who turned out to be drunks, like that tight-faced American wonder upstairs. It was true that no one could have known that the tight-lipped Wharton graduate had a drinking problem. It did not show on her face, and it was not written on her credentials, which were impeccable. When she was sober, she was very controlled. Too much so, in fact. But when she was drunk, she did things. Misplaced files. Shouted at the secretaries. And only last week she had knocked down a pedestrian while under the influence, and had said foul things to the policemen who took her into custody for her own safety. Only the timely intervention and a liberal greasing of the commissioner's palm by Prudentia had saved matters.

Martha was unable to deal with these things. She had no experience, just hope for a better world and more money than she knew what to do with; was in fact inhabited by a tenacious naïveté that made you want to shake her at times. In spite of all evidence to the contrary, she persisted in the belief that people were good; they only had to be told that they were.

She should have used some of that money to do background checks on the staff. Mrs. Ngallah suspected that Mrs. Morton's fondness for strong drink had something to do with the failure of her marriage. Here they were, saddled with her, and Martha only mouthed inanities about helping women in need. Mrs. Morton did not want to be helped. When Prudentia had hinted that perhaps it would be best to exorcise some ghosts, the woman, sober that morning, had looked at her frostily over her half-moons and told her that people's private lives would not be the subject of prurient interest on the part of people who had a job to do and ought to be doing it.

"Why not focus on those holy-rolling pep talks you are so good at? Hm?"

Why indeed, wondered Prudentia Ngallah. Because Martha, when told of the problem, said to give Gladys time. But there was no time.

And now this. The latest one. It had started quietly enough. A rough-looking woman had come to the front gate one day and demanded to see "the woman who has this place". Of course she was shunted off to Mrs. Ngallah, jenny of all trades.

"So, Mammy, wetin be the problem?"

The woman sat stony-faced in her white lace *kaba*, probably her communion-day church get-up. She said:

"You people have stolen my daughter. I hear she is here. I want her back home where she belongs."

That one Prudentia had heard many times.

"How old is your daughter?"

"I come here to take my daughter and you ask me questions! How do I know how old she is? I just want her back home where she belongs!"

"How can you not know the age of your own child?"

"She is not my flesh and blood. She is my son's wife and she ran away two year'go. She took his money and ran away. I did not want him to marry her. I wanted him to go to university. But she threw herself at him and dragged him down."

"If this is your son's wife, then he should be dealing with this, not you. But I can tell you that if she was less than sixteen when he married her, then your son is in trouble. Your son cannot marry a girl who is less than that age. It means that he has broken the law, and that is a case for the courts. If your son married the woman when she was the right age and he wants to divorce his wife, he can sue for desertion, and she will defend herself as she sees fit. But we did not keep your daughter-in-law here by force. All who come here do so of their own free will, and they can leave when they want."

"That is a fat lie! Where would that fool had found the courage to leave unless you helped her? She could not even keep her own house clean. I had to teach her how to wash herself!"

"You lived in her house?"

"My son's house, not her house. Where else do you expect me to live? She was killing him; I had to intervene."

"I cannot help you. I cannot force her to leave if she does not want to. You are not her husband. If he wants his wife, he can come and get her himself. I begin to understand why she left in the first place."

"Okay, you want to see trouble, then you will see trouble. I have come here in good faith and asked you nice to give my daughter back. But you want to show me white man book. You will see who is who."

The woman left, muttering imprecations.

Next thing, a tribal committee had come to "take our sequestered wife back home". Then a local rag carried the story that a woman was being kept against her will by the House, which would not let her family see her. Her two sons were pining for their mother, said the rag, with grainy photos to prove it.

Mrs. Ngallah was shocked to hear that children were involved, and was preparing to summon Alice when she herself asked for an appointment.

"So you did leave two sons behind you when you left?"

Alice squirmed. "Yes it is true. But I meant to go back for them later on; it's just that as I never said anything about them in the first place, I did not know how to manage it. I did not want to abandon them! It was just that...the suffering was too much, and when I heard on the radio that...that –" She wept.

"But you should have told us, and we would have made arrangements. We would have gone to court if necessary. You see that we have done so for many women. I see from your file

196

that you were two months short of your sixteenth birthday when you married. We could have asked for an annulment. The law is on our side on that one at least. Now public opinion will crucify you, and us too. You have placed the House in an untenable position, Alice. I wish you had told us earlier. We are made to look like wife-snatchers, and this will prevent men who would normally allow their wives to come to us from doing so in the future. So what do you want to do now?"

"I just want my children."

"And your husband?" It was only half a question.

Alice started to explain, but there was no way to put it into words for this woman. She remained silent.

"I see. We will make a case for you if you wish. We have too many lawsuits as it is, but that cannot be helped. You acted in ignorance and some selfishness, and you were still a child. Who says a little selfishness is not good for you?" She smiled. "But you see that a little truth from time to time won't hurt you, don't you?"

"Yes I understand, Auntie, it's just that..."

Mrs. Ngallah ended the meeting and Alice left, still weeping. Her case should be fairly easy, but there were other, more difficult ones.

Irate husbands demanding wives were pretty standard fare. Some families had daughters who had run away because they were about to be forced into marriage. Their demands for the daughters to be returned to them were dealt with pretty efficiently. Even the public outcry died down when some of the details were released.

But there had been one nightmare case of reported incest. The girl had claimed that her father had tried to force himself on her. It was found out later that the girl had had twins by an unknown father, thrown them down a latrine and refused to tell what had become of them. Her father tried to beat the information out of her, and she ran to the House. But some visitor had recognised her there, and she ran away again. Her father went to a willing reporter and charged the House with putting bad ideas into his daughter's head. Things had been rather sticky for a while and were only resolved when the truth came out. Luckily, the girl had been caught trying to cross over to Nigeria.

Other women with criminal pasts had also been smoked out, mainly by the press, and the House's image had taken a beating. It could be said to their credit that the House had changed the lives of nearly four hundred women for the better in just over two years. The Mechanical Department had become famous countrywide for its speed and efficiency, and some of the ill will came from people who were being squeezed out of business.

The Academic Department ran, thank God, almost on its own momentum. The House's candidates had performed well in public examinations, even though the head of department was a haughty drunk. She had once held a long harangue while under the influence and quoted Judith Butler at length to a bunch of bewildered backwoods escapees. Thank God that she did not teach too many courses. If the women realised that she drank, it would be the beginning of the end for all of them. No one would respect them any longer.

It was time to have a little talk with Martha about the state of affairs.

33

Martha remembered Sister Noreen with something akin to affection, though she had hated the long-chinned Irish nun at school.

Sister Noreen had a problem with the word *they*. She would ask a girl:

"And now, child, what happened to your brown sandals?"

The girl would of course reply: "Please Sister, they have stolen them."

Sister Noreen would roll her eyes heavenwards.

"Child, I have met people from many countries, but I have never yet met anyone called 'they'! Who are 'they'? Say you have lost the sandals and let's be done with it, child!

But Sister Noreen did not know the half of it. *They* existed. And right now, they were after her. They were formless and nameless, but they existed all right. Oh yes they did. They were everywhere. They were the ones who stole your sandals, your reader, and your needlework kit. And they were the ones who embezzled public funds. They were among the staff women, in public offices, in the bars and eating-houses, in the churches and schools. They were everywhere, and right now, they were out to get her.

She sipped her campari soda in the twilight. Her mind returned to what had just happened, like the tongue to a bit of mango fibre caught between one's teeth. She and Prudentia had just had a conversation. A shouting match. No, be frank: a screeching match.

Was Prudentia one of them? No, but they had frayed her nerves to breaking point, and caused Prudentia to yell at *her*. Unheard of. She owned this place, for God's sake. She contemplated sacking the woman for her monumental impertinence.

"Shouting at me like that," she slurred softly to the ice in her drink. "As – as if I were her bloody servant. Fat thing." But even through the red haze of the campari, she knew she would not sack her. The woman was just telling it like it was.

It had started mildly enough. Having gone round the premises, she was heading to her office when she passed a woman sobbing in the corridor leading to Prudentia's office.

"Why, what is the matter?" Unable to speak, the woman, whom she recognised as Alice, a quiet, sad-faced girl, pointed dumbly to Prudentia's office and stumbled off. Martha walked straight there. Prudentia was parked behind her large desk, massaging her temples with her fingertips.

"What happened? I passed a girl crying in the corridor."

"Ask me what has not happened instead, and perhaps I might be able to give you a short answer. Everything bad that could happen has happened. This place seems determined to prove that old pessimist Murphy true. That one you saw, she ran away from a husband and two kids to come here. Her mother–in–law has tracked her down here and is mobilising anything and everyone to see that she goes back home. Apparently, the husband is something of a wimp and the mum–in–law rules the roost. But there would have been no trouble if she had told us before." Prudentia sighed deeply and told her the story.

"Is that why she was crying?"

"She came to tell me about it just as I was about to send for her. The interview upset her. Or perhaps it was her conscience." She paused.

"Martha, I hate to be the one to say this; you know how much I believe in what you started. But things are getting tougher and tougher around here. You are not here all the time, so you cannot really know. Mrs. Morton's little problem is now a full-blown disaster. She is neglecting her duties. When I try to talk to her, she becomes all haughty and tells me through her nose to mind my own business. The engineer seems to have formed an exclusive attachment to one of the mechanic women and the others are beginning to murmur about it. There are stories, though I hesitate to credit them. That little cutesy doll in the kitchen is always overrunning her budget; the building permit we applied for to extend the staff quarters has been denied – again. Two of our trusted food suppliers have reneged on their contracts. The press crucifies us every day. The courts are against us. Those crazy new religions are preaching fire-and-brimstone sermons about us from their stupid makeshift pulpits. There have been cases of theft. Everything is going wrong at once!" Her voice had risen to a shout by now.

"Hm. Well tomorrow I'll call a meeting to sort—"

"Meetings won't do it. Posturing on television won't do it. Taking long vacations in the South Seas won't do it." She banged her well-cushioned fist on the desk.

"Wait wait wait! Are you suggesting that this is all *my* fault?"

"I am not *suggesting* anything." She mimicked Martha's voice. "I am telling you clearly that we need hands-on support from you here, right here. You cannot just provide the money and walk away to continue your life. This was your idea. You are the one who has to make it work. You cannot come to a society with your schoolgirl notions of justice and equal opportunity and expect things to change for you just because you have money. Money and high-falutin' notions are not enough. Visions are not enough. You should have prepared yourself to take the responsibility for implementing them. This place *cannot* fail. It cannot. You cannot show people a glimpse of paradise and then lose interest. Ideals that are implemented have to be followed through. Money alone cannot do it!"

"You guys are just incompetent. This is like running a boarding school. I mean, look at the nuns who were our teachers and principals. They did not have management degrees! You just have to find other people to work or provide supplies if the ones you have will not. And do not speak to me in that tone of voice."

Prudentia leaped up from her chair, eyes snapping. Her headdress began to unravel; but she finished the job and tossed it impatiently aside. "I will speak to you in any bloody tone of voice I choose. I am the one who is getting ulcers here. You come here frothing at the mouth about getting new suppliers. Well, go out and try getting them yourself! No one big enough to supply us is willing to do it. The word is out that we are troublemakers. The carpentry workshop you helped those six women set up along the coast there, do you even know what

201

happened? Do you? Well while you were going about in bikinis, strutting your stuff on the beach, someone burnt the place down."

"What!"

"Yes, what! That's what! And slashed the head carpenter's face from brow to lip.

"What you seem to find difficult to comprehend is that people do not like their women coming home and spewing newfangled nonsense about their right to a decent life. Look. You upset the state of things. You want women to be drivers and carpenters and mechanics in a world where men believe those to be male jobs, and where male jobs are scarce enough as it is. They feel that you are taking the food from their mouths and putting it in the mouths of the women. To make it worse, you are asking their God-given cooks to refuse to cook what little food there is to eat. You know that old thing about 'you have the yam but I have the knife'? Well, the economy has taken their yam and you have put the knife in the hands of the women. So what do you expect them to think? You want them to like you, and make it easier for them to lose their manhood? I told you in the beginning that we should have organised explanatory meetings with the village elders at least. Instead, you go on TV and speak English. How many of these people understand you?"

"You – you sound as if you are blaming me for trying to improve the lot of an important part of society. I mean, what is wrong with that?"

"No no no. Don't twist my words around. What I mean is that your intentions are good, but you must follow them through. And you must change your strategy. You do not just barge in and tell people what to do. You cannot start something and then lose interest. Everything seems to be on my head here. I cannot even go out and organise contact sessions with the people because I do not have the time. No one is doing what they are expected to do.

"And you most certainly should not have limited yourself to hiring so-called university professors to come here and make incendiary speeches about gender equity. How many of those women do you think understand university English? I

202

told you that we should move cautiously with our ideas. We should not have taken it all in one bite. First, you help the women learn how to do something lucrative, then you tell them to move on to the next stage. Teach them how to get food to eat; then afterwards they can demand to be part of the village council of elders or whatever. Don't you remember that in Europe before the advent of democracy, women were not allowed to vote mainly because they were not economically productive, or so it was thought? They did not pay taxes, they did not own anything, so they could not be allowed to vote! That was the reasoning. So when the women have economic influence, the political and social influence will come of its own accord. Do you see?" She paused to swallow. Martha opened her mouth, but Prudentia went on before she could speak.

"Another thing. You should have carried out a background check on the women you hired. I mean, just checking their references would have been something. Drunks and purported lesbians are bad for the image of this place. We are not in a society where women who hang about together are tolerated. People who cannot manage budgets are bad for an institution that claims to want to help women manage their own lives. And people who go swimming instead of pursuing their dreams are worst of all."

"Have you quite finished?" Perhaps icy disdain might stem the tide.

It did not.

"No, not by a long shot. You want some more? Okay. You asked for it. How about the fact that our enlightened founder is unable to keep her legs closed for five minutes together? How do you think I feel when my twenty-five year old nephew gleefully informs me that my highly moral boss has been keeping his friend up nights because she cannot get enough of it? Enh? How about the fact that you have an idea like this and you are unable to get your own parents on the bandwagon? Can you imagine the impact the support of people of their age would have had? In addition," Prudentia spoke to the ceiling, "she asks me if I have not finished. No, I have not finished. When I finish, you will know, I guarantee you. You will - "

But she was speaking to no one. Martha was gone.

Martha burst out of the office and ran up the stairs to the aerie. She did not notice Vera behind the stairwell, eyes almost glowing in the semi-darkness, not believing her luck. Trouble in paradise. It was unbelievable. She had heard ev-ery word. This was as good as money in the bank. She would look around and see who was willing to buy. Any one who could not use this to advantage was a fool. She, Vera, was not.

34

Martha's mind reached out a self-punishing finger and pressed the mental PLAY button again. The whole scene rolled forward in excruciating slow motion. How dare that fat cow suggest that she was sleeping around! The woman did not know what she was going through. Nobody knew. Even Ophelia was distressingly breezy about her problems.

Martha whimpered softly and sipped her drink. Nobody understood how you could lock yourself up in an ivory tower and throw away the key, and still find enough stupidity within yourself to chop off your long hair in a crew cut. How did she solve this one?

The painful bit was that it had all begun so well. Not so well, said the little voice. You should have taken account of your parents' reaction and realised that you had to prepare the terrain.

But she was not listening to little voices this evening.

And then she had again fallen into the trap the god of the heart-hunters had built specially for idiots like her. Why do these things happen only to me? Why do the men I am comfortable with drift off or break my heart? She had been content with Charles for a while, but Charles had moved to the capital hundreds of kilometres away. There was no use pretending that they could conduct a commuter relationship, so they parted amicably. They talked to each other on the phone for about six months after he left, and then the calls petered out.

After Charles, she had floated around for a while, and then she met the new bait in the trap. The bait in the trap had been especially appetizing this time. He was good-looking and discreet. He set much store by good solid values like honesty, fidelity, the work ethic and daily baths. He had his own money. He had ideals.

He worked for an NGO with ambitious ideas about the equal distribution of wealth. He was educated. He was well read. He was not looking for a pretty society wife who knew how to knit backrest covers. He just wanted a quiet, sincere relationship with someone mature and intelligent. He did not boast about how good he was, and how his boss was afraid of him because the top job by rights belonged to him and all the staff knew it. He made no demands she was unwilling or unable to satisfy.

He was also good in bed and the right age. They met at a baptism party. It seemed to her that most of the people who gave her grief were people she met at parties. Like at that fat cow downstairs bellowing at her.

Martha had been sitting in an easy chair in the living room of the house where the party had been organised, nursing a campari orange. She had been relegated to that limbo of honoured guests no one knows well enough or is willing to engage in conversation. The social small fry were too timorous and the big fish too disdainful. Her 'friend', a former classmate, harried hostess and mother of two, including the fractious baptismal baby, was rushing about in her over-embroidered boubou (I know a woman who brings them from Coutounou, 60.000; her prices are good, she had whispered to Martha when Martha complimented her politely), never finishing a sentence or a smile. Her husband sat on the veranda with his friends, his three-year old daughter rocking back and forth between his thick, hairless knees, drinking and swapping stories of personal expertise and open government secrets.

The wives alternately helped the hostess and gossiped.

About Brenda (the hostess, aged thirty-two, and inevitably a teacher): she had missed so many classes that the vice-principal had threatened to sanction her.

"So madam went and bought him a shirt and he forgave her. Who knows what else she gave him?"

Legs were crossed and uncrossed. Hems twitched. Eyelashes fluttered. Mouths sipped and jaws worked, and nibbled at reputations.

About Brenda's pelmet covers:

"Mama! Ugly –oh! And to think that you can get really good lace second-hand…"

About her husband:

"I hear he bought that Belinda a TV. Pays her rent."

"You don't mean it!"

"No, true. It even looks as if she's pregnant…"

When one of them took a plate of gnawed chicken bones to the kitchen, the others shifted and leaned forward.

"Be careful what you say about Belinda around that Bernadette, enh. They're second cousins on her mother's side."

"Ah-ah! I did not know-oh. Do you think she will tell her? Anyway, who cares? What can she do to me?"

And the women sat and shifted and gossiped, shredding one another to bits, angry and restless at they knew not what.

Wisps of this conversation floated to Martha on the hot, sad air. She was praying for six o'clock to be able to leave without it seeming as if she thought such functions were beneath her. It was only half past four.

Then a man walked in, wearing a bright Batik print shirt and black jeans. The chair next to hers had just been vacated (by a short wide man with a shiny face who had not spoken three words to her and who had said to Brenda on rising to leave: "Okay, let me go and talk to those people."

"Weh! Uncle Jake, we'll really miss your company…tell Sophie I am waiting for my share of the mission booty."

"I will. Bye."

"Bye, God bless."), so he sat down in it and a drink was brought for him.

One thing, as they say, led to another and carried them far out on a sea of what they agreed later would be adult desire.

He was recovering from a failed near-marriage. The girl had a bit of 'marriage insurance' on the side that became increasingly less bitty. He found out a week to the wedding that the 'insurance' was what she loved, even though she liked the financial security he would provide. End of story. She, Martha, was trying (and failing) to forget a spate of brief affairs after Charles that left no taste in the mouth at all.

He was a busy man. She herself, now that the House had found its sea legs, was not as busy as she might have been, but she was busy enough. So, as with Charles, they met about once a week. It went on like that for a year, this well-heeled urban almost-love.

207

She did not really notice when he stopped seeing her. She was still having an affair with him long after his mind had moved on to other things. It was an *adult* relationship, she scolded herself, when she was tempted to wonder whether they did not see too little of each other. There was no marathon sex and togetherness six days a week, and no long, smiley phone calls on the seventh day. So it was alright not to see him for a fortnight. No need to panic. It was a nice, laid-back relationship after all, and it gave her time to focus on the things that were important to her.

Except it lay back, stretched and expired without so much as a whimper. Faded to nothing, when she thought it was just taking a short nap.

She found out one evening when she went to his place, cute overnight bag in hand, and discovered an extremely delectable younger creature in ice-blue harem pants, with arched eyebrows and silver trinkets, eyeing her coolly from her vantage point on the sofa. It was ten p.m., too late for female cousins just dropping in. She immediately recognised that this was the competition.

Samuel came in. He was polite, giving her a peck on the cheek, but there was nothing in his manner to imply that he had done anything to be ashamed of.

While Martha was scrabbling about in her mind for some dignity to manage the situation, Samuel looked at her strained face and told himself that none of it was his fault. His was a warm soul that craved tenderness, and the careful treading of this most-holds-barred affair with Martha had ended up tiring him. He wanted to lose himself in someone, have someone consider him as important to her life. When he had met Martha, he was still licking his wounds from the business with the other girl, so he had not wanted a close relationship. When he healed, Martha seemed altogether too cool, so he looked around and found a warmer woman. That she was also younger was mere coincidence, he told himself. Martha was too contained and wrapped up in her own things. She did not need him. Now he had found the slim, elegant beauty who was ready to give anything, who knew that men must be pursued, no holds barred, and who was there so often that he knew what she was up to all the time. Martha was too far way, too much her own person for comfort. A man had to know exactly where a woman could be held to be able to keep her in thrall.

So it ended in the living room, with the two of them standing up and the girl on the sofa, unmoved.

Martha played the mature older woman, and left. Perhaps she might have stood a chance if she had thrown a fit. But all she said was that she had just dropped in to pick up some documents she needed for a study she was doing. It did not fool anyone, least of all the girl sitting on the sofa, but it helped Martha save face. Samuel walked her to the car and said good night. Though her car was out of earshot of the living room, he offered no explanation and she did not ask for one. For him, that was the final knell. She did not care enough about him to be jealous.

In the car, all she could do to ward off the darkness that threatened to engulf her was to murmur to herself, like a mantra: I want to go home and lie down, go home and lie down, lie down, lie down. She focussed her mind on this idea, knowing from experience that if she thought of anything else she would probably go mad. When she got home, her stomach was so hollow with misery she could barely walk up the stairs to the aerie. She stumbled into the bedroom and fell across the bed, face down, and tried to cry, but there were no tears. She knew this pain well, so well. She knew she would not be able to function until she got it under control.

It could not be reasoned away. She tried, though. She was too busy, he needed someone more present. It was just a passing temptation. He would realise what he was losing in letting her go like that. They were perfectly matched.

She admitted to herself that the pain she felt revealed what she had been hoping, unbeknownst even to her conscious self: she had hoped that this one would end in marriage and she would give up the unconscious search for an eligible male that she was sure every woman conducted without realising it. She had told herself in more lucid moments that part of this business of looking for a husband was biological programming, and that there was no need for an independent-minded woman to feel guilty about wanting to marry. The female animal of any species always examined the available males for the one who was most likely to bear healthy children, because that was how the future of the species was preserved. So it was alright to want to marry a guy. It was, like sex, a biological instinct.

At other times she felt a deep sense of shame that she who had been preaching to women about independence and managing their own lives and risking the loss of male companionship in the process yearned so secretly, so ardently for a permanent love.

Now, this evening, she not only had to admit outright that she had this hope, but she also had to face the fact that it was not going to be realised. Her eligible male had chosen someone else.

She fought a velvet-fisted pitched battle with the cool young beauty. She tried to organise romantic twosomes at her beach residence, which she rarely used. Samuel was too busy. She bought him things – a new car stereo, Gucci shoes. He took them, but he did not thaw. He thought she was trying to buy him. He wanted her to come off her high horse and tell him how she felt. She took a close interest in his work. He thought she was too aggressively intellectual.

She managed a scented-candle dinner of seafood with him once in the aerie, after which, in a rare moment of compassion, he slept with her. He went away again. He was not cheating on his new girl, he told himself; but he had not wanted to hurt Martha by seeming indifferent to her charms. Perhaps this last session would reconcile her to the idea of separation. He was not going back to her. She only wanted him now that she feared that she was about to lose him to someone else.

She never mentioned the girl during the dinner. Neither did he. After that night, she was unable to lure him back into her arms. She started dreading the time when she would wake up in the morning and find the loss looming above her, a presence at her bedside that had not gone away with the morning.

When she got up on three successive mornings and burst into tears at the thought of going through another day, she broke one of her cardinal rules and put out discreet tendrils on the grapevine. Mrs. Ngallah did not know the girl, but Ophelia knew her.

"Describe her."

"Tall, at least from what I could see; slim, dark, really dark. I could see that she had long legs, well shaped, because the trouser fabric was thin and she kept crossing and uncrossing her legs."

"Have you asked him anything?"

"God, no. It would be too humiliating to act jealous."

Ophelia stared at her incredulously. "I say *enh*, Martha, where you grow your own? I can guarantee you that if you had screamed and slapped him and torn the girl's clothes, you would have kept him. At least, you would have had a fighting chance. You are going around acting civilised when your heart is in shreds? Look at you, skinny like a market dog because you are suffering in silence! Wait. I will call someone and find out who she is."

She spoke to someone on the phone for some time, and then she hung up and turned to look at Martha.

"What did you find out?"

"Wait, let me replenish our drinks." She moved to the bar with their glasses.

"I'll give it to you straight. You're a big girl. It appears she is one of my students up there. And he has been seeing her for a bit. How long have you known him? A year and a half? Less. I see. Well it would seem that they have been going strong for the better part of a year."

He was going to marry the girl. He had already gone to see her parents, said Ophie, searching for a sign of pain on Martha's face.

Martha did not blink. Her face felt numb. She hoped that Ophelia would take her silence to mean that she was dealing with this new blow.

Through insensate lips, she heard herself telling Ophie that she would let him go. There was no logical explanation she could believe for his not wanting her; there was no need to fight what you could not understand. She had given him attention when she realised that she might have been neglecting him. He did not want it. Her love had come a little late; but she had not seen any sign of earlier love from him. Why had he not told her that she was too distant?

She was suitable for a semi-serious relationship, but she realised that his type did not marry nervy pioneers like her. He found too much of her imponderable. He wanted a woman with the trimmings: looks, education, manners – and a profound interest in him above all else.

"I guess I take myself too seriously, and I believe too strongly in what I do. Maybe he is a closet chauvinist and I scared him. As he has not seen fit to explain anything to me, what should I do? Kill myself?"

She decided that he wanted a successful woman, but not one whose personal beliefs would overshadow him. The thought made her feel hot all over.

"Why, the bastard! So I should limit my own horizons so that he can expand his? Why should one person decide that his own success has to come at the expense of his woman's self-fulfilment? Who the hell does he think he is? Let him go."

She could not waste her pain on him. He was unworthy.

"But this is what women have been saying all their lives," said Ophie. "The guy wants to be the most important thing in your life. If he is not, even though you love him, as I see is your case, he will leave you for someone who makes him the centre of her existence, someone who will get up at five a. m. sometimes to cook for him before going to work because he refuses to eat food not cooked by his wife, however busy she is, even if the servant cooks well. Is this not what you warn your girls against?"

"Yes, but this fool said he agreed with what I'm doing. He has even steered some funding opportunities my way."

"Yes, but it did not involve him. The women in this outfit of yours are not focussing on themselves to his detriment. He can afford to be generous with them. I see a correlation between this business and homosexuality. People will tell you how they do not mind homosexuals until they find out that their son is one. Then they *do* mind. Let me tell you, this business you have started is a lot more complex than you imagine. People are barely beginning to realise that their world is changing. You have to let their hearts and customs catch up with their thinking, and that will certainly take a while. As I have told you before, when it is expedient for me, I tell a guy what he wants to hear, and if I can get away with it, I do my own thing. Because even if men are bastards, the thought of being without one gives me the willies. I can go my own way a lot of the time, but I study the terrain very carefully before I do that. It is not very honest, but then that is what men do too."

Martha did not want to think now. She wanted to lock herself in the bedroom. She wanted to lie down. She felt queasy.

She got up and left the room.

In the days that followed, she decided that she would not cry for a man who did that to her.

She went back to her home in the capital and started hunting for victims of her own. In a couple of weeks, she had handpicked a couple of younger, penniless men. She vowed that she would never go out with only one man again. If one of them started acting difficult, she would focus on the other. If they were both recalcitrant, she would pick a third. Emotional insurance was the key to this business. She kept the young men on tenterhooks. She was alternately ice cold and lava-hot. She reduced their nerves to frazzles.

Then when they began to intimate ownership, she let them go and found someone else.

It did not help. The fear grew and grew like an ink stain on white cloth.

She went to the centre and raised hell. She started building a beauty clinic without waiting for a building permit and placed adverts in the media for more girls. She set up a scholarship fund for science-oriented girls. She built the carpenter's workshop for six fishermen's wives. She went on TV and made weighty pronouncements.

That lasted all of four months. But she could not stop thinking of Samuel. Why had he never said what he wanted? Why did he want emotional investment from her when she was not sure of obtaining any returns? Why should she be the one to take all the risks?

One day she attended a function organised by an international NGO. He was there too. So was his fiancée, looking good enough to eat in an all-black trouser suit with heavy silver jewellery and absolutely no makeup. She gave up and ran away halfway through the ceremony. She returned to

213

the centre and packed. She flew as far south as she could without actually falling off the face of the earth.

★ ★ ★

In the south, she gorged herself on seafood; the shellfish type and the two-legged type that hangs around on beaches waiting for rich dissatisfied thirty-somethings like her. She rented a boat and went sailing. She treated her hair with warm coconut oil. She went to the masseur in the daytime and prowled the waterfront bars at night, where she picked up the well-tanned and impecunious beach boys. It dulled the edge of her pain, but the bewilderment stayed.

She flew back home via Paris to replenish her wardrobe and buy a new car. Maybe new possessions would help her break with the sad past.

All roads to Cameroon lead through Paris, anyway, and many end there.

She detoured to the Netherlands and stood at Bertha's grave. She told her all on a cold, misty evening, but there was no flash of wisdom. The gravestone did not move. There was a white silence all around her. She walked through the snow to her rental car, and drove back to the hotel. She tried Cornelius's number, but he no longer lived at that address. No one knew where to find him. She flew back home with her new possessions.

She went straight to the centre and tried to get interested in what was going on. Maybe more work would help.

And here was Prudentia yelling at her like a fishwife. She knew that Ophie was out of the country as well, on a trip to Europe paid for by her boyfriend. So there was no one to tell that she was beginning to understand why people killed themselves. Who understood what she felt?

She needed to be alone, take stock and see what to do next. The day after the row with Mrs. Ngallah, she packed again in the early dawn and drove to her home on the beach. She needed to clear her head of this obsession. The beating waves and the swish of indifferent coconut palms, the voice of fishermen calling to each other over the water in the dark only made her aware of the peace she lacked. She packed up again and ran off to the capital.

Once there, she unhooked the phone and burrowed in.

While she was there, things were falling apart in her empire. The council struck on the pretext of overdue taxes. Vera went to the papers.

35

The narrow-faced reporter from the Weekly Correspondent could not believe his luck. Here was the scoop of his career dropping right into his lap, like ripe mangoes.

He looked at the diminutive, hard-faced girl dressed in incongruous innocent pink sitting before him.

"Let me summarize. The centre is falling apart. The founder is sleeping around with young men instead of trying to set the place right. The academic affairs officer is a drunk. The head engineer is conducting a lesbian relationship with one of her students. The founder and her parents do not get along.

"And you want me to pay you for the details so you can use the money to live your life as you wish, because you have finished your training and you want to move on. Is that it?"

"Well...yes."

"Why? I mean, this place has given you something, right? Before you went there, you were unemployed and there was no money for your fees at the university. I mean, you have learned new skills at no cost to yourself, you can set up – what, a catering business - because of what you learned there. So why are you doing this to the people who have given you a new lease on life? As far as I know, this woman, the founder, will help set you up in business if you ask. All you have to do is ask. So why, instead of asking, are you doing this to them?"

"Look, if you do not want to pay me, I can go somewhere else. I know people who would sell their mother for this info."

The reporter looked at her. "Yes, I suppose you *would* know that sort of person, seeing that there's not much to choose between you. Wait here. I'll talk to the bosses about it and see what we decide."

He left the office. Vera sat and waited. Why was he acting so uppity? A goat grazes where it is tethered. The centre was where she was tethered and it would be stupid not to graze because people would be hurt. It was a hard world. She had learned this the hard way, so no one was going to tell her what to think. This was empowerment. She was doing what she could with what she had.

The reporter came back. "Come with me. The boss wants to see you for himself."

The boss was a short, thin man with a salt-and pepper chin beard. He looked at the girl. She was about the age of his eldest daughter. Money. Women and money. That was all they ever thought of. Getting money for doing nothing. And this little viper expected him to pay for it. Well, she would see.

"So, Madam, they have taught you well, haven't they? You want to bite the hand that fed you and be paid for it, right? Well, first we have to check the information you want to sell so badly. You see, we cannot be sure that you are telling the truth. I do not see what your motive is, I mean, you will get what you want without doing this, so – why? Tell me why."

"I do not owe anyone any explanations. If you want to buy the information, say so and let's get on with it. If you do not, then I will be going somewhere else. You are not in a position to moralise. I know what the newspaper business is all about."

"Hm!" The editor's eyes flared briefly, and he looked her up and down. Little snake. "I regret to inform you that as we have no way of corroborating the information by independent means, it has no market value. We cannot pay you for something that is worthless. So, sorry, but we cannot do business with you. But let me give you a word of advice. As a man who is old enough to be your father, I would advise you to reconsider what you have done, or have tried to do. These things come back to haunt you, you know. Nothing goes for nothing."

"Save me the clichés, I get enough of that at the centre. I will go somewhere else, where they know how to do business, and then you will regret not accepting my offer. You will see." She stood up.

The men laughed loudly and incredulously. The boss said:

"Let me tell you something, little woman, to set you more firmly on your path of betrayal. No one will pay you for the information. You are a woman. You think you can threaten the hard men who sell newspapers? They will get it out of you for nothing, one way or another. As you yourself say, newspapermen are hardly saints. You have no power to threaten anyone. You can go on betraying people for as long as you live, but you are not smart enough. You will never get anything out of it. Now get out!"

When she had left, he said:

"Do we have any way of checking this information?"

"Well, I have the gateman. He claims to be sleeping with one of the staff, and he hears things from time to time."

"Okay. We'll test the waters with one general article, and then we'll see what to do with the rest of the information. Get busy."

Part Five

36

Nearly four hours after taking Hortense's morning call, Martha arrived at the centre a little before noon. She went up to her aerie and asked for Hortense first. They worked for hours. Towards evening, Martha took pity on her and asked her to go and rest. She herself ate some fruit, and immediately after, she sent for Mrs. Morton.

The woman came in, looking a little pale, her long face all planes and angles this evening, totally devoid of makeup, or emotion, for that matter. Her hair was drawn back tightly as usual. She stood stiffly in the middle of the living room until Martha invited her out onto the balcony.

"A drink?" Morton cast a quick, searching glance at her, but Martha did not blink. She shook her head.

"Tea or coffee, then?"

"Nothing, thanks."

"Alright! We'll get down to the nitty-gritty then. I have been hearing things about you. I have been told that you have a problem. A rather liquid one."

"Ah, I see you have been listening to that meddlesome cow."

"Mrs. Morton, I am not in the habit of hiring farm animals to work for me. Please avoid referring to members of staff in those terms. Obviously there is a problem, a very big one, with the way you are running your department and the way you conduct yourself in and out of this place. I have asked you to come here today so that we can see what is to be done about it. Comparing your colleagues to bovines will not get us anywhere. Let me tell you, I will settle the matter this evening, one way or another, once and for all. So I suggest we move on. Do you acknowledge that you have a drinking problem?"

"Since you have decided to listen to that inveterate bearer of false witness, what can I say? You have all the information. Do what you want with it." Morton shrugged and hunched her shoulders, looking out at the dusk.

"Gladys, listen to me. This is not a battle between you and me, or anyone else. You will have noticed that things have degenerated somewhat around here. You are not the only one with personal problems. Yours is not the only problem we have within this establishment. It may be one of the easiest, in fact. But it must be solved. There is no denying that you have not been working as well as you might. And the problem seems to be linked to your penchant for drink. I'm sorry to be blunt, but we have to solve our problems before our whole project collapses. Won't you talk to me about it? I want to help."

"If you want my resignation, it will be on your desk in an hour. I can leave before tomorrow."

Martha leaned forward. "Gladys, I do not want you to resign. I want you to stay and be as efficient as you were when I hired you. I only want to help. Something is worrying you. What is it?"

Morton was silent for a while. Then she shook her head and sighed.

"Let me tell you about my life before I came here, then perhaps you will understand." She paused.

"I was married to a man back in the United States, as you know. He was black and handsome, intelligent, considerate, successful, everything a woman could want. The beginning was – wonderful. My husband was a stockbroker. There are not too many Black ghetto kids who become stockbrokers, you know that. Ours was a match made in heaven. Two black yuppies with high incomes and a nice home in the suburbs; couldn't be better. A credit to the race, we were.

"But there are things that take their toll on a person that you cannot see and that he himself is unaware of. And sometimes even when he knows, he cannot escape them. For my husband, not being a white man, being the descendant of the slaves – he could never get rid of the feeling of inferiority. Believe me, for some black people, direct contact with white people is like catching a debilitating disease. They obsessively compare themselves with these people and worry that they are not measuring up. Every day he wondered what these people who had treated his ancestors like farm animals thought as he worked around them in the office. Everything they said, every

221

joke they cracked, seemed full of subtle meaning. He could not trust them. He became paranoid with the effort of hiding his distrust and keeping his job.

"To make it worse, he resented his classification as black. He was very light-skinned, more white than black. He was a man of mixed blood in a society that classifies its citizens based on race, whatever it says officially. He felt that if race was the issue, then a person has the right to choose which race he belongs to. He was only one quarter black, but he was not allowed to choose. The black reached up and took him for its own, staining his soul forever. And he could not forgive himself for being black. He could not tell anyone about his resentment. So he worked hard at the office and soon acquired a reputation. Then he came home and beat me to get rid of the stress. He transferred all his feelings of inferiority onto me. I was the inferior one. If he had a bad day at the office, he came home and I had a bad day out of the office.

"And I took it. I took it until he threatened me with a gun one day, then I left him. I ran away to a shelter for battered wives because I was ashamed to let my friends know that our perfect marriage was a nightmare. They were very kind to me there. I stayed there for a while, and then I decided to come to Africa to try and forget and to see where my people came from. Then I hard about this place and decided to stay. I did not divorce him. I am a lawyer! I know how to get a quickie divorce if I want one. But I did not do that. Sometimes I feel like a fraud here, trying to correct the lives of women whose only fault is that they are ignorant. I was not poor or ignorant, but I took the abuse for years. Compared to what opportunities I had, these women have nothing. But they have had the courage to break away from their fetters and try to make something of their lives. They have so little, but see what some of them have done for themselves!

"The difficult, humiliating part was that in spite of all the abuse, I still loved him. Still do, as a matter of fact. That is what I cannot understand about myself."

"But Gladys, you *did* leave. You left him. And you are doing something very important based on your experience with him. Even if your marriage was not a success, what you are doing for these girls is – something that they will be grateful for all their lives."

"Yes, but it took me eight long years to leave. Eight years of taking abuse when I could have been out in a trice. Who am I then to give lessons to people? If they knew my story, how would they see me? What would they think of me?"

"My dear, there is a woman who came here after eighteen years of taking abuse, and you know what? She went right back to take some more. No one can really say why women take abuse for so long when they have a way out. Perhaps they feel that they deserve it. Perhaps they feel that it is their lot in life. I do not know; I am not a psychologist. But the important thing is getting out. And you did that. Try not to be so hard on yourself.

"You may be a masochist, but try asking yourself how you came to be one. Were you not told when you were growing up that woman's lot is suffering, and that we are ennobled by our meek acceptance of it? If you have been told that without a man by her side, a woman is incomplete, why would you want to take the risk of living alone and being considered a failure? If someone has been repeating that to you from the time you were able to understand speech, how can you blame yourself for believing it?

"I realise that our acceptance of our lot is like belief in Christian doctrine. You now know that it is not possible for a woman to become pregnant without having sex, or for a man to rise up into the clouds and go to heaven. But you are prepared to believe it of the Virgin Mary or Jesus, because if you do not believe, what will you have to think of all those things your parents and teachers and priests told you? To take the step into unbelief is frightening. Even today, I still feel guilty about not going to confession like a good Catholic girl. I know it's nonsense, but I still feel guilty.

"Whatever your troubles, and remember that every one of us has hers, your contribution to this place is not something we can easily replace. So if that was your resignation you were offering me a while ago, I do not accept it. I need you here. You can have some time off and pull yourself together. But I want you back here. Okay?

"We all have private fears. We all have ghosts. But we have to go on, and I am counting on you to be part of my team."

"Well, I need a little time to sort this out in my head."

"Take a few weeks off. Maybe see a doctor. Or go back to the States and sort this out with this man."

Gladys rose. "Okay I'll try. Keep you posted." She walked to the door, and added as an afterthought: "Thank you for your trust."

Good. That was easier than I thought. One down and nine thousand to go.

★★★

Martha reached over to the phone on the side stool and dialled. Prudentia picked up the phone on the first ring.

"Could you come up to my apartments please?"

"Right now?"

"Yes."

"Alright. Be right there."

A few minutes later, she was there, dressed in a voluminous caftan of phosphorescent green.

"Sit down." Martha indicated the chair Gladys had just vacated.

"I wanted to talk about our…discussion last week."

"It was not a discussion and you know it."

"Alright, whatever. Let's not quibble about names, then. The quarrel."

"I'm listening."

"I'm having everyone of the senior staff that seems to be giving us major trouble here. I have talked to Gladys, and I think she will be alright. Less success with Grace, though, for the time being. I called her and she said she was too busy and she would get to me later." Martha smiled ruefully.

"I'm afraid if things do not change in that quarter, we'll have to replace her. Have you thought about it?"

Martha suppressed her irritation at the way Prudentia was assuming that she would naturally be involved in deciding who would go and who would stay. "Well, let's settle a few things and I'll see her again."

224

Prudentia took a deep breath. "Martha, I know that none of this is easy for you. When we …quarrelled, I said some very unpleasant things to you. I am sorry that I spoke in anger. But I still think you should give some thought to some of the comments I made regarding your attitude. I meant them. There is really no point in going on if you are frightened of fulfilling your dream. The - "

"It's okay, Prudentia, we were both upset. And I have thought seriously about what you said. However, I cannot change anything just by telling you what you want to hear. Only my actions will speak for me. Things are going to change around here. Let me say, instead that they have changed already. Are you willing to wait and see what I am about?"

Prudentia turned and looked at Martha. There were tears in her eyes. "In a way, you are the bravest of us. I wish I had your courage to try and try again when there seems to be no way out." She reached out and clasped Martha's hand. Martha let her hold it for as long as she felt was polite, then she shifted and pretended to rearrange her papers.

"Okay, so what is your strategy?" asked Prudentia.

Martha told her. It took a while. They were so engrossed they did not notice the time pass. When they finally looked up, the sun had gone home to roost behind the mangrove swamp, leaving the world in darkness. Prudentia called down and ordered lunch from the kitchen. While they waited for it to arrive, they chatted.

"You know, this will make waves. This will really make waves. Those bastards out there will be angrier than ever. "

"They can faint if they are so inclined. I have had enough of their whining." Martha sipped her lime juice.

"Do you know what they hate most?" asked Prudentia after a while. "It's the idea that there is a woman out there who does not think the way they would like her to. You know, someone who does not have the ambitions that they expect her to have. Life is so comfortable for them that they do not care how it is for other people. They want to be governors, ministers and all that; rule the world. But they do not think you can want that. In fact, they are frightened that someone, a female, will go and snatch the position from under their noses."

"No, it's not really that. It is not that they do not care. It is that they are used to thinking in a certain way. It is that they are unable to understand that you and I can have long-term ambitions beyond beautiful backrest covers and grandmotherhood. It is inconceivable to them that you are not satisfied with your lot. It frightens them when they realise that you want other things, because they don't know how to deal with ambitious women and they are not willing to try. We are manageable as long as we do what is expected of us. When we want other things, we are unnatural, crazed by too much education, unhappy, or troublesome. They cannot begin to believe that what they give us is not enough. That we want more. Many women declare loud and clear that they are completely satisfied with the way their lives are. So anyone who claims that they should not be is an unhappy, unfulfilled woman trying to break homes and upset the status quo because she cannot have what she wants."

"But the strange thing is that you will often hear a father say proudly of his daughter: she is tough. Where she works, she is the one who commands the men."

"Yes, but the father does not sleep with his daughter. It all boils down to sex, I think. He can handle a strong daughter's power. It reflects on him because he is her parent. If she is strong, then it is because he made her so. And he will not, unless he is twisted beyond repair, have his daughter as a sexual partner. He will never be asked to share his power with her. It is another man who will be forced to contend with her forcefulness. Everyone approved of what Mother Theresa was doing. She was a sexless nun who decided to bring succour to the needy. It is the sort of work women can do without upsetting anyone. What is more, she could not be viewed as a sex object. What enrages men is that their sex objects want to be something else."

"Ah!" Prudentia stretched. Her spine cracked. She was silent for a moment. "Remember that your father did not want you to be something else." She waited in some apprehension for Martha's reaction. The subject of her parents was taboo.

"He was furious!" Martha laughed, and Prudentia breathed more easily.

"Do you think it's rage he felt? I think it was fear. You were about to become someone that he could not classify, be pleased with, and then dismiss, however lovingly. I think the problem with most of them is that we are becoming something they fear they cannot control. In the old days, you could beat your woman if she got above herself. Nowadays, if you so much as insult them, they will take you to court for mental torture. Their world is falling apart, these men; that is why they are fighting so hard. It's the fear of losing control."

"Why should they be in control of everything? I remember one man telling me that it was important for him as the breadwinner in his family to maintain some degree of mystery about how much money he actually earned. He said it was so that when unexpected expenditure came up in the household, he could produce money like a magician and his wife, not knowing how he had managed it, would be in awe of him. She would see him as a worker of miracles. Can you imagine? He wants to be seen as a miracle worker, some kind of superior being who can make something out of nothing! That is what drives me nuts. Why do they want to be seen as something they are not? Okay - let them be what they want, gods or statesmen or whatever. Why can we not be what we want as well?"

"*Va savoir*, as Hortense would say. Who knows?"

There was a knock on the main door and Martha went to open it. It was the catering woman, with a trolley of food.

"Hello girls! I heard you were back, so I decided to bring up the food myself. Prue! You are up here too! A regular confab, is it?"

"Well, come in and join us. We were just going to eat something and rest, and ask you to come up. But since you're here, let's get it over and done with."

"Won't you girls eat first? The food will be cold, and the girls took *so* much trouble." She pouted prettily.

"No. This is more important. Come and sit down." Martha's tone alarmed her. She sat down, her eyes like a frightened rabbit's, looking from one to the other.

"Why, is there something wrong?"

"You mean you haven't noticed?"

227

Prudentia signalled to Martha that she would handle this. Martha bit back her refusal, sat back, and watched. If it did not go as she wished, she would step in.

"When was the last time you gave a coherent record of expenditure to the accountant?" Prudentia asked without preamble. Miss Robinson looked at her in surprise.

"Why – I mean – it's her job to balance the books, isn't it? I have my own job to do, don't I?"

"Yes, which includes keeping track of what you buy for the kitchens. You have not been doing that. You are driving the poor woman nuts. And there is a lot of wastage. How come some of the stuff you buy ends up being sold to dealers on the sly, eh?" At the woman's look of alarm, Prudentia snorted.

"Why are you looking surprised? You mean you haven't noticed?"

"You hired me to take care of the catering department. That is what I do. Our food is excellent. I might add that I have worked for much larger institutions, and no one, absolutely no one, ever complained about my management of the supplies."

"Your credentials were impeccable. That is why we thought that you could handle things on your own. This place exists to teach women self-reliance. What example do you think you are setting when you cannot even keep track of how many kilos of flour you use per week? What is even worse, I hear that you leave a lot of your duties to be looked after by that Vera."

"What? What do you mean?"

"I mean that I have heard alarming reports of what that girl has been up to in the kitchen and out of it on account of your negligence. I never trusted her; she seemed too much like a sewer rat: selfish and streetwise. I mean that you are incompetent and are doing a disservice to this place. If you, with all the opportunities you had, cannot run a damned kitchen, how do you expect women who were born with nothing to even begin to cope? I think you should make a serious effort to change. Things cannot go on as they are right now."

"I am sorry that you do not think my work is adequate. I am convinced that I have done my best. I have not been used to being the jack-of-all-trades, you know. I handle the catering, and someone takes care of the paperwork. I am doing my best. One cannot be everywhere at once."

"Your best is not enough. You have to try harder," said Prudentia.

"But I can't!" Miss Robinson wrung her hands and began to cry. "Why are you saying these things? Why do you hate me? I know you never liked me, don't deny it! You are always skulking about and spying on people and criticising everything. Try running my department and see how hard it is!"

"I don't see what is so hard about it. It's all a question of organisation and discipline. Especially self-discipline. Do you think we do not see girls amongst the lot that we like better than anyone else? But you go around with your favourites clinging happily to your skirts and you focus on them to the detriment of the others.

"If you are not ready to change, then I will be trying to run it, believe me. Look, this is very serious. We want clear commitment from you. What we would like to hear you say now is that you will try harder."

"I have done my best. I can do no better. What do you want from me?"

"Well, if that is the best you can do, then I am afraid we will have to find someone to do better. We cannot continue like this," said Martha.

"You are sending me away?"

"Yes." Martha looked at her squarely. "Since you refuse to acknowledge that there is a problem, I am afraid we have no choice."

The woman looked form one to the other, then suddenly rose and flounced to the door. She turned. She had dried her tears, and her mouth was a thin line between nose and chin.

"You are just like men! Always finding fault, finding fault. Can any of you do the work I do? You rush to occupy the moral high ground to preach to me from, as if you were better. I have heard things about you two that would make a porn star blush."

"That kind of scatological nonsense is unworthy of a member of this place," cut in Martha. "You have not made any proposals for improving the functioning of this place. We have enough problems from outside without people like you trying to wreck things from inside. I am afraid you will have to impress some other person with your skills. I myself am unmoved."

"Then you will certainly be hearing from me. You are such a disappointment. And you." She pointed at Prudentia. "Don't think you can roll your fat self all over me!" The door slammed.

They looked at each other.

"Why do people always bring up my weight?" They laughed together, a little nervously. They had hoped that every one of the staff would understand the need for change.

"Good. It is best this way. I expect her to go right to the Labour Court. But as she does not have a letter of dismissal, she cannot say that we sacked her unfairly or otherwise. We will sue back for dereliction of duty if she does not show up for work. In the meantime, who runs the kitchen? The new person you talked about?"

"Not for a while," Martha replied. "Things are a bit slow down there. You and I can handle it. The women are pretty competent on their own anyway. We'll give her time to make a fool of herself before we take on someone else. We don't want anyone saying that there was someone waiting in the wings to take her job."

"Good. That's settled. Can we eat? I'm so hungry, if they distributed my hunger to five cows they would all die immediately!"

As they were ending the meal, Hortense came in panting. She threw her weight into the free chair and mopped her face with a ragged tissue.

"News! But I will only tell if you give me a drink first."

When she had her drink, she said: "Good and bad news. The bad news is that a story has come out in the Correspondent with a lot of unflattering detail about our inner workings. The good news is that we got the mole."

"Who is it?" Martha and Prudence spoke in unison.

"Vera the kitchen rat."

"What!" shouted Martha.

"Oh, do calm down," said Prudentia. "Somehow I am not surprised. There was something about that girl. She was always where she ought not to be."

"But why? This place gave her everything. I thought when you mentioned her a while ago that you were referring to an exclusive friendship between her and Robinson."

"She wanted more. You know, there is a kind of person who cannot help taking, but who hates you for giving them what they want. They think they're smarter than you because they can make you give them things for nothing, since they themselves would never do that. That girl is like that. I think the poverty she lived through poisoned her outlook. People like her hate everyone who is better off than they are. They cannot accept the thought of being inferior to, or beholden to, anyone. They hate you for being something they think they would like to be. And they are never satisfied. I think she's like that. She will never be happy. Her whole life will be a perpetual battle to keep up with the Joneses long after the Joneses are dead and gone. Don't try to understand. It's just like that. It cannot be explained."

"But to go to the papers! So she was behind all this hue and cry."

"Ha! Wetin you done see? Wait until those people out there realise that you are not going to knuckle under, that you mean to fight back. Then you will see fire. This one is just gossip."

"Hortense, how did you find out?"

"Someone in the newspaper's offices. He's been after me for a while now and he hoped to get into my good books that way."

"What a rat!"

"*Alors*, what do we do?"

"Well, first of all, we amend our battle plans to take account of the defectors," said Martha. "And we hire a team of lawyers to take care of a possible libel suit and so on. We need a firm with an excellent reputation that charges the earth, you know, one of those well-known firms only the very rich or very bad can afford, to show that we mean business. Any ideas?"

231

"Ah!" said Hortense. "I can help you there. I compiled a list of firms we could use when the lawsuits began to pile up."

"How about Tarkang and Pritchard?" said Prudentia. "They have a reputation for tenacity and success. Their fees for one week could feed a large boarding school for one term. My nephew was a pupil there till he made a fool of himself and was asked to leave," said Prudentia.

"What'd he do?"

"Believe it or not, the young man felt that with his prospects, he could bed the wife of the one of the firm's senior partners. The lady was not amused, and informed her husband directly. He was lucky to have gotten off so lightly."

"Talk of vaulting ambition. We'll put out some feelers and see how it goes. Do you think they'll take us on? With all the notoriety of these past days. It would be embarrassing to ask and be refused. The news will be all about town in fifteen minutes, if I know men."

"No, they'll take us. I can guarantee you that," said Prue.

"Alright, so we go with Tarkang and whatever. Next thing is the replacements of the senior staff. I asked Gladys to take some time off and pull herself together. I expect she will be back with us soon. Anyone think otherwise, with reasons?"

Nobody did.

"Now, what is this business about Grace and a girl?"

"I hear on the very well-developed grapevine here that Grace has formed an attachment to Maggie. You remember her? That girl from the plantations who we thought might be retarded at first. She's made excellent progress. You wouldn't believe it if you saw her now. I think if we were a profit-making concern, she would be on our adverts."

"That's good, but what are the exact details of this attachment?"

"None, really," said Hortense. "You just hear that they spend a lot of time together. I think in the beginning Maggie followed Grace around like a puppy, and Grace did not object. Since she is such a grouch, any attachments she forms are bound to be noticed and talked about."

"That is not all," said Prudentia. "I think Grace buys Maggie things, and they spend most of their off hours in Grace's house. Something like that. You know we discourage too much closeness between the staff and the students because it might breed petty jealousies and stuff like that."

"Yes, but have there been any reports of fondling or public displays of affection?"

"Not that I know of," answered Prudentia. "But the rumours are pretty persistent. You remember how it was in school. In my dormitory, there were two form five girls whom we called lesbies because they spent all their time together, went to church together, ate together, and since they were senior students, could bend the rules far enough to share the same bed. No one actually saw anything, but the rumours were there."

"Then we should ignore them, if they are just rumours. We do not run this place on the basis of hearsay."

"Martha, I cannot agree with you there. We have to consider the context in which we operate. This society has no use for what it considers to be deviant behaviour, especially of a sexual type. And we have enough trouble as it is. I think Grace should go."

"I will send no one away on the basis of rumour! I mean, what should it matter what people do together as long as they do not hurt anyone? And we, considering our mission, should be especially tolerant of 'deviants', to use an odious term, because we are all deviants of a sort. I do not understand what homosexuality is all about, for example. I am, as you must know, quite desperately heterosexual. But the very fact that I do not understand homosexuality means that I should be careful in my response to it. How can I condemn something that I do not even begin to understand?

"Let's not forget that it is this same attitude that has placed women in the quandary that they face now. It is because people will not accept them for what they are. It is because people are always trying to fit them into uncomfortable moulds. So if we, who claim to want to liberate them, are behaving like their jailers, then what future do they have?"

"Let's not get things mixed up. Martha, you got your head too high up in the clouds! People have barely begun to accept the fact that you are good for anything but housework and childbearing, and you want to be a public lesbian? I think if we let this go, it would do us untold damage. And not only from the men. The women are even more conservative in such matters. That is indeed part of the overall problem, as you may have noticed. Their reputations hinge on the degree to which they conceal or express their sexuality, so they are very careful to keep it under wraps, and very critical of people who do not. What do you think they will say of someone who not only broadcasts her sexuality, but is rash enough not to do things like everyone else? Let's not lose sight of the fact that this is Africa oh! We're still behind on many issues. Overt sexuality is one of them."

She laughed suddenly.

"Ah-ah! I know women who would faint if you suggested that there was any way to make love other than with the man on top! Do you know that while you are agonising over your stretch marks, to some tribes it is a sign of beauty? You may not get a husband if you cannot show some stretch marks. It is a sign of fertility to them."

"Yes, that's true," said Hortense, who had kept quiet, wisely letting the elephants fight. "My mother told me that when they were growing up, if you did not have stretch marks, you had difficulty finding a husband. And slim women were frowned upon, so people were sent to fattening courses prior to marriage. Fat was a sign of beauty."

"Talk of the tyranny of beauty. Be thin, be fat, perm your hair, do not perm your hair. Wear wigs, do not wear wigs. Ah-ah!

"Anyway, to return to Grace, I still think we should let her express her sexuality in the way she sees fit. However, we have to find out if the girl is a minor, or was when she came here. We also have to ask Grace to be more discreet about it. And we have to find out if homosexuality is against the law in this country. God knows what that little reptile in the kitchen told the papers." As Prudentia made to speak: "No, I understand the merits of prudence. But if you want to eat a toad, eat a fat and juicy one. If they're going to call you names just because you want to do something slightly different, then you might as well have a fulfilling sex life, however different. We will stand by our women, whatever they are, as long as they stand by us. This may all be a storm in a teacup, besides. Nothing may have happened. Let's not condemn people before we know the facts. You go on a fishing expedition and tell me what you catch. Let's move on, the day is almost over.

'Hortense, you contact those lawyers tomorrow and ask for a meeting. We must go on the offensive. That carpenter woman who got slashed, did she see who did it?"

"There were several men and it was dark, but her ex-husband has been going around boasting about what he does to people who do not stay in their place."

"Good. Then we can start there. We'll sue him to hell and back. We have to make people know that we will stand by our own. And Vera. What do we do about her? As I see it, we can do little or nothing. She's too small for me to have a grand battle with her. It would look petty and vindictive. However, we can sue the newspaper for libel.

"Another thing we need to do is retain a firm of private investigators. We'll be needing them for our lawsuits. I know someone who can handle that. Hortense, remind me to give you the number so you can call them and set up an appointment for tomorrow. I think the lawyers should be called tonight, so that we see them first thing tomorrow. Hortense, note that. What next? Yes. Prudentia, you will see to the other members of staff, won't you? The instructors and all that. Rap some knuckles and then later we will organise a general staff meeting and lay down the new line of conduct. Anyone who does not like it can leave.

"Awwwright! Any other business? None? Okay Hortense, take down the number of the private dicks." They all laughed.

"Now, you people get your fat waists out of here, I need to rest."

37

The Courthouse was a medley of unkempt colonial buildings and post-colonial utilitarian tack-ons, a rabbit warren of office cubicles and courtrooms. The courtroom furniture was old, the varnish on the heavy seats cracked and peeling like the skin of a peasant who has stayed too close to the fire for too long.

Martha, Prudentia and Hortense sat in the car and waited for ten o'clock, when the case of Veronica Kumbong versus the Women's House would be called. More likely than not, the system, clogged up with ancient files and corrupt officials, would seize up again and refuse to move, as it had done several times before.

Today, they were lucky. At ten past the hour, the court clerk Prudentia had befriended pulled back his dirty brown curtain and signalled that the machine had been oiled and would move again, slow, cumbersome, to a conclusion often having little to do with the rule of law.

The three women got out of the car and went towards the courtroom. Just outside it, standing around in hostile clumps, one at each end of the long, narrow corridor, and murmuring amongst themselves, were the lawyers for both parties. Martha's camp was headed by Tarkang of Tarkang and Pritchard, with a gaggle of young lawyers in pinstriped suits carrying files and briefcases, trying to look important and only succeeding in looking young and bewildered. Pritchard, it was to be assumed, had stayed behind to look after the office.

Tarkang saw them and came forward, hand outstretched in greeting. He was a short, wide man, light-skinned, with a great dome of a forehead, shrewd, twinkling eyes and tiny hands and feet. His hair, what little there was of it, clung in iron-grey desperation, like the futile determination of a feeble, once-vigorous old man, to the edges of his rolled-fat nape, leaving the rest of his head shiny with oil and good living. His considerable girth was encased in a three-piece dark blue pinstripe, his huge gut taut, his oxfords smooth and shiny. He looked like a happy, ruthless shark.

"Miss Elive! Mrs. Ngallah. Good morning. How are you today?" He nodded at Hortense. "Hello Miss."

"Alright, I suppose. We seem to be about to make some progress. What's the situation?"

"We are going in a few minutes from now. I expect that after the preliminaries, there will be some minor skirmishing, but we'll make mincemeat of them, not to worry. It will be easy to prove that this is a case of a vindictive ex-pupil, or is she a student? No one will understand why she decided to bite the hand that fed her with such ferocity, and with no provocation whatsoever. Trust me; she will be out on her rear end before the day is out."

"I say, what exactly is she complaining about? I hear something about wrongful dismissal, but I don't get it. Why is she suing us at all? She is the one who left, you know."

"Yes, I am aware of that. I have discussed the facts in great detail with your two lovely staff members. He beamed beatifically at Hortense and Prudentia. "She does not have a case. I think someone is egging her on for his or her own reasons." He patted Martha on the arm. "Not to worry, my dear. All will be fine."

The two camps filed into the courtroom and waited, rearranging papers and muting coughs, feet scraping on the bare cement floor, for the magistrate to deign to grace the courtroom with his presence. He came in five minutes later, to general shuffling and scraping of furniture and the prolonged, lackadaisical yelp of the clerk: "Couuuuuurt!"

Everyone sat down and the opposing camp took the floor after the preliminaries. Vera was there in one of the simple, feminine frocks she affected since coming to the centre. She was sitting behind her lawyers, two seedy-looking men in brown suits.

The head of her team made his opening statement. He was a tall, shabby man of medium build, with a greyish complexion and a straggly beard. His language, in view of his appearance, was surprisingly good.

"You see before you a young girl of modest origin, naïve, impressionable, full of the girlish dreams of self–improvement and quite probably a happy, wholesome romance culminating in a suitable marriage. A good student at school, with good A levels, but the daughter of a yardman who cannot send his daughter on to university, even though she is more than qualified. Left to her own devices, as it were, the young girl, staring unemployment and a life of underachievement in a small town in the face, thirsting for knowledge, wanting to be free of the fetters of her social origin, hears an announcement on the radio. Come, it says. Come to the Women's House, where we will give you a reason to go on living, where we will give you self-respect and the ability to get a job. Come and get education and self-fulfilment. Come and be *better*.

"Which young girl with aspirations can resist that call, that call of the siren? What experience does she have of temptation, that she should know enough to stop her ears like Ulysses, against the call of certain perdition, to seal her lips against the poisonous nectar of mortal turpitude? None, ladies and gentlemen, none. What defence does she have against the insidious call of vice? None, my dear ladies and gentlemen, for she has no experience of these matters. She is easy prey for the hawkish, irresponsible, half-baked feminism of people who find it easier to destroy than to build, who spit and tear at the established social fabric, who shred the fabric rather than find the needles to darn it for the future of our society, nay, for the future of our whole nation.

"And so our young innocent falls among the harpies, their predatory instincts cloaked in the cloying candy of imported, irrelevant psychobabble, which flings the responsibility for personal failure on an undeserving society, providing easy excuses for those who cannot and will not work within the well-established, tried-and-tested, balanced and dynamic framework we have painstakingly developed throughout the ages of our not-insignificant history.

"Daniel in the lion's den, you might say, and ask why her God did not deliver her from the clutches of evil. We reply, dear ladies and gentlemen, that her God has sent her deliverance. That is what we have come to seek in this court, ladies and gents: we have come to deliver Vera Kumbong from the clutches of the lionesses, which as you know are far deadlier in their hunting instincts than their male counterparts. They will fight and claw, but, ladies and gentlemen, we will win because we fight the good fight. The bells toll in the school and churchyard, in our very *hearts*, calling all of society to join us in this eternal struggle against evil.

"We have come here, cap in hand, to humbly ask three things of you.

"First, that you deliver Vera Kumbong from the clutches of the evil genius, the Rasputin of our time, armed with money and resources, who flicks her forked tongue at our children and makes them forget their lessons.

"Second, that you make it impossible for this evil apostle of a material god to draw more unwary women into her clutches.

"Third and last, that you grant redress and reparation for moral and psychological damages inflicted on the person of Vera Kumbong in such amounts as to nip in the bud any such attempts by equally misguided citizens to destroy our society.

"We will bring to this courtroom unimpeachable witnesses, former disciples of evil who have recanted, the victims whose families have been sundered forever, and the workers, those drones who have broken their backs under the inclement elements to keep the evil bastion running, and for peanuts, as the Americans say.

"At the risk of repeating ourselves, we say that this fight is the good fight; I call on this court to help this poor girl root out and destroy the canker that threatens the future of our society and the world as we know it."

He sat down, pale, sweating, and not at all smug; Tarkang was a formidable adversary.

Tarkang got up and sauntered to the front of the court. He did not look in the least perturbed by the prosecution's outburst. He looked like a benevolent hippopotamus that had just had a satisfying meal and was looking forward to a little post-prandial wallow in the shallows before going on to take his siesta.

"Ladies and gentlemen of the court. My colleague on the other bench is learned. His education is well rooted in the classics; he speaks with the passion of the recent convert. From what he has said, I might just pack up and leave and never come near a courtroom for the rest of my life, for if I speak here, I should be defending a cause that goes against the tenets of decency inculcated in me from birth.

"But I will not pack up and leave, and I am going to tell you why." He smiled. "I may not be infused with the fiery fervour of my friend, to borrow his style, but what you need is the truth. As an old proverb says, evil shouts, and good whispers.

"The young lady who has come here today to bite the hand that fed her for over two years may just be a poor misguided soul, a mere puppet in the hands of certain vested interests, persuaded to speak against her mentor in exchange for nebulous promises of pecuniary or other reward.

"That is true, but that is only a small part of the matter. As far as matters go, the heart of this one is that a grasping, never-satisfied woman wishes to reap where she has not sown, a thief in the night who slinks and slithers, serpent-like, to undo what others have sweated to achieve, not for any particular end, but because she is the mind of evil.

"This young person here is of very humble origin, as you have heard. With his strident penchant for absolutes, my friend on the other side has painted her as a saint in the making, who has gone to the brink of the abyss and come back pure. She has done her forty days in the desert, and she has resisted the devil. How charmingly Christ-like! See her sitting there, demure and well bred." He chuckled in disbelief.

"However, that veneer was not acquired at home. Those clothes were not bought by her parents. The money in her pocket was not earned by her father. Such as she is, ladies and gentlemen, my client *made* her.

"So, you might ask, if my client did so much for her, then why has she turned? Ask yourself this: where did such a chaste, retiring little darling get the money and the courage to attack her benefactor? It is not logical.

"You are perfectly right. It is not logical. Something, to borrow my learned colleague's elegant, if slightly overwrought style, is rotten in the kingdom of Denmark. We are here to expose the rot. We will not dwell on the matter, because our evidence will speak for itself.

"My colleague has made much of the danger posed to the society by my client's institution as if the whole world were ready to chase out a few twisted aberrants, who are hanging out on a limb, ready to be flicked off and dropped into the eternal abyss where the ungodly pay their dues. Such neo-Miltonian visions have their value, of course. They belong to entertainment of rather questionable taste. I believe we should leave them there.

"I shall not take up more of the valuable time of this court. I do not claim that my client is perfect. Perfection, as many of us have discovered time and again to our chagrin, is not the lot of humanity. The evidence will speak for itself. Thank you."

The magistrate called a recess then and lumbered out of the courtroom.

Outside in the pale rainy-season sunlight, Vera's team shook hands with each other in self-righteous optimism, convinced that they had the public, which was the real judge anyway, on their sides. They could not, however, restrain a certain incipient quaking at the knees. The head of the team had tangled with Tarkang before, and he knew that nothing was beyond him. The actual client was not this half-baked slip of a girl, whom he did not like anyway; there was money coming in from somewhere, and the people providing it had asked him to spare no effort. He would spare none.

At the other end of the parking lot, Martha and her team got into their cars. She was riding in the Land Cruiser with Hortense and Prudentia.

"You will not be required to be present this afternoon unless you enjoy the kind of entertainment we provide. On the other hand, perhaps you should come along if you have time. It will give you a foretaste of the coming days, and that cannot hurt."

After that, they talked about other aspects of the case. They dropped him off at his offices. When he left, Martha said:

"Don't you think he was a little...subdued? I mean in court. The other guy was so fervent, so convincing. You could really see that he meant what he was saying."

"Ah-ah! Don't mind the courtroom theatricals. The judge has seen quite a few in his time and he won't be impressed. It's a lucky thing we got one of the straightforward ones. The guy is close to retirement anyway, in addition to his good record. He will make his determination based solely on the facts, believe me. Rest easy. Things will be okay. It means more negative publicity, but it will also give us a chance to show our mettle. People will be less eager to take us on if they lose. And they will, never fear."

"Hortense, who do you think they will be calling as witnesses? What did those detective people say?"

"From what they tell me, it would appear that the little kewpie doll in the kitchen would be present. As we expected, she has already sued us for wrongful dismissal in the labour court. The labour inspector who was supposed to seek an amicable settlement is so biased in her favour that he sent the matter directly to the court. We need to appear there early next week. Rumour has it that she's bankrolling this case as well."

"Who would have thought that that little idiot would find it in her to oppose me? I give her a job and a worthy cause and she turns around and spits in my face. Hortense, what results from the British end of the investigation?"

"Rumours of unseemly behaviour in Soho. We shall know how useful that will be in a few hours. The detective tells me there's someone who is being flown out here to provide details of her past."

"Have him liaise with the lawyer and see that the potential witness is placed on the witness list as soon as possible. Who's he, by the way?"

"The lawyers already know. In fact, they are expecting him. He is a very angry former boyfriend, who also has proof of kewpie's arrest whilst in the possession of psychotropic substances, etc. It will demolish her. As for the other two witnesses they are planning to call, one is Alice's mother-in-law."

"Yes," laughed Prudence. "That one. Tarkang will kill her. What language do you think he will cross-examine her in?"

"Probably a form of particularly insinuating Pidgin English that only he knows. All we need is Alice on the stand, and no crying or faltering – Prue you'll have to speak to her about that. Explain to her that much more that her shitty little marriage is in the balance here."

"One pep talk coming up!" sang Prudentia, and they all laughed again.

"No, she won't be a problem, I don't think so. The most unbelievable one is that gateman. That one is totally out of the blue. I wonder what he means to say."

"Ah! What can he say? He was not even allowed to come up into the premises; how could he have anything to say?"

"I suppose someone showed him a few bank notes and his pupils changed to dollar signs like in the cartoons. I suspect he will be peddling a lot of rumours."

"Rumours are not evidence," said Martha. "I hope this team really works for the high fees I'm paying them. If not…what do we have on the little rat herself?"

"I think Tarkang will capitalise on the fact that the kewpie doll will be demolished, and Vera herself does not appear to have found a character witness. She does not seem to have been terribly popular, poor neglected dear," finished Prudentia. "I don't see how we can possibly lose."

They came back to court two hours later. The weather had given up trying to be nice and the sky was sulking, ready to weep.

Tarkang was there, urbane as ever. He had good news for them.

"Let me introduce someone to you." He led Martha by the hand to his brood. There was a youngish-looking white man, mid-twenties with a hank of chestnut hair tied back in a ponytail, and a suit jacket over a tee shirt and jeans. He was not unattractive and Martha could understand kewpie doll being attracted to his robust, wide-shouldered, youthful charm. The court would understand too. So would public opinion.

She smiled at him and he smiled back. She pulled Tarkang to one side. "Have you briefed him?"

'Of course, dear lady, of course. But he will not be taking the stand today. In fact, I brought him here just to meet you. We will indicate to the court that we will be putting in for a couple of other witnesses, but we shall try not to reveal any details. We want it to come like a bombshell."

"So what is his story?"

"The dear old *détournement de mineur* thing. She met the youngster in a club, she introduced him to drink, drugs, she left him to them, and he climbed out of the hellhole himself. He went to rehab, now he has a decent job as a photographer's assistant.

"The young hunk is all of twenty-two. The excellent Miss Robertson is…what? Thirty-four? Thirty-five? So, five years ago, she was thirty or thirty-one and he was all of seventeen. Now, the age of consent is sixteen here and in any case, girls marry at thirteen in some places. But the men won't like it; they won't like it at all. Sleeping with a guy more than ten years your junior! Their prejudices will work for us this time. I never thought I'd live to bless them, but there you are. This afternoon, I absolutely love prejudices!" He waggled his fingers at her and smiled drolly.

Martha laughed back. The young man was spirited away in the Land Cruiser to a seaside hotel where he would have endless glasses of fruit juice and warm himself in the sun, if it bothered to come out in this season. His clean good looks would be a real boon.

"So who's on first this afternoon?"

"The inimitable mother-in-law of one of your charges, it would seem. Come to claim that you are a despicable wife-snatcher and you ought to rot in hell. Wants the daughter-in-law back on the rack, I shouldn't wonder. Ah, there she comes. I think I'd better go and get my act together. We start in fifteen minutes. One of the other lawyers will come and see you about preparing your testimony. Wouldn't do for me to hog the limelight, you know. See you in a while."

He left, walking quickly without seeming to do so.

244

Martha went back to Prudentia and Hortense and told them the news. Prudentia punched the air with a fat fist. "Yes! We've got them over a barrel." She hummed the first few lines of a requiem mass.

"Don't get excited. Wait till the whole thing's over before you celebrate."

Nevertheless, Martha herself was feeling buoyant. All seemed to be going rather well. They would make mincemeat of the other case in the labour court, then she would hit the headlines with her crushing of the carpenter's husband, and nothing else would ever touch her.

One of the young besuited men who hung around Tarkang like a cloud of flies, one of them came over to her.

"Good afternoon Madam. My name is Henry Eyong and I am to help you prepare your testimony for this case." Martha barely looked at him. Her mind was on other things.

"Of course. When do you think we should start?"

"As soon as can possibly be managed."

"I can spare you a couple of hours this evening, but I shall be looking up some people later. Between five and seven, perhaps? You may come to my hotel. I have a suite where we can meet."

They separated, he to his envious colleagues, who would have given a limb to be the one to prepare the controversial woman, and she to her friends. They walked into the courtroom together.

38

The stern-faced old woman had bought a new outfit for this court appearance. She looked out at the sea of faces, all waiting to hear what she would say. As anticipated, she knew little and cared less for court procedure. Both lawyers spoke to her in Pidgin English.

The oath was explained to her and she took it firmly, unequivocally. The prosecution had brought her to prove the moral-turpitude-destroyer-of-the-status-quo of the Women`s House.

"Mammy your name is Ernestine Tumanjong?"

"Yes."

"And you have a son called Herbert Tumanjong who married a woman called Alice Makia?"

"Yes."

"Where is your daughter-in-law now?"

"Them done fool 'am, I done run house pass two year now."

"Who fool 'am?"

The woman replied proudly, exactly as she had been coached: "That Women's House for Douala!"

"Have you tried to bring back your daughter-in-law?"

"Yes. I went there but a fat woman refused to let me see her."

"Why do you want her to come back?"

"Because her husband needs her. She left behind two small children. Two boys. They need her to look after them."

There was a swell of murmurs and a shuffling of feet. The judge banged his gavel once. Vera's lawyer could not resist a smirk at the defence.

"No further questions."

Tarkang rose languidly, taking his time. He strolled over to the witness box like a man out for his afternoon constitutional.

"Mammy Ernestine. Where do you live?"

"With my son, of course, where else do you think I should live? Someone has to take care of the children." The lawyer man had told her that a bad man working for the enemy would try to confuse her and make her tell lies when she did not mean to. She was going to show him who was who.

"So you live with your son," said Tarkang musingly. "Did you come to live there after his wife left or were you there before he got married?" He smiled kindly at the woman.

"I went to live there when I discovered that she was a bad wife."

"Bad wife? What did she do?"

"She did not know how to look after my son. She did not cook well, the house was always dirty, and she had bad blood and kept miscarrying."

Against her lawyer's advice, she went on. He had told her to answer only the questions that he or the other man would put to her, and not to volunteer any facts, but here was her chance to speak out and let the truth be known.

"She was a bad wife! I told my son never to marry a woman from that tribe, but she had seduced him and his body was hot for her."

"Did you try to tell her to change?"

"What did I not do? I spoke, I scolded, I advised many, many times. She tried to say bad things about me to my son and he beat her, but she refused to change."

By this time, the audience was rumbling its amusement, and the prosecution were holding their heads in their hands, praying for it to stop.

"So she was a bad wife?"

"Yes."

"If she was not a good wife for your son, why do you want her back? Why not let him marry another wife who will bring up his children for him?"

"Why should she go away like that? Who is she to run away? Now I hear that she is living well, she has money. She should pay back the money my son spent on her."

Tarkang turned and faced the courtroom. "This is strongly evocative of sturdy apron strings which refuse to let go. No further questions."

247

Mammy Ernestine left the witness box head high, unaware of the extent of the damage she had caused.

"Prosecution, call your next witness."

"You were employed at the centre as head of the catering department?"

"Yes."

"Why did you leave?"

"I did not leave; I was thrown out by the founder of the place and her lieutenant."

"How come? Were they not satisfied with your work?"

"On the contrary. My file will reveal no queries or disciplinary action. I started the department from scratch and made a name for it all over the country.

"I was thrown out because of the morally reprehensible policies of the Women's House, against which I spoke out repeatedly in our departmental meetings."

"When you talk of morally reprehensible policies, what do you refer to?"

"Mainly to the obsession with money that characterises all dealings within the establishment, but also to more intimate practices. There have been reports of unnatural sexual practices."

"Such as?"

"Lesbianism. There has also been widespread fornication between the female members of staff and the male manual employees."

The court was in uproar. The prosecution, feeling that its case had been adequately proven, signified to the judge that it had no further questions.

The embattled judge announced a five-minute recess. The defence was relaxed, even jovial, to the puzzlement of the prosecution, which felt it had dealt a deathblow to their case.

When the proceedings resumed, the defence went to cross-examine Miss Robinson.

"Miss Robinson, you claim that you were thrown out of the centre. Do you have any document attesting to your dismissal, wrongful or otherwise?

"No. That is to say - "

"Is it not true, Miss Robertson, that you were called to a meeting with the founder to discuss your management of the catering budget, and that you refused to recognise the fact that much of the funding for your department had not been used for the purpose for which it was intended?"

"I went to a meeting where I was threatened and browbeaten, I had to stand up for my rights."

"Do you recognise that there is a huge deficit in your department that you are unable to explain? A deficit that makes you liable to criminal proceedings should the centre decide to pursue the matter?"

"There is no proof to support any such allegations!"

"I am afraid there is, Miss Robinson. All sums disbursed are done so based on documents countersigned by yourself. You are in very hot water, Madam. Is it not true, then, that after flouncing out of the house, you have decided to throw, as it were, a spanner in their works, and get your revenge? Is it not true, Madam, that you have encouraged the young lady, Vera Kumbong, to bring this dastardly case against the centre, which has done wonders to improve the lot of countless women?

"Is it not true", roared Tarkang, now a raging lion, "that in your incompetence you have cost many women a chance to improve their lot?"

Then his voice dropped, soft and feline: "Miss Robinson," (who was now thoroughly frightened) "the moral turpitude you refer to. Is it not true that you yourself have been guilty arrested and fined, for possession of ecstasy in the past?"

"No! it's all a lie, lies! I - "

"Miss Robinson, should that be required by this court, we will provide the proof." He explained what proof he had, and asked whether the witness denied the facts. She sobbed into her lace handkerchief and refused to answer. The audience murmured.

"I have no further questions."

The judge banged his gavel. "Mr Tarkang. I am minded to hold you in contempt of court. This court is not a rehearsal ground for amateur theatricals."

"I stand corrected," said Barrister Samuel Tarkang, humbly. But he was not worried. The old judge was either on their side or he was genuinely interested in hearing the defence, otherwise he would have banged the gavel a lot earlier.

The witness left the stand in tears, looking pretty and helpless, but totally discredited. They might not need the testimony of the young Englishman after all, but there was no such thing as overkill in defence.

"Does the prosecution wish to call any more witnesses?"

"Yes my Lord."

The gateman came in looking apprehensive. He had a lot to lose. His job was already gone, of course. He had been promised a new position as head of security with the new catering firm that Miss Robinson was going to set up. But he had seen Miss Robinson come out in tears a while earlier, and he was not reassured. She had not even seemed to see him.

He was a university dropout who had found a job with the new security companies that sprung up in the wake of the explosion of crime and the inability of the police to deal with it. He had left his old job for the centre because it paid more, and he had living quarters to boot. He had been in love with Miss Robinson; her pert, girlish beauty made him feel protective.

He immediately felt less protective when the defence set about him. He ended up admitting that he had been promised a job with Miss Robinson after he left the centre. All his evidence was based on rumours. Sensing that he was in deep water, he vehemently denied having made any improper advances to, or entertaining a sexual relationship with any member of the centre's staff. The prosecution, which had been banking on its ability to suggest that certain better-off women of the centre had bought this young man's sexual favours, were hard put to it to explain his presence on the stand.

The old judge adjourned for the day and asked the defence to prepare its witnesses for the following day.

Martha and the women left the courthouse. Outside, the parking lot was now full of women who had been in the centre for some time and had now found employment elsewhere, as well as onlookers and the usual buzzards waiting for the kill. The media people were there as well, crowding around her in a gaggle and mobbing her with questions. Tarkang had asked her not to answer any questions until the end of the trial.

250

She and her team went out to their cars, heads high, and drove away.

★ ★ ★

Back at the hotel, she rested for an hour and then the reception called her to announce the young lawyer who was to help her with the defence. Tarkang himself was busy with the young Englishman, who would prove a more damaging witness. He'd said:

"Dear lady, I do not expect that you will have any problems. The case is all but won and I have confidence in my young associate. You just focus on producing a convincing manifesto and I'll do the rest."

The young lawyer, as she chose to think of him, was not as young as she had initially thought.

He came, she thought, in with the half defiant, half embarrassed air that men adopt in the presence of a woman who is richer than they are. He would not look at her. While he was fussily taking papers out of his briefcase, Martha studied him. He seemed to be about her age. He had the sort of dusty complexion that made you feel that he was unacquainted with body lotion, and did not care. He made her feel like pushing him into the shower and giving him a good scrub. He was fairly tall, and quite slim. Martha could see that his shirt collar was too big for his rather thin neck.

He had soft, thin hands with damp fingers and pale, rounded nails. He took out his papers nervously, not looking at her. She asked him if he would like a drink and he answered curtly: "No." Then he seemed to realise that he had been rude and he added grudgingly: "Thank you. I had one just before I came and I need to keep a clear head."

They went through the questions. He was good, and safely ensconced in the humdrum of his craft, he gained confidence in himself and relaxed. He began to look at her as he spoke. He even forgot himself and smiled a couple of times.

At the end of the discussion, he even permitted himself the luxury of summing it up.

"I think we've just about covered it. I do not foresee any surprises. The prosecution is not that good."

251

"Who will be leading me through the minefield, then?"

"That is for Mr. Tarkang to decide." But his tone and expression left her in no doubt that he hoped he would do it.

It was time for him to leave, but he shuffled his papers and shifted about on his seat. He did not get up.

Martha was amused. He had breached the first barrier, and now to him she was just another woman his age. She thought, with some bitterness, that if she had been a man, he would not have relaxed quite so quickly. But she had come to admit to herself that painful as it was, a woman, however exalted, would only ever be a woman to many men. Her femininity overshadowed any other qualities. The young lawyer had solved the problem of his awe by reducing her to the common denominator of sexuality, the universal solvent for all women, great and small. She could see his mind working, his covert glance at her legs, his awareness of her as a sexual being and not as his temporary employer. She had had a long day and this was not time for playing games. She put him in his place.

"If you have finished packing your stuff, then I am afraid I must ask you to leave. I have prior commitments that will not wait." She stood up and stared him down. He stood up too, mumbled a greeting and left.

She went to the bathroom to freshen up. To hell with him.

It was time to see her parents.

39

She had not seen them since the great debacle more than three years ago. Their contact had been limited to those painful, half guilty, accusatory phone calls. She wondered how it would be this time. She had called the day before to tell her mother that the trial was beginning and that she would be coming to the house in the evening. That had evinced a counterfeit enthusiasm. Mammy had come to terms with her daughter's refusal to be like other women, aided by the generous injections of money into her life. But she still did not understand what the girl was about.

In the meantime, money had blunted the edges of her parent's prejudices, making them condone without approving.

It was dark when she arrived.

The weather was the same as on that misty evening three years ago, when she had returned full of dreams, naiveté and determination.

They received her like an old couple welcoming a niece they did not know too well, who bewildered them, and whom they hoped would not stay too long. They smiled and nodded at all her city-girl attitudes, as if they were saying to themselves: thank God she's not our daughter, our flesh and blood, the fruit of our common loom, fashioned by us.

But she was theirs. They had listened with shy pride and ineffectual indignation as their friends either burnished her reputation or shredded it to bits. With the money had come a certain standing. Her father had resisted her mother's best efforts to convince him to build a bigger house with the money their daughter gave them. They lived in their old house, their ancient velvets and antimacassars replaced by rich-smelling leather, it is true, and they no longer bought cheap milk in plastic bags. Mama had tons of Indian wraps from Saudi Arabia and beyond, and had become a force in the Christian women's groups. Papa had bought a car and hired a driver - not Ngalle; his family had taken badly the fact that the new wealth was not more equitably distributed, and spread rumours of his daughter selling her soul in some unspeakable black magic ritual involving naked white women to get her money. That was why she would never marry, they said.

So she sat in their new dark brown leather chairs, with new, expensive lace stool covers and backrests. Conversation being tedious, her father turned on the TV.

"Let's see what they are saying about you on the news."

They could see her arriving at the courthouse with her posse of lawyers, and the shabby-looking opposition. Her mother offered the only sort of comfort she could give: "Look at that girl's lawyer: such an ugly man." Her father shushed her and leaned forward. They watched the news in silence. As such reports go, it was fairly balanced.

"What does that Kumbong girl really want?" asked her father.

"I do not think she herself really knows. I think it was just a plan to get some money; you know, sell the story of scandal and hit back at me. She is the sort of person who cannot stand people whom she feels are better than she is. They bring out the worst in her."

"I hear her father is a yardman up at the station."

"But you will win, won't you? You have more money," said her mother.

"The questions are more complex. The thing is that some people do not like the sort of work that I do. They think that I am turning women against them, making them headstrong. And they are trying to prove that I am a bad woman who teaches women to do bad things."

There was silence. She could feel them thinking that this view was not entirely unjustified.

She would never get through to them. She remembered the novel written by that British homosexual woman, Radclyffe Hall, and the relationship between Stephen, the protagonist, and her mother. One part of her understood their quandary. It was painful, but in a way, it was not their fault. If they crossed over onto her side, they too would be beyond the pale. This way, they could hide behind parental impotence: "Children these days, you know...you cannot control them." They were not equipped to withstand the juggernaut of accepted behaviour.

Another part of her was less charitable. They were content to spend the money that they had not earned, but they did not want to protect its source. But they would have to show more support now. She needed them to stand by her publicly. It would go a long way towards convincing the local population about the simple common sense behind her new set of projects.

She plunged right in.

"I have come to see you to ask for your help. I want to get involved in some community projects. You know, dispensaries, arts and crafts centres, building village meeting halls, that sort of thing. You have many influential friends in the church and your tribal meetings, I am sure that if you speak to them, they will listen to you. After all, you have become quite prominent. I would like to start a few pilot projects in this province, and then I will extend to other places."

The unspoken message hung in the air between them: I have bought you influence and social status with my money; now you have to pay back.

"What do you want of us?" The *this time* part of the question was not spoken, but it hovered over them, flapping apprehensive wings.

"I will send one of my women to come and help you organise meetings first within the neighbourhood groups, then within tribal groupings, then the churches, and so on. Each group will make proposals for projects, and then feasibility studies will be carried out. After that, the projects will be implemented.

"We realise that many of the problems we have faced are because men and the older parts of the population feel left out. They fear that if we take away their young women, then the continuity of their lives, as they know it, will be broken. They are afraid of change because they do not know what it will bring. So we have to show them that such change as we bring will benefit everyone." She waited. After a long pause, her father said:

"*M-hum*. So when will all this begin?"

255

"After the case. It is almost certain that we will win. The victory will help to put our message across. People love to be associated with winners, as you must know."

Mr Elive thought of a story he had read long ago in his schooldays. The bottle imp, it was called. It was the story of a man who had been given a magic bottle with an evil imp that made his life miserable until he could pass it on to someone else. This daughter of his was like the bottle imp, and he could not pass her on to anyone else. The time had come to pay, then. He would try.

40

She was early for court next morning. The mountain mist still clung to the far corners of building, like an unwelcome relative from the village skulking about the house. There were few people around yet. A few court functionaries prepared for the early cases with the permanently sour looks of people who were convinced that they were worth more than they were being paid. A couple of diehard photographers lounged against the wall. Waiting in her car, she saw Vera and her lawyers huddled in a corner of the parking lot. Bunch of losers. They did not even have a car, and had come to court in a rickety old communal taxi.

Suddenly, Martha was filled with anger. That girl could not be allowed to belittle all she had done just for a few francs. She thought of what it had cost her. She thought of her love, now married to someone else because of what she had chosen to do with her time and money. She was going to put on a public show. She would speak to the girl; make her express her grievances without the restrictions of court procedure and show that they did not exist. She wanted to expose the girl herself; she wanted to humiliate her. It was easy to say that she was one of those perpetually resentful beings who would never find satisfaction except at the expense of someone else and leave it at that, but what would ordinary people understand of such reasoning? She had to humiliate Vera.

She climbed out of the car, heart thudding, and walked towards them. The sidekick lawyer saw her approaching and pushed with his knuckles at the arm of his senior partner, whose back was to Martha. Vera looked up and their eyes met. Martha walked up to them.

"Good morning. Vera, I'd like to speak to you for a minute, if I may."

"You don't have to speak to her," said the senior partner. "As your lawyer I would advise you to…"

"No, wait. I will speak to her. There is no problem. She cannot do anything to me."

"I just want to know why." Martha looked directly into her eyes, hoping for a little shame. All she saw was unreasoning hate.

"We took you in, we looked after you, and everyone was good to you. Why do you want to destroy something that could help a lot of people? Why? Let's not hide behind lawyers. Tell me now why you are spreading these lies."

"I am not lying. Let me tell you, you bitch. You come here with your money and all, and you think you can buy people. You want to perform experiments on poor women who do not even know what you are doing to them. What do you put in their food, eh? You want people to think that you are good. You want be the bringer of light. Let me tell you, you are just like one of us! What have you got that I haven't got? Do you have two heads? Do you shit cake? Filth! Don't you menstruate? What right have you got to tell people what to do? Walking about acting as if you were our God." she mimicked Martha walk, speaking now to herself. "I don't believe a word of that nonsense you people were preaching in there."

"But you ate the food I bought with my money. You slept in my bed. You washed with my water. Why did you come there if you hated the place so much?"

"A fool and his money are soon parted, as even you must know. If you are stupid enough to give away your money, why should wise people not take it? You think those girls in there are there because they want to change? It is a place for free meals and no housework. Your stupid ideas do not concern them in the least. All they want is a place to be at peace for a while before they go on with life." She looked Martha up and down in contempt. "Don't think that you are any better than those girls because you have money and they don't. There is no part of your body that we do not have. There is nothing you are that we cannot be. You are just like us, so don't come all over moral with me. I know what you have between your skinny legs." She gave her one last look and turned away, dismissing her.

The two photographers had been roused by the commotion and were snapping away furiously. The court

258

people were watching avidly, open-mouthed. Martha took stock in a split second. She had banked on the girl being unable to face up to her, but the little serpent had gumption. A screaming match was not exactly dignified, but sometimes you had to get down into the muck to deliver a calf. She reached out and pulled Vera around to face her.

"Look at me and listen to what I say. If you resent me because I have been able to rise above mere bodily functions to fulfil my dream, then I am indeed sorry for you. You have just proven to me that you are moved not by any sense of injustice, or morality, however misguided, but by the ghosts of your own inadequacy. You are unable to make something of yourself. You are unable to seize the moment, so you hate those who can. You are pathetic." She spat out the word. "You will drag the world down with you because you are yourself unable to rise. You were given a unique opportunity to rise and shine, but the history of this country will know you as a failure.

"I would have had more respect for you if you could have pointed out a clear grievance about anything, anything at all. But you are just a sociopath. You should be locked up somewhere. You are a danger to yourself and the future of the human race. In case you fail to understand why I give my money to people I have never met, I suggest you complete your education by looking up the word philanthropy in the dictionary. You think only white people can create aid organisations to clean up after the mistakes of you and your ilk. If we were to count on people like you, Africa would never get anywhere." The girl glared at her over her shoulder, speechless with hate. Martha turned to leave, and then threw over her shoulder, nonchalantly, flicking her wrist in disgust:

"When I look at you, I understand why some animals eat their young."

There was spontaneous applause from the onlookers. The photographer snapped away. The little bitch stood there stiff and tight, speechless. Martha strode to her car and climbed back in. The thing had been just right. The girl had been caught unawares, just as planned, and she had finally shown people where her resentments lay. The image of the poor misled girl was scotched for ever. Sometimes it was good to get down on

259

the ground with them, show them that you were not hiding behind a team of aseptic lawyers. All the same, her hand trembled as she slammed the car door.

She could see the girl raging in the rear view mirror, and her shyster lawyers trying to restrain her. This was better than winning the case. It was as good as won, anyway. Now the news would spread around town at lightning speed and she would become a person. The public just saw her as a talking head on television or a grainy face in newspapers, but this was *nitty-gritty*, my dears! This was grassroots! Now they knew she was not just a vapid, moneyed woman divorced from reality, dispensing charity once removed, as if to a colony of lepers.

All the same, she had the tiniest headache, and she could not catch her breath back.

In a while, the courtyard filled up quickly, people standing in small groups and gesticulating wildly to each other, the witnesses of the scene enjoying their fifteen minutes of fame. Her young lawyer of the previous evening came up and knocked on the glass and she signalled him to get into the passenger side. Her heart was still pulsing strongly from the confrontation, and her eyes were bright with reminiscent anger. The young man took one look at her as she was and understood that he was talking to someone else this morning, not the relaxed woman of the evening before. He cut his coat accordingly.

"Er…Madam, I thought we should go over your statements one last time to see if anything needs to be added."

"Young man, you may not know it from looking at me, but I *have* been to school, you know. I can even read and write a little. We discussed these things at length yesterday and I had a copy of the script."

She stared at him till he looked away. Presumptuous little bugger.

"Now if you would go out and wait for your crowd somewhere else. My car is not a waiting lounge."

"Of course. Sorry to disturb." He climbed out gingerly and walked away slowly, his face hot with shame. God! How would she be in court? His dreams of a distinguished career as a trial lawyer looked somewhat dim this morning. Everyone knew that an unmanageable witness could bury you.

Not long after, Prudentia was wielding her bulk up into the front passenger seat.

"I say *enh*, what happened? They just called me at my sister's place *en catastrophe*. I tried to call you, but you phone is off."

"I just told that little bitch a few home truths." Martha's left knee swayed back and forth, left to right, left to right. She could not keep still. "I don't know. I was sitting here trying to gather my thoughts and then something just...snapped. I went out and asked her why she was doing this. She started telling me that I am no better than anyone else, and so I gave her what for. We can all play the media game."

Her eyes still flashed. "What did you hear?"

"About the same. That you 'washed' her good and proper."

"Yes, I did that. But the water that will clean that little animal is yet to be found. Anyway, the outburst was good in a way. It tells people that they cannot hide behind newspapers and opinions, if one can credit their jumbled half-thoughts with that name. I am telling you, from now on, anyone who attacks me personally will get a personalised response. I am tired of avoiding trouble. My whole life has been just that. All the time I try to avoid scenes or drawing attention to myself beyond my work. Do you know what that little fool said? She says my work is useless and than the girls think this is a sort of halfway house on the road to other things. You know, I think we shall put a lot more effort into the public relations drive. I shall be out there with the team. If anyone has something to say to me, they will tell me so to my face, and then they will know what I think. From now on, it will be face to face." She paused to catch her breath. "Anyway, let me not get too worked up.

"I saw my parents yesterday evening, and I told them about our grassroots operation."

"What did they say?"

"They were not wildly enthusiastic, but they'll do it. In any case, we need them just to introduce us to group leaders and ease the preliminaries, then we'll take it from there. How about your sister?"

"She's thrilled to bits. She'll be going to see her friends about it within the week. You know, I think there are lots of people who support our work. We just did not involve them before. You'd be surprised at the kind of men who hold liberal views about women. Somehow, we got tangled with the extremists. I mean, a lonely reporter accepts a bribe from some discontented higher-up who is afraid of losing his business, and writes a bad article, and we think the world is out to get us!"

"Well, let's not forget that there are a lot of diehard traditionalists, male and female."

"Yes but even there, all it takes is for the benefits to be explained to them, and they'll see."

"Look who's the starry-eyed idealist this morning!"

"And look who has become the flaming revolutionary goddess."

Mercifully, Tarkang came in a little late that morning, so she was spared his sharp-eyed smiling comments on the incident. She was really in no mood to be pleasant.

★ ★ ★

The morning began with witnesses for the defence. The Englishman was first. The courthouse was full to bursting this morning. There were actually people standing in the back. News had gone around that Martha would take the stand, and that there would be a star witness from abroad.

The Englishman took the oath and identified himself.

"Do you know a woman called Mathilda Robinson?"

"Yes, I do."

"Can you find her in the courtroom?"

"Yes, she is sitting over there." He pointed to her.

"Let the record show that the witness has identified Miss Robinson to the satisfaction of the court. What sort of relationship did you have with Miss Robinson?"

"We were lovers."

"Objection", cried the prosecution. "This testimony is not relevant to the case. Miss Robinson is not on trial here."

"My Lord, the defence aims to prove that Miss Robinson is not in a position to provide moral lessons to anyone, least of all to the founder of the Women's House, and that she contributed significantly to the malice that Miss Veronica Kumbong has displayed."

"Overruled. Please continue."

"For how long were you lovers?"

"For about nine months. From April to November 1994."

"How did the relationship end?"

"I was very ill. I was taking drugs and the police arrested me one night in a club. I was sent to a rehabilitation centre. Mathilda – Miss Robinson and I were arrested together. I never saw her again." He went on to reveal that Miss Robinson had been a habitual drug user, and she had provided the money for its purchase for both of them. They had lived together for the better part of a year, and when they had both been arrested, the matter had ended there. Miss Robinson had not visited him even once while he was in the rehabilitation clinic.

Lead counsel for the prosecution tried to cast doubt on the man's testimony, but Tarkang had pulled a few foreign strings and there were copies of the police report and the signed statement of Miss Robinson herself. It was soon over.

Next in the box was Prudentia Ngallah in all her embroidered orange splendour.

"What do you do for a living, Mrs. Ngallah?"

"I am a counsellor and head of logistics in the Women's House."

"Are you aware of the charges brought against Miss Martha Elive?"

"Yes I am."

"Do you think the charges have any basis in fact?"

"Not in the least. I am in fact appalled –"

"This court is not interested in the opinions of the witness. Please limit yourself to answering the questions. And the defence is warned not to ask leading questions."

Mr. Tarkang inclined his head graciously in the judge's direction.

"Were you present at the last meeting between Miss Robinson and the founder?"

"Yes I was."

"What *did* happen at that meeting?"

"I told Miss Robinson that the centre was not satisfied with her work and that she ought to do better. She said that she was doing her best and that she had come to us highly recommended, and consequently she did not see how her work could be improved upon. Then I told her she was to try harder and she got angry and threatened both of us. She accused me of spying on her and she walked out. Oh yes. And she called me a fat cow." The court roared. The old judge banged his gavel and threatened to send everyone out but those directly concerned in the case.

"I have nothing further."

"Cross-examine?"

The prosecution shook his head. This was turning into a nightmare. He just wanted it to end quickly so he could collect his fees, go home and get some sleep.

Then Martha was called. The court murmured and shuffled. The judge threatened, and the hubbub subsided.

Eyong breathed deeply, buttoned his jacket and walked to the front. This was his day. "Are the accusations of Miss Vera Kumbong true?"

"Most emphatically not."

"Why?"

"I set up the Women's House to improve the lot of women, not to drive them further down the road to ruin. I am aware that I bear some of the responsibility for this state of affairs."

"Indeed? How so?"

"In the sense that I chose to trust Miss Robinson's credentials on the basis of her certificates and experience. I did not ask for a police report on her. But we are not running a prison camp. One cannot be forever ferreting out the details of people's private lives, though perhaps in that lady's case some preliminary checks should have been carried out.

"As to the young lady, Miss Kumbong, who has seen fit to come to this courtroom and malign the noble work of the devoted people who have worked tirelessly to provide her with bed, board and solace for over two years, I can only say that her

264

actions are eloquent in themselves and require no elucidation. It is enough to say that without the assistance of my organisation, it is unlikely that she would ever have found a way to make a living that did not involve prostituting herself. If that is how she repays me, then, I can only be sorry for the parents who toiled to put her through secondary school."

"You have been accused of running a house of ill repute, in a way, have you not?"

"As to the accusations of moral turpitude and mismanagement, I can say that this is the case of the one with the log in his eye pointing to the speck in his neighbour's eye. The claim of lesbian relationships is the typical weapon of people who believe that women can only be happy when they are spread-eagled under a man with their clothes off. The general wisdom here is that women cannot get along, so when it is seen that they actually can work together without more than the normal friction inherent in human relationships, wicked minds begin to concoct stories of sexual deviancy.

"Beyond that, I can provide no defence apart from the work that I have done. I have here a list of three hundred and forty-eight women who are gainfully employed and fulfilled because they passed through my establishment. That means three hundred and forty-eight individuals brought back from the brink of despair, and on the premise that these women, some of whom are married with children, will pass on the advantages to their husbands and families, the benefits of their training cannot be overestimated. That means three hundred households with a stable income, or in the case of married women, two incomes.

"It means that on the day a man loses his job, his woman can help to run the house until he is able to find another job and split the responsibility with her. It means that children will no longer go without food or medicine or school needs because their father is dead or out of a job. It means that a man does not forever have to go and kiss the feet of his rich relatives for school fees at the beginning of the academic year. It means that a family can hold its head up in the town square because they know they are united and that the work together for their well-being.

"There have also been accusations of general moral turpitude."

"If what I have told you I have sought to do is moral turpitude, then I do not know what moral code this country should subscribe to. I have been accused, I am told, of peddling a brand of feminism that threatens to rip the society apart. I say to those who would bandy labels about to be careful of them. Is it feminism, which those who hide their heads in the sand dismiss as the ravings of hysterical women, to ask that fully half of this country's population should not die in ignorance, or is it plain common sense? What is better, to have your children die in your arms because you do not want your wife to go to a place where she can learn to take better care of them or to see your children grow up to look after you in your old age? What is better: to teach women to know how their bodies work and be able to have better control over the reproduction process or to have more and more children when you are unable to feed them ones you have? What is better: to have a family with two incomes, where the wife can be the breadwinner if the husband loses his job in these troubled times, or to ask one man, one solitary man, to bear the burden of feeding eight, nine or ten people alone? If that is feminism, then I am proud to be a feminist. If that is moral turpitude, then may the Lord preserve me from morality. If that is what the prosecution call turning a young girl away from the path of righteousness, then bring back the death penalty and have me shot at once, because I will corrupt more of your young women.

"The people who have come to accuse me in this court are not here because I am at fault. It is because they are unable to face the fact that they have been given the yam and the knife, and even with that, they could not cook themselves a meal. They had the opportunity to be part of a great experience, and they bungled it. So, they would like to transfer their sins onto other people to find relief from their feeling of failure. I am not, and shall not be held responsible for the inadequacies of others. The people who have egged them on are guilty of an even more grievous sin. They have tried to rob a whole nation of its right to development because they put their egos before everything else. They are the cankerworm that is destroying our nation from

266

within. They must be made to change, or they must be rooted out.

"And I will not be daunted in my task. If anything, I shall go on with greater determination because I am even more aware of the task that awaits me. I shall work till I drop!"

"I have nothing further."

She stood up in the deafening silence and went back to her seat. Prudentia leaned over and whispered: "You know, you could have been a revivalist preacher! Sure you didn't miss your calling?"

The rest was anti climax. The judge called for a recess, and the verdict in her favour was announced not long after. Outside the courthouse, there was a dance group, a group of portly women swaying gracefully and singing in one of the grassfield languages.

"Who on earth are they?"

"My sister's meeting. I told you we should get to know these people. We have to strike while the iron is hot, you know. Verdicts, in case you did not know, are a bit of a circus around here. Go down and plaster a banknote on the brow of the lead singer."

There was a crowd of people milling about, snack vendors had appeared as if by magic. Martha felt divorced from it all.

The young lawyer who had coached her through her defence came up to her. Martha stuck her hand out and shook his firmly. "Good job. I was a little jittery earlier on, as you may have noticed."

"I should be congratulating you. You made my task very easy. You did it all yourself, you know. You spoke with such conviction than the judge did not dare interrupt you."

"I spoke from the heart. Thank you for your help." A newspaperman moved towards them, followed by a photographer. Martha recognised the narrow-faced reporter from the Weekly Correspondent. "Ah, it is our fire-and-brimstone friend. So are you going to publish all I said faithfully, or are you going to continue with your diatribes? You can see what happens to those who tamper with the truth."

267

Martha waved in the general direction of where Vera and her bunch had been last seen.

The reporter smiled at her, unfazed. "I was hoping for an interview."

Martha turned to the lawyer. "Let's give him something to write about." She turned back to the reporter. "This man is one of my team of lawyers. So you know what will be happening to you if you go and write your own thing."

41

Away from the courthouse, another minor drama was being played out in the Clerks' Quarters neighbourhood. Fortified by her new money and her prolonged, painful, search for independence, Alice had gone home to see her children.

Not long after the fraught meeting with Mrs. Ngallah, she had left the centre and found employment with a foreign aid organisation. The pay was good; better than she had ever dreamed of getting in her whole life. So, she had come back to her hometown, if not a conquering heroine, at least a solvent one.

She had rented a nice little house on the outskirts, not far from her office. She had not dared to go to her former home until the scandal broke and her mother-in-law went to court and wrecked the case for the prosecution, if the papers were to be believed. Then she had lain awake in the evening after work, pondering what to do. After the verdict was announced, she decided that she had been a coward for long enough. That evening, she changed into jeans and a tee shirt, took her cash purse and got into a communal taxi. When she got to the Quarters, it was almost dark. The houses looked so small, pathetic really. It looked like a scene from another life; nothing to do with her. She walked slowly down the path between the little houses with their chimneys darkened by ancient smoke.

There was a light in the parlour of her former home. She went up the steps and knocked on the door. At first, there was no answer, then there was the patter of small, bare feet and a young voice piped up:

"Who is dere?"

She pushed the door open. Her first son was standing next to the scarred coffee table. He was dressed in faded blue trousers and a dog-eared tee shirt. He frowned at her quizzically. His memory struggled with something, an old love, then his face cleared, and childlike, his mind moved on to other things. He had a small, battered plastic green dinosaur in his hand to which he had been giving urgent instructions before she knocked. He went back to his game on the coffee table, and said as an afterthought: "Papa is in the room".

The armchairs had faded to a dull shade only faintly reminiscent of their former yellow, stained with random maps of old piss and spilled liquids. There was dust on the junk covering the table under the window. It did not seem to have been cleaned since she left. The bare cement floor was dark with grime. The holy pictures were torn and filthy; the children had scribbled meandering strings of numbers and the alphabet on the sections they could reach.

"Paul?" He looked up, surprised. His eyes stared at her with the vacancy of childhood. Should he relax and admit to himself that this was his mother come home?

"Hm?"

"Look at me." He looked at her. Again, in his eyes a vague sign of something, like smoke in a mirror.

"Don't you know me?" He shook his head, his mouth open. He knew who she was, but would she stay?

"Where is your brother?"

"'E's sleepin'"

"Where is your father?"

"'As gone to buy bread. Is in the room."

"Where is your grandma?"

"Sh'as gone."

"To where?"

"To her house."

"Come and sit here, next to me. Come!"

He did not. Instead, he stood there, looking at her, his dinosaur rubbing absently on the table. Then she heard to swish of footsteps through the stubby grass, and someone came up the steps. Herbert came in.

Alice stood up. He was wearing an old shirt, its cuffs folded back to the elbows. He looked thinner, darker. He had a French loaf wrapped up in a bit of cement paper. He was almost at the bedroom door before he realised that there was someone in the room other than his son. They looked at each other in silence. Then he turned and went into the bedroom. The little boy looked at his father, and then went on giving last-minute instructions to his dino, as he called it.

She followed him to the bedroom. He was standing by the old cot, the loaf still in his hand, doing nothing. She pushed the door closed behind her. She took a step towards him, and suddenly he turned to her, eyes wild. He pulled her to him by the front of her tee shirt and squeezed her neck with both hands, the forgotten loaf crackling between their torsos. His face was twisted, his teeth bared in a wordless snarl.

She did not struggle. Then he released her suddenly, causing her to stumble. And turned away to the window, his back to her. His shoulders slumped.

She said: "I've come back."

He stood there silent for a while, and then he whirled around again and came back at her. He threw her across the bed and hit her with the flat of his hand. It was a good sign. If he had really wanted to hurt her, he would have hit her with his fists. She covered her head with her hands and waited for the storm to pass. He grew tired and collapsed on the bed next to her, chest heaving. He waited. Then:

"Why did you leave me?"

"It was not you I left. It was the situation. I couldn't bear it any longer."

"You leave me for almost three years, then you come in here and act as if nothing happened. What do you expect? You did not even care about your children! Who do you think has been looking after them all this while? You think you can just come and go like that." He snapped his fingers. "I have come back, she says, I have come back. We have lived without you for three years, and you see we are not dead. Three years. What did you think you were doing? How do you think I felt? You disgraced me in front of my friends. You made me the laughing stock of the town. And you want me to take you back. What will they say? How will I seem to them? Like a weakling. My wife leaves me, and three years later, she walks in, just like that and I take her - " His voice broke. He swallowed painfully, audibly. She knew his throat hurt from the unshed tears. She did not want to see him weeping. But she was afraid to move; afraid it would set him off again.

271

The door creaked on its hinges and opened. Her other son came in.

"Papa?" Alice sat up. He was wearing nothing but a ragged pair of shorts. His eyes were swollen with sleep. Catarrh had dried on his face, white and scaly. He shuffled slowly towards the bed, his finger picking at the mess on his face.

"Junior." She held out her hands, but he swerved past her and went to lean against his father's legs.

"I want to eat," he whined.

"Paul! Paul!" called his father.

Paul came in. "Go and give Junior food."

Paul took his brother by the hand and they went out. She could hear their high, childish voices talking in the kitchen. Junior cried for a while; there was the sound of pots and pans, and then silence.

"I left because I was unhappy. I do not know whether you understood just how unhappy I was. I think the main problem was that we did not know what we were getting into. We were too young. And your mother's presence did not help." She paused and waited for the explosion. It did not come.

"I felt useless in my own house. You mother took over our lives and ran them as if we were bugs on her farm. I could not stay.

"I have found a job. I have rented a bigger house. I hope we can live together again. I know that some of the things that happened were my fault, because I was too weak. But the main problem was that you let your mother come between us, you gave her too much power over our lives, and you did not care what I thought. You beat me.

"Part of the problem was also that there was not enough money. But – well, I have a job now, and I will contribute to the running of the household."

He did not answer. He lay there and tears coursed down his face, unchecked. He could not speak. She decided to leave the rest for later.

She went out to the living room. The children had finished eating. She sat down and called them.

"Come and sit here. Here. Next to me. Come." Paul came and sat down, and she hugged him to her. He smelled of young

272

sweat and unwashed clothes. Junior looked at her suspiciously and then, since his big brother was already sitting down next to the woman, he came and sat down too. Next to his brother, away from her.

"Where is your mother?"

"Sh'as gone," said Paul.

"Sh'as gone," echoed Junior faintly.

"To where?"

"Don' know."

"Don' know," repeated junior.

"Do you know me?"

No answer.

"I am your mother. Of course you know me. I have come back." They looked at each other, then at her.

"Is a lie," decided Junior.

"No. Grown ups do not lie. You say, 'you are joking' if you do not believe what an adult says."

"You a' joking."

She laughed, but her voice was laced with tears.

"I am not joking. I am back. I will stay with you and we will go to a big new house. I will look after you, wash your clothes, and cook for you. And I will never leave you again."

"A new house?"" asked Paul.

"Yes, a new house."

"Will we have a car like Jimmy their car?"

"Yes."

"A big big car?" asked Junior.

"Well, perhaps a small one to start with."

"Will you buy me groundnut sweet?" asked Junior.

"No, I want coconut sweet!"

"You'll buy me a red gun?"

"You'll buy me a tricycle?"

"No! A story book!"

"*Enh-enh!*"

They fought. Junior cried and looked towards his mother, wanting her to beat Paul.

"Paul, say sorry to Junior. You should not fight with your small brother."

"I wu' not."

273

She was home.

274

42

Vera left the court like a wounded animal, in a skulking hurry. They had won again. The rich, scornful women. Her lawyers packed their things, not looking at each other or at anyone else, and disappeared into the crowd.

She walked to the main road and caught a bus to the big city. She went to the new apartment she was sharing with Miss Robinson. She let herself in. Miss Robinson was lying on the couch with a face towel soaked in ice water covering her brow. She did not take it off as Vera came in.

Vera threw her bag onto the floor and sank into a chair.

"We lost."

Robinson did not answer.

"I said we lost."

"So what else is new? Who did they bring as witnesses?"

"A man from England. Said he knew you. Rather well, in fact."

"His name."

"Keith or something like that.'

"Oh...*that* one." She took the towel off her face and sat up tiredly. "How did they find him?" She passed her hand over her face. "I suppose this means we're back to square one."

"What does that mean?"

"We lost, you said so yourself. I feel sorriest for you."

"Why? We can start again. We can go into business as arranged. People will not refuse to eat in your restaurant because you lost a court case. It is only a temporary setback. In a few years..."

"Well, it's not that simple. You see, my savings have rather...diminished and I was hoping that if we won the case, you know, they would pay us damages. But right now there is nothing I can do for you. I just have this terrible headache. I want to rest.

"We have to be out of here by month's end. I only paid a month's rent, you know."

275

After a pause, she said: "I think I shall go back to London. This country is too backward. Narrow-minded. I am sorry it did not work out for you. But you will find something. You are still young."

"Find something. What something? Where will I go now?"

A hint of impatience crept into Robinson's voice. "Go back to university or whatever, finish your credits and get a job. You have some money from the centre, don't you?"

"But you know I spent that on my wardrobe for the case! I have nothing left. And I never went to university."

"Well, then perhaps you should go and see your parents. I don't know…I have such a headache!"

"You know my parents have nothing! Where do you want me to go now? What am I going to do?"

"Look. I haven't the faintest. You are a big girl now. You find something to do. I am not your mother."

"Yes," said Vera bitterly, "that you are not."

"Would you please leave me alone now? I need to rest. I am very tired."

Vera went to the bedroom she had been occupying and lay down on the bed. She considered her options. Limited was a polite way to describe them. She had none to speak of. But she would have to work with what she had. Somehow, the stress of the past few days overcame her and she went to sleep. When she woke up, it was close to nine p.m. She went to the bathroom. She came out to the living room and peeped around the corner. The bitch was not there. She went to her bedroom and knocked. No answer. She tried the door. It opened onto an unmade bed and clothes scattered all over the place. Who would have thought that this dainty porcelain doll would be so untidy? There was an open suitcase on the floor. Vera checked through it. Clothes, mostly. A few cosmetics.

On a shelf in the closet, she found the woman's documents. There was an air ticket amongst them, for three days hence, bought earlier in the afternoon. The sneaky, cowardly little bitch! Vera swept the stuff off the shelf and ransacked the closet. Clothes and accessories.

276

No money. She turned back into the room and kicked at the suitcase, overturning it.

She seized a bare pillow and threw it across the room, cursing the woman.

Wait.

There was a sequined evening purse under the pillow. She opened it. It was filled with crisp foreign currency. Pounds sterling. She counted. Three thousand four hundred and seventy. Jeez! She knew that a pound was about one thousand CFA. That made it...Wow!

She snickered to herself. Everything comes to she who searches. There could be more. She resolved to go through the room more carefully. But first, she went out into the paved yard with the wad of notes. Where to hide the booty? There was a small heap of dried concrete mix covered with old cement paper. She found a bit of plastic wrapping, wrapped the money up and hid it in the cement paper.

Then she went in and searched the room more thoroughly. Among the documents she had swept off the shelf were traveller's cheques. She did not know exactly what they were, but that meant another two thousand pounds. Where she was going, they could be exchanged for hard cash. Who said she was done for?

They would *know* her.

She went back, retrieved the money from the cache, and put it in her bra, along with the cheques. She would wait for the idiot and try to get more money out of her. The bitch was rich; she had said so herself on many occasions. This was just pin money. She went back into the bedroom and put everything back they way it had been, save for the money. She came back to the living room.

Where had she gone out to? Vera stretched out on the couch and waited.

Miss Robinson came in an hour or so later and found Vera lying on her couch with her shoes on. The cheek!

"Would you mind sitting somewhere else? I rather like the couch, you know. And the fabric is rather hard to clean. I suggest you remove your shoes if you want to get up on it,

277

though I don't think you'll be doing that for long. I've arranged for my furniture to be sold."

Vera decided to play along for a while. She sat up.

"Sold? So you are really leaving me here?"

"I believe I said so earlier," said Miss Robinson shortly. "Now, you can stay here for a few days, till the end of the month, and then you can find a place for yourself."

"Bb...but Miss Robinson, you promised that if things did not go well, you would help me! You said you would start a business for the two of us! What shall I do now? And the gateman?"

"Look. I can't be bothered with all that now, alright? I have other things to think about." She flung her bag on a chair. Okay, I'll give you something to buy food for a few days. But that's all I can do."

"How much?"

"Ten."

"Ten thousand. Ten thousand? Keep it. You will know me one day, and sooner than you think."

"Are you threatening me? I have resources at my disposal that would reduce you to nothing. Now get out!"

"With pleasure. I dust my feet of you."

Miss Robinson stared at her, stony-faced, as she walked to the door. At the door, Vera turned.

"Bye-bye!" she said gaily. She could not resist wriggling her fingers just a *little* bit.

Miss Robinson sighed and passed a hand over her brow. These natives. Be glad to get away from all this. She lay on the sofa for a while, thinking. It would be nice to be back in London, somewhere civilised. Damn Keith. Why did he have to come out here and disgrace her? Without him, the court case would have collapsed like a punctured balloon. Anyway. She would go back to London and rest for a while. It was all so tiring. And then maybe the south of Spain. Yes, somewhere exciting.

She really should finish packing. She dragged herself off the couch and went to the bedroom. Hope that little thief has not gone through my things, she thought to herself. At the thought of her money, her heart skipped a beat. But what would she do with pounds sterling? Wouldn't even know what it was. Her

278

mouth twisted scornfully. She went to check her money and papers, all the same. One never knew.

Vera let herself out of the gate and walked to the main street, a couple of hundred yards away. She would go to an inn and stay there for the night, and then the next day, Nigeria here I come! She would show them all.

43

Martha was in her office. It would be nice to have a quiet weekend somewhere with a nice man and no noise, she thought. Her last great love was an old ache that hurt from time to time, but the gut-wrenching misery had been forgotten in the heat of the court case. The fortnight, in spite of its successes, had been exhausting. And there was still one problem to be dealt with, back here at the centre. She reached out her hand to summon Prudentia, but thought better of it. It would be good to do a couple of things on her own for a change. With her new-found resolve, it seemed better to act independently from time to time.

She pulled the phone towards her, but it was Grace the graceless she called.

"Would you come up to my office, please?"

"Now? What for?"

"Right now."

Time to show some claws around here.

Grace came in, in her dog-eared tee shirt as usual. She did not wait to be asked to sit down; She pulled back a chair and dropped into it.

"Heard you did alright in court."

"Do sit down, Grace and thanks for the concern.

"Much as your support warms my heart, I did not call you here to talk about our success in court." Martha felt a little breathless, so she took a couple of covert deep breaths. When she spoke again, her voice was firmer.

"Now, Grace. I do not know whether you have heard any of the rumours that are going about on your account." She raised her eyebrows and waited.

"What rumours?" asked Grace carelessly. She was not interested in gossip.

"About you conducting an inappropriate relationship with one of your students."

"Drop the innuendo and come out straight. What is an inappropriate relationship?" She grimaced and waggled her head from side to side in mockery, a look of challenge in her eyes.

Can they smell the coward in me? Martha wondered. Aloud, she said:

"Look, stop shitting about and face the thing squarely. There is a girl called Maggie with whom, from what I gather, you spend most of your waking hours. You are always cooped up in the workshop together long after everyone else has gone off to their quarters. Worse, you take her to your place, and you know that is breaking the rules. If you think that no one notices such things, then you are more stupid than I thought.

"So now I am asking you, what kind of a relationship do you have with the girl? Are you having an affair with her?"

Grace looked at her up and down. "If that is what you called me here for, then I guess I'll be going. I have better things to do with my time." She looked at Martha straight in the face as if to say: now let's see how you'll handle that. Then she stood up slowly and turned to go.

"Sit down." Martha's voice was deadly quiet. It penetrated even the thick skin of the woman. She half turned. For the first time, Martha caught a look of uncertainty in her eyes. She decided to press home the advantage.

She looked straight at her, unwavering. Grace dropped her eyes first, and sat down again. This time she did not slouch in her chair.

"I will tell you a few things. I will say them once. I will never have to repeat them again, because if you cross me, you will have me on your back for the rest of your life, and I won't be talking; I'll be acting.

"One. Your attitude. You work in an institution where contact with other people is unavoidable. You will henceforth adjust your conduct to suit this environment. When you are greeted, you will reply politely.

"You will fraternise with other members of staff. If there is a staff party, you will attend. You will be civil. You will participate in the other activities of this institution to the best of

281

your abilities. You will endeavour to groom yourself and not go about smelling of sweat and wearing those horrible tee shirts.

"Two. This girl. You will not invite her to your bungalow again. You will spread your attentions as equitably as possible amongst the other students under your charge. I am not sure whether you are a lesbian or not. I do not really care. However, if you are, and you are lovers with this kid, you will stop it. Now. Not tomorrow, not next week. Now. If you wish to conduct relationships of any sort, homosexual or heterosexual, or both, whatever your inclination, you will do that outside these walls.

"Three. The day you talk to me with such lack of respect as you have shown now, I'll rearrange your facial bones for you. I doubt I can actually improve your face, but I'll certainly change it.

"And now, if you are unable to clear up this situation to my satisfaction within the next few minutes, you are out. You will leave this campus within the hour, and you will not come back. You will either adjust to living with people here, or you will live, but elsewhere. You can choose now.

"Have I made myself clear?"

There was a pause, during which Martha's heart lurched painfully against her ribs.

"Yes, perfectly so." Martha could have hugged her, she was so relieved. She had feared that she would have to repeat the question, like a principal to a recalcitrant pupil.

"However, I would like to say something."

Martha spread her forearms, palms up. "It's a free world."

"I have not, and have never, had a lesbian or other sexual relationship with Maggie or anyone else on this campus. On my honour. And I would like to go on working here."

Martha let her fret for a full minute. Then:

"Very well. On your honour, you stay. We will see what it is worth." As the woman remained seated, she said:

"That will be all. Thank you for your time." Hands clasped on the blotter, she watched the woman leave. Then she punched the air in silent triumph.

The phone rang. It was Gladys.

"You're back!"

"Yes. Could I come see you for a minute?"

She came in and the first thing Martha noticed was that she had her hair down. It framed her face, softening it. Her cheekbones were less prominent, her skin looked fresh. She was wearing a loose yellow shirt and brown slacks.

"Hear you've been belling cats all over the place." She smiled at Martha. "Now take that will-she-won't-she look off your face. She will, no fear. Now, you've done the dirty work, I can come in and be part of the dream team, eh? Smart thinking, in my view. As the ship has not sunk, the rats have come back."

Martha racked her brain, but she could not remember Gladys ever joking before this.

"You're alright." It was not a question.

"Buried the ghosts. They're not quite dead yet, but I think they'll slowly suffocate. Need to sit on the coffin lid for a while, though. I got a quickie divorce. I did not have the courage to see the bastard, but I guess that will come with time."

"I have a few ghosts of my own that are very hard to bury. I'm working on it too." They smiled at each other.

"I'm calling a staff meeting. An extended one. Teaching and ground staff as well."

"To lay down the line."

"Sort of. Evaluate and adjust our sights."

"Well, I'm off to unpack. Just came to report for duty."

"We'll put you on the roster."

She got up to leave. As she stretched out her hand to open the door, Martha spoke.

"Gladys."

"Hm?" She turned.

"I'm glad."

Gladys did not answer. She just waved at Martha and shut the door.

Martha leaned back. The midmorning sunlight filtered through her peach curtains, bathing the room in pale yellow light. An old elementary school marching song meandered into her mind, and she began to hum softly to herself.

The day is bright,
Is bright and fair,

283

Oh happy day,
The day is bright,
The day is bright is bright and fair,
Oh happy day the day is bright.

It conjured up memories of long-break time playing in the mounds of cut grass, inhaling the earthy green smell, clambering out, running a distance to take a flying leap and diving in again, laughing and shouting. One day a girl called Mirabelle (no one bothered with the *-lle*: they called her Mirabeh) had come and fainted onto the heap of grass. There was a delicious, exciting panic, and the headmaster, a short, solid, crusty man with bushy eyebrows who loved farming (they had the best school farm in the district) was called. One of the big class seven boys was sent to fetch *manyanga* (palm kernel oil) from a neighbouring house. It was forced down Mirabelle's throat and, after a while, she coughed, spitting out the chewing gum that had blocked her air passage. She was made to sit on a teacher's chair, and the whole school went and stood around her, staring at her; it was all so *new*.

She remembered the thrill of going to steal guavas in the yards of rich, absent homeowners and being chased by their 'watch-days' - the caretakers, running through the tall grass, giggling, the guavas pushed into the space between the school uniform and her skin, cool and knobby against her bare back, a rope around her waist to hold them in.

Returning from school to find her lunch ready on one enamel plate covered by another (before the advent of food flasks), eating hungrily as her mother scolded her about the state of her school uniform (you'll wash it yourself this time, and then next time you'll know not to dirty it like that), and rushing out to play 'dodging': two girls about ten metres apart on a straight line, a third in the middle; one throwing a plastic-wrapping ball at the girl in the middle, which she dodged, the other one catching it and throwing it again. If the girl in the middle dodged ten balls, she won. If the ball touched her once, she was 'out'.

She remembered sneaking back to the school farm to steal the headmaster's string beans and precious sweet white corn, imported from America. Eating them hungrily between the long earth ridges and drinking clear rainwater caught between the ridges of fertile earth. Going to the vegetable farm, skirting the stinking compost heap, to eat cabbage leaves, washing them down with huge sweet tomatoes.

Going home in the gloaming, the smell of cookfires reheating cocoyams for the evening meal, the sound of mothers calling their children, passing people returning from evening mass, and arriving home to mother, who made you wash before evening prayers and bed.

A happy, thought-free life, the days of innocence before knowledge of good and evil came.

There were still brighter says ahead, if she would stop daydreaming and get to work. She called Hortense.

"Call a staff meeting for this afternoon."

"Any hints about the agenda?"

"Nope. Will be disclosed at the meeting." Might as well put the positive adrenaline to good use. In the meantime, she had things to do. Private things. She dialled the switchboard of Tarkang and Pritchard.

"Extension 128 please."

"Hello?"

"Hello, good morning. This is Martha Elive. How are you doing?"

"F-fine, thank you. And how are you?"

Pause.

"I wonder if you have time to meet with me this evening. There is some professional matter I'd like to pick your brains on. What time do you get off work?"

"In theory, at five, but I usually stay on if I have work."

"Do you have a lot of work right now?"

"Well, no, but – "

"Then perhaps we should meet here at the centre. Do you want me to send a car for you?"

He thought of his twelve-year old Lancer whose drive shaft had broken again. He considered taking a minibus and arriving hot and smelling of sweat.

"Er, send the car. Thanks."

Bingo!

"Alright then, let's say that the car will arrive about six. You should be here by seven, right? Okay, see you then."

There. She'd done it. No going back now. She wondered whether she was not making a mistake. Her instincts might be wrong. Maybe he was not attracted to her. He might be hard to manage. She thought about it for a while longer, then she took a sheet of paper and drew a table, plus side and minus side. Slowly, she began to write down what she knew about him.

Not much. But this evening would decide whether she could go on or not. She smiled ruefully to herself. If someone had told her, when she was eighteen, that she would ever try to rope in a man so blatantly! Now the small-town Madonna was on the prowl for male flesh, eh? What? It was they way of the world. You had to choose the most suitable male specimen. She would not let this one go.

44

Six o'clock. She remembered the poem *Prelude*, by T.S. Eliot. The burnt-out ends of smoky days, she thought. The morning's euphoria had been dampened somewhat by the tedious staff meeting. It had not been difficult, just long and detailed. All the department heads had attended, seated on either side of her on the dais of the small hall behind the main offices. All the staff had attended the meeting too, and they had all declared that they would prefer to stay on. And she had established her authority more firmly. Prudentia had been helpful, but Martha had kept the reins of the meeting firmly in her own hands. New control, new woman. Gladys had participated and Hortense had diligently recorded everything, as usual. Grace had attended too. Usually she ignored calls to attend meetings, but this afternoon she had been there, and had actually made suggestions. She was also wearing a denim dress, which caused quite a stir when she came in.

Decisions had been made. Martha had decided not to adopt Prudentia's suggestion for the new head of the catering department. Instead, she had announced that she would hire a hotel chef (after having him checked out by the private detective; lessons must be learnt). Prudentia looked slightly surprised and Martha, speaking to her, but addressing the whole room, said:

"Unlike Miss Robinson, whom we hired chiefly on the basis of her certificates and experience, I have had this gentleman thoroughly checked out. I thought putting a man on the staff would be good for our image. And I think the brand of affirmative action we have been applying here with regard to staff hiring will have to stop. This institution must function properly. The important thing is to train women who can function independently in the outside world. It does not matter, I think, who trains them. So, this is a major shift in policy. It means that we are not going to hire people chiefly because they are women. If there are men who are ready to work with us and who are good at their job, then we take them. That means staffing will be a lot more competitive. I hope you will all take account of that when you do your jobs. I don't want lame ducks among the staff. We have enough trouble with the students as it is."

There had been laughter, some of it uneasy.

After the meeting, Martha had sent for Prudentia, ostensibly to ask about Maggie, but actually to see how Prudentia had taken her declaration of independence.

She had taken it well, it seemed. She asked when they were to expect see the new man. Martha told he would be coming in the afternoon. "You talk to him about the details. He's married with kids in their early twenties, most of whom have left home. Check with Hortense." She waited. Prudence did not complain. Okay, the message had passed. I am now the boss of this place. She decided to relax a little.

"After I see Maggie, I'll rest awhile. There's a little fish I want to bait." She smiled.

Prudentia sat up. "Who?"

"You will see. Massa, I am tired of being alone, *dis donc.*" They pondered the prospect of loneliness for a while.

"You know, the worst part about men is that they can make you very happy. And once you have been very happy with one, you keep wanting to try again to see if you can recapture the magic with someone else.'

"What you mean is that you need them."

"No. Not need. No human being needs another unless they're a baby. Well, I mean you need men to have babies and all that. What I mean is that sometimes, you are filled with a debilitating kind of loneliness, a kind of yearning."

"I call it sex drive. That happens when you have not been to bed with someone for a while."

"No, well, it's true that sex comes into it sometimes. But even when you sleep with a guy, if there is not a certain... companionship, you know that there is something missing. Maybe that's what people call love."

"No, my view is that it's just a natural instinct to pair up. You know, the basic unit, make a family, perpetuate the species. Realities intrude, however. Finding the right partner, of the right age, money, class, colour, language, attitude, whatever. That's the hard part."

She stopped and looked at Martha shrewdly.

"Let me intrude and tell you something. It's all right to feel lonely from time to time. It's all right to feel drawn to men. They feel drawn to us too, in case you haven't noticed the bulge in their trousers. They are lonely too. They also want companionship. That is why even though they are chronic cheats, they come back to the person they feel at ease with. As a friend of mine said, the woman outside who thinks she is the ultimate seduction machine and can take my husband from me if she wished should wonder how come I'm pregnant every two years. Because, like you said, you can sleep with someone, but he or she may not arouse the feeling of companionship, call it love if you like. The reason nature created males and females is that they can and need to supplement each other. No one sex can perpetuate the race on its own. Wanting to have a permanent or steady partner is not a sign of weakness. The important thing is the rules of companionship. That is where you must not give ground."

"Thus spake the eminent predicant socio-psycho-moral sexologist," said Martha mockingly, but she was grateful to hear it from someone other than Ophie. Sometimes she was afraid to take Ophie's views seriously because they were so outlandish. "Talking about companionship, who is your companion?"

"And this from the one who would not reveal her *little secret*." Prudentia mimicked Jeremy Irons as Scar in *The Lion King*. "My dair," she continued in a poor imitation of an English upper-class voice, "unlike certain segments of the population, I do not discuss my intimate affairs." They laughed. Then she sobered up and said: "Actually, I have a very satisfying relationship with a certain urbane, potbellied individual who was instrumental to the current high ratings you enjoy in the polls." She wrinkled her nose coquettishly at Martha.

"Wha...Hey, you rascal, you are sleeping with my lawyer!"

"*Shhh!*"

"Whooooo, Prudentia! Ça! You be real pussycat. I would never have dreamt it."

289

"You too! How did you think my nephew got to be a pupil in Tarkang and Pritchard?"

Martha leaned forward. "I just have to ask this. How do you reconcile your respective, er, girths?"

"You'd be surprised at the human body's capacity to adapt to certain situations. And now, I'll have no more prurient questions from you, Madam. Who is this individual you hanker after?"

Martha looked up at her from under her eyelashes. "One of his junior partners. The one who prepared the case with me. But I just have aims, I have not caught him yet."

"Ahhh, the plot thickeneth"

"That's not grammar."

"Who gives a shit? Now let me do a little more preaching. I know your big Latin lover left you and you sort of went to pieces. I'm glad you think you can start again. There is no point burying yourself or pretending that the guys are unworthy so you will not dignify them with your attention, eh? Take what you need from them, and ignore the rest if it is not criminal or life-threatening or unhygienic. I got to a stage where I decided that if a guy showered daily, I'd take him. You know the high ideals are good for the theory books, but the bottom line is living with the guy, eh? Don't demand of him that he should know the history of origami. Not all people can be as cultivated as you would like them. You'd be surprised at the number of men who still cannot handle a fork properly. But if they are decent, caring individuals, who cares?

"And I'll tell you a secret. You know why many women stay married? It is the fear of loneliness. They all say it's the children, but that is the real thing. More of them- us - are getting divorced these days because the rules are becoming more flexible; they have other things to make them feel less lonely when a man is not around. Also, African women are experiencing their own sexual revolution. But for the threat of AIDS, I think we would be able to hope for a certain amount of happiness from time to time. It means that you can get divorced and marry someone else. People can have affairs after divorce. Divorced women can remarry. They are no longer pariahs. In short, more sexual freedom, more options. Men have always had more sexual freedom, now women are getting it too. The only drawback is disease, but if you can avoid that, go ahead! As good old T.S. said, neither fear nor courage saves us. If you sit there and wait for them to come and get you, my dear, you'll have mushrooms growing all over down there before you know it.

"Men are not as intrepid as they once were. With your status, you terrify about ninety-two percent of the menfolk, and while some males still believe in the senior-district-officer-marries-his-subservient-kitchen-maid kind of relationship, it no longer works so well these days. The economic pressures are too strong for single-income homes. We who have our own incomes have a fighting chance at any age. And marriage is not always the ultimate aim. Get someone you can relax with from time to time. So you have to rope in someone and then show him your soft underbelly, pun not intended."

"Gee thanks," said Martha. "I mean that. I really needed someone to tell me just how right I am. I mean, frankly, I'm a genius." She joked, but Prudentia could see that she was wanted to convey her gratitude. It was also a way of saying: I may have decided to take over control here, but we're still partners. "Now clear out and let me see this Maggie girl."

Ten minutes later, Maggie came in. Martha thought she remembered seeing the big, slow girl once or twice, but she did not think she had ever spoken to her.

"Sit down."

The girl sat, slowly, both hands beneath her buttocks.

Maggie had never been to the founder's office before. Things like visiting the high and mighty, sufficient to send some girls into transports, meant little or nothing to her. Except of course, for Miss Grace.

"I have asked you to come up here because I have heard that you are very close friends with Miss Grace. Is she your friend?"

"Yes."

"What do you do together?"

"Work and talk."

"You go to her house?"

"Yes."

"You know that you should not go to her house. It's against the rules."

"She said I could come whenever I wanted to."

"Yes, but she is wrong. That is against the rules. What do you do when you go to her house?"

"We eat and we watch TV. We play chess." Maggie's face lit up.

"Does...do you and Miss Grace do other things?"

"Other things? Yes, we play cards."

"Now, I want you to tell me something. You know what making love is? To sleep with someone. I want you to tell me something. I will not be angry with you, and I will not tell anyone else. I will not send you away. You can stay here for as long as you like. You understand that?"

"Yes."

"You know what making love is?"

"Yes, to do foolish." Martha tried not to laugh. She decided to switch to Pidgin English.

"Men and women can do foolish. Do you know that women and women can do it too?"

Maggie pondered this for a while. "Hermaphrodite?" That was one of the local names for homosexuality.

"Good. Now, I said I would not be angry with you and I would not send you away. Has Miss Grace tried to make hermaphrodite with you?"

"*Mh-mh!*" Maggie shook her head violently, the disgust evident on her face. "*Ish!*" she said, using the ultimate expression of disgust in Pidgin.

"But have you heard people talking about it? About you and Miss Grace?"

"Yes, a girl in our unit said so."

"What did you do?"

"Nothing. I told Miss Grace. She cried." Maggie's face lengthened.

"Okay, you can go now. Do not tell anyone about what we discussed here, not even Miss Grace. But do not go to her house again. You hear? If she asks you, tell her that I said you should not go to her house again because it is against the rules.

Then you come and tell me, you hear? And if someone calls you a hermaphrodite again, you tell Mrs. Ngallah or me. Hm?"

"Yes, Ma."

"Okay, go now."

Maggie walked out of the founder's office, her brain whirling. What was that all about? It was true that some girl had called her a hermaphrodite because of an altercation over a broken dish in the kitchen unit. She had told Miss Grace, who was her friend, and Miss Grace had cried and asked her to go back to her room.

But she was not a hermaphrodite, and Miss Grace had not asked her to be one. Did people think she and Miss Grace – the thought filled her with anger. To say things like that about Miss Grace! The founder had asked her not to tell Miss Grace, so she would not. But if anyone made another comment like that again, she, Maggie, would beat her.

She pounded up the stairs to her unit and lay down on the bed, thinking.

It was not true. She had a boyfriend. A few months ago, she had gone back home to Mile 18 to visit her mother. She had been there once before, when she started earning money. Her mother had wept and alternately hugged and called her names, as was her wont. Flo was there too, dressed in skin-tight flowered trousers, cheap-looking shoes and plastic jewellery.

"*Madam*," she said in scornful, envious greeting, and looked Maggie up and down. She lived in Douala, she said.

"You di waka *akpara* (you're a streetwalker)," said Flo's mother in disgust and disappointment. "If your father were alive, he would have killed you." Flo looked away. She had heard that many times before.

Maggie had given her mother money. Whereupon, Flo's mother began to cry and talk about daughters who never did anything for their poor parents, and Flo walked out in a rage, threatening never to come back home again.

In the evening, walking along the narrow paths of the village, Maggie had met a prison warder, whose parents lived in the village too. He talked. She listened. She liked him. They were fast friends by the time she was leaving. He promised to write to her at the centre. She grew to look forward to his letters.

293

That same evening, when they were in bed, Flo had asked her about the centre. "You are looking fresh. What do you people do there?" Flo could not read and she was not interested in the news. If she watched any TV at all in the city, it was the very popular Latin American soap operas. Maggie had told her about how they lived and how you could earn some money of your own. Flo was silent for a long time and Maggie fell asleep. When she went back the next day, Florence followed her.

Maggie got up and fetched some lime juice from the fridge. The thought that people would say things like that about Miss Grace filled her with anger. She wished she could catch someone and squeeze her neck.

When she went back last month, her warder was in the village, visiting. He came to see her. He held her hand, and in the evening, when he came to see her off, he kissed her. It felt good. She let him. He promised to write her again.

When she finished here, in a few months, she meant to team up with some other girls and open a garage. Then they would get married. She was not a hermaphrodite. If someone said so, she would beat her.

45

Martha had come upstairs for a short nap before her visitor came, but she was too keyed up to sleep. She lay on the bed and indulged in a tentative erotic daydream with a faceless stranger and finally dozed off. At six, she woke up to prepare for her visitor. She had given the driver instructions earlier.

She showered and changed into a sleeveless cream blouse tucked into loose-fitting wine-coloured trousers. No short skirt to show legs. Too obvious. She was beyond that now. *So why did you oil your upper arms specially to make them shine*, said the Owen Meany voice, *and wear a sleeveless blouse?* Because that's not obvious, you idiot said Martha, and then she realised that she had spoken aloud. Goodness. The voices had gone back to their lair this past week, leaving her brain free for other things. She thought she would retire them permanently. Imagine that she became so used to listening to them that she talked back when people were around! Thank heaven she lived alone.

She added cream satin ballerinas. She used a sweet-smelling hand cream she had brought back from Samoa. This was calculated. He would shake her hand when he came in, and each time he raised his hand to drink, he would smell her perfume. With luck, he would smell her all the way home and all night, if he didn't wash his hands when he got home. No makeup. African men liked to think of women as natural, unaided by cosmetics. Actually, what they did not want were visible cosmetics. So, just a hint of eye shadow. No earrings. However, a thin gold chain around her neck. Pure gold, glowing softly in the light from the cleverly shaded lamp.

She did not straighten the bed on which she had been sleeping. Things would not get that far. I am not that sort of girl, she caught herself thinking, and smiled at her self-delusion. Good old traditional at heart, aren't you, my dear. No modern bed-hopping for you.

The bell rang at three minutes past seven. Leonarda the driver was there, with her booty hovering behind her. She let him in.

"Hello, how was your trip?"

"Comfortable, thank you." They shook hands. Round one to me. He sat where she indicated, and she sat in relative shade, upper arms and gold chain gleaming. Pretending that this evening, she was Cleopatra, suave and seductive.

Round two.

"Drink?"

He moved; one arm half crooked, resting on its fist, the other on the arm of the chair, he pushed himself forward. Martha watched without seeming to do so. The signs were good. He was ill at ease and a little in awe of her. He would be grateful if she laughed with him, and friendly. *Just friends*, shrilled Meany. Martha slapped *him* away with the back of a mental hand.

"Yes, please. A beer."

She smiled at him; a closed lipped approving-dowager-duchess-to-estate-overseer smile, eyes drooping slightly, a hint of seduction. *You hope*, said Owen. *He's probably wondering why you are making faces at him.* Martha resisted the impulse to slap herself on the side of the face to silence Owen forever, and reached for the cunningly concealed bell-pull instead.

Martha had gambled on his wanting a beer, so she had ordered something expensive and foreign. Even if he did not like the taste, he would be too scared of offending her to say so. If he said so, then she was in deep shit. She would have to change her approach.

While waiting for the drinks to be brought in, she made small talk. "How are you recovering from the excitement of my case?" She did not wait for an answer. She wanted to do the talking. "I am glad to rest for a bit, relax. It was a tense fortnight." *I am the troublemaker worth lots of lolly, but also a flesh and blood human being*, said another voice, and Martha smiled to herself.

"Yes, quite tense. This is where you live when you are here?"

"Most of the time, But I have a bungalow in town that I use occasionally." *So actually I brought you here to my lair, see. I have plans for you.*

"How's it like, being a lawyer in this country? I suppose it's tough."

"Well, if you are in a good firm, like mine, then it's not too bad. You can make quite a living and get comprehensive hands-on experience..."

Round two to her.

They discussed cases. The drinks came, with peanuts, coconut candy and olives. He relaxed after his first beer. He unbuttoned his suit jacket. He began to wave his hands as he talked. He expressed opinions at variance with hers, politely. He looked at her directly.

She came to her excuse for the evening. The carpenter woman's case. He advised her to take up the matter with the village elders first and then with the customary court if that did not work. This is what she had decided to do herself anyway. They discussed, skirting around the edges, the obstacles that women faced in setting up small and medium-sized enterprises: lack of access to credit, lack of education, bureaucratic bottlenecks. She did not bring up the business of irate husbands, and he did not either. It meant two things. Either he did not think of it as a problem, or he had his own opinion that he was unwilling to share with her. So be it. She was not interested in his ideology; she was interested in other things more physical.

That done with, they talked about school. He was a private missionary school product, Nigeria for law (LL.M.), and then pupillage, the Bar and now five years at work. She fished around for dates, and finally put his age at thirty-three, a few months above hers.

She tried him on current events. He listened to the news. He liked football, but not too much. He went to church sometimes.

One hour and forty-three minutes. Time for him to leave. She began to leave longer and longer gaps between her responses. She asked no new questions. He was sharp in his way. He looked at his watch and exclaimed at the time. He had to prepare a brief for tomorrow; he had better be going. She did

297

not object. She rang for Leonarda, who came upstairs with another girl.

"It's been a pleasant evening," said he, like a decent mission schoolboy.

"I'm glad you came," said she, like a pleasant mission schoolgirl.

He left with Leonarda, and the other girl cleared up the glasses and stuff. She mixed herself another drink and went out onto the balcony. She replayed as much of the conversation as she could remember. Then she went back in and looked through her papers for the rough table she had started in the morning. She sat down at her small desk and added some things to the list. Then she read over it.

Plus	Minus
1.Age (about the same as me)	1. Attitude in hotel room (macho): can be amended
2.Employment (gainfully employed) likes his job – I think	2.lacking in refinement about some things (calls all Latin American music Patchanga). Thinks Robert Ludlum ought to win the Nobel
3.looks: bearable	3.Calls December Dixember
4.Brains in a diligent, unimaginative way	4.Don't like his hands
Conclusion: go ahead and find out more.	

She locked the list up in a drawer and went to the bedroom. Owen and the others wanted to chat, but she pushed them away and read a paperback instead. Then she went to sleep.

46

The rest of the week was taken up with the case of the carpenter woman. Martha and Prudentia travelled over to the West Coast to her village. It was one of the numerous fishing hamlets straggling along the coastline. Most of the houses were built of either *caraboard* (thin, narrow, rough-hewn boards) with thatched roofs, or entirely of thatch. The children chased each other around the ancient trees against which the houses nestled.

She was a tall, bony woman, the left side of her face puckered up hideously by the scar, which ran from the cheekbone to the side of her mouth. Her name was Catherine.

The village elders spoke to them with the shallow deference the poor reserve for rich people they do not respect. The headman led them to sit on some rough benches under a spreading tree. "It is true that our daughter has been disfigured, sad, but she came here boasting about how she was better off than the men, now that she had a job. It is no surprise that she raised a few hackles..."

Did they know who did it?

They looked at one another, old gnarled fishermen, their faces carved by the sea air, monolithic. They did not, but it was best to let sleeping dogs lie, bringing the matter up again would upset the whole village.

"I intend," said Martha, "to take the matter as far as it will go. This woman has been disfigured because of the help I gave her. I shall not relent until the culprit is brought to justice. She herself tells me that she was just expressing joy at her good fortune. Even if she were boastful, is it right to go out and tear up someone's face like that?"

"It means that when a man boasts that he has caught a bigger fish than he actually did, you should dissect his face?" asked Prudentia.

Faced with such childish intransigence, the old men went off into a corner by themselves and conferred for a while. Finally, they agreed to hold a meeting between the woman and her attackers.

The husband, both fearful and defiant, finally admitted to the crime. His uncles begged for clemency. He promised not to do it again. It was just that his wife had been disrespectful.

In what way?

Well, she was boasting about how she could take care of herself now, made a fool of him all over the village.

"Is that enough reason to attack her with a machete? What if you had killed her?"

He did not want to kill anyone, he said, his was not a family of murderers; he had just wanted to teach her a lesson.

"Well, the lesson has not been learnt. If you try to force your wife to go to your school of violence again, you will bear the consequences."

He stood there in repentance born of being found out, his hands twitching. The elders made him apologize to his former wife. He would buy a pig for her, they said; that was the custom.

Afterwards, Martha bought a crate of beer for the headman and the elders and explained to them that she wanted to open a sawmill along the coast so that the timber harvested in the hinterland would at least be sawn into boards before it left the area. A good portion of the timber would then be locally processed into furniture.

"I am hoping to find some people with some experience with hard work to run the sawmill, which will be separate from the carpentry workshop. If you go about tearing open the faces of those who can give you jobs, how will you encourage investors?"

The elders hastily assured her that no such nonsense would be tolerated in future. If there was anyone in this village or the neighbouring ones who tried anything, well, they were people of the sea, and the sea takes care of its own.

When they got up to leave, after having promised that work on both projects would begin in under a month, the villagers gave them a huge basket of smoked fish of all types, and walked them to the car in a large group, with the children darting in and out around the edges.

300

47

On a crowded coaster bus heading for the Nigerian border, Vera tried to doze as the bus lurched this way and that, dodging the potholes. She had managed to grab a window seat so she could breath a little fresh air, but she might as well be locked in a box in a very hot sauna. The warm, humid air seeped through her light cotton frock, soaking it. The merchant with bleached skin and eczema on his neck sitting next to her cast covetous looks at the outline of her bra under the thin dress. Vera was waiting for him the next time he raised his eyes to her face. She imbued her look with all the scorn and disgust she could muster for this blotchy, saggy bag of poorly maintained flesh. How could a creature like this even have a soul? She looked at him till he removed his gaze, and then she turned to look out of the window for the rest of the trip to the border. She did not think he had recognised her, because she had dyed her hair auburn and shaved her eyebrows for the trip.

Three hours later, at the border crossing, all passengers were asked to descend. The drawn-out ritual of haggling between traders and customs officers began. Each side went through the motions, protestations on one side and counterfeit official sternness on the other, but they already knew the price. Vera stood in line with her small carryall. When her turn came, she said she had nothing to declare.

The blotchy trader cast her a look and drew a customs man aside. They muttered. The customs official came back and asked Vera to follow him to the office. When they got there, he asked her name.

"Evelyne Ekellem."

"Your identification." He held out his hand.

Vera produced a school ID she had picked up one day on a path at the Women's House, and had not declared found. It showed her to be a darker woman who bore a passing resemblance to her real self. The customs man looked at her carefully. His questions were no longer bored. The trader had whispered to him that he ought to take the girl down a peg or two, harass her a little and may be earn enough for an extra beer in the evening. But this smelled fishy. He grilled her for a quarter of an hour or so, but she stuck to her story. She was going to Lagos at the invitation of her aunt. It was her first trip. Yes this was her ID. It was expired because the school had not yet started issuing new ones for this academic year.

He asked her to step out on the veranda so he could make a call.

As Vera got out, one of the women passengers got a good look at her for the first time. She nudged her friend.

"I say, does she not look a little like that girl on TV?"

"...big court case."

"Yes. Lost it..."

"Stole her money..."

The blotchy trader joined them. They walked to the customs shed and went inside. Worried that her ID would cause her to pay more bribe money than she was willing to part with, Vera had not noticed the discussion. So when she looked up and saw two border guards facing her, there was nothing she could do.

She was hauled to the outpost. She promised money, sex, anything, babbling a little. They ignored her and took the money anyway, after searching her bag. They cuffed her and put her in the holding cell.

In the evening of the next day, Hortense called Martha and told her the news.

"This one deserves some Moet."

Martha thanked her and hung up. It did not really interest her. She had already won the battle with the girl. Let society punish the monster it had spawned. As long as they did not drag her into it.

48

On her return from France, Ophelia went straight to her apartment near the university. She would have liked to stop at Martha's and give her all the juicy details of the trip, but she felt bone-tired. She had managed to get her hands on three of the tiny bottles of the plonk they served on the plane and it had tired her out.

Her new boyfriend had stayed back to finish some business in Europe. In the taxi, she thought that it would be nice to keep them, Brown Trail and the new boyfriend, together. That way she had insurance against any unpleasant surprises from any of them. It had been nice to take a few weeks off from Nora's husband, though. He was becoming too intense. He talked of leaving his wife. Even if he were lying, which was highly probable, she did not want to be stuck with the remains of someone else's marriage. There might be better pickings elsewhere. Besides, her enemies at the university would certainly know how to use that against her. Imagine breaking up the marriage of the son of a prominent son of the soil!

The taxi left her at the door and she let herself in. She headed for the bathroom as she checked her messages on her cell phone. She sighed as she sat on the bowl. Oh sweet release. Nothing like the pleasure of emptying your bladder in the right place. She had been plagued by bedwetting till she was twelve; she would never underestimate the special pleasure of urinating in the right place after her mother once held her over a bonfire to cure her affliction. No unpacking this evening. Tomorrow would take care of that. She changed into her dressing gown, a bright red silk embroidered with peacocks and slant-eyed maidens.

As she was moving towards the kitchen to mix herself a drink, the doorbell pealed. Cursing, she went over to the door. Who knew that she was back? She and her neighbours did not get along. They disapproved of her bohemian way of life. Hope to God it's not Brown Trail. I don't want any soulful reunions and questions about what I've been up to.

"Who is it?"

"It's me," said a female voice she did not know.

She opened the door prepared to send the student packing.

Nora pushed roughly past her once the door started opening, and moved straight into the living room. Ophie followed her and found her seated on the sofa, her arms crossed tightly over her breasts, a plastic bag dangling from her left hand. She stared at Ophelia in silence. She was wearing a short-sleeved pale blue boubou.

Ophie's brain clicked and whirred. Claim ignorance and bully her out.

"I don't know which of my courses you are attending, but I can assure you that I have nothing to say to you right now, and that I cannot help you with whichever problem you have come here to present. I am just returning from an exhausting trip, so I shall have to ask you to leave. Who are you anyway?"

Nora looked her up and down. "Hm! So, you don't know me."

"I am afraid you have the advantage over me. However, I am not currently in the mood for introductions, so perhaps you should come over to the faculty on Monday. I will be in a better frame of mind then."

"Ah. You still don't know who I am, do you? Liar." Nora drew out the word. Her voice was still calm, but her right foot was beating a rapid tattoo on the rug. It was obvious that she was keeping calm with an effort. How to get rid of this hippopotamus?

"Alright. Cards on table. I know you. But I do not have any problem with who you are. This business with your husband is not personal at all. I neither like nor do not like you. I just take what I can from where I see it. Alright? And I have absolutely nothing to say to you, so if you would please leave –"

"If I don't leave, what will you do? Call the police?" Nora snorted and her foot tapped even faster. "I am not leaving. We'll settle this business today like this." She unplugged her right hand from under her armpit and pointed to the floor in emphasis.

"You carry your thin self and steal people's husbands with you evil charms. You think I don't know you free women? You are depriving my children of the love and support that is theirs by right. You have disgraced me in this town." She paused, beginning to pant. "Look at you, stupid fool. Dry as a bone. Take your AIDS and go and spread it elsewhere. Leave my husband alone."

"Hey, I did not approach your husband. He approached me. You ought to have taken better care of him if you care about him so much."

"Better care, enh? I will show you better care. I did not approach him. What d'you mean you did not approach him? You and your witchcraft. I am just telling you, leave him alone! If not – "

"If not, what? Are you going to chain him to the kitchen table? You think your threats impress me? Why don't you lose some weight for a start? If you could hold him, he would not have broken free. He's not so hot anyway. I give him back to you. I have other fish to fry. Take him and both of you get out of my life. Nonsense!"

"Who are you talking to like that?"

"Is your eyesight as defective as your understanding? Do you see anyone else here?"

Nora stood up, still clutching the plastic bag. "Who are you talking to?"

"Out of my house. Out. Get out!" Ophie pointed a shaking finger at the front door. "Iddddiot."

"You call who idiot? You are insulting me? You steal my husband and you are insulting me? You are insulting – me?"

"It's a compliment to your mental abilities, in fact. Take it and leave. It's the best you are likely to get around here."

Muttering to herself, Nora plunged her hand into the plastic bag and pulled out a black-handled knife. "I am going to tear your mouth all the way to your ears so that your insults can come out better. I am going to plunge this into your privates so you can screw my husband better." She moved towards Ophie, knife steady in her hand. Ophie turned and ran towards her

305

bedroom, meaning to lock herself in. But as she reached for the door handle, Nora grabbed her dressing gown at the nape. Ophie strained forward. They tangled and fell into the bedroom together, Ophie on top. She rose and ran to the other side of the bed. Nora rolled over and stood up.

"You want me to get out of your house. *You* will get out. You will get out of my life." She rushed around the bed, brandishing the knife. Ophie leaped onto the bed and tried to run across to the door. Nora dived forward and caught her ankle. Ophie fell heavily, banging her lower face on the edge of the bed.

★ ★ ★

Next door, Mr. and Mrs. Atabong were just sitting down to dinner when they heard the screams. Mrs. Atabong looked at her husband.

"What was that?"

"It's that harlot again."

"It sounds like a fight. Let me go and see."

"Go where? If you step one foot out of this house, you will stay out forever. Why do you want to go and help a harlot whose boyfriend is beating her? It is none of your business what free girls like that do. Let them kill each other if they like."

"But – "

"If you open that pit latrine of a mouth again, you will feel the back of my hand. Sit down!" He glared at her until she subsided, head bent over her food.

★ ★ ★

Her teeth jarred. Blood spurted from her nose, covering her mouth and chin. She screamed. The blood stained her teeth. It dripped onto the robe. Nora threw back her arm and swung. The knife plunged into the back of Ophie's leg, just above the knee. She screamed again, and scrabbled forward on her hands. She kicked out with her unhurt leg. It caught Nora square in the middle of her face. Nora let go of Ophie's ankle and put her hands to her face, wailing loudly. The knife wiped against her cheek, leaving a wedge-shaped stain. Ophie got to her feet and rushed out into the bathroom, slammed the door shut and twisted the knob, sobbing loudly, hoping the door would hold.

Feeling safer, she stopped sobbing and listened. Silence. She looked around for a weapon. There was nothing heavier than a six-pack of soap. She picked it up, hefting it in her hand. She caught a glimpse of herself in the mirror. Her nose looked soft; blood covered her lower face. The dressing gown was ruined. Her swollen eyes blinked back at her. They looked around and fell on a small black mass on the edge of the sink. She stared at it for a moment, then her brain registered. Still holding the bar of soap, she picked the phone up, flipped it open. She speed-dialled Martha's number. The phone squeaked, connecting her call.

Please God please please please let her pick it up -

A heavy blow fell on the bathroom door. Ophie started, dropping the phone. She hugged the bar of soap to her chest. She crouched down, picked up the phone. Put it to her ear.

"Hello!"

She swallowed. Another blow fell on the door.

"Ophie, why are you not talking? Hello!"

"M –Marsha."

"What, drunk already? You this girl!"

"No. Dora. Ish tryig to kill be."

"What? Who is Dora?"

"Prown Trail. Wife." Her breath whistled through her nose. "Tryig to kill be. Help."

"Nora? Where are you?"

"Pathroob. She's tryig to preak de door." She began to whimper. "Help."

"Alright. Wait. Don't worry, she won't get to you. I'm sending someone, okay? Just be cool."

She nodded at the phone, then realised that Martha could not hear that.

"Okay." She let the phone go and it slid into the sink. Another heavy blow thudded into the door, then another. And another. The door trembled. She backed into the angled nook between the sink and the bathtub and slid to the floor. The blows stopped. She could hear Nora breathing heavily on the other side of the wood. Please let the door hold. Please Papa God let the door hold.

"Ophelia?"

307

Oh God, she would kill him. Brown Trail.

"Ophie, where are y – hey! What is this? What have you done? What has happened? Have you killed her?"

Ophelia crept to the door and put her ear to the wood. The knife clattered onto the tiles. No one said anything for a while.

"Let's go home," said Nora's voice.

"Where is she?"

"In there."

Footsteps approached.

"Ophelia, are you okay?"

"Alive."

"Open the door. It's alright. You're safe."

She opened the door. He looked at her. She pointed to her nose and twisted around to show the back of her leg.

"Come."

He walked her to the front door. Nora was sitting on the sofa. Calm again. No expression on her face. She did not move as they went out. He hammered on the neighbour's door.

Inside, Mr. and Mrs. Atabong looked up from their dinner. Mrs. Atabong made as if to rise. Her husband pointed his fork at her and signalled imperiously that she should sit down. She sank back, eyes lowered. He kept his eyes on her until she started eating again. The hammering ceased.

Brown trail put his arm around Ophelia. She was beginning to limp. They walked to the nearest house, which was some distance away. It was inhabited by another faculty member, his wife and their five children. The door was opened by a small girl of three, who ran back into the living room, yelling to her parents to "come an' see Auntie Ophiya with blood blood blood!" She was bundled into their station wagon and driven to hospital.

Nora's husband went back to fetch his wife.

49

In the course of the next few weeks, Martha met with Eyong several times. Each time they were more relaxed with each other. Now that it was clear that he was totally taken with her, she sat back and let him do the chasing. He had an apartment just two streets down from his office, to which he invited Martha one day. When she got there, the place was spotless, which made her wonder for one sickening moment whether there was a girlfriend in the background. But the neatness was explained when, after half an hour or so, the door was pushed open and a middle-aged woman came in. She was dressed in a dark red traditional wrapper outfit, and her good-humoured face was shiny with sweat.

She greeted them breathlessly, walked across the room and threw herself in a wicker chair next to the whirring fan.

"Weh, this heat go kill man oh! You this child, when are you going to install air conditioning?"

Martha looked at her again and wondered how she could have missed the resemblance in the first place. It was his mother, of course. After she had caught her breath, he performed the introductions. She immediately darted across the room and shook Martha's hand vigorously.

"Mayyyyyy, my daughter! So it's you. The work you are doing, my daughter, I don't know if we can ever thank you enough, oh. I am in one common initiative group and the other day we were asked by some of your people to compile a list of things we could do to increase our revenue. My daughter! You this Eyong, I came in and you could not even tell me it was she. My dear, have you eaten?"

" Well, we just arrived…"

"I made some eru for this one. You know, if I do not come and see what he is eating, he will starve to death. See how skinny he is."

Eyong got up and, putting his arm around his mother, propelled her to the kitchen. "Go and make your noise there", he said affectionately.

He shut the door and came back to sit down next to her. "Don't mind her," he said, smiling. "She is having her house painted and I invited her to come and stay here for the smell of the paint to fade. She is slightly asthmatic.

"You know, I don't think I mentioned it, but I did not have a father. I mean, of course I must have had one, but I never knew him. My mother sold garri in the daytime and roasted fish at night so I could go to school. At one point, she sold foo-foo and eru in the market. I used to meet her there after school and I continued to sell while she went home to prepare the fish. I cooked for us on most days. Don't mind her griping about my not eating; I am probably a better cook than she is, not so, Mammy," he asked as his mother came back into the room with plates, preparing to set the table for dinner. She flapped her hand at him and snorted.

When she went back in to the kitchen, he added: "So when I see all that you are trying to do for these women, I think that if someone had helped my mother, it would have made life easier for her. You know, I admire you a lot. Those first days when Tarkang asked me to prepare the case with you; I was literally speechless with admiration for your courage. I guess you must have found me stupid."

"I just thought that you were one of those idiots out there who will always reduce me to a sum of my private parts. But I should say that at the time, I was taking a beating from public opinion, and I was suspicious of everyone. How wrong I was!"

"Indeed. I am your number one fan. No. I forget. Number two. My mother is definitely number one. She is supposed to go back to her house this evening." He took her hand. "Maybe you would care to stay? It's getting dark."

Just as she was about to reply, his mother came in with the food. He did not let go of her hand as they stood up to move to the table. After the meal, his mother said she had to leave and Martha offered to drive her back home, as Eyong's car was in the garage.

310

When they got back to his apartment, she asked him: "What do you think your mother is thinking now that you have gone and told her that I will be here till tomorrow?."

"That's her affair. She is relaxed about these things. I told you she has never married. I got used to a few uncles in my time. So. Are you staying?"

"What does it look like I want to do?" she said, unbuttoning her blouse slowly, her eyes on his. He stood there, mesmerised. Then he strode forward and lifted her off her feet, carrying her to his bedroom.

Martha could not resist a giggle.

50

Ophelia was sitting up in bed, wearing a tee shirt, her legs under the sheets, a thick bandage over the middle of her face.

"So how's our patient?"

"Losing her patience. I want to go home. I'm well now."

"Doctor says no. Your leg is not healing as quickly as it should. You want to go home like a poorly-bandaged mummy?"

"Have you ever slept in a hospital?"

"No."

"Then shut up. You would last about two hours."

"Stop being cantankerous. You are lucky that man came when he did, or you might not be alive to whine today."

"Yes. Then he abandoned me to the neighbours and took his wife away."

"What did you expect? For him to leave her there and take you away? Come on, be serious. You went to Paris with another man, without his knowledge, and he kept vigil for your return. Is it his fault that his wife also did? I think you should stop whining and admit that there is something the matter with you."

"If you've come here with your compulsive moralising…"

"I have. And you will listen." She plucked the book from Ophelia's hand and flung it to the floor. She glared at Ophelia till she lowered her eyes.

"You've got to pull your life together. I am usually wary of giving advice, but I think I would be doing you a disservice if I pretended that all was fine. One. Your drinking. You act as if you are the only one with problems to drown. You claim to enjoy your life as a single woman, but I think you have not been able to come to terms with the fact of your spinsterhood. In spite of your claims, you are not proud of being an unmarried woman. You are actually scared that after a while, no one will want you, aren't you? That is why you are so hard on men; you are punishing them for what you know they will do to you later. You are rude to everyone so that they can think that you don't care about anything. But you do. If you did not spend so much money on your family, you would have bought a new car a long time ago."

"Have I asked you for money?"

"Shut up. It's alright to be soft and feminine. You *are* soft and feminine. You are a woman. Nothing wrong with that. There is no need to go around trying to prove that you are tough and you can drink most men under the table. There is no need to treat men like toilet tissue to prove that you can be as hard as they. I know women who are a lot harder than you will ever hope to be, but they are not pretending. They are real. And I do not necessarily approve of them. It is not by adopting the habits of men that we will solve our problems. We have to d it our way. We will not grow muscles or coarsen our voices. We will work with what we have. And for an intellectual, you disappoint me. A deep voice or mannishness does not mean that you are automatically right. It is as if you were saying that the only way to be right is to be male. You are playing right into the hands of our detractors. In any case, though you think that your behaviour reflects what men do, I can tell you that there are men who would never be as amoral as you are. By trying to act like you think they do, you are saying that *woman* is wrong by definition. By existence.

"Sleeping with someone's husband and displaying him as if he were not married is a short cut to the cemetery, as you almost found out."

"He has not even come to see me."

"Then he has more brains that I gave him credit for. I told him if he comes anywhere near you, I would arrange for all his fingers to be snipped off at the first joint, one dark night. Look. You and Nora are both my friends. I want you both to be at peace. She will not be happy without him. You are just playing with him. I told him to go and do a Samuel Pepys, complete with tears and protestations of love."

"It's not fair.'

"Not fair to whom? You call him Brown Trail. Is that fair? His wife does not call him that. She needs him more than you do. She has, rightly or wrongly, built her life around him. And I think you are a bed-hopper because you are afraid of being alone. You are in fact buying love insurance. But I think you should try and develop the backbone to be alone from time to time, sexually speaking, at least. Loneliness is the permanent condition of humans, whatever they do and whoever shares their lives. You can never move into a person's body and live there. You cannot share his lungs. These men you sleep with, what kind of real companionship do they provide you with? Each time you switch partners, you are even lonelier than you were before. Note. This is not a moral judgment. I am more afraid of the reasons why you sleep around. If you were happy doing it, I would not mind. But you are not. You have never confessed to being in love with anyone. Even if it is self-delusion, it is still mostly a happy feeling while it lasts.

"Ah, stop crying. You will get salt water into your wound. Think about all that. And think about what you are going to do when you get out of here. I went to see your Dean, and he has been listening to Atabong, so good-bye to the university. I guess you expected that, anyway."

"But it's not fair. Would they sack a man for beating his wife? Do they sack married people for domestic quarrels?"

"Probably not. So, come with me and help me make sure that such things will not be happening to women again. I think you can do a great job at the centre."

"Comparing the literary merits of *Kwabena and the Leopard* with those of *Lukong and the Leopard*?"

"Talking of that, I seem to remember that you had a work in progress once. What happened to it?"

"Forget about that."

"I will not. You know, Ophelia, for all your talk about musts and must nots, you are the most confused woman I know. You act like a rebel, but you have not charted the course of your rebellion. You just hit out at whatever man comes your way. I will reverse your charge about my lack of a proper ideology. You have to have a personal ideology. Without one, you will always grope in the dark."

"If what I find in the dark grows larger when it is stroked, that's good enough for me."

314

"Don't be coarse. And stop trying to act tougher than you feel. I know you think I preachify too much, but you have to have a personal morality to guide you. I know we have all lied and cheated and slept with people's husbands. But we should not pretend as some women do, that we do not do these things or, like you, that in this way we attain fulfilment because we are punishing men. Wanting to punish them is giving them too much importance in our lives. It means that our thoughts will be dominated by them. Do you think that kind of prison of the mind is better than the prison of the body that we live in now? To return to this book of yours."

"Look. I have tried to write, but what can I say that is new?"

"What did you plan on saying?"

"Something abut women and religion in a revolutionary way. I want it to be something that only I have written.'

"How do you know that someone else has?"

"That's the problem. I cannot be sure. And I do not know how it will be received."

"Writing about religion can only be a reaction to what you have seen and read. How can your reaction get you into trouble?

"Ask Salman Rushdie."

"Ophelia, you are such a wimp. What is the difference now between you and those women who will not take risks for fear of standing out? You must take the risk that what you write will not be liked by all. You must not deny yourself your destiny because people won't like it. Do not let life interfere with the art in you."

Ophelia sighed. "Martha, leave me. I do not know where I am at right now. I even thought of writing poetry, but a look at the high-minded paroxysms of Milton cured me of that impulse." She sniffed. "Concerning art, for me, it can only imitate life."

"That is too highbrow for me, but do what ever you need to do for this book to be written."

"You were always an ignorant provincial."

"So be it. But this ignorant provincial wants you to do something with your talents."

315

"We'll see," sighed Ophelia.

"Ophelia. Think of all those women who cannot read or write, and see the dreadful waste you are making of your abilities. Your life will be permanently diminished if you can write, but choose not to. Take the risk, Ophelia. As Florence Nightingale said, better pain than paralysis."

"Now you're quoting my books back at me."

"That shows I read them. I'm going over to see Nora now. When I return, you should be telling me another story."

★ ★ ★

Nora was lying on the sofa, her face bandaged exactly like Ophie's.

"You both look more or less the same, that's for sure. What on earth possessed you to go and disgrace yourself like that?"

"Ah beg, leave me!"

"I no go leave you. Look at you. You are the joke of the town. Irate wives went out with disco music, let me tell you. What kind of stupid desperation is it that pushes you to try to kill the wrong person? A man cheats on you, and you try to kill his girlfriend. Are you married to her? You are lucky that the police were not called."

"My in-laws would have got me out."

"So that is your own insurance. Why can you not stand on your own two feet? What is the use of going to school only to come back and hunt yourself a rich husband to support you, and kiss up to your in-laws? Why do you have to lean on your marriage for everything? Is that all you are, a wife? Where is the rest of you that God made? Marriages are made on earth, never mind the church nonsense. God gives you a job to do, regardless of whether you are married or not."

"I bring up my children well."

"So nuns and people like us are useless. Thank you."

"Take it any way you like. If you have come here to support your friend, just leave. If she touches my husband again, I'll kill her."

"If your husband touches her again, I'll kill him first, never fear. Then you'll have nothing left to kill for. In the

316

unlikely event that your husband goes back to her, and you touch even a hair of her head, I'll make sure that you never see the outside of a prison again. Look at you. Your husband sleeps with your housegirl. You do not fight him. You do not fight the house girl who has betrayed your trust. He cheats on you with a stranger and you try to kill her. Where's the logic in that? I think you felt threatened by Ophelia because she is independent, and she seems to hold your man with no effort at all. You know how she does that? She does not care what he thinks of her. She does not go fawning over him like you do. If she were married to him, she would probably insult his parents if they visited too often. She plays with your husband like one does with a puppy. When she is tired of him, she kicks him away. You ought to tear a leaf from her book and show him that you are not his doormat."

"But I did that. I left. He did not even come to look for me."

"Then you should have stayed away for a lot longer. After a while, he would have begun to wonder. In any case, he was nothing much to Ophelia. He was beginning to bore her. She was going to leave him anyway. Since you want to be married at all costs, all you had to do was wait for him to come back to you after she threw him out. Instead, you went and showed him that you would kill for him. You're good with histrionics, but bad on tactics."

"*You* can talk. Who made you the expert on marriage? Who will marry you, with your crazy ideas? You were always a little odd. I knew you would come to a bad end."

"It's not worse than yours, attempted murder. It may be a bad end I come to. But it is *my* end. Anyway, I am not here to defend myself. Look at you. You teach six hours a week and you eat and get fat and have babies. Get a life, Nora. If you had independent interests, you would not be so desperate. If you valued yourself, you would not take shit from this man. Find something to keep you busy, something that will be yours and yours alone. Now that you have lost your position of respected queen termite, people will not be inviting you to their houses again. What will you do? Tell me. I am listening.

317

"Why do you choose to live in limbo? Why are you burying yourself in the uncertainty of emotional dependence on a man who, as experience has shown you, will always cheat on you? You used to describe how you had a handle on him with your sexuality. Now that the handle has broken off, what do you have left? Nothing.

"I beg, leave me with plenty talk."

"Plenty talk is what you will get from me, Nora. You do not have the courage to either submit entirely and be content with your lot, working with the system as it is, or to come right out and resist. You have to choose. You have to find that courage. If the status quo, which allows married men to have mistresses more or less in public, does not satisfy you, then you must do something about it. Such as you are, Nora, you are all set to be an eternal victim of a system you perpetuate by your refusal to work for its elimination. As long as you are happy in your marriage, you can be disdainful of those women who are not as happy as you are. Now that you are no longer happy, what will you do to change the situation? Now that the meaning has been leached out of your life, what will you do? Who are you now that you are not a satisfied wife?

When there was no answer, Martha stood up. "Call me when you recover. I may help you find some answers."

★ ★ ★

Back in the car, she dialled Eyong's number.

"Yes?"

"Guess who's coming for dinner."

318